ISBN 978-1-331-98721-5
PIBN 10161219

English
Français
Deutsche
Italiano
Español
Português

www.forgottenbooks.com

Mythology Photography **Fiction**
Fishing Christianity **Art** Cooking
Essays Buddhism Freemasonry
Medicine **Biology** Music **Ancient
Egypt** Evolution Carpentry Physics
Dance Geology **Mathematics** Fitness
Shakespeare **Folklore** Yoga Marketing
Confidence Immortality Biographies
Poetry **Psychology** Witchcraft
Electronics Chemistry History **Law**
Accounting **Philosophy** Anthropology
Alchemy Drama Quantum Mechanics
Atheism Sexual Health **Ancient History**
Entrepreneurship Languages Sport
Paleontology Needlework Islam
Metaphysics Investment Archaeology
Parenting Statistics Criminology
Motivational

OUR VICEREGAL LIFE

IN INDIA

SELECTIONS FROM MY JOURNAL

1884–1888

BY THE

MARCHIONESS OF DUFFERIN & AVA

IN TWO VOLUMES——VOL. I.

FOURTH THOUSAND

WITH PORTRAIT AND MAP

LONDON
JOHN MURRAY, ALBEMARLE STREET
1890

THESE   JOURNAL - LETTERS   WERE   ORIGINALLY

ADDRESSED TO MY MOTHER : TO HER THEREFORE

I DEDICATE THIS SELECTION FROM THEM

HARRIOT DUFFERIN & AVA

CLANDEBOYE
August 31, 1889

CONTENTS

OF

THE FIRST VOLUME

—•◦•—

CHAPTER I.

ARRIVAL IN INDIA

December 2, 1884, to January 29, 1885

CHAPTER II.

FIRST SEASON IN CALCUTTA

January 31 to March 18, 1885

PAGE

CHAPTER *III*

RAWAL PINDI DURBAR AND VISIT TO LAHORE

March 23 to April 20, 1885

CHAPTER IV

SIMLA DURING THE RAINS

April 22 to October 19, 1885

CHAPTER V

AUTUMN TOUR, 1885 : NAHUN, DELHI, RAJPUTANA,
CENTRAL INDIA, AGRA, AND LUCKNOW

October 20 to December 16, 1885

CHAPTER VI

CALCUTTA, 1885–1886

December 17, 1885, to February 2, 1886

CHAPTER VII

BURMAH AND MADRAS

February 3 to March 8, 1886

OUR VICEREGAL LIFE
IN INDIA

CHAPTER I

ARRIVAL IN INDIA

DECEMBER 2, 1884, TO JANUARY 29, 1885

Aden : Tuesday, December 2nd, 1884.—We have had a
delightful day, and, although I feel rather tired, I will try
to give you some account of it now, for, should the weather
be bad to-morrow, I might be unable to write. To-day it
has been perfect, bright and warm enough, but with a
fresh wind, so that the much-abused Aden was at its best,
and we have come away with the highest opinion of its
charms.

Directly after breakfast we came on deck to admire
the beautiful rocks that are known by the name of Little
Aden. They are islands, barren-looking, but carved by
volcanic convulsions into the most wonderful shapes;
they rise straight out of the green sea into high needles,
or curve away from the sandy shore so as to form caves
and bays; their colouring is varied and beautiful, purple
and red, with a greenish tinge sometimes, which does not

appear to be the result of vegetation. This place does not look fit for human habitation, but there are wild Arabs upon it, and it is used by Aden itself as a sort of convict settlement.

Aden has the beauty of form and colour. It is absolutely barren, but nothing could be more lovely than it looked to-day as we approached it.

As soon as we hove in sight, the Viceroy's flag was hauled up for the first time, the Captain 'breaking' it himself; and as we anchored, the thirty-one guns, which are now D.'s due, were fired from the various batteries ashore.

Our ship was soon surrounded by funny little brown boys, in small dug-out canoes of the same colour as themselves. These little creatures paddle about in the most fearless way; they come quite up to the still moving steamer, first one side, then the other, call to the passengers, 'Have a dive,' ' Give a dive,' bail out the water with their hands as they speak, jump in headlong after any coin that is thrown them, and catch it long before it reaches the bottom. Many of them dye their hair yellow, which has a curious effect, and a little rag round their waists is all their clothing, so I wonder where they keep the money they pick up—certainly not in the boat, which is often upset. One of the boys had his leg taken off some time ago by a Rock cod, but he still plies his trade, and is said not so much to feel the loss of his leg as the ingratitude of the cod, who had often met him under water, and who ought to have had a friendly feeling for him.

The Resident, General Blair, Mrs. and Miss Blair,

and a number of officers came on board, and we soon
went ashore with them. We passed two of our men-
of-war and a Frenchman, all dressed with flags, and
on the English ships the men manned the yards—
always a pretty sight. We landed under an awning ornamented with flags and with green reeds which had been
brought thirty miles on camels for the purpose. Here
we found the dignitaries of the place, soldiers, natives,
and guards of honour—one was formed by the English
regiment here (the 40th). Next to them were the 'Aden
Troop,' most picturesque-looking men, mounted on white
horses, wearing red turbans and white uniforms. When
D. drove away they rode by him with drawn swords.
There were also some native infantry troops at the
landing-place. Here we separated.

D. started on a long drive to see the Tanks and the
place generally, and we ladies went at once to the Resident's house. It is a charming one, but what volumes
it speaks for the climate! It is literally a roof supported
by pillars, with wooden latticework between them, even
the bedrooms being on the horse-box principle, with the
air blowing about, around, above and below, in every
direction. Certainly in a hot climate you must give up
your prejudice against draughts.

To-day it was delightful in this summer-house,
the room looking like a gigantic balcony; but there *are*
drawbacks to this open-air existence, for sometimes there
are sand-storms, and the sand blows in and covers up
everything in the most hopeless way. It is almost
impossible to make any plant grow even indoors, for,
as you may perceive from my description of the house,

there is very little difference between indoors and out-of-doors, and the hot wind reaches everywhere.

When the gentlemen came back we were given a big lunch, for about thirty people; and after it D. had a little business to do, and it was five before we came on board our ship again. Then we said good-night to the Blairs, who had been most kind to us, and stood on deck to see all those splendid rocks and serrated peaks against the setting sun.

I must not forget to say that there was another native regiment up at the Residency, whose band played during lunch. They were the 4th Bombay Rifles and were dressed like our Rifle regiments, but wore black turbans.

Bombay: December 8th.—I wish it were possible for me to give you even a faint idea of the splendour of the landing at Bombay, but it was such a magnificent sight that it seems almost useless to try to describe it. I believe that we shall never, even in India, see anything to compare with it again, so I must do the best I can in the way of putting my impressions upon paper. The *Tasmania* anchored at 11 A.M.; but as we were not to land till 4.30, we remained quietly watching the departure of the other passengers and admiring the splendid harbour in which we found ourselves. It was extremely amusing to see the crowds of boats alongside, full of various coloured people on various business; of expectant husbands come out to meet the ' grass widows ' who have travelled with us, messengers with letters for persons on board, natives vainly trying to get up the sides, the police, in bright yellow caps, trying to keep order; noise and bustle everywhere!

Sir James Fergusson came on board to see us and to let us know all the arrangements made. There was one very sad thing to mar the day. Mr. Balfour got a telegram telling him of his mother's death. He seemed to be devoted to her, and is very unhappy, so it is very hard upon him to be amongst comparative strangers, and in the midst of so much gaiety.

After lunch we rested a little, and then, arraying ourselves in our best, awaited the arrival of the Admiral, Sir W. Hewett, and Captain Ritchie (Secretary to the Bombay Government), who came to fetch us off. As we left the ship the Lascars manned the yards, and a roaring salute from the three men-of-war began to thunder forth. Everything looked beautiful in the bright sunshine—the ships dressed and the yards manned, the white smoke curling about them, the quantities of yachts, boats, and other vessels, and then the brilliantly clothed natives squatting on the quay. The steps down to the water were covered with scarlet cloth, and at the top of them we found the prominent personages who had come to meet the new Viceroy, they also adding to the mass of colour with their uniforms. Turning to the right, the scarlet cloth was laid down for a couple of hundred yards, with an arch at each end, and tropical plants on either side showed off their green leaves against the carpet and the scarlet balustrade behind them; when we had advanced a few steps down this path we stopped to have the address read and answered.

Sir J. Fergusson stood behind D. and I close to him

the Staff at one side.   The address was read by a Parsee, and there was a group of natives round him.

When this was over, D. and I and Sir James walked through the second arch and got into the carriages. My heart leapt into my mouth for a moment when I saw the four horses in combination with the crowds and the noise, but I will tell you now that I soon got over my nervousness and was not the least frightened during the drive.   Some of the A.D.C.s went first in a sort of wagonette, then Nelly, Rachel, and *I*, with Captain Dean; Sir James Fergusson's Military Secretary went next, and then followed the two Governors. Between and about the carriages were mounted native soldiers.

And now comes the difficult moment to describe, but I must appeal to your imagination to fill in the details of the scene.   Fancy a drive of five miles through a town: in the first part some very fine buildings and large houses, occasionally an open space or a short bit of avenue with fine trees, and then a long bazaar, or native town, with curious old houses and strange balconies; and then fill the whole—the streets, the windows, the rows and rows of balconies, the trees, the tops of carriages—with a teeming crowd, almost every individual of which is a study in himself: natives of every shape and colour, dresses of the most brilliant hues, little children clothed in the whole rainbow, and with a large nose-ring added to that; children clothed in nothing at all, and parents with the nearest approach to nothing at all that *I* ever saw before; one window filled with ladies draped in brilliant stuffs, and a little further on four or five naked bodies decorating another window; and when you can't imagine any more, add the five miles of cheering and the ever-recurring bands sending forth 'God save the Queen,' the handkerchiefs waving, and all the incidents of a crowd—in fact, put life into the masses of colour your imagination has brought before you, and say if it was not an exciting scene!

The Government House was once a Jesuit monastery; it is very pretty and curious—large rooms, wide staircases, but, oh dear! it's very cold! Now I really did expect to be warm at Bombay, but the temperature actually is cool. In England it would be nice and pleasant, but there you don't live in a room in which the walls are cut up into arches opening on to large corridors where all the windows are wide open; and you would sooner die than sit in (not one, but) twenty draughts at a time; and you don't dine in a room which seems to have no side-wall at all; and you don't expect to find that your bedroom has four very large windows and three doors, *all* wide open at once; but that is what you do find here.

When we reached Parell we were received by Miss Fergusson and by Mrs. Dean, the wife of the Military Secretary. After some tea (very nearly in the open air and certainly in many draughts) we went out to look at the garden. It is left as the monks laid it out, and is very pretty; there are some palms that I never saw before, the top of the straight bare stem being like a large flat fan. While we were walking through the garden the electric light illuminated it. I then went up to my airy bedroom, and found three new ayahs arrived from Calcutta—one for Rachel, and one for each of our maids. I was amused to see the gently moving ayah following the active Blackwell about like a shadow, and I began to hope my Hindustani would make great progress, but the ayah is banished, at any rate from my room, while the girls will get on fast with their languages.

There were twenty at dinner, mostly Staff. I sat between Sir James and General Hardinge. When I told the latter who Rachel was, he told me a funny story about her grandmother, the 'Queen of Beauty' (Duchess of Somerset). She had a little Japanese dog, and she went one day with it to the Zoo; the man at the door stopped her, saying, 'No dogs allowed in,' at which she looked at him scornfully, and said in tragic tones, 'Man, it is not a dog, it's a bird!'

Tuesday, 9th.—At 9.30 there were prayers, and then we breakfasted in the verandah dining-room, which in the morning was delightful, and after that we were photographed in a group. The number of frightful caricatures of us which is being called into existence is fearful, for we never move anywhere that we don't see a photographer pointing at us from the top of a carriage, or from some unexpected vantage-ground.

We next visited all the horses, and then came in to write letters till lunch. I was warm and comfortable all the day, and felt no draughts. At four His Excellency laid a foundation-stone, and in the evening Sir James had a great dinner and a party for us, and we all put on our very best—I my Order and diamonds and Nelly hers, and D. his uniform, &c. I like Sir James very much, and found the dinner very pleasant.

The reception was a little fatiguing; 600 people came, and we stood on a golden carpet and shook hands with all the ladies and bowed to all the gentlemen. There were many natives, and their dresses are very handsome. The Parsee ladies look very nice, and wear most beautiful colours.

I stayed for about half-an-hour after the presentations were over, and then slipped away, as we have an early function to-morrow.

Wednesday, 10th.—I must close this letter before lunch to-day, but I shall have time to tell you of our doings this morning. D. was to open a Hospital for Sick Animals at 8.30 A.M., and as I heard many native ladies would be there, I settled to go too. When we arrived at the place we found an enormous awning spread, under which all the people were sitting, and as there were flags and colours about it, and rows of Parsee ladies and native men seated under it, it all looked very gay and charming in the sunny fresh morning.

A little history of the charity was read first. It is a branch of a ' Prevention of Cruelty to Animals Organisation,' the idea being that instead of fining a poor man for ill-treating his bullocks, and thus almost necessitating his working them still harder, it would be better to provide a place where the unfortunate animals could be cured ; and, aided by some rich citizens, this Hospital and a Veterinary College have been started. After the usual speeches we were conducted to one of the ' Hospital wards,' and there we saw a curious Brahmin ceremonial : eggs and cocoanuts were broken on the floor, and the posts and lintels of the doors were smeared with egg, oil, and some other stuff. Then great trays of flowers were brought, and the chief man—the host in fact—taking a large wreath or necklace of jessamine and roses, put it over His Excellency's head, handed him a bouquet, and sprinkled it with rosewater; he adorned me in the same way, then Sir James, and then Nelly, who wished to sink into the ground on the spot, and then the host himself was thus decorated. Rachel too had her necklace and bouquet. The wreaths are beautifully made, and are better described as ropes of flowers; each flower is tied separately to the next one, and a few silver threads are mixed. They are really very pretty; the bouquets are a stiff shape with some tinsel in the centre. You may imagine how odd the gentlemen looked in their frock coats and garlands of flowers.

I have told you about the early part of this day, and must now tell you how hard we worked during the afternoon.

We were to lunch with General Hardinge at Malabar Point, which really belongs to the Governor of Bombay, and which is the most lovely place ! It is a promontory, with the sea on one side and a bay on the other. The sitting-rooms are very pretty, divided from each other by enormous carved open-work doors. The living rooms are all about the garden in different bungalows. Sir James Fergusson drove me in a mail phaeton, the rest of the party following with carriages and four.

After lunch we visited a large boys' school, Miss

Pechey's dispensary, a Parsee girls' school, and the School of Art. Then *I* was tired out and went home, while D. went to see a market. The only one of these institutions which I will stop to tell you about is the girls' school. The Parsee young ladies wear such very pretty colours, while the little girls are all dressed like boys, with coloured jackets and trousers and round hats. The pupils sang, and a tiny little creature came forward and recited in very broken English, with lots of gesticulation, a little poem about a rabbit. I think it was a conversation between a rabbit and a sportsman; at any rate it was a charming little performance. Everywhere we were decorated with garlands of flowers, and sometimes had bracelets as well. In the evening there was a big dinner and a ball.

Friday, 12th.—We had to leave very early on Thursday morning, the train starting at eight. We found our carriages most comfortable, indeed the whole train was ours. We had a sitting-room, my bedroom, bath-room, and beds for two maids in one carriage. D. had a bedroom and a place for his servant in another. There was a large dining-room in a third, and the Staff and all the servants had carriages provided for them. Our beds were very comfortable, and our food good. The scenery the first day, when we were going over the Ghauts, was very fine, curious-shaped basaltic hills, with odd little pinnacles, or domes, or excrescences of some sort on the top of each; the rest of the way it was not remarkable. Last night was cold, and this morning very much so, winter dresses and shawls required. D. was not very well in the day, and was quite ill in the night, when his temperature rose to 102.

Saturday, 13*th.*—He seemed very unfit this morning for all he was to go through ; however, as four o'clock approached he got up and prepared for his entry into Calcutta.

There was a magnificent array of uniforms at the station, fine turns-out of carriage and horses, and guards and outriders, and the whole way to the house was crowded with people, who received us with cheers. We crossed a bridge over the Hooghly and drove through part of the town, looking with the greatest interest at all we could see of this place, which is to be our home for the present.

When we arrived at Government House we found a large guard of honour drawn up before it, and the flight of steps leading to the door was covered with gentlemen in uniform and natives in gay dresses. Lord Ripon received us most cordially, and presented all the Council to the new Excellency.

Lady Ripon met us in the Throne-room, and we all went to the Council Chamber to hear D. sworn in. It is not an imposing ceremony. Several gentlemen stood round a table while the Warrant was read, then they sat down while D. signed it, *et voilà tout.*

We went to have some tea, and after it D. was fetched to go and seat himself on the throne to hear the address read—such a funny little throne with no back. He replied, and all was over. I believe this throne was once Tippoo Sahib's howdah. For the rest of the time we spent together Lady Ripon and I never knew who was the lady of the house, and we could not catch each other's eye, we were both so afraid of appearing to take upon ourselves! She was a great comfort to me and so kind in helping me with information.

In the evening Lord Ripon sent D. the insignia of the Star of India to wear at the big official dinner of 100 people. Everyone asked was expected to come, and some native gentlemen who cannot eat with us sat in another room till dinner was over.

Monday, 15th.—We went early this morning to see the Ripons off. We are quite sorry to lose them, and feel rather lonely now.

Yesterday we went to the Cathedral; it is rather like a railway station, the punkah rods representing the iron framework of that sort of building; the walls are quite white, while the windows are a bluish colour, which makes everyone look pale. In deference to the hot climate the service was short.

Tuesday, 16th, *to Sunday,* 21st.—Both my time and my thoughts have been so entirely occupied with furnishing that I have little else to tell you of. We are performing wonders in the way of settling down, and I have arranged myself a very pretty drawing-room, with another room next door, which can be thrown open if there are people to dinner.

I was very unhappy yesterday about the house, which I should then have described as gigantic, with *no* room in it. I thought my rooms intolerably uncomfortable (I should have to enter into too many details to explain why), but I have had an idea which I have this moment carried out, and now I feel that there is hope left. I have thrown all conservative principles to the winds, have abandoned the rooms used by all previous Viceroys, and have moved into the visitors' wing. So that I have now a lovely boudoir looking on to the garden, instead of a dull room upstairs, without a balcony or a view, and a nice room next to it for the girls, who would otherwise have sat in their bedrooms. I am close to my own staircase, and nothing can be nicer. Having thus packed myself and my belongings into one of the elephant's paws (or wings) of this house, we are really comfortable.

I will now tell you how I spend the day, and then you will learn casually about some of my arrangements. D. gets up pretty early to work, and I am generally ready at 8.30. We breakfast at nine o'clock on the balcony outside my pink drawing-room—we four (family) together. D. stays and walks about for a little, while the green parrots and the crows look down upon us from the capitals of the pillars which support the roof of the verandah. At ten o'clock Lord William Beresford has an interview with His Excellency, and then comes on to me. I always write down the things I want to ask him about, and as he settles everything the list is very curious and miscellaneous.

Each A.D.C. has his own department. Major Cooper is 'Household,' and he and I see to everything, and make ourselves generally fussy and useful.

Captain Harbord has the kitchen and the cook to see

after. Captain Balfour is a musician, so he manages the band, and I have asked him to make it play every night from eight till nine while we are at dinner. Captain Burn does the invitations. Lord William has the stables, and all the A.D.C.s are under him, and every detail is brought before him. From the highest military affairs in the land to a mosquito inside my Excellency's curtain or a bolt on my door, all is the business of this invaluable person, and he does all equally well. He jots everything down in his book, or on his shirt-sleeve, and never rests till the order is carried out. He has the stables. very well arranged, and the 'turns out' are very handsome. The carriages are plain, without gilding or ornament, but we nearly always drive with four horses, postillions, footmen, outriders, and escort, all in scarlet and gold liveries.

The principal servants in the house also wear scarlet and gold. The 'khidmatgars,' or men who wait at table, have long red cloth tunics, white trousers, bare feet, white or red and gold sashes wound round their waists, and white turbans. The smarter ones have gold embroidered breastplates, and the lower ones have a D. and coronet embroidered on their chests. We each have a 'jemadar,' or body servant, who attends to us at other times. Mine stands outside my door and sees to all I want, goes in my carriage with me, and never leaves me till I am safe inside my room. I daren't move a chair unless I am quite sure the door is well shut, else he would be upon me, and I am sure he would even arrange my papers and my photographs for me.

Nelly and Rachel also have their jemadars, and all

the housemaids (and they are legion) are men with long red tunics, turbans, and gold braid—oh, so smart!—while every now and then in one's best drawing-room, or in one's most private apartments, a creature very lightly clad in a dingy white cotton rag makes his appearance, and seems to feel as much at home there as his smarter brethren do. He is probably a gardener, and he most likely presents you with a bouquet of violets! Then we each have a magnificent sentry in the passage near our bedrooms—they are very tall men, in handsome uniforms; and then there are heaps of servants, 'some in rags, and some in tags, and some in no clothes at all.' One 'caste' arranges the flowers, another cleans the plate, a third puts candles into the candlesticks, but a fourth lights them; one fills a jug of water, while it requires either a higher or a lower man to pour it out. The man who cleans your boots would not condescend to hand you a cup of tea, and the person who makes your bed would be dishonoured were he to take any other part in doing your room. The consequence is that, instead of one neat housemaid at work, when you go up to 'my lady's chamber' you find seven or eight men in various stages of dress, each putting a hand to some little thing which has to be done; and you may imagine the energetic Blackwell's feelings, and how her ayah tells her that 'she much too strong, strong as four Hindustani women.'

I have wandered away from 'my day' to give you an account of the household. As I said before, I have been attending to our comforts, and my room really is pretty now. The furniture is pink silk, and I have made the room look 'homey' with little tables, screens, plants, photographs. The girls have a very nice little boudoir next door, and I also have a second small drawing-room, which I open into mine with three big doors when we have any dinner party. These rooms are, to a certain extent, my creation, for there was no private house before, and after dinner the party sat in the long, dreary throne-room. This I have converted into our usual dining room ; it has carpets and curtains, and is decidedly preferable to a barren marble hall, where we should shiver. We still lunch in that cold place, but it is very nice in the middle of the day.

Off my room there is a delightful balcony, frequented by wild parrots and crows, and soon to be inhabited by all sorts of captive creatures. I am going to have an aviary made, and I already have several birds.

All these arrangements fill my morning, and at two we lunch. We sit at round tables, and are usually fourteen in number.

When I drive, I go out at 3.30, and so get a little sunshine, but the fashion here is for no one to venture out until it is damp and dark, which it is after five o'clock.

We have some difficulty in finding an object for our drive. Sometimes we go to the Zoo, and sometimes there is a game of polo going on, which we sit and watch.

We dine at eight, and the Staff comes and spends the evening with us, or does *not* come, as it chooses.

On Saturday, 20th, His Excellency had his first levée. It was very large, and though the people passed at the rate of twenty-five a minute, which was quicker than usual, it took twenty minutes longer than any levée for the last ten years. D. liked the end of it very much, when the native officers were presented. He says they are very fine men, and that they came forward in a smiling, frank way; they salute and present the hilt of their swords, which the Viceroy touches, and then they pass on.

I think there were about 1,800 men at this levée.

His Excellency was very smart! He wore his Lord-Lieutenant's uniform, with four stars and the Indian Empire (a sort of medal like a flat rose) on his coat, and the diamond medallion of the Star of India hanging from his throat, with the grand cordon of that Order. It is a very pale blue, with a white border. The medallion is a portrait of the Queen on a cameo surrounded by diamonds.

We got our first mail from home on Friday, the 19th; a very great pleasure.

On Sunday we went to our parish church in the morning and to the cathedral in the evening, and Prince Oscar of Sweden with his Commodore and an A.D.C. lunched with us.

I cut my fingers very badly, taking a knife out of a sheath, and am bandaged up by the doctor. I fear I shall not be able to wear a glove at my drawing-room. I am *not* to wear a train, lest I should encourage extravagance, and so a smart one I had brought from England has to be packed away!

Monday, 22nd.—I paid my visit to the wife of the Lieutenant-Governor, Mrs. Rivers Thompson. They have a very pretty place just out of Calcutta, with a capital house and one of the largest lawns in India.

Lawns are precious things in hot countries. They have an artificial river in their grounds; so have we, ours having been made by Lord Lytton. Their river is rather larger than ours, and they had a predecessor who was interested in plants, so I think they have more to show in that respect than we have. They gave us tea on the balcony, and we saw the younger girls of the family, and had altogether a pleasant little visit.

Tuesday, 23*rd.*—We spent this day in a very official manner. The Viceroy was to hold a durbar in the afternoon; that is, in plain English, he was to receive three Rajahs, who pay their morning visits in state, every particular of the reception being carefully arranged beforehand. General Wilkinson and two of his Staff were to be present, so they lunched with us, and then the Marble Hall was prepared for the arrival of the first Rajah, His Highness the Maharajah of Jodhpore, whose rank required that 'the Military Secretary, the Under-Secretary in the Foreign Department, and an A.D.C. to the Viceroy' should drive to his residence to fetch him. Scarlet cloth was laid down for him; a guard of honour was at the door; a band played on the steps, and between each pillar down the hall stood a gigantic trooper of the body-guard, in his scarlet uniform, holding a lance in his hand. As the Maharajah arrived a salute of twenty-one guns was fired from the Fort.

We ladies were hidden behind a screen that we might look on.

A still grander throne than usual was placed for the

Viceroy—it was a silver one, with large gold lions for arms; an attendant with a white yak's tail in his hand stood by, lest a fly should trouble His Excellency's composure; a gold embroidered carpet was laid before the daïs, and chairs were arranged on either side of it. Some attendants held bunches of peacock feathers set in gold, and others had very big gilt maces in their hands. General Wilkinson and the Staff, and one native A.D.C., who wore a large turban and a broad band of red on his forehead, sat on the left of the throne. When the Maharajah reached the door, the Viceroy got up and walked to the middle of the room to meet him, shook hands with him, and motioned him to a chair on his right, while his followers took lower places on the same side. The Maharajah's dress was green and gold; he spoke through an interpreter, and the dialogue with him went on pretty well. No one else attempts to speak. 'After a short conversation,' say the regulations, 'the Maharajah's attendants are presented to the Viceroy, and each one holds out to him one gold mohur,' which he touches, thus politely expressing 'You may keep it though you are so anxious to give it to me.' Then there was another short conversation before the leave-taking. At a signal the Viceroy's attendants brought in two silver vessels; one contained attar of roses, the other some very sticky leaves wrapped up in silver and gold paper. I believe that when carefully unwrapped a small piece of betel-nut is found in each. The Viceroy puts a small spoonful of attar of roses on the Maharajah's hand, and gives him a sticky thing to take away with him, and they sit down again, while the Under-

Secretary in the Foreign Department does the same
for His Highness's attendants, and then they make
a final move. The Viceroy again takes a few steps
to conduct the Maharajah to the middle of the room,
bows to his followers, and they depart with the
'same ceremonies as those observed on His Highness's
arrival.'

For the second one, 'the Maharajah of Bhurtpur,
G.C.S.I.' two A.D.C.s went, seventeen guns were fired,
and His Excellency stood at the foot of the daïs to receive
His Highness, who had to offer '101 gold mohurs' to be
touched.

His Highness the Rajah of Faridkot was fetched by
two A.D.C.s. His Excellency remained on the daïs to
receive him. The salute was only eleven guns, and he
only presented eleven gold mohurs to 'be touched and
remitted.' All the other ceremonies were the same.
I have not told you much about the dresses, as we sat
behind the native guests and could not see them well.
It was very curious and interesting to see this once
in a way. I don't suppose we shall want to look on
often.

His Excellency went and unbent himself over a game
of tennis, but I rested all the afternoon with the prospect of several hundred curtseys to be made in the
evening.

We dined alone and dressed afterwards for the
drawing-room. When all was ready, a procession came
to fetch us, and preceded us into the throne-room.
D. and I stood on the daïs, and we found in the room
the gentlemen who have the entrée; their ladies passed

us first, and also remained in the room till the drawing-room was over. I told you *I* was not allowed to wear my train, but I found numbers of ladies had them on, to say nothing of lappets and feathers !

Most of the ladies were very smart, and I think everything went off as well as possible. I got rather hot with the exercise of making so many curtseys, but otherwise I did not feel the fatigue much. When it was over, the procession formed again and we went upstairs. This was the first time we had seen the large reception rooms peopled. They were quite full, and looked very nice. There was a buffet with light refreshments at one side of the ball-room, and the band played there too. We walked about for some time, making new acquaintances and speaking to some of the people we have already met, and then when I began to feel very tired we went away.

Wednesday, 24*th.*—Prince Karl, of Sweden, arrived from Delhi this morning to join his brother, Prince Oscar, who is in a man-of-war here. The one stays in the house, and the other came to meet him at breakfast. Prince Charles is very nice-looking and extremely tall We shall not see much of our guests, for they have to keep Christmas on the Swedish ship, and it takes two whole afternoons and evenings to do that properly.

The Calcutta races began to-day. We went to see them privately, but next Thursday week we go in state. The course is very pretty, and the stand is nicely arranged with plants and flowers. The races only go on between the hours of four and six. There will be polo and racing for alternate days all the week. The ladies were very smartly dressed, and it was a gay and pretty sight.

Thursday, 25th.—We should have spent a very pleasant Christmas Day indeed but for the absence of the children, who have hitherto always helped to make it 'merry;' and I think that all the little presents they had provided for us, and which, according to their directions, were laid out for us this morning, only served to mark the blank. The missing of them was an under-current running through the day. But it is of our doings, and not of our repinings, *I* must tell you.

Lord William Beresford had suggested that we should go and see Barrackpore in the afternoon, and as we were very glad to find some way of spending our Christmas with an appearance of gaiety we arranged to do so. We started in the steam launch as soon after church as possible, and enjoyed the trip up the river very much. With Barrackpore we were quite delighted. I suppose you know that it is a place the Viceroy has about twelve miles from Calcutta. It is situated on the river, and is quite like an English park, with beautiful single trees of different kinds, and it is all so pretty and so completely in the country that I long to go and stay there. It reminds me of the Duke of Westminster's place on the Thames, Cliveden, and we happened to have two of his sons with us, who thought so too. On landing, there is a short walk arched over by bamboos; then comes a pretty garden with a little fountain in it, and quantities of large blue convolvulus creeping over everything; then, to the right, lawn and shrubs, palms, and strange plants, and a gigantic banian-tree covering a great space of ground, its branches and offshoots forming arches and galleries, and a fine dining-room, which we used for luncheon. The scarlet liveries looked very beautiful moving in and out of this natural arbour, and we fell in love with Barrackpore on the spot.

Quantities of hawks collected in the branches above, and when we had finished our meal we threw up some bits of meat, which they swooped upon and caught before they fell, in the most graceful way.

I had heard the house was a perfect barn, but I was delighted with it. It is simply furnished, but there is quite enough in it for the little visits we pay, and I hope we shall often spend Sunday there. The Staff have bungalows in the grounds. I took the two maids down there, and they were pleased, which is a good thing, as they are the people to whom the constant packing up to go there will be troublesome.

We drove round the park and saw the rose-gardens and the monument to Lady Canning. *I*t was designed by Lady Waterford, her sister, and is placed over a favourite spot of hers, where she used to sit and draw. Coming home we had tea on the launch, and saw a fine sunset, in which the temples on the banks and the queer-shaped boats, with their picturesque rowers, looked lovely against the brilliant sky.

I sat down to write, so full of Barrackpore that I omitted to say that the family has received into its bosom a monkey ! *I* confess that when Nelly expressed her intention of setting up a monkey I was horrified, but I must say that the pleading eyes and gentle manners of the little creature she was given to-day have quite won my heart. Rachel has a parrot, and I received a little deer. Happily mine is not alive, and is only a beautiful specimen of Delhi enamel, the spots on his precious back being diamonds, his body being blue, and the ground on which he stands being gold inlaid with green.

The day did not pass without a misfortune. The wretched hawks, of whom I wrote a few minutes ago with enthusiasm, came down upon my balcony and, seizing a small cage, managed to abstract one of my canaries. The details were harrowing, but I have refused to hear them.

We had the great good fortune to receive our mail to-day, so all the Christmas good wishes came exactly at the right moment. From England, Canada, and Turkey Christmas cards and letters arrived, and all were very welcome.

Friday, 26th.—We have been to see our stables. They are across the road and next to the kitchen. Did I ever tell you that the kitchen is somewhere in Calcutta, but not in this house? There are fifty-five horses in the stable, and each horse has a man to himself, who lives with him and sleeps at the foot of his stall. I went over there in a bath-chair, drawn by two men, which is one of my Simla carriages.

Saturday, 27th.—We went again to the races and saw a very exciting dead-heat, and also a steeplechase in which Lord William rode.

So far we look somewhat isolated in the Grand Stand, for even the people we know don't come and speak to us, and I can't wander about after them. They think it is not proper to come up, but I hope they will soon lose that idea.

We had a 'small' dinner in the evening. We sat down thirty-six people. I was pleased to find that everyone highly approved the throne-room arrangement, and told me they had never seen it look so habitable before.

Thursday, January 1*st*, 1885.—I think my New Year really began on November 13. It was then we turned over a leaf, and I am not ready for a fresh epoch! However, we had a long and hard day's work with which to open 1885, for in India January 1 is not only New Year's Day, it is also 'Empress Day,' and, as such, is kept as a great holiday.

At eight o'clock in the morning we began our duties. I began them in a carriage and four, and the Viceroy on horseback. We went to the Maidan, and there assisted at a review. Although D. 'took the salute' and rode up and down the lines, and was the principal figure there, I consider that I had much the most trying part to play, for I was in great terror of my horses, and suffered much in anticipation of the *feu-de-joie*. They behaved very well, and nothing happened. The morning was lovely, and the military display went off well. The Staff was, of course, brilliant; the native regiments looked very fine, and especially one which has buff facings; there were Volunteers too, dressed in brown (khaki) to match the grass, some artillery, a 'regular' regiment, and a very small company of irregular sailors. I know they volunteer, and that they dress as seamen, but whether they ever go in a boat, or know the bow from the stern, I can't tell; still I feel quite sure that H.E. the Vice-Admiral of Ulster took great interest in them.

We got home to breakfast before ten, and the next public performance was a state visit to the races to see the Viceroy's Cup run for. We had two carriages and four, and a strong escort and outriders, so that the procession must really have looked very pretty driving up the course. There were crowds of people, and D. was very well received indeed. We are no longer so solitary on the stand, as we are rapidly making acquaintances, and people begin to understand that we don't wish to be cloistered. They have seen a great deal of us this gay week.

In the evening we made a great innovation. There was to be a large official dinner for 100 men, and D. thought he would like his three ladies to dine at it, so we broke through all traditions, and did so, and I think the experiment was successful, and, at any rate, we made it appear less of a public dinner and more of a private entertainment. We also took great pains with the room, put down a carpet in the Marble Hall, and got out our plate, and ornamented and lighted the table, so that it really looked very handsome. Nowell was quite excited over his first dinner of 100, and all his talents for organisation came into full play. I forget if I told you that he is now put in charge of the household, and we find it the greatest comfort to have one European head.   The natives are excellent servants, but they want a master hand over them.

Saturday, 3rd.—There are three ways of getting to Barrackpore, by road, by river, or by rail, and we settled to try the road this time.   We drove for about six miles through the town and through native bazaars, and then got on our riding horses for about six more.   The whole way there were splendid trees on either side of the road, a perfect avenue, and as I had gained confidence in my pony 'The Duke,' I enjoyed my ride extremely.   We reached Barrackpore about six o'clock, and found it looking quite lovely.   A splendid sunset, reflected in the river, added to its natural beauty, and our Christmas Day enthusiasm suffered no diminution.

Sunday, 4th.—We are, if possible, still more en-chanted this morning.   Everything here seems to be perfect—the weather, the air, the trees, flowers, shrubs, creepers, sunshine !

The place is beautifully kept.   The trees are very fine and of infinite variety ; roses are in the greatest profusion, and some of them are quite enrmoous ; the large blue convolvulus climbs all over a long low wall, which surrounds a little garden full of heliotrope and other sweet flowers, and where a little fountain plays in a marble basin ; there are bushes of red and purple blossom, and a lovely orange creeper covers the balcony near which I write.   I am sitting in a sort of open room, which has the drawing-room behind it, and the square uncovered balcony in front.   This, you must remember, is the depth of winter ! I believe that once upon a time I used to skate in January, and that a fur cap and sealskin were necessary to my well-being then ; but now I have to 'mind the sun' and to wear a double felt hat, and to carry a white umbrella. I am glad to be able to say that I have thoroughly enjoyed both extremes, and that, although I delighted in a Canadian winter, I have the greatest pleasure in drinking in the sunshine of an Indian one. D. and I took a little stroll early in the morning, and greatly admired our demesne, and then we sat under the celebrated banian-tree for breakfast, and Nelly's monkey perched on a branch and enjoyed itself too. Later we walked on and looked at Lady Canning's tomb, and examined the plants that were new to us on the way. There is a marble monument over the grave, with an inscription written by Lord Canning on one side and a text on the other. The enclosure is large, and the railing round it is composed of twisted C.s with a coronet across them.

As we spend Sunday here, it is well to find that the church is as satisfactory as the rest of the place. It is close to our gate, so we walk there, passing a piece of water, on which lovely red water-lilies grow. The service and sermon were both very nice, and the whole thing felt home-like, simple and quiet.

There is absolute pleasure in existing in a place like this, and I am always wishing I could show it to those at home.

I have not taken much exercise lately, but I made up for it to-day. Directly after lunch, in despite of all Indian rules and regulations, we began to walk about,

and we walked the whole afternoon, visiting first a temple
in the grounds erected ' to the Memory of the Brave.'
It is built in Grecian style, and on the walls inside are
tablets, on which are inscribed the names of the officers
who were killed in an Indian war.   Then we looked at
the Flagstaff Bungalow, and made our way over to a
place where elephants were to be seen.   They are used
for commissariat purposes, and it was very interesting
to us to come upon thirty-six of these animals ' at home,'
each one being fed by his special attendant, or mahout,
who makes up his food into little bundles and insists upon
his eating it so ; for it seems that, when left to himself,
the elephant wastes his provender, and does not make
the most of it.   He used to be given rice, of which he is
very fond, but alas ! these are economical days, and now
he has to content himself with sugar-cane and straw.
It is funny to see how, while munching up a mouthful,
the elephant takes up a wisp of straw and brushes
away all the flies which annoy him.   We asked the man
in charge to send an elephant over for us to ride in
the morning.

On our way back we explored the plant-houses and
the garden, then had tea on the verandah, and started
off on a still longer walk to visit a Hindu temple.

The people there received us most civilly, and we
found the old gentleman in charge could speak English
very well.   He told us he built the temple, but *I* think
he must have been mistaken.   We could not enter the
sacred precincts, but from outside we were allowed to
peep at the shrine, where under a silver canopy a metal
goddess sits, a crown on her head and a plate of rice in

her hand, while the god, who is made of eight kinds of metal, stands by and holds out his hands to her, asking for gifts. There were six more small temples round, but we did not try to look into them, as we are not quite sure whether the people like it.

We discovered a fireplace in our house, and as it is rather chilly in the evening we were glad to sit by a fire when we came in.

Monday, 5th.—We went for a nice ride on our horses at 7.30 this morning, and after breakfast we mounted our elephant! He knelt down, and a ladder was placed against his side for us to mount, while the servants made a loop of his tail and climbed up by it. When we were shut up in the howdah, the elephant was told to rise, and as he got on his front legs it seemed as if everything must slip off behind, and we had to hold on very tight until he had reached an even keel; then he looked very grand with his scarlet cloth and the howdah full of people, marching over the grass and towering above the shrubs, and we felt quite comfortable and enjoyed our elevated ride very much. The mahout sits on the elephant's neck and guides him with his feet.

We returned to Calcutta by river and drove on to the polo grounds for a little. The Viceroy was away the whole day opening a small railway. He enjoyed the expedition very much. He travelled up twenty miles of new line, lunched in a tent, and visited a shrine, The story they tell of this sacred place is this: A man found that his cow never gave any milk, so he watched her proceedings, and saw her pour it out as a libation before a certain stone, and henceforth all people follow her example, and come and present offerings to the god there, so that the priest in charge makes his fortune out of pilgrims. This man had just been let out of prison, having committed a serious crime, and it was explained to the Viceroy that he must be very civil to him because he was a great man, but not too civil as he was a bad man. I believe D. managed this delicate ' nuance ' perfectly.

Don't suppose that we all came home to rest. No, we had to go to the theatre, and though everything else is early here, the theatre is late, and we did not get home till one o'clock. 'Artful Cards' was rather nicely played, but the artists are starving, and we must go again to help them.

Tuesday, 6th.—During my absence I had my balcony wired in, for I found the impertinence of the crows was becoming intolerable ; and you should have seen the fearful excitement of the green parrots this morning when they found their accustomed haunt closed to them.

Wednesday, 7th.—Colonel Euan-Smith, the Resident at Bhurtpore, breakfasted with us. We sat a long time and ranged over many subjects, from lieutenant-governors down to tigers, and from elephants to the weather. Talking of the English spoken by natives, he told us he once received a letter beginning ' Honoured Enormity.' The writer had evidently looked in the dictionary and found this expression suitable. One man, during an examination, was told to write an essay upon

the horse, which he did in the following brief terms :
' The horse is a very noble animal, but when irritated,
he ceases to do so.'   Another had to write upon the
difference between riches and poverty, and he ended by
saying—' In short, the rich man welters on crimson
velvet, while the poor man snorts on flint.'

Colonel Euan-Smith also told us of an officer's adventures with a tiger, by which he lost an arm.   He had
climbed along the trunk of a tree which was slanting
over a pond, and had fired at a tiger from the end of it ;
the tiger was wounded, but, to his horror, Captain X.
saw the beast walking across the tree towards him.   He
dropped into the water, the tiger fell on him, and he was
pulled ashore by the animal, who was just well enough
to lie on him and munch away at the arm which he put
up to protect his face.   Presently the tiger, feeling very
bad, retired a little way, and Captain X. had sufficient
presence of mind to roll gently back into the water, where
some men came to his rescue.

In the afternoon I visited the General Hospital and
the Lady Canning Home.   The Clewer Sisters live at the
Home and train nurses.   Most of the women are Eura-
sians, and they seem to make very good sick nurses
when once they have learned by precept and example
that it is not beneath them to hand a glass of water to
a patient, and that such little offices may be performed
without the intervention of a coolie.   The climate at
this time of year is a great help to hospital management,
for when you can have all the windows wide open and
a bright sun streaming in, you require fewer comforts,
less furniture, and everything looks cheerful for the

patients.   There were some very sad cases of accident and illness; it is so hard to be laid up far from home, and we saw several men who, having families to provide for, have lost, with their health, all means of making a living for them, and don't even know how to get back to England themselves.

We dined at the Lieutenant-Governor's, and they had a party after.   They have such a nice house, and we spent a very pleasant evening.

Thursday, *8th*.—We had one of the usual dinners for about sixty-four people.   I don't think there was anything remarkable about it.   It went off very well, and Mrs. Euan-Smith played the piano for us.   We let the guests go instead of retiring ourselves; it is less stiff, and besides I never can get His Excellency away, so it is much shorter and easier to let him be left.

Friday, *9th*.—We went to see Lady Stewart in the Fort.   It is a very large one, and we wound in and out of arches and drove over many drawbridges before reaching the Commander-in-Chief's quarters.

Saturday, *10th*.—I consented heroically to drive to the races on Lord William's coach, and I bore the ordeal with fortitude.   I must allow that the horses went like lambs, and that he is a first-rate whip.   He even retained my confidence after he had put out his left shoulder riding in a steeplechase, and when crowds returning home, and darkness coming on, made the journey back much more perilous.   There were three steeplechases, and in each one there were falls, but happily no serious accident to anyone. Lord William's was the worst, but he does not mind such a trivial discomfort as having a shoulder dislocated, and, as I said before, he drove us through the most populous streets safely to the railway station. There we met Judge and Mrs. Cunningham (Lord Lawrence's daughter), who were coming to stay with us at Barrackpore, and we had a nice little dinner of ten.

Sunday, 11*th.*—Sir Auckland Colvin and Mr. Lyall (Resident at Mysore) came out in time for breakfast; then some of us walked to church, and afterwards we sat under the trees till lunch time.

We again fed the hawks and again visited the elephants, and on our way home looked into an English cemetery. It is crowded with rather large and very dilapidated monuments. Two of the inscriptions rather amused me. One began with the French words ' Ici repose,' all the rest being English, and another had on it—

' John Taylor,

A wretched, poor and helpless worm,

Into Thy kind arms I fall.

———

Erected as a mark of respect by his wife.'

The word ' respect ' seems to come in funnily after the melancholy description of him given above.

I gathered one anecdote from Judge Cunningham which is amusing. It is an illustration of true native politeness. A judge, who was a very bad shot, had been

out for a day's sport, and on his return the man who
went with him was asked—'Well, how did the judge
shoot to-day?' 'Oh!' he replied, 'the judge shot beautifully, but God was very merciful to the birds.'

Monday, 12*th.*—D. and the rest of the party went off
in the launch directly after breakfast—for the Viceroy is
hard at work all and every day, and has to hurry back
to his office early on Monday morning—but I remained
behind for a couple of hours, which I spent in arranging
all the rooms for the Duke and Duchess of Connaught,
who come to stay with us next week. I returned by
train.

Tuesday, 13*th.*—My aviary being finished, I went
early in the morning to look for some birds to put in it.
There were such curious beasts at the place, and one
monkey which looked as if some Barnum had been at
work upon him, so extraordinary was his complexion
and general colouring. He had a good coat of brown
fur, and his hair stood out round his head. His nose
and mouth were a brilliant scarlet, his cheeks a bright
blue, and on his back he had two large patches of purple
opalescent colour, as if the sun were shining through
a purple glass window on to his fur. I never saw anything so strange.

On my return, I did much housekeeping, hung pictures, arranged rooms, and saw that all was in apple-pie
order for to-morrow.

In the afternoon I went to visit two hospitals, one
the Medical College, the other the Eden. They are

very large and airy, but I don't think it will profit
you much for me to describe them. Medical students,
swathed in sheets and with bare heads, stood on the
steps to receive me. 'Sister Lucy' and her nurses
were there, and native women who have taken nursing
diplomas were in attendance, wrapped in washing silk
saris; and in the Eden, which is a lying-in hospital,
there were some very tiny brown babies to be seen. In
the other all sorts of ills are mixed up together, and
even the cholera patients are not isolated. I suppose
that, being able to have the air rushing in on every side,
the danger of contagion is not so great as at home.

Wednesday, 14*th.*—I was down at 7.30, looked at all
the rooms, saw that my balcony and my charming new
toy, the aviary, looked nice, and then, when the salute
began, I went out on the steps to receive the Duke
and Duchess of Connaught. They were very kind in
their appreciation of the efforts we had made to make
them comfortable, and they seemed to notice everything that had been done for them. They breakfasted
with us.

After luncheon we looked on from behind a screen at
a large deputation of Mahometans who came to present
an address. They were all in fine costumes, and wore
great varieties of headdresses.

As soon as D. was free, we started off for the Botanical Gardens. We had settled to go up in the steam
launch and to drive back. When passing the King of
Oude's Palace, which is opposite the Botanical Gardens,
we saw a man standing on the top of a house waving

a flag, with which he was directing the movements of hundreds of pigeons. It was very pretty to see them wheeling about and executing manœuvres in the air in obedience to his signals.

The Botanical Gardens are very beautiful and interesting, and we went round them with Dr. King, who is an enthusiastic gardener. We had tea under a large, but very much less pretty banian-tree than our own, and then drove home in the char-à-banc.

A 'small' dinner of forty-three ended the day—a military dinner: the Duke told me he had not been in the room with so many Generals for a long time.

Thursday, 15*th.*—There is nothing like energy. The Duke and the Duchess and all of us except D. were on the coach by seven o'clock A.M., and on our way to the paper chase, which we found a very amusing scene. There were crowds of spectators in carriages and on horseback, besides the hunters themselves, who were arrayed in most sporting costumes. The 'double' puzzled many of them, and I never saw anything funnier than the knot of unwilling horses who remained for about five minutes 'refusing,' and causing the greatest anxiety to their riders. The chase was very fast, and Lord William came in first, but he had missed a fence, and so Mrs. Cooke was declared the winner. We got home for breakfast, and then the energetic Duchess said she required exercise, so I took her all over the house. After that she went out shopping till lunch time, and at four we drove out to see a game of polo.

We had a state dinner of seventy-three, and a great

reception after. There were many natives in fine dresses, and I thought it all looked very pretty and gay. The Duchess enjoyed it very much, and of course she was a great attraction. The party filled all the reception rooms upstairs, and the buffet was in the Marble Hall where we had dined.

Friday, 16*th.*—More energy! Military manœuvres at 7.30. We were all out again, and D. and the Duke rode, the Viceroy having to take the salute; then there was a march past, and a sham fight. As we were in the thick of it with four horses I felt it more prudent to descend from the carriage, and the Duchess walked about with me, and we inspected the killed and wounded who lay in our path, and who looked very picturesque and comfortable. A large square red flag represented the enemy, and we were pleased to see it utterly routed. Not until we felt sure of victory did we return home. The Duke went on to see an Army Clothing place, and we came home to breakfast and to read our letters.

We were just going out in the afternoon when a dreadful dust-storm came on unexpectedly, and I feared that it would be followed by rain. Happily it cleared, and the Duke and Duchess played tennis, and we had tea in the garden. We dined a little earlier than usual, and dressed afterwards for the ball. *It* began about ten o'clock, when we all met in my rooms, and went up in procession to the ball-room, which was already full of people. 'God save the Queen' was played as we came in, and we immediately danced a state quadrille. I had managed to get a great deal more light into the room;

the floor and music were good, and I think, on the whole, it was a very nice ball, pretty and gay and bright.

Saturday, 17*th*.—I was very tired, and so took the day easy; but the Duchess, in spite of a headache, did the most fatiguing things. She and the Duke, with Nelly in waiting, went and hunted about in the hot sun for the Chinese Bazaar, which, it appears, does not exist; and after luncheon they all went with D. on the coach to the steeplechases; Lady Downe, the Bishop, Major Cooper, and *I* going up in the launch to Barrackpore. I was anxious to see that all was in order for our guests, and *I* was rewarded for giving up the races by having a very nice quiet afternoon. The others arrived at 7.30, and we dined a little later than usual, so as to give them time to dress. I was glad to find that no accident happened to Lord William, who had again ridden in a race.

Sunday, 18*th*.—We spent our day as usual here, and the Duke and Duchess seemed to enjoy it thoroughly. We asked the clergyman and his wife and the Commanding Officer and his wife to lunch, and the only variety made in the hawk amusement afterwards was the experiment, tried successfully, of putting a bit of meat on the top of Dr. Scott's hat as he sat at table under the banian-tree. Twice a hawk came down and carried it off, and the birds swarmed round us as they saw that there was food to be had. When, however, the gentlemen all went and sat in a row, their helmets surmounted with tempting bait, the hawks suspected a trick and would not come down.

Monday, 19th.—To-day we visited French territory, and were received by the Governor and given a grand lunch by the authorities. It took us about an hour in the steam launch to get to Chandernagore, and when we landed and had climbed in safety over a dangerous pathway of carpet and red cloth, we found ourselves in the tiniest and most uninteresting of little towns. The possession is only about three miles in size, and the French have to keep up a governor, magistrates, and a miniature army there, all of whom are excessively bored, having neither business nor pleasure with which to fill their time, and not sufficient space to supply mischief for their idle hands. Their wildest dissipation is sitting on a ghat looking at the sunset to the accompaniment of a glass of sherry. They were all very kind to us, and the Governor drank the healths of our Queen and country while we drank prosperity to the Republic.

The lunch, which was very good, took longer than we expected, but the sights took no time at all, and so when we got to Calcutta the sun had not quite disappeared, but was sleepily gilding the river, while the approaching darkness gave to all the ships and barges a sort of beautiful mystery. After this little gleam of poetry came the prose of dressing for a ball, and then the ball itself.

It was given by the city to the Duke and Duchess of Connaught, was arranged in the Town Hall, and was a great success. Everyone had lent things to help the decoration, and in addition to the ball-room, which was hung with white and yellow, and which had a military trophy at one end and raised seats covered with bright carpets at the other, there were several beautifully furnished sitting-rooms. The supper was in a great hall with columns, on each one of which was a shield with arms on it. The whole was brilliantly lighted. The Duke and Duchess did their duty thoroughly in the dancing way, and stayed late, so that everyone was pleased.

Tuesday, 20th.—I took the Duchess in the morning to see the Economic Museum. Perhaps some day, when *I* have less to say, *I* may do a little ' Murray ' and tell you about it, but now I will only say that one can see specimens of the commoner Indian materials there, and that *I* shall certainly return when I have more time to go through it.

The Maharanee of Kuch Behar came to see the Duchess and stayed to lunch. She is very nice, and seems so pleased to come here, and keeps telling me she feels so at home. She brought the little boy, who is so early to be made an English schoolboy ; he is a most precocious little creature, not three years old, but he already speaks English and rides a pony.

We all drove to the Zoological Gardens in the afternoon, and a monkey there was a great success. He is quite a character, and goes on in such a human fashion, and does such absurd things with such a solemn face, that it is really very amusing to watch him. We gave him a newspaper, which he appeared to read, and which he opened and turned over and smoothed and studied, and then he put it on his head and looked at us from under it, chewing a tooth-pick meanwhile.

From the Zoo to the Bishop's Palace ! — a very fine house. We had tea there, and then went to see the monuments in the cathedral and to hear the organ. This closed the Royal visit, for we dined in morning dress, and they left after dinner. We were all quite sorry to part with them. They are both so nice, and seem to enjoy everything, and no *contretemps* of any kind occurred to spoil the visit. I must mention that we all wrote in each others' books, that we exchanged photographs and were photographed in a group, and were weighed, all our lightnesses and our heavinesses being duly recorded; and that, in addition to all I have told you, there were some little rides and walks and games of lawn tennis to fill the spare moments.

Wednesday, 21st.—A complete day of rest for me, but the Viceroy, who is always at work, gets none. I did not go out at all until the evening, when we went on board an old ship to attend a concert given for the sailors. It is a sort of mission, and the place is called ' Bethel.' The chaplain is very energetic, and several ladies sing and take trouble in getting up these weekly concerts. We thought it was a good thing to encourage, and I believe the Viceroy's presence gave great pleasure to the ' river.' I was given a lovely bouquet with an anchor in the centre made of white roses, and a pretty programme was painted for us, and flags covered in and ornamented the place. The sailors joined in the chorus, and they sang a song themselves in which the solo part was, ' Where are you going to, my pretty maid ? ' and the chorus always replied something about ' Rio Grande.'

Saturday, 24th.— In the afternoon our new guests, the Duke and Duchess of Mecklenburg-Schwerin and Don Carlos, went to the races. D. stayed at home to work, and I went to give prizes at some native schools, Lord Radstock presiding.

It was rather an interesting sight. There was a little platform put up for me in a garden, on one side of which were the Hindu Christian girls belonging to the Normal School. Many of these become teachers, and some of them looked about sixteen years of age. They were dressed in white, the older ones wearing white veils over their heads. Near them, and on the other side of the daïs, were three more schools. All the girls in these were small and wore native dresses; that is to say, coloured wraps and lots of jewels—bracelets on their wrists and ankles, earrings and nose-rings. Their hair was drawn tight back and was done up in a large knob, nature's deficiencies being made up with ribbon; this knob was sometimes covered with a coloured net, and sometimes the whole head and ears were hidden with gold ornaments; but the teachers discourage the wearing of much jewellery at school, as the responsibility is too great for them. None of these girls looked more than ten or eleven, nor are they more developed in appearance than children of that age at home; and it was sad to give a doll as a prize to some poor little creature who, young as she is, is probably on the very verge of matrimony, who may any moment leave her own parents for the tender mercies of a mother-in-law or of an elderly husband, or who as a child-widow may be condemned to a sort of outcast existence all the rest of her days.

The ceremonies consisted in singing hymns and songs in various languages, then an interesting report was read, and Lord Radstock spoke. After this came my part of the proceedings, and I dealt out dolls, little boxès, and picture-books, as rewards for 'Scripture, Geography, Literature, Bengali, and Usefulness.'

We all met at the station and came to Barrackpore by train.

Sunday, 25th.—Sir Thomas Baker, the Adjutant-General, is with us here. The Bougainvilleas, a lovely purple creeper, and the Bignonia, an orange one, are in perfection, and a large cotton tree, which looked dead ten days ago, is now covered with beautiful large bunches of a bright flame-coloured lily-shaped flower.

Monday, 26th.—I think that in this climate one should record a fog, and we went out riding this morning in the thickest and dampest mist possible, and had to light a lamp for breakfast! *It* cleared off soon after nine, and we had a pleasant voyage back to Calcutta by the river.

Tuesday, 27th.—I shan't record fogs any more, for they appear to be common enough at this time of year, and this morning again we had to move the breakfast table into the house; my balcony was dripping, and I felt anxious as to the health of my birds!

D. was happy this afternoon in opening his own particular tennis court. It has been made in the space between two wings of the house; it has a red composition floor and wooden walls, which are eventually to be covered with creepers. Several gentlemen in scarlet uniforms attend to pick up the balls, but they are to be exchanged for small boys, lightly clad. D.'s artistic eye is in perpetual delight here, either over the muscles exhibited by those who wear few garments, such as the Bheesties, or over the majestic folds of the ' Roman toga,' for that is the name we ignorantly give to the costume of the ordinary native of Calcutta. I think it was to their brown colour and to their muscles that the Viceroy was looking forward when he ordered his little boys, but a higher authority has commanded that they shall be draped.

Having mentioned him casually, *I* must, *I* think, introduce you formally to the ' Bheestie.' He is quite a character, and a feature in every landscape. Look where you will, out of your window or out of your carriage, you are sure to see a bronze athlete, with a large turban on his head, a short garment round his waist, and a heavy skin full of water over his back, laying the dust on every side and defying in his own person all such modern inventions as water-carts or hose. His is real, hard, uninterrupted labour. His calling is honourable, his caste high—everyone will accept water from a Bheestie ; and those attached to regiments have served so well in time of war that now they are eligible for decorations given for service in the field.

I fear *I* see too distinctly to share His Excellency's admiration for the ' Roman toga.' *I* like bright colours, handsome stuffs, and beautiful jewels—in my frivolous feminine way—and although spotless sheets, an occasional laurel wreath, and the primitive sandal may have added something to the dignity of the heroes and emperors of ancient days, I am not very sanguine on the subject, for in my experience classic and æsthetic dress always loses by translation from theory into practice.

In the evening we all went in different directions : I patronised a concert in aid of Roman Catholic schools, D. went to the circus, and others attended a party at the Bishop's.

Wednesday, 28th.—I saw a very horrid sight this afternoon. It was the last day of the races, and Lord William was to ride in some ' consolation stakes ' which, I thought, sounded like an easy little race for unlucky horses. We went to the course in time to see him ride, and at the very first fence, straight in front of the stand, he had an awful fall. I shut my eyes through part of it ; but when I looked up he was lying perfectly motionless, and when he was lifted his face was covered with blood. He has hurt himself badly, but the doctors think his head is uninjured. We shall not allow him to ride steeplechases any more. I had had quite enough of the races after this, and came home.

Thursday, 29th.—I took the Duchess of Mecklenburg-Schwerin to a great jeweller's shop by way of entertainment, and I was much interested myself by all we saw there. The jewels set in Europe for the Eastern market are a curious mixture of splendour and childishness : watches encrusted with diamonds, and with such complicated interiors that, besides telling you all you can

possibly want to know about the time of the day or of
the year, they play you a tune, and give you a representation of the conductor waving about his bâton as he
sits somewhere on the face, mixed up with the seconds
and the hours.   Then there are ornaments for turbans,
on which the diamond flowers, being wound up, whirl
round and round till you can no longer see their shape.
It would be difficult to keep up an argument with a
man whose jewels were behaving in such an eccentric
manner!

We also saw a fine collection of native jewels which
are to be sold by auction in a few weeks.   To our ideas
they are positively ugly, and one can only wonder at the
way in which the precious stones are treated— enormous
rubies, emeralds, and pearls bored through and strung
together like ordinary beads; diamonds cut perfectly
flat and looking like very common glass.   There were
some buttercups, the petals of which were diamonds cut
quite thin and utterly destroyed.   There are ornaments
set double—that is, with rubies on one side and emeralds
on the other; and there are precious stones in all sorts
of useless things, such as small boxes, mouthpieces, &c.
When we had looked at all these things, the jeweller
took us into the workshops to see the silver repoussé
work done.   The men draw the pattern on a flat piece
of silver, and then beat down the background.

The day ended with a large dinner here, and a
pretty cheery little dance.

CHAPTER II

FIRST SEASON IN CALCUTTA

JANUARY 31 TO MARCH 18, 1885

Saturday, January 31st.—The Duke and Duchess of Mecklenburg-Schwerin and Don Carlos have left us.

The girls and I came down to Barrackpore early by train, as I wanted to see the 'institutions' here. They are of a nice small size, so that a little tea and tobacco and a plum cake are sufficient to give pleasure. Four very old women are entirely provided for, and there are a few other pensioners and a school for native Christian children. There were some fascinating infants there, and the teaching seemed wonderfully good. The pupils, who had only been learning a year, wrote English and Hindustani characters remarkably well, and they sang in English, pronouncing it most distinctly.

The afternoon was lovely, and we enjoyed it much, as we sat under the banian-tree waiting for D. and our guests. This week Sir Donald and Lady Stewart and their two daughters, and Captain Haines their A.D.C., came to us.

We are a party of twelve, and we only brought the young members of our Staff with us, so in the evening they play games and enjoy themselves, though I must say that no one is more lively than Sir Donald himself, who is not young. He is such a nice man.

Sunday, February 1st.—Heavy rain this morning! One has to be glad because it is good for the country and because it is right to be unselfish, otherwise I should complain bitterly. This place is only intended for outdoor life, for as none of the rooms have real windows, they are extremely dismal in the daytime. Some have skylights, and some have windows opening on to verandahs.

Happily the day cleared, and we were able to get to church and once more to sit under the trees, and the girls insisted upon having a net dragged through a sort of tank which I have once before described as being covered with red water-lilies, and to our surprise ten or twelve very large fish were taken. We put back some, and ate others. This seems a good place to give you the practical information that there is only one fish to be had in Calcutta, and day after day ' becti' appears upon the bill of fare—becti hot, becti cold, becti of course. In April one more comes in, the mango fish by name, but by that time we shall be at Simla, where there is not even the becti. I have eaten him too often to be able to tell you whether he is good or not, but I will remember to consult some tourist on the subject.

A few new birds have joined the company of hawks at Barrackpore. I can't say they sing, but they are not dumb. The ' copper-head's' ' coo' sounds exactly like a blow upon a piece of metal. The 'brainfever' bird repeats his name over and over again until he nearly gives you the malady itself. The 'mynas' make a sound like intensified crickets, and I am sure that I have heard a bird that says 'Baccarat' constantly, but he does not seem to be known to fame. The oriole's lovely golden plumage is sometimes to be seen flitting through the branches; there are also squirrels in the trees, and at night there are jackals 'prowling around'! So much for the zoology of Barrackpore as far as I know it.

After church I looked at the Zenana Mission House and the Sunday School. Widows are the most numerous of the converts, which is easy to understand, for going over to Christianity means the sacrifice of home, and therefore those who have the fewest ties, and whose position at home is unhappy, naturally leave it more willingly than women who have husbands to consider.

It is a curious thing that there is no opposition whatever made to the teaching of the Bible in the schools, and all the children are instructed in it and in no other religion. Some people say that the parents do not object because they feel that caste prejudice is too strong to permit of many conversions; others that the children lose their own superstitions and do not gain a new religion; while some persons believe that the ground is prepared, and that it requires very little to bring the people over to Christianity in a mass.

Monday, 2nd, to Friday, 6th.—I do not think the events of the rest of the week have been interesting enough to give them to you in detail. D. paid his return visit to the

Maharajah of Jeypore, and was hung with garlands of flowers and gold braid.   Admiral Sir W. Hewitt arrived with two ships, and sleeps in our house, but spends most of his days on board.

Sir James and Miss Fergusson, Mrs. Dean, and two A.D.C.s have also come; and as we expect Lord Randolph Churchill on Saturday, we have had to put up tents in the garden for the accommodation of some of these visitors.

I have had a little durbar of my own, and have received the Maharajah of Jeypore in solemn conclave. The girls had taken Miss Fergusson and Mrs. Dean out for a drive, and I was alone in my boudoir, when Mr. Wallace sent to ask when I could receive His Highness. 'Now,' I replied, and so he was ushered in, and, quite after the manner of the Viceroy, I advanced to meet him on the threshold, waved him to a pink silk chair, paid him 'all the compliments of the season,' mentioned the satisfaction it gave me to see him and to find him well, said how much I had heard of Jeypore, and how much various guests of mine had spoken of his kindness to them, accepted an invitation for myself to go there, and accepted His Highness's photograph in return for my own which the Viceroy had given him.

His remarks and mine were interpreted by a sombre Babu all in black, while the Maharajah wore a pink moiré frock coat, pompadour trousers, white satin waistcoat, diamond and emerald necklace, and a turban made of red silk cord, put on so as to show a good deal of his long black hair.   I must warn you that the words 'frock coat and trousers,' when applied to the costume of the

Maharajah, might not be accepted as correct by the great Mr. Poole, but if you can imagine the first to be old-fashioned and short-waisted, and the second to be tight and in wrinkles, and finally to be lost in a pair of European boots, you will have a very fair idea of His Highness's appearance. His manners were quite as beautiful as my own, and he made his exit most gracefully.

The dinner was for about seventy people, but the dance was a little larger than usual in honour of Sir James Fergusson. It ended nevertheless at twelve. Happily the early hours are very popular with the men, and even with the ladies, who are very gay here and have to sit up almost too many nights of the week. These small dances have been most successful, but this is the last of them, as we have a ball next week, and then comes Lent. During the evening there was a great thunder and hailstorm.

Please to remember that I am in India, for if you don't keep that fact before your eyes you will not find the following description of a flower show at all interesting. You will only imagine that I am in the County Down, and will wonder why I should tell you anything so commonplace.

On Friday afternoon I, being at Calcutta, started off for the Agri-Horticultural Gardens, armed with an umbrella and a mackintosh. A few steps from the gate I put up the hood of the carriage; a few steps farther I put on the mackintosh; and on alighting I put up an umbrella and proceeded to walk through a very damp tent, looking at the various exhibits which had been

more or less damaged by the weather last night; then
made a rapid passage across the wet grass to another
tent to look at cut flowers, but was entreated to hurry
through my inspection, as the tent was likely to come
down, and so made haste back to the carriage and home.
Of course it is forty years since such a thing happened
before, but I can only speak from experience, and it is
very unfortunate for the weather that I happen to keep
a journal.

I really was very sorry for the people interested, as
it quite ruined the show, and *I* wanted myself, from
practical motives, to see what ought to grow here.

By the evening, wet streets and very beautiful summer
lightning fitfully illuminating the sky were all that remained of the storm, and *I* was very glad of it, for it
was one of our outgoing nights. We were patronising an
amateur performance of ' Pygmalion and Galatea,' given
' to aid the advancement of dramatic art in India ; ' which
means, in plainer English than that of the programme,
that the amateurs wished to act, that they originally
intended to look out for a charity to act for, but that before
that object was decided upon it was discovered that their
three nights' performances would completely empty the
already nearly empty theatres of the place, and therefore it was arranged that the money should go to them ;
and we saw some of the unsuccessful professionals throw-
ing bouquets at these self-sacrificing amateurs.

Saturday, 7th.—We gave a Barrackpore garden and
children's party. Had two elephants with smart howdahs
on for the infants to ride, a band playing, a little

target to shoot at, and tea. If it does rain in India it also can dry up, and my party was not at all spoilt by yesterday's downpour.

Sunday, 8th.—Sir Charles and Lady Macgregor, Sir Auckland Colvin, Lord Randolph Churchill, and two Frenchmen—the Marquis de la Grange and the ' Prince de Lucigne, Count de Faucigny '—all came to lunch. The foreigners have piles of letters of introduction, and will come and stay with us as soon as we have room for them Lord Randolph remains here, and the rest of the party returned to Calcutta in the evening. They all liked their day in the country, and all thought Barrackpore perfectly lovely.

Monday, 9th.—I had an afternoon visit from Mr. Broughton, ' Administrator-General here, and son of a very old friend of ours. He told me what he was doing, and how he had little ventures in silk and tea; and, while discoursing on local topics, he mentioned casually that he was trustee for an idol, to which he paid 250 rupees a month. This ' idol ' is a sacred stone, and can perhaps scarcely be dignified with the name of ' god,' but the account of it was rather interesting. A deputation was sent to look for two sacred stones in some river, and when they were brought back, a meeting was held to decide whether they were really sacred or not. Mr. Broughton had to be present, while a Fakir and some other learned personages squatted on the floor, with a book and the stones before them, and compared them with a rea old, undoubted ' idol ' which was brought in for the purpose. This jury gave it against the new candidates, but I suppose the stones appealed, for the verdict was somehow or other reversed, and a suitable throne was procured upon which the three now sit and receive their monthly stipend.

We had a very pleasant dinner at the Fort; all the family (the Commander-in-Chief's) are bright and cheerful, and everyone seemed to be happy. Miss Stewart took our profiles on a blank wall, and I hear my portrait is admirable. She has quite a gallery of these heads. The shadow is thrown on the wall, and the outline is done in pencil and then filled in with black; the effect is very good. The victim's head rests against a wineglass to keep it steady, and the artist has, after the manner of photographers, to put the chin a little more up or a little more down, which process of arrangement, as performed by a lovely young lady, seemed to amuse and gratify the gentlemen much. Lord Randolph raised his eyebrows a little as he sat under this treatment the day of his first introduction to society here.

Tuesday, 10*th.*—I am afraid you will begin to doubt my veracity if I tell you that the rain rather interfered with tennis this afternoon, and quite prevented the use of a refreshment tent at the Lieutenant-Governor's ball! But I assure you it is true. So we did very little in the day; at night we had a small dinner of people specially asked to meet Sir James Fergusson, and then put up an umbrella and dashed into the carriage to drive to Belvedere. The ball was very nice indeed, and I enjoyed it, for at last I do believe I am making a few acquaintances. Hitherto it has been most uphill work. I may talk all through a dinner on Monday to some persons, but when I see them on Tuesday, they not only don't speak to me, but I can't feel sure that a gleam of recognition passes over their faces, and all the labour of remembering them and of trying to bow to them or to speak to them falls upon me. I am told it is shyness, training, fear of what other people will say, &c., &c.; but, whatever the reason of it may be, the result is that it makes this the most difficult of all the societies I have ever had to do with. Well, last night I saw a glimmer of improvement, and at any rate a few of the great lords and ladies (Burra Sahib and Burra Mem Sahib) did speak to me without being driven to it. I assure you this sense of progress made me feel quite cheerful.

Wednesday, 11*th.*—Nelly took Miss Fergusson out to pay visits in the morning, and they played tennis in the afternoon.

I went to give prizes at a Zenana Mission. This one is managed by Miss Hoare, a very energetic lady, 'with no nonsense about her.' She nearly made me laugh by nodding at me after I had distributed a certain number of dolls and boxes, and saying, 'Those are the prizes, now these are the bribes.'

The little Hindu girls are most attractive! They do look such miniature women with their coil of hair (or ribbon), the jewels on their heads, necklaces, bracelets and anklets; and then their drapery of different-coloured muslins variously put on.

It was most amusing to see them come up for their

prizes, but I grieve to say that symptoms of European costume are to be seen amongst them. I had just dealt out a reward or a bribe to a real little Oriental picture, when a horrid calico frock of a purely English pattern appeared before me! And, alas! even some who began well ended in patent-leather shoes, over which seven or eight silver anklets fell in the most incongruous manner! One child coming forward appeared so lame that *I* inquired about her, and found she was only suffering from new shoes! Is it not dreadful?—jewels, and green and gold garments wound round with crimson muslin, and then striped cotton stockings and shoes!—and I was made a most unwilling accomplice, for *I* had to give out English cotton jackets, and dolls dressed in the ' height of the fashion ' and well calculated to spoil the taste of the rising generation. These atrocities are sent out by kind people at home. *I* wish they would get patterns of *I*ndian garments, and make them both for the children and the dolls! Unfortunately the latter are manufactured with chignons and boots, and I suppose they can't be bought without them.

From this function I went on to a party at Mrs. Ilbert's. On driving up to the house, I found two girls in bright native dress playing badminton. Everyone was introduced to me. I was most interested in the two medical students who were there, and in a girl who has taken a degree and is now a teacher in a large school.

Our guests from Bombay left us after dinner to return home, and we went to the circus which we were patronising.

The rain came through the tent and pattered on the backs of our chairs.

When I hear the familiar sound, my mind reverts to the 'crops,' and to the effect it will produce upon turnips and mangold wurzel; but then I read of 'rabi crops,' of 'rahar, linseed, indigo, and poppy,' of 'the harvesting of paddy' and 'the threshing of jowari,' and these new names make me realise, in spite of the homely rain, that I am in a new world.

Thursday, 12th.—The girls and I went on board the *Euryalus* to see Admiral Hewitt and his ship. He had the decks 'cleared for action,' worked the guns, and gave us tea. He also showed us the Order given him by King John of Abyssinia. It consists of a gold Masonic cross set with jewels, and worn round the neck with a silken cord, and a great lion's mane by way of a collar.

We had a ball in the evening. About 1,000 people were asked, but *I* don't think there can have been more than 600 present, and there was plenty of room for dancing—almost too much, I thought, for at supper time the room was nearly empty and never filled again. Like a good chaperon I stayed till the very end, and Nelly and Rachel and their partners danced the last galop alone. D. having had hard work all day was tired, and disappeared before supper.

Friday, 13th.—I fear the subject of Zenana Missions will begin to bore you, but this is the prize-giving month, and even to-day does not bring me to the end of these functions. This afternoon the schools were seated in rows on the grass at Belvedere, and very picturesque they looked.   I am never tired of seeing the curious little girls with their strange garments, stranger life, and mysterious future, and find all that I can see and hear of them most interesting.   There was a very striking child, whose costume really deserves to be described.   She looked about twelve.   Her hair was elaborately plaited at the back, and had worsted flowers stuck into it in the form of a high comb.   A broad band of gold covered her parting and ended in an ornament falling over her forehead, with similar bands from each side and similar ornaments covering the ears.   She wore a jacket of blue and gold with short sleeves; and a thin black scarf with green and red stripes and broad gold edges came over each shoulder, was confined to the waist by a belt, and was arranged in such a way as to entirely drape her figure, covering her to the feet in graceful folds.   On each brown arm were at least fifteen gold bracelets, anklets on her feet, and a pearl drop in her nose.   She had a very interesting face, and was dignified to the verge of being cross !   None of the children really understand English, but they repeat ' *I* love little pussy and ' Mary had a little lamb ' in monotonous and tragic tones.

Lord Randolph Churchill left us in the evening.

Monday, 16*th.* — There was an afternoon dance on board the *Euryalus.*   When we arrived the yards were manned, and then we found ourselves in a beautiful room covered in with flags.   The party was a great success, and the ship is off to-morrow, leaving behind a Lieutenant Lindsey, who is going to join Sir Gerald Graham at Suakim.

Tuesday, 17th.—I have been giving new colours, and making a speech, and assisting at a garden party in the Fort.

The regiment I gave the colours to is known to you as the 8th, but is now the 'King's Liverpool Regiment,' commanded by Colonel Le Mesurier. The solemn 'being off with the old love' is indicated by the marching of the tattered rags down the line, saluting them, and retiring them to the music of 'Auld Lang Syne.' Then follows the equally serious 'coming on with the new,' when the Bishop consecrates the colours, which rest against the drums piled in the centre of the square; then they are unfurled and an officer receives them from me on bended knee; and then comes her ladyship's speech to this effect :—

'COLONEL LE MESURIER, OFFICERS, NON-COMMISSIONED OFFICERS, AND MEN OF THE KING'S LIVERPOOL REGIMENT,—I confide these colours to your keeping, in the full assurance that you will guard them faithfully, and that a regiment already so famous for its distinguished conduct on the historical battlefields of Europe, and in many an *I*ndian combat, will not fail to add fresh lustre to the glorious record inscribed upon their folds, whenever called upon to defend the honour of our Queen and country.' The Colonel's very nice reply follows, the receiving and saluting of the new colours, and a march past to finish with.

The officers had a garden party afterwards, which was most successful. Very few of the people had ever seen colours presented before, so it was quite an event.

I felt rather nervous over it, but was especially glad

to do it, remembering that it was George's regiment, and that he had served under the old colours.

Wednesday, 18*th.*—I went to tea with the Maharanee of Kuch Behar, and had a very pleasant visit.   Her house is extremely pretty and furnished in the European style. She herself wears native dress, but has very smart shoes and stockings, while her sisters and sister-in-law had bare feet.   Three of her sisters were children, very pretty, with such lovely eyes and sweet expressions, and her sister-in-law, who spoke English perfectly, was a remarkably nice person.

I was very glad of the opportunity of seeing them. The Maharanee herself is very cheerful and pleasant, laughs very merrily, and must be very intelligent—she has so quickly and completely got into European ways and never seems the least awkward or put out.

D. lets me send you a copy of a letter he received from one of the two great Llamas of Thibet.   The style is delightful, the translation is literal :—

‘ To the great and most opulent Governor, who turns the wheel of power all over this wide world, Ruler of Asia and Pillar of the Faith to his Throne.

‘ With reverence, and with the full three mundane essentials (the heart, the speech, and the body),

‘ This most humble and insignificant self, who from his infancy, applying himself to study, has acquired only a minute jot of learning, such as may be compared with an insect's mouthful of water, has been favoured with a golden robe of honour in the shape of a present of Rs. 2,500 for him, for which he presents his most cordial thanks.

'This year there has appeared the incarnation of that divine personage who is the crown ornament of this world of men and gods. Next year His Holiness's incarnation will be identified. This humble self has been discharging with the utmost zeal and devotion all the religious duties of the Penchen Rimboochay as the Minister of the great Buddhist Church, and moreover as the representative of the late all-knowing Penchen, in upholding, protecting, and propagating the religion of the Victor. Together with this piece of news he respectfully sends scarves and the mitre of the late Penchen for acceptance.

'Dated Tashi Lunpo, the 5th of the 10th Lunar Month, Wood-monkey year.' [Corresponding with the 22nd November, 1884.]

Friday, 20th.—I visited the Loretto Convent Orphanage this afternoon, and, on entering it, felt myself transported back to Canada. There were the nuns, and there was the Archbishop, and there were the good little girls ' Vouées au Bleu,' and the indifferent little girls all in white, and there was the little song of welcome, and the flattering address, and the bit of convent embroidery as a souvenir, and myself on a platform and the purple priestly robes beside me—all exactly as it used to be. What wonder then that I fell back naturally into the ancient groove, and obtained a holiday for the whole array of little pupils—who appear to me to have gone on curtseying at every mention of my name for the last twelve years—or that I felt quite sentimental over this sudden return to Canada and all its pleasant memories ?

I also visited the establishment of the Little Sisters of the Poor this afternoon. They do much good, and make a home for about fifty helpless old people. Then on to another prize-giving. The schools were all squatting on the roof of a long verandah and looked, as usual, very picturesque. Several of the dolls had to be kept back, as the girls for whom they were destined were being married.

I saw three European hats and feathers in one school ; that was almost too much for me, and *I* was glad to look away in the direction of a child whose attention was greatly distracted from the Bengali prayer by the difficulties of arranging its yards and yards of muslin into the proper drapery.

We had what *I* call a 'small' dinner, thirty people. The difference between the small and the large is not only in numbers. I choose the guests for the small, and really know who they are, and we sit in my room and dine in the throne-room, instead of using the state apartments. I sat by Salar Jung, the Nizam's Minister.

In the evening D. went to a Mahometan conversazione, where they had scientific amusements and exhibited various things, such as telephones and phonographs.

Saturday, 21st.—I gave away prizes at some athletic sports. It was a pleasant afternoon. We sat out, and then drove back on the coach, and took Sir Frederick and Lady Roberts, two of their A.D.C.s, and two Miss Stewarts up to Barrackpore.

We spent a quiet day (Sunday, 22nd) under our trees, our party being enlarged by the arrival of Mr. and Mrs. Delves Broughton, who came by an early morning train.

Monday, 23rd.—Invited by Rai Juggodanund Mookerjee, we went in the evening to a native entertainment in his house. To get there we drove through the bazaars—long streets of mud and bamboo hovels, where native colouring and local smells were rampant. Groups of people were standing about, and greeted us with clapping of hands as we passed; near the gate of the house there was a great crowd, and a military band was playing there.

Our host met us and conducted us through a bit of garden brilliantly illuminated, a sort of roof being made to it by quantities of large white lotus flowers, which were, I suppose, attached to a net; this led into an enormous tent lined with flags, blazing with candles and electric lights, full of all the ' beauty and fashion ' of the neighbourhood, and with a sprinkling of smart native dresses to orientalise the scene. We were seated in front of the stage, and when the curtain drew up, some very substantial fairies were revealed standing on equally substantial flowers, and they sang the following lines in Bengali :—

> As stars round Luna's bright throne wait,
>   When the blue vault from clouds is free,
> Thus girt with officers of State,
>   Our noble Viceroy here we see.

We bless our Empress-Queen who sent
   A Peer so just this realm to sway;
With hearts and feelings reverent
   Let us to him our homage pay.

And gladly now 'twill be our task
   By art dramatic to beguile
This noble audience—we but ask
   Your kind applause, your lenient smile.

Then the play began. It was called the 'Matrimonial Fix,' and we were provided with an English *résumé* of the plot. It is a farcical satire upon the native who goes to England for ten months, and who is supposed to come back dressed in European clothes and having forgotten his own language; and upon the educated female, who is represented as giving her husband a scientific lecture upon heat, which drives him out of the house, while she, during his absence, makes love to a kindred and educated soul, with whom, in the last scene, she absconds. The dress and absence of dress look more remarkable on the stage than off it. D. still saw ancient Romans in their togas. I still saw ordinary men in cotton sheets. In one scene a bridegroom appeared naked to the waist, with a red loin-cloth as a costume, while in the next he was clothed in a full suit of broadcloth; the match-maker was lightly clad, the bridegroom's father wore the sheet or toga, the women were fully ' draped.'

The best actor was a maid-servant, who seemed to say very sharp things, and when she and her mistress had a disagreement the scolding on both sides was loud and stormy.

As a study of manners and customs, the play was

most interesting. It was in two acts, and at the end of
the first we were taken into the house and upstairs, where
a new joy awaited us.

'A Nautch in the Upper Hall,' says the programme!
The old and *blasé* Anglo-Indian despised this one, and
whispered something about music-halls; but as we are
not *blasé*, it amused us very much. There were about
five musicians, who stood just behind the two girls, and
who seemed always to have to prompt them about something. These played little stringed instruments of the
mandolin order. One of the women was very good-
looking, and was heavily clothed from head to foot in
velvet and gold, and a great scarf of green and gold; the
other wore rather short pink petticoats, but when she did
whirl round, one saw that she had on a regular suit of
armour, cloth of gold down to the ankles. Nothing could
be more strictly proper, and nothing could possibly be
more languid and gentle and almost motionless than the
dancing, if dancing it can be called. The first performer,
without moving from her place, squares her elbows
slightly, and with her two hands, palms downwards,
their fingers almost touching at the points, moves them
almost imperceptibly, and manages gradually to glide a
few steps forward, then to make one turn, to raise her
arms and wave them gently for a moment, to glide the
few steps back, and to end abruptly. The second does
the same, while the first performer, come to life in the
background, shows that she is hot, and tries to cool herself much more vigorously than she danced. There
really is so *very* little movement that there is scarcely
evidence sufficient to decide whether it is graceful or not.

The elder one had an uncanny way of *lifting* her throat from side to side as if it was disjointed, which was more in the Egyptian style than the rest of the performance. The girls then sang, and a song in English, with a good deal of gesticulation and some play with the eyes, was very amusing. It related how the band was playing, and how the lady peeped out from her curtain at the 'captain' (he apparently played the drum in that regiment), and how he 'with his whiskers' and tattooing all the time cast side-glances at her window.

In addition to this 'Nautch,' there was native music of various kinds—a man who played on bowls of water, accompanied by an old gentleman who held two small drums and played upon each with his fingers ; one who made two trumpets sound by placing them against the muscles of his throat (I can't explain further), and one who played well on a sort of metallic 'bones.' At the end of this part of the entertainment a great supper awaited us, a thoroughly European meal, which we played with for a while, and then we were admitted to the zenana. I thought that nothing in the male line lower than a lieutenant-governor would be allowed to enter, but several inferior mortals did. There were four ladies waiting to receive us—our host's wife, daughter, and two relations—and a crowd of females peeping in behind. The ladies wore very smart draperies and numbers of bracelets and rings, and seemed very pleased to see us, but a little shy. Over the chimneypiece hung an oil-painting of me, done from a photograph and really very good. After talking a little, the lady of the house presented us with bouquets, hung us with garlands, saturated our handkerchiefs with rosewater and attar of roses, and presented us each with one of the sticky parcels of betel-nut which I have before described.

After this, begarlanded as we were, we returned to the tent, and saw the last act of the play, and then home, feeling that we had been well entertained.

Wednesday, 25th.—This afternoon we had a garden party by advertisement—a notice in the papers announcing that *I* should be at home to all those who had the *entrée* to Government House taking the place of any invitation.

We put up a large awning as a sort of drawing-room on the grass, had tents for refreshment, chairs placed two and two all over the grounds, a band playing, and an assortment of conjurors who appeared to me, when I had a moment to go and see them, as the feeblest specimens of the genus wizard that I had ever seen. I arrived at one performance in time to learn that a girl who was sitting with her head back and her mouth much smeared with brickdust had just had her tongue cut off, and a bit of meat on a skewer was being carried about preparatory to being put on again as the missing piece. After a very clumsy pretence of performing this operation, the young lady got up and exhibited the unruly member whole and uninjured. I was decidedly unlucky, for I believe there were some better tricks ; but it took time to see even one, for they were performed in a sort of Arabian Nights way, one trick inside another, so that one never knew when the original one would be finished. The party itself was pretty and bright, and went off very well. The

afternoon was perfect, and I stood in the shade and
said ' How do you do ? ' to everyone before going to see
the sights.

Friday, 27th.—D. had his first long Council over
the Rent Bill, about which you are all being so troublesome and so agitating in England.

The sittings are public, but *I* was unable to attend
this time, as I had a little engagement of my own, one
which had in my eyes the additional merit of obtaining
for me an extra day at Barrackpore. My destination
was the old Dutch settlement of Chinsurah, which is
some way higher up the river than Barrackpore, and
therefore it was decidedly convenient to stop there on
my way down, and to be met by D., who came on after
sitting in his Council from eleven to six. The Council
will sit four times a week, and D. will have all this in
addition to his usual heavy work.

My expedition had for its object more zenana prize-
givings. We left Calcutta at twelve, taking with us Mrs.
Wilson, the wife of a merchant in Calcutta. We lunched
at Barrackpore, and then went on our way again to
Chinsurah. The entertainment was in a large house
borrowed for the occasion. All the school children sat
in the open central court ; a raised passage ran all round
it, on three sides of which the fathers and the brothers
and the low caste maid-servants were grouped, and on
the fourth I sat, literally in the seat of the gods, supported by the ' quality ' of the place. Lady Lytton had
been there seven years ago, and the people had refused
then to remove their gods. Now, either gods have gone

down in the world, or 'Vicereines' have gone up, for unasked they removed the former to make way for the latter. I suppose this is called 'being more enlightened'; and a further proof of progression they gave, for the married women were on the top of the house looking down upon the court, and although a sort of screen was put up, it was very defective in places, and they made large holes for themselves in others. I was glad they were able to have this amusement, though I am not a very great advocate for 'progress' in such matters, for I think that Eastern women cannot be too slowly brought forward, and that gods, so long as they are objects of faith, should be disturbed for no one. There was also a passage round the second floor of the house, where European school children sat.

The function consisted in listening to much Bengali poetry repeated by little girls, who stood up, one by one, on a chair to recite it; in hearing a report read, and in giving away the prizes. The report told us that the examiner thought the children said their poetry in rather a sing-song manner, 'which should be dis- couraged;' that he found these small native girls 'very well up in the history of the Jews;' that they were 'intimately acquainted' with the multiplication table, and were being 'initiated into the mysteries' of grammar and geography. After this satisfactory account of the pupils I stood on the steps and dealt out dolls, the small and ugly ones being received with evident dissatisfaction. The children only consent to attend school on condition that they get a prize, and they naturally feel aggrieved if the hire is not worthy of the labourer. To do lessons a whole year and then to be fobbed off with a very inferior doll to that you see in the arms of a not more industrious neighbour must indeed be irritating! One very discontented child returned to the charge at the very end, but I had nothing left to give her.

I was allowed after this to go up and see the zenana ladies, who had come down from the roof to a room in the house, and when I got there I was very sorry only to have a few moments to spare. They all seemed so pleased to see me, crowded round to shake hands with me, made me sit down and held my hands, and were delightfully cordial; but darkness comes on so quickly that I had to be off, and, had there not been a moon, I should have met with difficulties on the river.

Mr. Wilson joined his wife at Barrackpore, and they both stayed the night. They are very pleasant people. He has something to do with the Zoo, and told us that two tigers there had just committed suicide. It is a very curious thing. They came in large cages, in which they remained for some weeks, but directly they were moved into the permanent cages they refused to eat. The best mutton could not tempt them, and they actually died!

The travelling cages had been sent away, else they would have been put back into them, to see if that would cure their home sickness.

Sunday, March 1st.—Whenever during the last month we have ventured to feel chilly, we have been assured that by the 1st of March we should be gasping under punkahs; but no, I have put on a woollen shawl—the day is dull and dark, and the sky has decidedly tears in its eyes, for they brim over occasionally. What a mysterious, changeable, incomprehensible, and disappointing thing is climate!

Circumstances were too strong for D. in spite of his desire to keep Sunday as a holiday, and he had to do some business to-day with Mr. Hope, who came out for the purpose. The wind changed in the evening and made all things pleasanter, and D. and I took a nice walk in the park. We came across a large pepul-tree, which had a very big palm growing straight up from the centre of it, the palm's roots being wound round the pepul's trunk and branches. There is another in the place which has four fine straight palms growing up through it, but their roots are in the ground.

Monday, 2nd.—The girls and I came home a new way to-day. We rode and drove back to Calcutta before breakfast. The morning was lovely, and we liked it very much.

After lunch we went into the Council Room for a little. The big table forms a 'hollow square.' The Viceroy sits at the top, with the Lieutenant-Governor on one side of him, other Councillors at the sides, and reporters at the bottom, spectators behind them. The speakers mostly read their speeches, and they sit while delivering them. It is not easy to hear, and the proceedings are dull. The room is a very good one, and, with the passage leading to it, is hung with the portraits of old Viceroys. The most interesting picture is that of Warren Hastings, who looks rather like Shakespeare. I was sorry that I did not stay longer at the

Council, for all the speeches were over at five, and
D. said a few words. This ends the preliminary proceedings of the Bengal Rent Bill, and now the 193
amendments have to be discussed.

We are all very full of the great durbar which is to·
be held at Rawal Pindi for the Amir. Our big camp·
will be out ; about 20,000 troops will be collected there,
and it will be quite an historical event. The Councillors,.
their wives, and several other people come, and we wonder
whether the present Amir will agree with Shere Ali, who,
after seeing all the beauty and fashion of our society,
said, ' You English are very proud of not shutting up
your women, but you are very clever about it, for I see·
you only let out the ugly ones.'

Wednesday, 4th.—I had a small garden party for·
lawn tennis and badminton, and succeeded in getting
people to come in the necessary flannels. *I* played
badminton, D. showed off his new court with wooden
walls, and Nelly played tennis with the best of them.
We had the band ' discoursing,' and spent a very pleasant
afternoon. The Council was only just over in time.
They sit almost every day, and all lunch with us, with
the exception of Mahometans and Hindus, who sit in
different chambers downstairs and eat sweets and drink
cold water.

In the evening we went to a Parsee theatre. A beautiful box was made for us in the very centre of the stalls,
close to the stage. The piece was an operetta called
' The Padlock.' The singing was of the most sing-song,.
monotonous, and unmusical character. All the per—

formers, including the heroine, wore black velvet tunics and trousers covered with spangles. *She* was a man, and not lovely. We were amused by it, but the orchestra was a melancholy moan resembling bagpipes. The second piece was called ' A Fancy Ball.' One man kept the stage, while the guests at the ball performed the well-known stage-army trick, and, after passing through one way, reappeared again in a different dress, but without any attempt at disguise. The piece ended with a loyal song and a most unflattering transparency of our gracious Queen.

Thursday, 5th.—The thermometer now is about 85° in the shade. I don't find it at all too hot ; but before we go on the 23rd it will probably be 95°. We had a plague of flying ants in the drawing-room just before dinner ; they were swarming round a lamp and lying in layers on the table. They made such a mess that the room had to be shut up. They drop their wings, and appear as crawling things, and in every stage of their existence they are extremely disagreeable.

Friday, 6th.—Goaded on by my family to take exercise, and having no engagements for the day, I rode in the morning and played tennis in the afternoon, and found it rather too much for me.

Sir Samuel and Lady Baker arrived. They come on a shooting expedition, and are so full of all their preparations that they actually do not appreciate the prospective delights of Barrackpore, and elect to remain here for Sunday.

Saturday, 7th.—The Calcutta Volunteers were inspected by the Viceroy this afternoon. He went in uniform, and walked up and down their ranks, and then made a speech to them while *I* remained on the dais, and afterwards gave away the prizes. D. is honorary colonel of the regiment. The small company of Naval Volunteers was also there.

From this function we drove straight to the train, and were at Barrackpore in an hour's time.

Sunday, 8th.—A perfectly heavenly day, the air delightful, and the temperature agreeably warm; the sun was, however, hot enough to make driving to church more prudent than walking. When we got there we found the whole upper part of the building swaying about—from north to south, from east to west swing, swing, swing, the punkahs. As I got into my place I heard behind me a very audible, ' These horrid things ! ' from D., and he immediately had ours stopped, a proceeding which the punkahwallah found difficult to understand, and he stood all through the service grinning and expectant, with the rope in his hand. The rest of the sky, however, kept waving, and *I* felt doubtful for some time whether the surrounding oscillations would produce sleep or sea-sickness. Punkahs are very ugly things—heavy bars of wood with very thick and unornamental flounces of brown holland, swung by ropes from the ceiling, and just high enough to escape a short person and to disarrange the curls of a tall one. Next Sunday midday services will be abolished, and if we don't get up at 7.30 we must wait till the evening for our church. And yet so far the thermometer is seldom over 80°. Decidedly we make a great fuss over heat here.

Tuesday, 10th.—The Viceroy had another deputation of zemindars protesting against the Bill, which will probably be made law to-morrow. I don't think they can have expected to gain much by it, but they are very sanguine and have great faith in agitation.

Wednesday, 11th.—The Bengal Rent Bill was passed to-day. I went into the Council Room to hear the final orations. D. spoke last and very well.

Having heard that the Bill had become law, I went off to lay the foundation-stone of a home for girls studying medicine. The money for it has been given by the Maharanee Surnomoyee, who seems to be a most charitable lady. The ceremony was the same as usual, and I was given a very handsome trowel.

In the morning I had an interview with a high authority about doing up some of the rooms in the house. I will tell you more about that when I have quite decided where I shall begin.

Thursday, 12th.—I got a great deal of work into this day. I went in the morning to see the Economic Museum, which I have mentioned to you before, and after looking through the two rooms of which I thought it consisted—the one containing pretty things bought from the exhibition, and the other models of various natives from Assam, the Nicobar, and the Andaman

Islands, with their fishing, shooting, and household implements—I found that there were two more rooms in this part of the building, and that beyond there was a great museum of which I had never even heard before, though the gentleman with me told me it was of ' world-wide' celebrity. I just walked through it, and was very glad to find there was such a place, for there is not very much to see in Calcutta, and here one could spend many days in looking at all the things. This morning I did not attempt to do more than find out that there was a big room full of minerals, one of stuffed animals, one of birds, and large collections of shells, insects, fossils, carvings, musical instruments, &c., &c. Two of the small ideas I carried away were gathered over the insects and the poisons. The butterflies exactly representing green leaves were quite new to me, and *I* could not have believed that the resemblance could be so exact between an animal and a plant. The poison of the cobra was shown us in a small bottle, on which was written that the quantity contained in it would kill 7,450 chickens or 46 dogs. The gentleman who showed it to us had himself collected it, and the process must have been exciting. One man held the snake by the head and the tail, which naturally irritated it, and our friend presented a spoon covered by a palm-leaf to its mouth; the angry snake bit through the leaf, and the fluid fell into the spoon. Another external poison is a small red berry which goldsmiths use here as a weight; when mixed up with water it can be worked into a point, and a prick from that point is certain death.

The sun was very powerful this morning, and one

felt obliged to get very quickly into the covered carriage so as not to be exposed to it for a moment.

In the afternoon I paid my first visit to a zenana. We drove through the native town to the house. The master of it met us at the door, and conducted us up to the room where the ladies were. The whole space seemed to be cut up into very small rooms furnished in the European way, and with punkahs swinging so low that one had to be perpetually dodging them. His wife wore a violet and gold silk garment over her, a black velvet jacket underneath, and jewels everywhere, a quantity hanging over her forehead, enormous rings encircling and depending from her ears, a very big one in her nose, eight or nine fine necklaces, at least sixteen bracelets on her arms, and a large ornament on the back of each hand, to which chains and a ring for each finger were attached. A grown-up daughter-in-law swathed in black and gold was very shy, and kept her face covered, but the father-in-law kept saying, 'You may look at her,' so we lifted the veil and peeped. She was rather a fine-looking girl. A little granddaughter, also magnificently bedizened, and a married daughter completed the party. We spoke a little, and fingered and admired the jewels, and then the veiled lady was sent away in order that her brother-in-law might be admitted.

The second part of the entertainment was 'Five o'clock tea,' in the shape of cocoanut and other cakes made with ghi (a sort of melted butter, which renders them almost uneatable to us), champagne and ices. I boldly tasted all the cakes, which had been made by the lady

of the house, but I did not get very far with them.
Then we returned to the zenana, and the wife put
wreaths of very strong-smelling flowers round our necks ;
then she put a still stronger odour on our handkerchiefs,
and gave us each a large bouquet of roses ornamented
with tinsel ; and so adorned we drove through the streets
of Calcutta. I am sure we must have perfumed the
whole town, and I know I was glad when I could escape
from my wreath, my pocket-handkerchief, and from the
whole carriage full of scent.

In the evening we had a big 'walk round,' that is,
a 'drum' of great dimensions. We opened the first
floor of the house right through from verandah to
verandah, had the band and a buffet in the Marble Hall,
and invited everybody. I thought it a very pretty
party ; there was so much space, and the Oriental
dresses always beautify the crowd. I walked and talked
all the time, but D. was obliged to mix some business
with his pleasure, and to 'sit out' with a man. He
only comes in at the end of our dinner, has his breakfasts
and luncheons cut short, and is altogether busy. What
peace the two-ton boat on the Bosphorus was, to be sure !

Friday, 13*th.*—I had been most anxious for D. to
see one of my picturesque Hindu schools, and had
persuaded him to engage himself for the prize-giving at
the 'Bethune School,' which is a secular one for girls,
where they teach the 'higher branches,' take degrees,
&c., so I was much disappointed to find that it was not
at all picturesque. With education unfortunately comes
a taste for English millinery, and a departure from the

good taste generally inherent to a national costume, and I could really *groan* when princess frocks, marabout feathers, and other shabby finery are flaunted before me. D. and I sat on a dais with a very big table in front of us, which interfered with our view, and the prize-winners who appeared before us had to overcome fearful obstacles to reach us : many a foot of native arrangement was displayed under the European varnish as the unfortunate wearer struggled up on to the platform. It gave me time, however, to consider the costume question fully, and to come to even stronger opinions upon the subject than *I* held before ; it also made me look at the needle-work in a very unsympathetic spirit. Why should we introduce into this country the crochet and woolwork of which we are so sick at home ? But we do, and take great trouble to din it into the fingers of these poor children instead of encouraging their own beautiful embroideries.

We listened to several ' tunes ' on the piano, to some songs, and to a report ; but the most pleasing thing to me in this particular function was the nice face of the first ' B.A.' She is a teacher in the school now, and happily keeps to her own graceful garments. A very excellent education is given to girls at this school, and I hope to visit it some day when the pupils are at work.

Saturday, 14*th.*—We were to have gone to Barrack-pore yesterday, but put it off, as Nelly had hurt her foot and could not move. To-day I was obliged to leave her, as I had a school feast to see after. Rachel and *I* went up in the launch, and lunched under the banian-tree, and then soon after four the children began to arrive. The object of the feast was, what I call my own little school. I told you about it once before, and I will just say now that it contains the most delightful infant of four years old that I ever saw. She is such a very pretty little thing, with a brown skin, such white teeth, pretty brown eyes, and short black hair, and with her muslin garment over her head, and covering her down to the feet, she looks a regular little woman. She clung to Rachel or me all the day, chattered away in her unknown tongue, played games most merrily, and tied up a quantity of sweets in the corner of her muslin to take home to her mother, which sweets being full of liqueur soon came to grief; and when Rachel put a rose in front of her dress she looked so amused, and so pleased with it ; and then at tea she managed the unaccustomed food and silver spoon most cleverly. I never saw such a duck as she is—Shusil Bala by name. The children in this school are mostly Christian ; the boys, who were Hindu, could not come lest they should break their caste by eating, but the girls did, and the teacher let them eat, thinking that if the parents were very particular they would not have allowed them to come. The other guests were Sunday-school children, some Roman Catholic children, and some pensioners. It was a feast indeed, and I hope no one is the worse for it. The most showy cakes and shapes of various kinds had been saved up from our last big party, and you never saw such a quantity of pink and white sugar, jams, and all that is unwholesome ; while the way in which the guests mixed everything, and ate chocolate, and jelly, and ice, and bonbons, and plum, sponge, and seed cakes all together, made one shudder.

The pensioners were given meat and beer—and thereby hangs a tale, for the beer rather elated a poor old man, who says the 'Amens' loudly in church every Sunday, and he began to pray for me and for everyone else in such an obstreperous manner that he had to be sat upon and sent home. We thought it had also rather excited some soldiers' wives who slipped in, and one was heard enthusiastically to declare ' that she wished she had come here without her children ! ' We had elephants, which were extremely popular, everyone wanting to have a ride, but unfortunately the animals got cross over the constant kneeling down and getting up again, and *I* had to stop the rides for fear of accidents. Lord Herbrand Russell (who was most good-natured the whole day) began, at my request, to hurry down all the children from out of a howdah, and was wondering how on earth one howdah could hold so many, when he discovered that Major Cooper was as rapidly lifting them up on the other side.

My little school played games very nicely, but the Europeans were rather grand and dull. *I* dealt round more cakes before they went, and they all looked very happy and pleased. The band was nearly as attractive as the elephants, and the soldiers' wives danced to the music, their performance in that line helping to amuse the little ones.

D. came out in the evening.

Monday, 16*th.*—Yesterday was the warmest day we

have had, 90° where we sat all the morning. A very big snake, over six feet in length, fell out of a tree on to a sentry, who killed it and showed it to us.

We went to church in the evening, and our bonnets were perpetually swept by the punkahs. They are dreadful things, I think. There is a sort of confusion which is bewildering. Some swing across you, and some to and from you, and they are pulled by different men, who keep different time, and one feels as if one never could get accustomed to the unsteady appearance of everything overhead. They made the church quite cool, and I was not at all conscious of having felt the heat, but I suppose I did, for when I got up this morning I found myself staggering about, and was really far from well all day. The doctor kept me lying down, and gave me a great deal of stimulant; and as *I* am not supposed to have believed in the heat, *I* am triumphed over. I have not really *felt* it, but one melts in the most rapid manner at night, and I suppose that takes it out of one.

Tuesday, 17*th.*—We are still somewhat of invalids ; Nelly, having made her foot worse by over-exertion, has to be careful, and I found that a few guests at dinner tired me much. We dined out on the balcony, but it was mail day, and D. was so busy that he ran in and out of dinner, and did not manage to dress for it.

Wednesday, 18*th.*—The packing has begun, and our rooms are once more denuded, and I feel that before

going I ought to give you a short retrospective account
of our life here as it appears to me at the end of the
season.

The house I like very much, and we have been very
comfortable in it, and hope by degrees to do it up and
make it very pretty. My own rooms are charming, and
the balcony delightful, and, though I never go into it,
there is a very nice garden. The tennis court I do
frequent sometimes, and D. plays almost every day in
his. He works all day, with the exception of this hour's
play, and only appears at breakfast, luncheon, and
again at dinner, but happily he seldom does anything
after that. The girls have their little boudoir and very
nice big rooms upstairs, and are very happy and merry
together.

Though we live in the same house, and have our
meals together, I do not really see much of the Staff
here. They are all young, and all have their own
friends and amusements; and as they have nothing to
do with the Government business it is quite different
from an embassy.

I don't think I have quite enough to do, and there
seems a difficulty in Calcutta in ever getting hold of
anything one can do. I have, I hope, got the society
on rather a better footing, and I have managed to have
some small entertainments, instead of always asking
everybody to everything, and the parties have been
pleasant, and not stiff.

For my day, I write more or less all the morning,
occasionally going out on my balcony and commun-
ing with my birds; and in the afternoon, if there is no

function, I sit on the tennis ground, and then come in and read till dressing time. Now that it is hot we dine on a verandah, and sometimes we sit out in the evening, sometimes manage to get up a game of some kind, and always go to bed early and go through a process of melting till the morning.

This afternoon I had a final small garden party to say good-bye to a few people here. I had meant to play badminton, but was not up to it.

A native gentleman sent me what they call a ' Dolly,' which is really a tray full of little presents. It was a very interesting one, and he wrote a nice letter with it, saying that we had ' evinced a kindly feeling towards our Eastern customs and the welfare of our women ; therefore I venture to send these presents at the earnest request of my wife. . . . The greater part are held auspicious by our women as conducing to the success and long life of their husbands.' One tray contained bouquets and wreaths of flowers, and then there were a quantity of puzzle boxes, bangles cut in bone, two toilet baskets covered with cowrie shells, and containing small mirrors, combs, red powder, &c.—mothers present these to their daughters on the occasion of marriage ; two large conch shells, one of them a sacred blowing instrument used at marriages, births, &c., and one used at the time of coronation by pouring water from it on the head of the king. ' It dispels all evils where water is drunk out of it or poured on the head.' The red powder is used by Hindu women from the day of their marriage. The bridegroom with his own hand puts this powder on his bride's forehead where the hair is parted, and she always wears it until she becomes a widow. With these things were some models of fish, frogs, serpents, &c., made in clay.

We are going to ask the Duke and Duchess of Connaught to come to Rawal Pindi. We had not asked them before, as we thought all their plans for going to England had been made.

CHAPTER III

RAWAL PINDI DURBAR AND VISIT TO LAHORE

MARCH 23 TO APRIL 20, 1885

Monday, March 23rd.—Our last days at Calcutta have been too much taken up with packing to be very interesting. Emptying drawers and filling tin-lined cases occupy our time, and the whole house looks untidy and dismantled.

We managed to go to church on Sunday morning and to walk in the Zoo in the afternoon, and, coming home from there, I noticed that Nelly looked tired, but unluckily she managed to put off my budding alarm by tolerably reasonable excuses, and I did not make the doctor see her till this morning, when he found her temperature was 100° and declared that she must not travel. This came upon us like a bombshell, for it was difficult to know what to do, with a special train waiting and every sort of preparation made for our departure. The doctor thought she was 'almost sure' to be able to travel the next day, so I decided that, on the whole, it was best to leave her and Rachel and the doctor behind, and myself to go on with D. to Allahabad, where we were to remain twenty-four hours, and then either to be joined there by Nelly, or to return to her, as the thermometer might suggest. It was a choice of evils, but this was the plan we carried out. His Excellency and *I* left at 8.30 P.M.; and as we walked down the steps of Government House, with the carriages there, and the large Guard of Honour, we almost felt as if we must have got through the five years very quickly and were already homeward bound!

The people in the streets outside gave D. quite a warm reception, and, though our departure was 'private,' there were a great many at the station to see us off.

Tuesday, 24th.—The night was quite cool, and we almost wished for more blankets, but to-day the sun was very powerful, and one required all one's cooling and sun-protecting comforts. Our carriage was the coolest of all. In several of the windows there are khus-khus tatties, that is, pieces of matting set in frames which revolve, and as they revolve they get wet with water, which is arranged to trickle through them, and the air coming through this is very pleasant to the hot and dusty passenger. In our compartment it was never above 90°, but in that of the A.D.C.s it got up to 96°. At the stations one felt the necessity of a very big hat! I wish you could see mine! It is an enormous 'coal-heaver' made of thick pith. On the way we got a telegram saying that Nelly was just the same and was not fit to move. I am very anxious she should be got away from Calcutta, as it is getting hotter and hotter; how fearful it would be if we were shut up there and could not get to Simla!

At Allahabad, the Lieutenant-Governor, Sir Alfred Lyall, the local government, and a number of natives met us. An address was read, and D. took the opportunity of saying with what pride we had heard of the gallantry of our Indian troops in Egypt.

Allahabad is very uninteresting; there is nothing at all to see, and there is nothing very characteristic about it. The crowd is rather more picturesque than that of Calcutta, but all we saw of the town was brown and dusty and muddy-looking—mud houses, a tank with mud banks, and two mud islands in the centre of it, with a muddy-looking tree and little temple upon them, a long dusty road and a bit of park—the grass part struggling to be green, but only managing it by contrasting itself with the asphalte tennis courts which cut into it—then the Government House, which is nice. *It* is of the bungalow type, but has high and large rooms opening on to the prettiest flower-garden I have seen in India. The dining-room is rather like a church, especially when a church is hung with punkahs. Lady Lyall is in England, and one daughter is left with her father here. There was a big dinner and a party in the evening. I was rather sleepy after my journey, but I was carried off to bed just as I had found some one I knew something of—Mr. Hackett, a missionary. We had begun to talk of Bray, and then of his work here, when the party ended. We had better news of Nelly before dinner, so I shall not have to go back to her.

Wednesday, 25*th.*—D. had a durbar for the Maharajah Holkar, and a private conversation with him afterwards, and later in the day the Viceroy returned his visit. I drove to see the Fort. The only points of interest there are the view from the ramparts of the junction of the Jumna and the Ganges, and a shrine. Thousands of pilgrims come here to bathe in the sacred river and to propitiate the gods at the shrine. The view, as a view, is an ugly one ; there is no excitement over the meeting of the rivers, and there is much sand, and no high ground to be seen. The shrine is an underground place supported by small columns and thickly populated with gods. One is a brass face, another is a lump of stone ; the favourite one had several bits of money and some rings lying before her ; and a piece of stone with a split in it is shown, which a great king said was no god, but when he struck it with his sword, blood proceeded from the wound, and then he said it was a god.

The air here is hotter, but much drier than that of Calcutta, and mosquitoes are plentiful, but not very poisonous. We have just heard that the Duke and Duchess of Connaught will come to the camp, and there is very little time to make preparations for them. We left Allahabad late in the evening, and had a cool night in the train.

Thursday, 26th.—Another day and night of travelling, but the air is getting so refreshing that it really does one good. I won't say much about our journey, as I shall have so many things to tell you in this letter. Nelly leaves Calcutta to-night.

Friday, 27th.—We had a perfectly delightful day in

the train; rain had fallen in the neighbourhood, and
everything was fresh-looking, no dust and no heat.
I feel so very much better than I have ever done at
Calcutta, and quite free from a sort of depression that I
suffered a little from there. The scenery was very interesting as we came along, the stations gay with flowers,
the trees with their fresh spring foliage on, and the
country peopled with a new, more picturesque, and much
more stalwart set of beings than one sees in Bengal.
There were great stretches of land so carved out by water
that the mud banks looked just like the volcanic rocks
at Aden, only that we were on a level with the tops of
them, and could see the patches of grass growing on
their summits; then there were mud villages, just like
the Egyptian ones; and at last the mountains, and
glimpses of snowy peaks, and trees in the foreground,
and all toned down by the recent rain into blues and
purples and mysterious tints.

As we approached Rawal Pindi we could see a whole
town of tents before us, and we kept passing groups of
strange figures sitting on house-tops or gaping up at us
from the wayside, impromptu stables full of horses and
mules, yards full of camels and fine white cattle; and
when we actually reached the station there was a magnificent array of British uniforms—the Commander-in-
Chief, Sir Donald Stewart, General Hardinge from
Bombay, Sir F. Roberts from Madras, Sir Michael
Biddulph the General in command here, many more
officers, heaps of aides-de-camp, governors, members
of Council, &c., and behind them a long line of native
princes, the Punjab chiefs. They were presented one

by one to the Viceroy, which gave me time to admire
their clothes and their splendid jewellery. One had a
great crown on, something like a bishop's mitre, but,
magnificent though it looked, it is by no means his best
one ! We walked on a little, and were met by the ' Mayor
and Aldermen ' of Rawal Pindi in full Oriental costume.
They read the address from the municipality in Hindustani, His Excellency replying in English.   Then we got
into our own carriages, which have come down here,
and, preceded by our own magnificent body-guard and
escorted by the 9th Lancers, we drove to our camp.   It
was a mile from the station, and the whole way soldiers
stood shoulder to shoulder on either side of the road,
English and native regiments alternately, ten thousand
men ; and as the carriage approached each new regiment
saluted, and ' God save the Queen ' went on from band to
band all down the line.   The mere fact of seeing all these
different uniforms and races of men was most interesting.
Seaforth Highlanders, Light Infantry, Irish Fusiliers,
Rifles, Bengal Cavalry, Dragoons, Carabineers, the celebrated Guide Corps, the Mooltan Horse, and the warlike
and bellicose little Goorkhas, were all there ; and behind
their lines were crowds of natives ; camels wearing smart
red saddlecloths and red Marie-Stuart caps upon their
heads, with their ears coming coquettishly and becomingly
out of them ; a big carriage drawn by four camels belonging to Sir Charles Aitchison, and mule batteries,
and occasional groups of English people—such a
combination of military and Oriental pomp as I feel
it impossible to give you any but the very faintest
idea of.   And as we reached our camp came the

last honour in the shape of a salute booming in our very ears.

The Viceroy's camp consists of thirty-six tents for Staff and for guests, and these form a street, eighteen on each side, with a broad strip of grass in front of them, and two wide roads with another wide stretch of grass down the centre, the length of which is broken with fountains and rockeries and ferneries. At the top of this double street is our tent palace. The first room in it is an enormous drawing-room, then comes a still bigger 'durbar tent,' and then—always under cover—you pass on to Her Excellency's boudoir, His Excellency's office, her bedroom, his room, with dressing-rooms and bath-rooms; and then there is the 'young ladies' boudoir' and their bedrooms, and a tent for Miss Blackwell, one for Mr. Nowell, one for Miss M'Donald, and one for His Excellency's bearer (or under-valet), and one for our ayahs (or under-maids); and my boudoir opens on to a square, full of pots of flowers, where a little fountain sprinkles a bed of maiden-hair; and in all the rooms there are Persian carpets and sofas and armchairs; in the bedrooms pier glasses, chests of drawers, and wardrobes. The 'street' has lamp-posts all down it and water laid on; there are telephones and a post-office, messengers on camels, and six extra aides-de-camp in waiting on us—and that is the way we are 'roughing it' in camp!

In addition to this, you must imagine the kitchen department, and our band, and our numbers of servants, and then our guards! I believe we have rows and rows of body-guard and policemen and Seaforth Highlanders keeping watch over us here. And this that I have

been describing to you is only our own camp. The
Commander-in-Chief's camp is a mile away, and there
is the Lieutenant-Governor's camp nearly as far off, and
the native camp still farther, and the Civil camp somewhere about; and then all the various regiments quite
out of sight of our establishment, some of them nine
miles off.

The only drawback to our comfort is that after the
heat of Calcutta we find the tents cold. D. and I dined
alone and sat over a little stove, while all the guests dined
in the mess tent.

Saturday, 28th.—From eleven till one o'clock the
Viceroy sat in durbar, while *I* managed to see all
that was interesting and to omit what was tiresome.
He received seven of the Punjab chiefs one by one,
each one with all the ceremonies *I* have described
to you before. As each Rajah approached, a gun at
the bottom of the 'street' announced his arrival,
while his departure was signalled by another at the
top. These gentlemen all came in their proper order
of precedence.

First Patiala, a boy of twelve, who arrived in a wonderful silver and gold carriage. Then Bahawalpur, the
owner of the two crowns! He was worth seeing. He
wore white trousers, a heavily embroidered gold coat,
and then such a tiara, encircling such a picturesque
head! His hair is long and black, and the lowest
part of this diamond crown must be three inches
high, while the front of it cannot be less than seven.
There is a black cap inside of it, but being the same colour

as his hair it does not show. Jhind was a fine old man, also with some splendid jewels; and then there came Nabha, who disputes with Jhind the third place, and therefore it is arranged that while Jhind visits the Viceroy first, the return visit is paid to Nabha first. Kapurthalla is twelve years old, but he weighs fourteen stone, and is at present 'learning English, Persian, Urdu, and Gurmukhi.' So far in the list I watched their arrivals, and was amused and interested in their 'turns out.' Some had scarlet runners before them carrying lances, some had mounted lancers, and gentlemen playing the 'tom-tom' as they rode. Some had great state umbrellas over their heads. All had four horses, and Patiala and Kapurthalla both drove in silver carriages. Each had a European gentleman with him, who led him by the hand into the presence of the Viceroy. There sat D. on his golden throne during seven long visits, making conversation, touching and remitting mohurs, giving attar and pan. It was a hard morning's work, followed by a hard afternoon, when he had to return all these visits. The number of guns fired during the day was 499, that is 127 for the Rajahs who came, and 372 for the Viceroy's return visits.

I received a few people (without guns) at four o'clock and then went for a drive, taking Lady Roberts and Mrs. Paget with me. There is a very pretty park here, and the lovely mountain view and bracing air made it very pleasant. In the evening we had a small dinner of fourteen, and afterwards D. had a levée at which 1,100 presentations were made.

Sunday, 29th.—We are cold, very cold indeed. It rains and blows, and we sit over our little stoves, and put on extra garments and winter underclothing, and Mr. Balfour, who does not take these precautions, immediately falls ill. D. and I thought the church very draughty, for in India it is always supposed to be hot, and windows and doors are dealt with accordingly.

This is a good moment just to tell you about our extra Staff. We have Colonel Fitzgerald and Captain Gubbins, both of the Hyderabad Contingent, Mr. Lawrence, 17th Lancers, a son of the late Lord Lawrence, Mr. Goad of the Bengal Cavalry, and Colonel Fergus-Graham, who is always an Honorary A.D.C. Our guests are Sir F. and Lady Roberts, General Hardinge, General and Mrs. Paget (travellers), the Hopes, Bayleys, Mr. Gibbs, General Wilson, and Mr. Ilbert, Councillors.

In the afternoon D. and I went over to see the house and camp arranged for the Amir. If it continues to be so chilly, I am sure he will appreciate a house. For durbars he has two magnificent red tents lined with Kashmir shawls which have been lent by the Maharajah of Kashmir. They are supported by silver pillars, and are altogether beautiful. We had a few young men to lunch, have a small number of people to dine, and expect Nelly and Rachel to arrive about ten o'clock.

Monday, 30th.—We were awoke this morning by the rain pattering on our tent, and were kept awake by the noisiness of a crow who sat on our roof and discoursed to the surrounding colony. It is really dreadful that it should be so damp and cold!

We could do nothing all day on account of the weather, and when the Duke and Duchess of Connaught came late at night, I had to get into a waterproof to go across to their tent.

Tuesday, 31st.—Alas! alas! Such a night! Thunder and pouring rain, and such torrents in the morning that there was no use in getting up to see the Amir's entry. As it turned out there was nothing to see, for under the circumstances he naturally preferred a close carriage to a state elephant, and the procession had to be given up. The fifty elephants were sent home, and the troops in great coats looked miserable; the only cheerful and appropriate part of the proceedings was the tune to which the Amir was marched to his house—'He might have been a Russian, he might have been a Prussian, but, in spite of all temptation, he is an Englishman!'

Our condition in our tents is very bad: all the passages between one room and another are wet, and one has to rush past every join to avoid receiving a cold drop down one's back. The great Shamiana (a flat-roofed tent) is so destroyed that it is impossible to have the durbar to-day, and the prospects for the review are very bad, as the ground is in such a fearful state of mud. When once it was decided to postpone the durbar, it was arranged that the Amir should come and see the Viceroy privately. I was taking the Duchess a drive, between showers, and saw him both going and coming. He seems to be a very fine-looking man, and his uniform has something of a Russian character. D. asked the Duke of Connaught to be present at this visit, as it was purely complimentary.

We had an enormous dinner in the 'durbar tent,' the biggest tent in India; it is long and narrow, lined with blue and white, and considered very smart. There are great chandeliers round the gold and white pillars, and these come up through the table. We had brought our ornamental plate, and the table looked very nice, and the room got comfortably warm—but oh! the bitter cold of the sitting-room! And the drippings as we got to it! We all sent for woollen shawls and wrapped up.

Wednesday, April 1st.—Things got worse and worse all day, until at last, when dinner-time came, we were in a hopeless condition, and decided to go into houses at once. We did not attempt to change our dresses, and even to pass from one room to the other we had to put on waterproofs and thick boots; and every time any one attempted to come through a door he had to put up an umbrella and jump a ditch, and when I, clad as if for a country walk, put my foot out of my bed-room, I sank in the mud and had to go back to change. The Duchess and Lady Downe had to be carried across to dinner; the girls were told to pack their things and to sleep in the sitting-room as a drier place than their own tent. The Downes and Bayleys were washed quite out of their tents, and everyone was in a more or less dismal condition.

You can scarcely imagine how dreadful a well-soaked camp is—how everything you touch is wet, and how odious the drippings are. Early in the day we had hoped for better things, and had settled to ride at five,

but by that time the rain was coming down in torrents
and a thunderstorm was in full swing. The Commander-
in-Chief managed to ride over to dine with us, and we
had two other officers and Colonel Bradford and Major
Lang, who travelled with us from England, to make up
our party, but we are all getting depressed by this
odious weather. *It* is extraordinary how the servants
manage everything, and bring the dinner unharmed
through the seas of mud—but one feels very sorry for
them and for their muslin-covered legs, for they all
wear white trousers. One of the funniest sights is the
man who attends to my stove. His duty is to sit outside
and to come creeping in every few moments to poke it
up, and to put on more fuel. He is anything but smart :
his garments consist of a turban, a jacket, a loin-cloth,
and a sheet, all of a very dirty white ; thus lightly clad,
I cannot bear to know that he is squatting in wet and mud
outside, so I request him to 'baitho' in the room—that
is, to roll himself in his sheet and to sit huddled up in a
corner ; there he squats, eyeing the princes, governors,
commanders-in-chief, and ladies into whose society he
finds himself introduced, and every now and then he
throws off his sheet and stalks with his bare brown legs
over to the fire, then returns to ruminate in his warm
corner. This is a specimen of the mixture of shabbiness
and finery which one notices so much in Eastern life ;
for what would the most modest little householder in
England think if he saw a beggar coming in to do up
his grate during an evening party ! And yet here we
are, with scores of servants in gorgeous liveries at hand,
considering this quite a natural apparition and no blot

upon our household arrangements.　D. did laugh, however, when he found him and me *tête-à-tête* over the stove before dinner, I reading and he looking on.

The maids have really been miserable, and Nowell has a touch of fever.　We take quinine every morning and are keeping well.

Thursday, 2nd.—Hurrah! The rain is over, the sun is shining, all the wet passages are opened out, and currents of nice dry air are allowed to penetrate into our rooms. Everyone has brightened up, and the way is clear now for making our plans.　Yesterday it was impossible to think of the durbar, or the review, or anything but mud.

Directly after breakfast we went out to revel in the sunshine and to see the world, and there we saw a *really* Indian sight.　While all our thoughts were fixed on *drying* things, the indefatigable Bheestie was hard at work watering the muddy grass in front of the tents! He filled his skin with water from the nearest puddle and spilt it out again at the doors of our guests!

The mountains look perfectly lovely to-day, and the more distant snowy range is visible in this clear atmosphere.

I ought to tell you that the Amir was pleased with our wet weather; some unkind people say because, being in a house himself, it gratified him to think of the discomforts other people suffer. The natives too, though they can't like it, always consider rain as a good omen, and many people here prefer it to heat and dust.　Yesterday I could not forgive them for expressing this preference, which seemed to me absurd.

The Amir is in great good humour, and almost wants to go on to England. He would like to dine here, and altogether wishes to enjoy himself. He was to come and see His Excellency at three o'clock, so we stood near to see him arrive; our own carriage had been sent for him, and he had two others behind full of his followers. He himself is a stout man, not very tall, and suffering either from gout, rheumatism, or Russian boots, so that he walks lame.

He and the Viceroy, an interpreter, our Foreign Secretary and his, sat in a tent carefully guarded on all sides, and there they discussed matters for three hours. The Amir took a good deal of snuff, but had no other refreshment, though his pipe-bearer duly arrived by himself in a carriage to prepare his 'Hubble bubble' for him should he want it. All that passed is wrapped in mystery, and D. only told us that after he had explained the English intentions, and propounded our views upon the 'Afghan question,' he said to the Amir, 'And now what are your proposals and opinions?' upon which the great man replied, '*I* don't think that is a fair question.'

The Amir has a very curious guard, which came to ride back with him. The steeds are small and thin, and their little rats' tails are tied in knots; the riders are splendid specimens of the genus ragamuffin. They wear bright orange tunics, tall Russian boots, and on their heads an imitation of our guards' bearskin, only made in the loose long wool of the black sheep. We walked round them to look at them, and the odour that pervaded their neighbourhood was terrible! I must tell you one nice gentle little trait in the Amir's character. He spent three hours yesterday morning arranging cut flowers in forty vases, and he expressed a wish to have large supplies sent him daily! And this is the man who cuts off heads and hangs people when at home, and who is accompanied here by his executioner, who, dressed in red velvet, and wearing his axe and strangling rope, helps at other times to put up the tents.

The Rajah of Bahawalpur sent us up (by request of course) his great crown to look at. *It* is quite magnificent. Some of the very largest are Cape diamonds, but as they are arranged in alternate rows with the white ones, their yellow colour does not look amiss.

Another Punjab chief, Nabha, let his pipers play to us at luncheon. *It* was very amusing to see them, as the whole costume is Scotch, but pink silk tights have to be worn to simulate the delicate complexion of the ordinary Highlander's knee.

We have people to dinner and luncheon every day, and we ride, or drive, or walk, and always spend much time in considering the weather, which continues to look uncertain. We are quite frightened when a gun goes off, lest it should bring down the rain. Sometimes, however, the sun shines a little, and the snowy range of the Himalaya looks quite lovely.

Saturday, 4th.—There was a durbar in the Shamiana this morning for the smaller chiefs, who may not be able to remain on for the great durbar. Even this one was a fine sight. There must have been over a hundred of these men, each one in a different costume; an array of beautiful colours, curious turbans, and different types of faces. The Shamiana is a great room, ninety feet square; the throne was placed opposite the entrance, and one side of it was filled with these natives, the other with officers and spectators. When all were assembled, the Viceroy walked up the centre, preceded by his Staff, and seated himself on the throne, and then the chiefs passed one by one before him, each one offering gold mohurs to be touched. At the end the Viceroy told the interpreter what to say, and he made a speech in Hindustani. As soon as this was over, the tent was arranged for an evening party, and then down came the rain again, and the carpets had to be taken up and the furniture removed. Don't let me speak any more upon this odious subject.

We had a big dinner of seventy. It is wonderful how well everything is managed; all looks as nice and is as good as it could be at home. A dinner for forty is going on at the same time in the mess tent, and breakfasts, luncheons for eighty persons, and occasional buffets have also to be prepared, so the cook's post is certainly no sinecure.

Sunday, 5th.—A dreary, showery Easter Day. We got to church in the morning and managed to take a walk in the afternoon.

Monday, 6th.—As all hope of having a real review is over, owing to the muddy state of the ground, it was decided to do the best that could be done with the roads, and to have a mere march past to-day. It was a really splendid sight. No one could have imagined under what difficulties the troops made so fine an appearance. There was the horrid wet weather in which they have lived for ten days, and the perpetual showers actually going on, and there was the tactical difficulty of getting them all to march past in order and at regular intervals when they only had the roads to form in. Everything went off as well as possible. Our military ardour was greatly inflamed by the sight, and we felt very proud both of our own and our native troops.

The parade was 20,000 strong, a larger number than has been got together here before, and there were the Viceroy, the Queen's son, three Commanders-in-Chief, Sir Donald Stewart, Sir Frederick Roberts, General Hardinge, and the Amir to show off before. The marching lasted an hour and forty minutes. The elephant, mule, and bullock batteries interested us much. There were four guns, and three elephants to each gun, and the twelve enormous beasts looked very solid and steady as they passed. The bullocks stand fire better, however, and have to take the elephants' place in times of danger. When our troops had all passed, the native contingents came to the tune of ' We don't want to fight, but by Jingo if we do.' They also looked extremely well.

The rain was not quite sufficient really to spoil anything, but just as we drove away it came down heavily, and then suddenly cleared away and allowed a bright sun to appear.

The Amir wore a white uniform, and was, *I* hope,

impressed with all he saw. We thought his Commander-in-Chief looked bored, but that may have been his guile.

The afternoon continued lovely, and His Excellency took the Amir out for a drive and showed him the park, which is really very pretty, and from which there is a fine view. The Duke and Duchess of Connaught rode, accompanied by the girls, and Lady Downe and I went out quietly together. We visited the native camp, and saw how very uncomfortable and miserable its inhabitants must have been during the rains, for the ground is low and looks quite swampy. The general effect of the camp is that of a great show, for at the entrance to each chief's own encampment is a bright red arch ; these, and the kannats to all their tents, being made of cotton printed in colours, while some of the tents themselves have patterns on them. Bands were playing in all directions, and the soldiers did not seem to have quite settled down since the morning. The background of lovely mountains served to raise the scene in one's estimation and to give grandeur to it, but *I* watched with anxiety a black cloud, 'no larger than a man's hand,' which grew and grew and still hung over us even at dinner time. *I* said fervently, '*If* it will only not come down till half-past eleven'—and that is exactly what it did.

There were two big dinners going on, one for the Amir in the durbar tent, all the guests being men, and one for us in the mess tent.

The official dinner went off extremely well. The Amir watched D. all through, and did as he did, while his personal attendant, a boy of sixteen, who always goes about with him, stood behind his chair and smoked cigarettes! The interpreter also sat behind, and His Excellency's conversation was transmitted by him. After the Queen's health had been drunk, D. gave the Amir's, when, to everybody's surprise, His Highness got up and made a very nice little speech, full of the friendship that existed between England and Afghanistan, and of good wishes for the success of the British army everywhere. The only way of returning this civility was by having 'three cheers for the Amir,' and the Duchess and I just arrived from the mess tent in time to hear these truly national sounds.

The Seaforth Highlanders walked round the table playing their pipes with tremendous swagger; and all this time my evening party was collecting in the Shamiana. As it was quite full of people, the Duchess and I thought we might as well go in, but we soon began to wish the gentlemen would come to our assistance; for when our guests saw that introductions were being made to us, they all pushed forward, and we were soon entirely surrounded by the most picturesque medley of faces and dresses that you can conceive. There were native officers of different regiments, from the very tall men in the Mooltan Horse, with their great blue and white or red turbans, to the tiny Goorkha, all in black. There were guests dressed in gold brocades, others all in white, with big turbans and long black hair and beards; and there were the Rajahs resplendent with jewels. But it would be quite hopeless to attempt to describe the dress of an assembly where each individual is able to consult his own idiosyncrasies, where he is tied to no particular colour, form, or material, and where every creature is picturesque, whether in a luxurious or in a simple fashion.

I will just describe one or two specimen costumes, and the rest you will have to imagine. I have often mentioned the Rajah of Bahawalpur, but he is such a magnificent-looking Rajah that I must tell you again about him. His dark-coloured face is handsome. He has straight features and fine eyes, a short black beard, and long black hair resting on his shoulders. In front of his gold-embroidered cap he wore a most magnificent aigrette of European-cut diamonds, round his waist a diamond belt, and round his neck about seven rows of splendid jewels—emeralds and pearls and rubies and pearls strung alternately. His coat was velvet and gold, and the skirt of it stood out a little over large loose white trousers. I have also seen him in a beautiful sage-green moiré coat embroidered in silver. His taste for gorgeous display makes him as interesting as a prince in the Arabian Nights!

Of a very different type was a little Sikh 'high priest,' who was swaddled in shirts and sheets, with a bit of black shawl to relieve the white, and who went about producing from underneath his wrappings a picture of Sir Donald McLeod, whose memory he adores. The old Rajah, Nabha, is another interesting man—wearing a tight green and gold tunic with short sleeves to the elbow, the long sleeves of some under-garment, also of rich material, showing from underneath. I have seen him on horseback in this dress, with a shield on his back, and he looked quite like an old knight in the days of the Crusaders. Jhind, too, is magnificent, an old man with very fine features and long grey beard ; he wears a white close sort of turban which rather frames the face, and a handsome aigrette in it; the rest of his dress is like that of Nabha. Kapurthalla wore a large pink and gold muslin turban, with big aigrettes and diamond brooches in it, and a loose red and gold coat. Patiala also wears this dress—but that is enough millinery for the present!

As *I* was saying, the Duchess and I were beginning to feel quite oppressed by our surroundings, when the doors lifted (they do lift in a tent) and the Viceroy and his guests came in. The Amir was in a dull brown uniform and grey Astrakan cap. We spoke to him, exchanging a few compliments, and as soon as His Excellency had seen some of the principal people we were glad to make our way to the front of the tents for air and space. A great bonfire was burning there, and we had a quantity of wild men to dance their own peculiar savage war dance round it. *It* was a curious sight, that enormous circle of natives and Europeans, all in full dress and uniforms, collected round this fire, while a hundred most cut-throat-looking creatures, indifferently clothed and with long hair hanging down, went shrieking and jumping and dancing and brandishing their swords to the sound of a horrible tom-tom and some worse pipes.

The Duchess and I went back to the tent again after this, and made several tours of the room, and many more acquaintances, and then by a happy inspiration, at a particular moment, *I* suggested that we might retire, and we had scarcely reached our own tent when down came my thunderstorm !

Tuesday, 7th.—Yesterday we had the march past; to-day we had a real review, for the ground dries so quickly that it was found to be possible to move the troops a little. As we had to go over rough roads and ploughed fields, our barouche and char-à-banc had artillery horses put into them; and I felt very happy with such well-seasoned campaigners in my carriage. As usual here, the mountains made a lovely background to the picture, while the foreground was well filled with Oriental and military colouring. There were elephants and camels, and native costumes and beautiful uniforms, and carriages and riders, and grand stands—quite a gala day it was—and then in the middle distance our long, long line of splendid troops!. The Viceroy with a very large Staff rode down the lines, and I was allowed to drive after them, so that I saw everything quite as well as the Commander-in-Chief did; and then I was placed close to the Staff at the saluting post, and the troops went by in brigades—Infantry, English and native, mule and elephant batteries, then at a trot all the Cavalry and Artillery, the latter passing once more at a gallop, the whole ending with the royal salute.

Everything went off without a hitch; the troops looked splendid, and twice as numerous as they did yesterday, owing to the different formation. There was but one opinion on the subject : both soldiers and spectators were delighted to have seen such a magnificent sight. We only got home at two, and were glad of a little time to rest before my garden party, to which we had asked everyone staying here to come this afternoon.

Our state elephants were ordered out, and were stationed like a magnificent guard of honour down either side of the approach, the party taking place between the lines. There were twenty elephants on each side, all with scarlet and gold howdahs on, while the Viceroy's own elephant with its attendant small one, and two other particularly fine animals, stood opposite and on either side of our tent door. The state elephant is gigantic, and he is almost entirely covered by a scarlet cloth very thickly embroidered with gold. The howdah is silver, and is a great weight; the cushions are scarlet; one man sits behind holding a large state umbrella, while the mahout, also in scarlet and gold, sits on the elephant's neck and guides it. The attendant elephant carries what appears to be a silver ladder, and he also is magnificently clad. The elephants have never been used in this way before, but they were considered to look so splendid to-day that they are to re-appear at the durbar to-morrow.

The same gorgeous dresses attended the party, and one could see them better out of doors than in a room. Bands from the various regiments played, and we had some Highlanders to dance reels and sword dances. I had all the native officers presented to me, and touched the hilts of their swords which they held out to me. This is the first time they have ever been presented to a 'Lady Sahib,' or even to the Viceroy except at a levée. We had a few people to dinner, and so ended a very full day.

Wednesday, 8th.—I have now to try and give you some idea of the great durbar. For this occasion the division between the durbar tent and the great

Shamiana was taken down, and they were thrown into
one. A dais, with three thrones on it, was at the extreme end, facing the entrance, while the whole space in
both tents was filled with guests, leaving only a broad
passage down the middle covered with scarlet cloth.
The Punjab chiefs had seats placed for them, and
arrived each under his own salute, and each one more
splendid than the other. Patiala sat first; he had a
canary-coloured turban with chains of emeralds and
diamond drops hanging about it. Bahawalpur surpassed
himself. His white puggaree was quite gigantic, and was
a mass of jewels, the most enormous aigrettes of diamonds round it, and strings of emeralds and pearls. *It*
came quite over his forehead, and the height of the
aigrette in the centre was quite twice that of the face
beneath it. His coat was black velvet embroidered with
seed pearls, and I believe he was covered with jewels in
front, but I could only get a general view of things, and
could not see all the details. Besides these chiefs, there
were crowds of other durbaries (natives who have the
right of attending durbars), officers in uniform, and
ladies; and as the sun shone brightly, everybody and
everything looked its best, and we all admired and sat in
breathless expectation to see the thrones filled! At last
a 'boom' sounded from a cannon, and the Viceroy's
Staff was seen marching up, and then appeared the
Viceroy himself, very gorgeous indeed in his Lord-
Lieutenant's uniform, the Star of India and the
four collars of his various Orders ornamenting him
richly both back and front! The Duke, who walked on
his left, had his stars and collars on, and the Amir on

his right wore a very dull plain brown uniform. When the three were seated, the Viceroy turned slightly to the Amir, and probably said that he was glad to see him, and that he hoped he had slept well; and the interpreter having passed this on, the Amir most likely made some equally new remarks; and we all watched their nods and bows and 'wreathed smiles,' when a voice was heard to say, 'The Dresses of Honour for His Highness the Amir!' and then servants poured in with trays full of very nice things which we should all like to possess, and each tray was laid down on the floor till the display reached right down to the door, where horses and elephants, and cannon and mountain batteries joined the company of presents. Those on the floor consisted of watches and clocks, guns, jewellery, cabinets, musical boxes, silver cups, and quantities of beautiful stuffs; and I particularly liked a good ebony walking-stick with a watch in its ivory handle. Well, these having been exhibited, the Amir taking pains not to look at them, the trays were all removed, and then more came on for His Highness's sons, and more for His Highness's followers, until we all got quite tired of seeing other people's presents. Though the Amir did not appear to notice these little offerings, I am sure they warmed his heart, for he suddenly began to make a speech, which was translated by the Foreign Secretary, and which proved to be a hearty declaration of friendship for England, with a warlike flavour in the expression of it. This quite 'fetched' the audience, which broke out into enthusiastic plaudits, such as have probably never been heard in durbar before. I am sorry to say that at this most critical juncture one of the presents behaved badly, and, a birdcage having been brought in, its mechanical inmate set off at intervals to sing a little song, 'Afghanistan will ever be a true friend to England.' Chirp, chirp, chirp, chirp, said the bird, and so on! An effective present was a portrait of D., which was borne in by two men, who held it opposite to the Amir for a moment and then backed it out again, and one heard a whisper all over the place, 'The Viceroy, the Viceroy,' as it was recognised all down the line. Last of all the sword of honour was carried in on a cushion, and D., taking it in his hand, said that he presented this to His Highness as a mark of his own personal esteem, and in recognition of the friendship for England which His Highness had just expressed so forcibly. In reply, the Amir was still more friendly to us and more warlike to others, so the British soldier again applauded vehemently.

The sword is a Damascus blade with a gold hilt set with diamonds, the scabbard is red velvet and gold also with diamonds on it, and it bears an inscription, which says that it was presented to the Amir 'by his friend, the Earl of Dufferin, Viceroy of India.' This ended the durbar; the chief actors marched away, each member of Council was led down and bowed out by Foreign Office officers, and each chief in his turn was handed to his carriage. We rushed to the door just to have a private view of the silver and gold carriages, and the jewels and the finery, but we were called away to be photographed in a group, and had only time to see that wonderful head of Bahawalpur's drive away in a barouche. Would not you like to see a sight of that kind driving down Regent Street?

D. and I and the girls went a family drive in the afternoon, the A.D.C.s following in another carriage. This was a rest, as we both felt tired with big and little anxieties, and we are so glad that all is so well over. The last three days have been lovely, and it has all been so interesting and so fine! Those wild dancers came again in the evening, and we sat round the bonfires till bedtime. I thought we were rather courageous, for 100 swords flourishing wildly in the air, in the hands of complete savages, look rather terrific.

April 10*th,* 11*th,* 12*th.*—There have been no very stirring events the last few days, so I shall be able to put very shortly all we have been doing. The Viceroy had a small parade one morning to see his escort, which consists of the 9th Lancers, the Corps of Guides, the Seaforth Highlanders, the 1st Bengal Infantry, and a battery of Artillery, and with these the Native Contingent. They are troops kept up by native princes. There were about 4,000 men on parade.

At other times we have ridden and driven, and written our letters, and paid one or two visits, and the girls have tried elephants and camels, and there have been races and polo matches; only, as our camp is exactly in the centre of the racecourse, no one can see anything of the races. This morning the Amir left, and before D. was up he got a telegram from home telling him to invest His Highness with the Star of India. So he very hurriedly got his own ribbon and star,

collected A.D.C.s and cushions, and sent off a deputation to present the Amir with this Order. He was
delighted, and put them on to go away in. It poured
again with rain when he was leaving, but he expressed
himself as truly grateful and pleased, and said he had
not expected to be treated with so much honour. He in-
tends to remain some days at Peshawar, so we have to
give up our trip there, as we cannot wait until he goes on.

In the evening the Duke and Duchess of Connaught
went off, and to-morrow we start ourselves, and so ends
our camp life at Rawal Pindi.

Tuesday, 14*th*.—I told you that we had to give up
our expedition to Peshawar ; but as we were determined
to have one day's rest before entering upon further
duties, we decided to go and see the Attock Bridge and
to drop down the Indus in boats for about sixty miles.
In pursuance of this plan, we slept in our train at Rawal
Pindi, and just awoke for a moment at four o'clock to
feel it gently moving on, and again about eight in the
morning, when we found ourselves at our destination.
We walked across the iron bridge, which is very high on
account of the great rise in the river after the rains.
Underneath the railroad there is a subway for carriages.
The train followed us across, and we breakfasted in it,
and then got into our boats, the servants remaining in
their carriages and going by rail to meet us, a journey
of about 100 miles. The fortress of Attock was just
opposite our breakfast place, and we were sorry not to
visit it, for the walls and towers climb up a great hill,
and enclose a large space of ground, looking very ancient

and picturesque. We had three boats, with six rowers in each, and a man in the stern, steering with a long oar. The river is extremely swift, and, in spite of my Canadian experiences, I sometimes felt quite frightened, especially as in our very first rapid a solid wave came in and drenched Rachel and me completely. Nelly's dress got wetted too, but the Viceroy was respected! We were in such a condition that we were obliged to land, and, after taking off as many clothes as possible, we got into ulsters and spread our dresses and etceteras on the awning of the boat, to dry in the sun as we went along. By luncheon time we were able to put them on again, and to enjoy our picnic on the sand and a little climb about the rocks. Then we proceeded on our perilous way, and had a most delightful afternoon in the sunshine and fresh air. The scenery was beautiful —the rapid river, and the high rocks, and the innumerable little bays, and the distant mountains—and all so bright that, even with my tinted spectacles, which I found it prudent to wear, there seemed a perpetual blaze of light on everything. We landed at a picturesque spot, where the river made a sudden turn, and where there was a bridge of boats across it, and a road passing between two immensely high rocks. We drove up to the station in a tonga, and had tea there before our train arrived. We dined, and then started off again, and, travelling all night, reached Lahore at two o'clock next day.

Wednesday, 15*th.*—There was an address at the station, and then we came on to the Lieutenant-

Governor's house, where we are staying. It is a very curious house, being, in fact, an old Moslem tomb. The dining-room is a square Moresque chamber, vaulted and high, with a row of windows near the top. It is all done in blue and red patterns, which look very like the tiles in old mosques. The rest of the rooms form an octagon round this, so that on each side there is one good room and two odd-shaped long ones. We found everyone complaining bitterly of the heat, and fanning themselves, and shutting up the house to keep it cool, but in my room, to which I gave the sun free access, my thermometer never went above 85°. It was considered safe to go out about five, and then we started in two big chars-à-bancs to drive to Jehangir's tomb at Shahdera, a distance of about five miles.

My first impression of Lahore is one of luxuriant foliage and flowers and cultivation. I don't feel that I have seen any *town*, but we drove through gardens and along roads with double avenues of trees, and there were palms, and nurseries of roses, and fertile-looking fields, and then we reached the garden in which Jehangir built his tomb. First we saw the Serai, or great house of entertainment for men and beasts, a place such as the Arabian Nights' travellers used to put up in. These establishments existed about every fifteen miles on the great high roads, and they were all built on the same plan; there are three gateways, the principal one being made of red sandstone with marble inlaid in patterns, and the rest of the building encloses a large square, which must have looked very grand when it was filled with equipages and travellers in gorgeous Eastern dresses. These buildings are all in a very ruinous condition now.

The tomb itself is a very large square building, with four high minarets at the corners; the covered passages are much decorated, and all the entrances to the tomb have carved and perforated white marble doors. The sarcophagus is white, inlaid with coloured marbles in the Italian fashion, the sides of it being covered with the name of God ninety-nine times repeated in very beautiful characters. The roof of this building is also tiled with marble, and from it we proceeded still farther, up to the top of one of the minarets, in order to get a view of the city. Even from this elevated position Lahore seemed too much enveloped in trees to show much *town,* and we only carried away an idea of one or two mosques rising out of the misty distance. It was prosaic of us to have tea on the roof of Jehangir's tomb, but we did both have it and enjoy it.

In the evening there was a big dinner and a levée, and oh! we were so sleepy, and so glad to get into a quiet and stationary bed!

I must tell you that the roses at Lahore are things to rave about. *I* never saw such a profusion; one drives through hedges of them, and there are great bushes, and arches, and trees covered with them; it seems to me to be a real city of gardens. There are several public ones through which one drives in a perpetual state of exclamation and admiration; and then there is a garden five miles long surrounding the walls of the city, so that whenever a Lahore cockney chooses to step out from his close dwelling and narrow street, he finds himself amongst plantains, and roses, and palms, and mangoes, and pepul-trees, and lovely flowering pomegranates.

Thursday, 16th.—I have a great deal too much to tell you, and I long for the pens of ever so many ready writers to give you even faint ideas of all we see and all we do and all we appreciate and enjoy! In the afternoon the Viceroy received the Maharajah of Kashmir in durbar. He is such a fine old man, with a handsome and distinguished-looking face and courtly manners. He is very ill, I fear, and his eldest son does not look a worthy successor. He and his people all wear muslin petticoats, and these look very well when a handsome loose coat is worn over them; but without the coat I think it is an ugly dress.

When the visit was over, we began some sight-seeing, and visited the gaol, where we saw the prisoners making handsome carpets, which are said to be everlasting, and are sold for as much as 2*l.* 10*s.* a yard. It is an enormous place, holding nearly 2,000 prisoners. Our inspection of it was very imperfect, but it looked clean and cheerful in the blazing sun.

Then we saw the Museum and the School of Art; but there is no use telling you about things which are everywhere much alike, and in the latter place the only uncommon sight was a row of juvenile carpenters, about eight years of age, learning their trade. They begin with carving, and they sit on the floor as only an Oriental can sit, working away with a chisel and hammer on a sort of wooden copy-book and using their toes almost as much as their hands. I went home after this, but D. visited the Oriental College, which interested him much.

Now, how am *I* to describe our evening entertain-ment in the Shalimar Gardens? We started off in time for dinner, expecting nothing in particular, and only knowing that we were to dine in a garden, and that there were to be two addresses presented, and a party afterwards. We drove about five miles along a road, which was lighted the whole way by torches, and as we approached our destination, we found the wall of the garden, which covers about seventy acres, designated by a line of illumination. Then, when we got down from the carriage and stopped under an archway, we looked down upon a real garden of light! Straight away from us went a pathway of water, down the centre of which played a succession of little fountains, giving a sort of misty mysteriousness to the scene. On either side of this fairy-like canal were broad bands of fire, and walks, and great rows of large trees with quantities of Chinese lanterns and various illuminating devices intermixed. These lines of fire and water crossed the gardens in every direction, and at the end of the first terrace we found ourselves in a sort of open colonnade, where dinner-tables were spread, and on the other side of which we looked down upon another great illuminated water-garden. It was too lovely: the water from the first garden passed immediately under the place whereon we sat, and fell as a waterfall out at the other side down to the terrace below; and moving about and standing in the illuminated kiosks one could see the figures of the attendants adding their mite to the completeness of the picture!

In spite of the poetic nature of our surroundings, we sat down and ate an ordinary dinner! Then the native guests began to arrive—the Rajahs of Jhind and Faridkote, the Maharajah of Kashmir, &c., &c., and *I* need not tell you these finely clad men always add to the beauty of the scene. While they were assembling I walked round the gardens and saw how the beds of light were managed. There must have been hundreds of thousands of tiny earthenware jars full of oil placed quite close one to the other, and a wick burning in each. The lines of light round all the buildings were done in the same way. Then I returned to hear the addresses. The first was presented by a deputation of five old Sikhs, with handsome faces and long grey beards turned over their ears and fastened away under their turbans, Sikh fashion, all of them dressed in their artistic Oriental garb ; and then came the representatives of the ' modern school.' The young man of the period in India surely never looks in a pier-glass, or he could not possibly show himself in his black alpaca square-cut coat and trousers by the side of his gorgeous elders. The one dress is ugly and undistinguished, the other all that is beautiful and comfortable and fine. D. spoke in answer to each ; and as I watched the two parties listening, I was struck by the superior dignity of the elder group—their manners are so good, their expression so grave and sensible.

We left this lovely scene with regret, and had a nice drive home, the night being only pleasantly warm.

Friday, 17*th*.—We have had such a day of sight-seeing that *I* take up my pen with a feeling of despair.

Everything we saw was so interesting; and yet it is so impossible to convey to you a tithe of the pleasure we had in seeing, or to describe at all minutely, all the wonders and beauties that delighted and surprised us !

The sun was slightly veiled, and so we were able, with unheard-of audacity, to be out from nine till 12.30 in the day. We began by driving through many gardens and shady roads to the Delhi gate, and, passing through that, entered immediately into another world. We drove through narrow streets, where strange old houses and curious carved windows were filled with crowds of people, and through which we could only slowly move along, until we passed another archway, and found ourselves in the outer court of a mosque, the face of which is decorated with inlaid pottery in brilliant colours and beautiful designs. The inner court, the mosque itself, and the minarets were once entirely covered with these splendid colours, and, though much has been destroyed, there is enough left to make one feel how supremely beautiful it must have been in its original state of perfection. Leaving this, which is the mosque of Wazir Khan, we looked into a smaller one with golden domes, and had rose-leaves dropped upon our heads as we got down from the carriage. After this came some modern waterworks, then another mosque, within whose large and quiet court sat a boys' school learning the Koran. The decoration of this mosque is a white marble-looking material with a raised pattern on it, the whole having rather the effect of chintz.

Next we saw the tomb of Runjeet Singh. This is very beautiful indeed; the tomb itself is marble, with a large round covered vessel on the top to contain his ashes. Round this were eleven knobs of marble, some plain and some ornamented. The latter hold the ashes of his queens, the former those of his slave girls, all of whom were burnt as his widows ; and at the corners were two more of those round tombstones over the ashes of two pigeons which had flown on to his funeral pile. The roof of the dome itself was of gold, very slightly ornamented with colour, and the colonnade outside had a lovely sort of decoration which we had never seen before ; it had the effect of a beautiful soft grey, and was made with small convex pieces of looking-glass imbedded in a pattern of delicate white plaster leaves and flowers. Runjeet Singh seems to have been fond of both these styles of decoration, for when we went on to his palace in the Fort, we found a great many rooms there done both with the gold and with the glass.

From a single view of these lovely creations one can only carry away a general impression and a great sense of pleasure, and it is difficult to resolve the expression of it into any real description. One feels that the mere recapitulation of perforated marble doors, and inlaid marble floors, and carved marble pillars, and golden domes, and arches decorated with painted illustrations of the stories of the gods, and splendid coloured tiles, gives no idea of a morning spent in passing from one thing which is beautiful and interesting to another which is still more so ! Nor can *I* impress you with my view of these sights unless I can make you add to the actual things *I* am attempting to describe the crowd which is always present. You have to picture to yourself the most

curiously built and characteristic streets, and then to fill
every nook and corner, and to cover all the roofs, with men,
women, and children, each individual being a picture in
himself. We pass through them going into the mosques,
and look out at them from the mosques, and as we move
on from one beautiful building to another there is
always this swarm of human beings adding to the
interest and picturesqueness of the scene.

The Fort and Runjeet Singh's palace, which I have
mentioned, came next, and then we visited a native girls'
school, which, at his own special request, the Viceroy
was allowed to see. It was in such a narrow street that
the carriage could not go up it, so I. got into a palanquin and followed D., who was on horseback. We could
have touched the houses on either side, and, as usual,
felt much interested in the inhabitants. I need not tell
you about the school, as my former letters have given
you some idea what the children look like in these
establishments.

On our way home we had to see a modern building,
an Assembly Room built in memory of Sir Robert Mont-
gomery, and a Reading Room to Sir John Lawrence; but
it was like descending from 'Ivanhoe' to 'Aurora Floyd,'
and I could not appreciate either! This was the sight-
seeing of the morning, and one felt quite 'exalted' after
it. We went home, and the Viceroy immediately started
off to pay a return visit to the Maharajah of Kashmir
and to look in at the new cathedral; then came lunch,
and good-bye! At the door some people from the
Rajah brought a beautiful bundle of shawls for my acceptance, which I graciously took, and passed on to the

Foreign Secretary, to be sold for the good of the Government! Sir Charles and Lady Aitchison, our host and hostess, have been so kind to us, and have done everything to make our visit pleasant.

This would seem a good place to explain to you the Indian system of gifts. When money is presented to the Viceroy, he always 'remits' it, but when presents of jewels, arms, stuffs, horses, or other things of value are given him, they are accepted, and are immediately handed over to the Tosh Khana or Government Treasury, where they are sold, return presents of equal value being made to the donor.

A 'dolly' generally consists of trays upon trays of fruit and vegetables and sugar-candy; these are offered at every place and are accepted and divided amongst the servants, who enjoy the good things immensely.

We had an hour and a half in the train, and then got to Amritsar for our afternoon sight-seeing. More beautiful narrow streets, the houses almost swathed in Indian shawls, brilliant phulkarries, and bright-coloured cottons; more overflowing windows and crowded house-tops, and then the Golden Temple! The name is not at all too poetical for the place. There it stands, a golden building in the very centre of a large square sheet of water, only to be reached by a narrow marble pathway. Nothing more fairy-like can be conceived. Viewing it from a distance, you get its reflection in the water, and see all the picturesque houses on the further side and the great minarets in the town beyond, and this temple really does seem to be a dream! No wonder that to approach it you must take off your earthly shoes and put on embroidered slippers, then you descend the stairs and walk a long way round the banks of the water. First you visit a sort of chapel where the high priest sits, and he shows you the swords of the great Sikh warriors, for this is the religious capital of the Sikhs; and still about, and above, and around you are always the ornamental people; the nice old Sikh priests offer you silver coins which you ' touch and remit,' then they produce some puggarees and sugar-plums for your acceptance, which you are actually allowed to take; then they perform for you the Sikh baptism! It sounds strange, but it seems to be quite within their customs to show off the ceremony. The son of a Sikh is not a Sikh until he has received the baptism of steel. Two young men were the objects of the ceremony. They stood below the priest, who stirred water and sugar in a bowl with a steel dagger; this he poured into their hands, and they drank it; he poured it on to their faces and over their heads; he exhorted, and they repeated vows, and thus the steel entered into their souls; and they sat down together with a bowl of sugar-candy between them, and fed each other with it to show that they were brothers. Henceforth they are Sikhs; they will never cut their hair, and can easily be known by that, and by a peculiarly shaped turban.

While this was going on, there sat immovable, below a little marble archway, a holy man in a pink turban, who looked exactly like a carved god in a niche, and in the balcony above were some very holy Sikhs wearing curious yellow and black turbans covered with steel; and everywhere we looked there seemed to be fresh interest, and not half enough time to realise it all. We next passed through a golden gateway on to the marble path to the Golden Temple. Priests sit there all day singing to most primitive music, and reading the ' granth ' (pronounced grunt), which is their bible. The book is covered with gold-embroidered cloth, and over it is a jewelled arch, in which diamonds and emeralds and rubies are set, and from which hang countless strings of pearls; and again I. must tell you of golden roofs and solid gold doors, and silver doors and inlaid marble walls, and yet you will have no idea of this lovely Golden Temple!

We drove back through a different set of streets, and out of the town to the Fort and to a large garden, and, like Lahore, we found here, at Amritsar, a profusion of flowers, and great spaces of green, and avenues of trees, so that when we got back to the train we were really worn out *admiring.* Our minds had been on the stretch all day, and very delightful it was!

Saturday, 18*th.*—We breakfasted at Umballa, which we reached in the night, and then left railways and took to open carriages and four. We changed horses very often, and in about four hours arrived at Pinjore, where we are to be the guests of the Maharajah of Patiala for two nights. He met us near the place, and D. got into his carriage. This is another fairy scene. The gardens are just like those at Shalimar, but on a smaller scale; there is the same succession of terraces, and straight sheets of water, and fountains, and kiosks at the end of each terrace, through which the water flows. We

live in one of these on the top of the waterfall, and you
can't think how pretty it is. The central room is
entirely open, but furnished like a drawing-room; there
are three great arches on each side with muslin curtains
lined with pink, and great crimson blinds which can be
dropped if necessary; at one end of them is a dining-
room, and at the other a bedroom, and the girls are in
tents. This is a real Capua at the bottom of the
mountains.

The Maharajah entertains us right royally, and every
meal is a banquet: his pipers played for us at dinner,
and walked round the table afterwards. They are really
rather good, but they played several different tunes in
the room, and the bagpipes groaned in such a fearful
manner at the beginning of each that, in spite of the
Viceregal gravity of D.'s face, *I* could not help laughing.
Our host came in after dinner to see some conjuring he
had provided for us; he is such a nice boy, and speaks
English very well. It was very pretty, sitting at the
edge of our drawing-room, looking down the illuminated
garden at a waterfall which was lighted at the back,
and watching the crowd of retainers who looked on
with us.

Sunday, 19th.—We had rather a heathenish Sunday,
for there was no church, and there were fireworks in
the garden after dinner; but the most extraordinary
'firework' was a natural one. There came on suddenly
a storm of thunder, lightning, and wind, which in two
minutes upset our open drawing-room and sent our
muslin curtains flying all over the place; candles and

lamps had quickly to be extinguished, a tent outside was burnt, and for the space of ten minutes everything was confusion and desolation.

With the exception of this pyrotechnic display and the boisterous and *mauvais quart d'heure,* we had a very quiet, peaceful, and nice warm day.

Tuesday, 21st.—I have now to give you my first impressions of Simla—impressions greatly tempered by the consideration that it is to be our home for the greater part of every year. We breakfasted early, and then started off on our long eight hours' drive—D. and I in one victoria, the girls in another, and the rest of our party in much less comfortable machines called tongas. Yesterday was lovely, and we saw the mountains looking their very best.

We went at a great pace, ascending and descending, and twisting and turning round the most fearful corners, always at the edge of a precipice! Sometimes our road was exactly opposite to us, either very much higher or very much lower on the other side of a ravine; sometimes it appeared to be altogether lost, and was only to be found again by pursuing it round some very sharp angle. There were patches of cultivation almost all the way up, culminating in beautiful and enormous rhododendron-trees here. For the rest, the scenery is that of a real sea of mountains, rolling hills of various heights, with snowy peaks in the distance, but no very striking range or particular peak to appeal to one's imagination.

We changed horses every four miles, but even so our last pair seemed to feel the ascent to Government House

very severely ; indeed, the road had become more precipi-
tous and more angular than ever ! The only place that
I have ever imagined at all like this spot is Mount
Ararat with the Ark balanced on the top of it, and I am
sure that when the rains come *I* shall feel still more like
Mrs. Noah.

The house itself is a cottage, and would be very suitable for any family desiring to lead a domestic and not
an official life—so, personally, we are comfortable ; but
when I look round my small drawing-room, and consider
all the other diminutive apartments, I do feel that it is
very unfit for a Viceregal establishment. Altogether it is
the funniest place ! At the back of the house you have
about a yard to spare before you tumble down a precipice,
and in front there is just room for one tennis court before
you go over another. The A.D.C.s are all slipping off
the hill in various little bungalows, and go through most
perilous adventures to come to dinner. Walking, riding,
driving, all seem to me to be indulged in at the risk of one's
life, and even of unsafe roads there is a limited variety.
I have three leading ideas on the subject of Simla at
present. First, I feel that I never have been in such an
out-of-the-way place before ; secondly, that I never have
lived in such a small house ; and thirdly, that I never
saw a place so cramped in every way out of doors. I
fear this last sensation will grow upon me. There is
one drive which I tried to take yesterday, but had to
turn back on account of a thunderstorm ; mine is almost
the only carriage allowed here, most people going about
in jinrickshaws or dandys. The former is a sort of
bath-chair pushed and pulled by four men, and the latter

is an invalid chair carried on their shoulders.   All these men have liveries, and it looks so funny to see them coming along.   Sometimes you meet three ladies sociably in a row, and their men in brilliant colours like a quantity of gaudy birds—blue breasts, yellow breasts, red caps, &c., &c.   They go at a great pace, and I shall have to use mine whenever I forsake the one carriage road.

CHAPTER IV

SIMLA DURING THE RAINS

APRIL 22 TO OCTOBER 19, 1885

Wednesday, April 22nd.—The Duke and Duchess of Connaught are staying with Sir Thomas Baker (Adjutant-General), and he asked us to go and lunch with them, and afterwards to join them in an expedition to Mushobra. Our neighbours here look very near to us, and so they would be had we the wings of a dove wherewith to fly from our ark to their eyries on the surrounding hills; but as we have to toil up and down in jinrickshaws or on ponies, it takes time to go anywhere and we were three-quarters of an hour reaching our destination. You will be really amused to hear that I require six men to take me along in my bath-chair, and a jemadar to look after them, so that when Nelly, Rachel, and I take a little gentle exercise together we have a small regiment of nineteen men in scarlet liveries pulling and pushing our three machines! In spite of these numerous attendants, locomotion here is most unsociable: there is only room for one at a time, and I must say I think a long expedition in a jinrickshaw is decidedly dull. We went to a place some seven miles off, following each other and occasionally shouting a remark; and when we got to

Mushobra we had tea, and then, finding it extremely cold for sitting out, we set off to walk ' a little way' back.. The Duchess and I led, and as we thought everyone had his or her own conveyance, we felt at liberty to follow our inclinations, and on we walked for quite four miles. It appears, however, that we made one of our party very miserable, for he had on a pair of tight, thin, patent-leather riding-boots; the stones were very rough on the road, and as he watched us disappearing round turn after turn on the mountainous path, he groaned aloud, but did not dare to mount his steed while ladies and Royal Dukes walked.

D. and I visited ' Observatory Hill,' which is a site Lord Lytton chose for the new Government House. At Calcutta it was proposed that we should alter this cottage into a fitting Viceregal residence, but the moment we saw the proximity of our precipices and the smallness of the house, we began to think that it would be a mistake to build here, and now that we have seen the new site we are convinced of it! There is a splendid view from it, and a large space of vacant ground to build on, and I should say it has every possible advantage over this.

We were very much amused, while walking about there, to see that it requires two men to use one spade. The first man digs in the ordinary way, but the second pulls a rope which is attached to the spade, and thus helps his friend up with his shovelful! These men come from Ladak, and are curious-looking creatures. They shave the front part of the head, and wear long curls at the back and sides; they have flat ugly features, and look dirty. The women are not pretty, and their dress, which consists of a straight blouse, and trousers gradually tightening down to the ankle, is most unbecoming. Their nose-rings are of thick silver, and are as large as bangles.

We had a small dinner for the Duke and Duchess of Connaught, who are to leave for England on Saturday. I found my little house was very comfortable for a party of twenty-three, but *I* fear that when we get beyond that number people will grumble over the ' horrible crushes ' at Government House.

Sunday, 26th.—Going to church is a matter of difficulty here, and I am not sure but that strict Sabbatarians would forbid one's attempting it, seeing how much labour it involves. There are two jinrickshaws for the girls and one between the maids = 19 men. There is a pony carriage for me, a horse for His Excellency, and ponies for all the A.D.C.s, while at the church door the congregation of bath-chair men in all their various costumes standing by rows of these machines, and the collection of horses held by their syces, give more of a festive than of a serious character to the outside of the building, and a lady stepping into her pew, booted and spurred and habited, disturbs all one's conventional notions of a ' Sunday gown.'

We walked up to the Military Secretary's bungalow for tea. The lucky man has really a charming house, and I wish the proper owner was in it. We miss Lord William very much. He is at home on leave.

Monday, 27th.—The girls and I energetically got up

early to see the snow mountains. They rode all the way, and I drove to the bottom of ' Jakko ' a very high hill, and was carried up it in a jhampan. I tried to walk a little, but one is so easily put out of breath here that I could not manage the climb. Besides the view of the mountains, we were to see an old Fakir surrounded by all the monkeys of the neighbourhood, who assemble at his call, but we were most unlucky—the snows were not visible, and the monkeys were otherwise engaged, so we saw nothing, and must make the expedition again while the weather is still cold.

In the afternoon Captain Harbord drove me to tea with Lady Stewart, and we were going on to a ' Monday Pop.' Fancy having a ' Monday Pop ' in the heart of the Himalayas! The tea we managed, but on our way from it we were caught by the most terrific dust-storm. Anything more completely disagreeable I never felt. It quite frightened one by its vivacity, and both blinded and choked us. We drove on as fast and as well as we could to the nearest shelter, opening one eye at a time to peep at our situation, coughing, and holding on to our flapping garments, and altogether miserable. We just got into the photographer s shop when the dust ceased, and a bad thunder and rain-storm succeeded it. We did not mind this so much, and thought the mud only too delightful after the dust.

The night was still worse, and there was a squall of wind and rain in the middle of it which made one quite tremble for the roof. The cold returns after all this ' weather,' and we want our warmest clothes and fires to keep us at all comfortable.

Tuesday, 28th.—I was to receive visitors to-day between the fashionable hours of twelve and two, but the first detachment had only just arrived when rain, hail, and thunder came on with such ' impetuous rage ' that those who had come were obliged to stay, and those who had not started could not come at all. The hail rattled on our iron roof in the most deafening fashion ; the ground was quite white when we looked out after the storm, and we picked up lumps of ice as large as cherries on the lawn. We thought that this must really be the climax and the end of all our meteorological troubles, and in this mistaken idea we started out riding and walking in the afternoon. Those on horseback got wet through, and D. and I had a very adventurous walk, the only improvement since the morning being that the hailstones were now no larger than currants ; pelted by them, enveloped in cloud, dazzled by lightning, and listening to the growling thunder, we plodded on, greatly admiring by the way the big trees of crimson rhododendrons, which will be sadly dashed by the ice-balling they have received ; and, on the whole, we quite enjoyed the tempests !

The Stewarts came to tea with me, and we had Mrs. Cunningham, General Wilson, and General Gordon to dine with us. The latter has come to report the safe departure of the Amir. He received from His Highness two Orders—the one a little gold medal with ' Honour ' written on it, the other an extremely pretty ornament with large flat diamonds set in enamel. As the Amir calls it an ' Order,' General Gordon is allowed to accept it, but his daughter will wear it. He told us that the first night the Amir entered his own territory six new Martini-Henry rifles were stolen from him, whereas in our country he lost nothing. He must have felt very safe and happy here, and he said himself, 'One need not wear a sword in a friend's house.'

Thursday, 30th.—I felt that the happiness of my life here depended upon my having some thoroughly steady, safe, and yet fast means of locomotion, so I have set up a mule. Her name is 'Begum,' and she is a treasure! She walks very fast and canters beautifully, and the gentle expression of her eye is most reassuring. To-day I tried her for the first time, and though I fear she is not Viceregal-looking, I maintain she is sensible and useful; and when she wears a blue necklace and has a few red tassels about her, she will look lovely. I shall be glad when she has become an established fact, and when people cease to gaze at her long ears.

Friday, May 1st.—A most lovely May morning for see-ing the snows! We all got up early, and I on my Begum,. and the Viceroy and his Suite on nobler but not better animals, went up 'Jakko' before breakfast! At the top we saw the funniest sight. The old Fakir called 'A'o, A'o' (Come, come), and the monkeys arrived, whole families of them— fathers, children, and mothers with their little ones clasped to their breasts (only it is the baby that does the clasping, so that the mother moves about quite freely); and when grain was thrown to them they scrambled for it and ate it up very quickly, while they even ventured to.

take food from out of our hands. All the time they gave
a sort of little gentle cry; and the infants looked too funny,
gazing upside down at one from between their mothers'
arms—their little wrinkled faces and neatly parted hair
make them look so old-fashioned. The view was magnificent—such an immense range of snow mountains
against the background of blue sky, and such a varied
foreground of hills and woods, with the sun shining
brilliantly on all. Still I shan't do it often, for expeditions
in the early morning don't suit me, and I had to go to
bed for a little on my return.

Thursday, 7th.—I told you that I did not think my
domestic and countrified life here would provide material
for a weekly journal, nor is it important enough to be
divided up into days; so I will just give you a retrospective
account of a week at Simla, and will begin by telling you
that I really think it is a very nice place, and that
it is growing larger and larger in my estimation. The
roads seem more numerous and much safer than
they did at first, and I find the riding and the walks
delightful.

Besides going up ' Jakko,' one can go round it, and a
lovely ride we found it, and much did my Begum astonish
the rather scoffingly-inclined girls by keeping up with
their steeds at a canter, and outstripping them altogether
at a walk.

We had one very amusing afternoon. By dint of much
levelling, great labour, and considerable expense, a playground has been made in a valley here, where races and
gymkhana meetings can be held, and where cricket and

football can be played. It is called Annandale, and it is the only place I have seen in Simla from which you don't look down upon the world; it is so surrounded by hills that for a moment you can forget that you are yourself upon a mountain. This playground is a creation of Lord William's, and our A.D.C.s are the principal promoters and supporters of the sports there, so we went down to have tea and to watch them practising for a gymkhana, while the girls were to try tilting at the ring. Nelly was very successful, and enjoyed it immensely. The two Miss Stewarts were there, and they all galloped about, lances in hand, their hats falling off, and their hair much dishevelled, looking very energetic and very much amused. The men, meanwhile, were tent-pegging, or riding wildly round the course leading one or two ponies, going over hurdles, or simply racing. Lady Stewart and I sat and looked on, and 'Begum' was led out to tilt and covered herself with glory, Nelly being her rider.

The descent to this playground is of course very steep, but the road lies through a lovely forest of deodars and rhododendrons, with several of our most precious ferns growing at their roots. The most common tree about here is a white oak, whose only claim to relationship with our oak is that it bears acorns. In other districts near there are green oaks and brown oaks, but none of them really resemble their English namesake. This white one covers many of the hills; it looks grey in the distance, and is not a pretty tree.

I am at home one morning a week from twelve till two, those being the extraordinary hours at which visits are paid all over India. As houses here are so difficult of access, people kindly put up little ' Not at home ' boxes at the bottom of their hills, and you may imagine how the unsociable ride about in search of these !

Our daily life is much as follows : We breakfast in a little room upstairs, which at other times serves Nelly as a studio, and then we step out on the balcony and admire the magnificent range of snow mountains, which at this time of year are nearly always visible. After that we are all busy till lunch-time in our various sanctums, then come these rides or walks, and in the evening the girls manage to have some game, while D. and I generally sit quiet enjoying a book. We found an old bagatelle board here, on which they play a most simple game of ninepins, but it appears to afford all the young party endless interest and excitement.

Captain Harbord and Mr. Balfour have gone down to the plains to shoot tigers.

We do not begin to entertain until the Queen's Birth-day, when a levée is held and a dinner and ball given ; to the latter everybody here is asked, and our house appears in all its incompetence. I have not mentioned D.'s work, which is continuous. I am wondering whether a settled peace will diminish it at all. Thunderstorms have come on again, and we begin to hear for the first time of ' little rains,' which may possibly precede the certain deluge.

Friday, 8th, to Friday, 15*th.*—I am sorry to write about the weather, and *I* would not do so were the subject com-monplace ; but it really is such remarkable and unrivalled weather, it obtrudes itself so much upon one's attention, it interferes with so many plans, it is so noisy and obstreperous, so industrious and indefatigable in pouring and thundering and making itself generally disagreeable, that I am compelled to take some notice of it—more especially as, when the ' weather permits ' itself such vagaries, it prevents everyone else from doing anything. A gymkhana meeting, church, the Sipi Fair, the ' Monday Pop,' are some of the little pleasures with which it has interfered, so you see that every other interesting topic has been flooded out of my journal, and therefore it only remains for me to tell you how the storms are conducted.

The clouds lead off ; they rise in smoky columns from behind the woods, they wander lightly over the hillsides, they lie in the valleys like great bales of cotton wool, or float in tufts over the housetops ; they playfully invade one's boudoir, or in the form of a dense fog they darken and envelope everything ; then they collect overhead in great black threatening masses ready for action ! Next is heard a distant rumbling which, instead of being a short, sharp ejaculation of meteorological wrath, is a long, continuous remonstrance carried on from hill to hill, with angry flashes of lightning to accentuate its meaning ; and then comes the rain ! Such rain ! Not the soft and genial Irish shower, but a malignant downpour which resounds upon the iron roof, rattles on the balcony, and rustles through the air like a very Cataract of Lodore.

This is the way in which Friday, Saturday, Sunday, and Monday were spent by the weather, while we kept up a running commentary upon it, expressive of displeasure, disappointment, discouragement, and dismay!—for these rains, you must know, are only the 'little rains,' and we still have the 'great rains' to look forward to. They begin about June 20, and pour on and on for ten weeks; for them we are storing up a fund of resignation and a supply of mackintoshes and umbrellas, but for this rehearsal we were unprepared, and we cannot even comfort ourselves with the reflection that the present rain is good for the country. On the contrary, some people fear that the extraordinary cold of the season may put off the monsoon; and should that be the case, there would be a famine next year. This is too dreadful to think of; so I will take a more cheerful view, and although Tuesday, Wednesday, and Thursday have only been slight improvements upon the preceding days, I will go on hoping that a new moon may do something for us, and that the sunshine of this morning (Friday, 15th) may continue in spite of the too abundant clouds pervading the sky.

The Ripon Hospital was opened yesterday. It is a very pretty building, divided into five blocks, with accommodation for natives, Europeans, and paying patients. They hope to use one wing for a lying-in hospital. After walking through it we sat under a Shamiana and listened to a speech from a Mr. Hume, who expatiated upon the perfections and beauty of the new building. He said that only 7,000*l.* was wanted now to complete it, and he hoped we should make it up by next year. D. also said a few words and declared the building open, and then we all started off for church (Ascension Day),

our umbrellas and mackintoshes being greatly needed ;
and when we returned it was through, if not under, a
cloud that we drove home.

Tuesday, between showers, we rode over to call upon
the Aitchisons, with whom we stayed at Lahore. They
live quite at the other end of Simla, and have a beautiful
view and pretty garden. They have also (happy people !)
built a ball-room, and can now do their necessary
entertainments in some comfort. We then went to tea
with Lady Stewart, and succeeded in only getting a little
damp going there.

Wednesday I walked to one of the Staff bungalows
to see the ' Langours,' monkeys with white whiskers and
black faces, who live all round here. There were quantities about, and it was very amusing to see them take
headers from tree to tree. It struck me as a most
delightful athletic sport. Fancy seeing fifty heaven-born
Leotards flying from branch to branch down a precipice,
many of them with babies clinging to them ! They
occasionally sat still and looked at us ; sometimes they
throw stones at passers-by, but we could not excite them
to any such evil practice.

I was nearly forgetting to tell you of one of the great
events of the day. The tennis court is open ! The rain
makes D. appreciate it immensely, and it will really be
a great boon to all the young men in Simla.

This morning the heavy silver thrones are being
lugged up some precipitous paths to a hill Rajah's house,
and his Excellency and Staff have ridden after them. I
thought you would like to know that even to this mountainous region we carry our state chairs and that,

although we live in a cottage, we hold durbars and are accompanied by all the symbols of our official dignity.

Nelly, Rachel, and I have begun to take lessons in Hindustani from a Munshi, who tells us we shall speak it in a month; but as he gives us such sentiments as 'Evil communications corrupt good manners' to translate, I fear our conversation in this language will be more stilted than useful.

Nelly is doing a series of portraits in chalk, and Major Cooper provides her with models. She did one of the jhampani men with great success, but at the first sitting given her by a second model, a wild man wrapped in a sheet, he fainted, and having first subsided into an arm-chair he next rolled on to the floor and lay with his head under his wing. The jemadar had gone to dinner, and Nelly and her maid were left for some time vainly calling for assistance, and doing their little best to resuscitate the victim, who declined all their pressing offers of brandy and water, and would have no remedy but fresh air!

Saturday, 16*th.*—The first gymkhana went off successfully to-day. It was really a gymkhana *à deux,* for as no outsiders took part in it, and as some of the Staff were absent—some ill, and some not sporting characters—the burden of the day fell upon Captains Burn and Gordon, who manfully steeplechased, flatraced, rode postillion races, and submitted to being carried in jhampans through a water jump. People might have complained of a want of variety, but *I* am sure they did not, for after so much rain we are all too glad to get out again, and should enjoy any outdoor amusement provided for us. On my way to this entertainment I looked in at a charity bazaar, which in all countries is a trying ordeal to go through.

Monday, 18th.—Our little Sipi Fair outing began to-day. We had to ride eight miles to Wildflower Hall, along a narrow road at the edge of a precipice. I am not afraid of precipices, however, when mounted on Begum, though even she shied once at a Fakir who sat on the wayside, shaking his long red locks about and looking most uncanny. This country villa of ours is 1,000 feet higher than Simla. It is on the top of a hill, and is in the midst of most sweet-smelling pine-woods. The mountain view from it is magnificent. A great range of snowy peaks bounds the horizon, and shuts in a world of rugged and sharply-outlined hills and rocks and dales, a much more accentuated world than any I have lived in heretofore.

Our house is a real cottage, the biggest things about it being the fireplaces, which happily (for it is very cold) are quite out of proportion to the tiny rooms. We were a party of eight, and were very merry at dinner and at some games afterwards.

Tuesday, 19th.—At eleven o'clock we mounted our steeds and commenced our descent to the valley. A most delightful ride we had through the forest of oak and pine, the hillsides covered with maidenhair and other lovely ferns, the sun shining through the trees upon us, and the mountain view just visible between the branches.

Our path was such a zigzag one that I felt as if *I* was trying to dance a quadrille on horseback, there were such sharp turns in it, bringing one face to face with one's partner either above or below; and then we passed picturesque groups of people bound for the fair, and could hear the sounds of revelry from the people already there, and as we approached the place we saw such a lively scene! There were about twenty merry-go-rounds, all revolving at once, carrying basketsful of men, women, and children round and round through the air; there were little shops selling the latest things in the way of novelties from Birmingham; there were serpent charmers, and performing monkeys, and men beating tom-toms with all their might and main; there was an elephant beautifully got up, and there was a little brass god seated in an arm-chair receiving small coin; then there were of course crowds of natives, some Europeans, and all the horses and jhampanis that had brought the people down, and last, but most important of all, there was 'the bank of brides.' Matrimony is supposed to be the object of this fair, and so in a sort of amphitheatre on the hillside sit the candidates for hymeneal honours! I will not declare absolutely that they were all brides; but, at any rate, there were rows and rows of women and girls dressed in their very best. Bright-coloured jackets and scarves and nether garments adorned them, while their heads, noses, ears, throats, arms, and ankles were all heavily laden with jewellery. A really smart woman wears silver or gold ornaments falling over her forehead, and almost concealing her hair; rings of great size and weight hanging from every available space in her ear;

one of such gigantic dimensions in her nose that it requires to be kept in its place by a broad chain across the face attaching it to the already overladen ear; necklaces innumerable reach from her throat to her waist; quantities of rings adorn her fingers, and on her thumb she wears a looking-glass set in silver, a most practical ornament for so well-decorated a lady; bracelets and anklets of course.

Many of these women are very good-looking, and have refined and intelligent faces, but those of the Mongol type are extremely ugly, while their dresses do nothing to improve their appearance, being dark in colour and suspiciously dirty-looking. They wear flat round cloth caps on their unkempt hair, but they have jewels too, and like very much to have quantities of rough turquoises sewn on to their headdresses. They sat together the whole day, and I made many excursions through them, airing my few words of Hindustani, and presenting some nose-rings and toys to the children, which were always received with great pleasure. We bought a few of the ornaments from the women, but they are sufficiently sophisticated to make us pay dear for our purchases, and I even suspect that some of the jewellery is put on to attract and defraud the unwary European; many of the things look much better on than off, and are evidently new and rough copies of the old patterns.

We enjoyed the fair immensely; it was all so gay and bright, with so much colour and life and novelty about it. However, I was glad when lunch was announced, for the sun was shining on the valley, and as we had not allowed the police to push everyone out of our way according to their desire, I was exhausted with wandering through the crowd.

The lunch was given by our aides-de-camp, and was quite a banquet. I was saying to my neighbour that one never was allowed to 'rough it' in India, and that a picnic in our sense of the term seemed to be quite unknown here. He told me that the native word for a real picnic is a 'poggle-khana,' that is, a fool's dinner; so I suppose that if we will dine out of doors we shall be obliged to do our folly in as wise a manner as possible, with tables, and chairs, and silver, and every luxury that we are accustomed to at home.

After lunch I made one more tour through the beauties, and then a hill Rana, the lord of the soil, had some tricks performed for us, while the Rajah of Rutlam, a really gorgeous figure, sat and looked on. He wore a crimson velvet jacket or tunic embroidered in gold and silver, and on his long smooth black hair a bright yellow turban covered with jewels. The first performance consisted in one man shooting with a bow and arrow at the legs of another man, who danced and jumped and capered about so as to make the shot as difficult as possible. It was a most infantine amusement. We also saw some performing birds and a dancing girl, and then we turned homewards, and mounting our steeds began the ascent. It was so pretty to see the thin line of people zigzagging up the hillside, some riding, some walking, and some being carried, the Rajah looking very stately and magnificent on a fine Arab horse. Altogether we had a most delightful day, and enjoyed it very much. It was fine too until the night, when one of our real heavy rains came on with the usual thunder, and lasted some sixteen hours.

Wednesday, 20th.—A most desperate outlook of mist and rain this morning. However, we resolved to get home, so, wrapping ourselves up in ulsters and water-proofs, we started off, and I believe we really found our very wet ride rather amusing ; it took us about an hour and a half. Wildflower Hall was so exceedingly cold this morning that we are glad to be back in our own warm room. Need I add that the oldest inhabitant has never seen such weather ?

In the evening we went to the theatre. It is a nice little building, ' run ' by Lord William for amateurs to act in. ' The Palace of Truth ' was acted to-night—a bad piece for private theatricals ; so, although nicely put on the stage, we found it rather dull and long. We drove part of the way there in the brougham, and then got into rickshaws to make an otherwise impossible descent to the theatre. We did not get back till half-past twelve, which was extremely late for us, who generally go to bed at half-past ten.

The mail day changes this week owing to the coming monsoon, and I have to send this off on Saturday instead of Tuesday morning.

Thursday, 21st.—The weather continues its unnatural conduct, and it kept me in great uncertainty all the morning as to how my first garden party here would go off. Will, or won't it clear up ? Will, or won't people come ? were the questions we ' wondered ' over. I determined to have something to fall back upon, should both rain and guests attend, so had the dining-room cleared for dancing and put tea in the house. However, we had Queen's luck, and about four o'clock it settled down to be fine for the afternoon. The garden party was a small and select one; badminton and tennis were played, and the band, perched upon my balcony, discoursed to us. *I* think it went off very well.

Saturday, 23rd.—Too many clouds about, and in the afternoon a deluge. *It* was raining after lunch, but we settled to ride at four, if it cleared. We got out, but in about half-an-hour we had to turn back, and through a pretty heavy thunder-shower we rode home, and just escaped a most terrific hailstorm. The bits of ice hopped into my room from the window-sill; the rattle on the roof was so great that we had to scream to each other to make ourselves heard, and when we looked out the ground was quite white. *You* are probably basking in sunshine in England.

The Stewarts, Barrington Footes, and Major and Mrs. Keith dined with us, and we had a musical evening. Captain Foote also recited for us. Captains Balfour and Harbord came back from their tiger-shooting expedition; they did not get nearly so much sport as they expected. Mr. Balfour killed one tiger, and they all had a very exciting search after him on foot. The beast was wounded one day, and was only captured at the end of the second day, after having knocked down a man. Happily he only struck him with a broken paw, and so did not hurt him much. The description of all their doings is very interesting.   Even in the plains this is a cool year, and so, except that the rocks were too hot to sit upon, they don't seem to have noticed the heat much.

Monday, 25th.—We kept the Queen's Birthday by a large official dinner and a levée, difficult things to manage in a small house.   Forty-eight people dined in the ball-room and sixteen in the dining-room, and my drawing-room was cleared for the levée.   We three ladies dined; and as the room was very light, as the table was covered with plate and flowers, and as all the guests were in uniform, it was very pretty and very gay for an official performance.   We disappeared directly after, while the guests who had dined smoked, and those who were just arriving collected in a large Shamiana (some-what damp) erected on the lawn outside.   Then the Viceroy placed himself in front of his silver throne, and everybody passed before him.

Tuesday, 26th.—Our thoughts are centred upon the state ball, and upon the problem of expanding our limited space.   As you don't know the house, it would be useless to try and describe our arrangements to you, but *I* hope next mail to tell you how the event went off.

Wednesday, 27th.—The day was a lovely one, and we all went down to Annandale to enjoy ourselves. We tilted at the ring and tent-pegged. *I* actually tried the former amusement on Begum, and D. was very successful with his first essay at the latter. *It* was most delightful down there, and we enjoyed it very much.

Thursday, 28th.—The morning of the ball, the day fine, and not much fear for the supper Shamiana! What a piece of luck!

I did very little all the day except to take an active interest in the arrangements for the ball, and particularly to superintend the decoration of the conservatory, which I did up like a sitting-room. It is at one end of the drawing-room, opening into it; so, when furnished, it added greatly to the available space and was really very pretty. Unfortunately at night it was rather cold, and the frequenters of 'kala jagah' (or dark places) were unable to enjoy it as much as I had hoped they would. There were many more odd corners curtained in, and whole verandahs utilised in the same way, and for supper we had a big Shamiana, which held places for 100, and which was very well lighted, and looked very nice. Dancing was intended to be in two rooms, but there was a misfortune with the floor of one of them, so that practically the dancers were confined to one. Before dinner, I received from my English guests at Rawal Pindi a most lovely Indian necklace and bangles as a souvenir of their stay with us there. The necklace is a real Oriental one, with all sorts of precious stones set flat in a collar shape, and with fringes of pearls at each side of it; the inside is beautifully enamelled. Each bangle is a single row of stones of different kinds—turquoise, diamond, cat's-eye, ruby, &c. They are very pretty and uncommon, and I wore my new jewels at the ball with great pride and pleasure.

We four dined alone, and dressed afterwards, and then, when sufficient people were collected, we marched down in solemn procession, and took our places in a state quadrille. There must have been nearly 450 people—all the men in uniforms, and the ladies very smart—and all seemed to enjoy themselves and to dance with great spirit. His Excellency did his share, and we only retired at two o'clock, and were able to go to sleep to the distant sounds of music, the dancing being kept up for some time longer.

Friday, 29th.—A quiet ride of an exploring nature was considered to be the best thing after a ball, so we went up Prospect Hill, a peak very close to our own, and had from it a most magnificent view, the best I have seen here. Nothing gets in the way on any side, and one can see all round the ruggedness of the earth's surface near, and the high, higher, highest ranges of mountains in the far distance, the superlative degree of comparison being covered with snow. *I*t was a rough kind of mountain path to the top, and we thought it prudent to have our horses led down and to walk ourselves.

Saturday, 30th.—Our lovely weather seems about to break up again. It was very cold in the evening, and it rained this morning and is most gloomy; but the greatest convulsion of nature was in the night, when we had an earthquake, shaking about our beds and making us very uncomfortable. I thought it most alarming, and was somewhat relieved by the consideration that our house is a wooden one; but then, *en revanche*, it is quite at the edge of a khud. We have since heard that at some place in Kashmir eighty persons were killed, and about the same number injured.

An ominous sound of thunder and a shower at five o'clock threatened to stop the gymkhana, but it soon cleared away, and there were sufficient races to ensure the wounding of one man. Mr. Balfour was the victim this time, and he had a nasty fall riding one and leading another pony over some rails. It is in vain that we entreat everybody to have safe and easy jumps; they seem to enjoy the element of danger.

I am getting up a garden fête for the hospital here; it is to be a mixture of garden party, fish-pond, shooting at targets, band, and indoor concerts. If only the day is fine, I think it will be very successful; but who can answer for the weather this year? and the 25th of June is perilously near the rains!

Wednesday, June 3rd.—Mrs. Ilbert is giving six lectures on sick-nursing; the proceeds to go to the Hospital Fund. The girls and I attended, and the forty pupils sat in rows, listening and taking notes; and then, having learnt how to arrange a sick-room, they proceeded to make a bed in the proper manner and to answer questions. Mrs. Ilbert did it very well, and her lecture was both interesting and useful.

In the evening we had a big dinner and a dance after. We only asked the dancing people, and it was most successful, everyone appearing to be in the best of spirits. It ended at twelve, which is a comfort, and I am so glad that early dances do succeed, for then one is not incompetent to perform one's ordinary duties next day, and can even compass one's Hindustani exercises in the morning.

Sunday, 7th, to Tuesday, 9th.—I am afraid you will soon begin to find the history of my life at Simla extremely dull, for although it is in reality almost too gay for a country place, yet perpetual short notices of garden parties, gymkhanas, Monday Pops, small dances, dinners, lectures on nursing, and rides will pall upon you ere long; and even were I to enter into more particulars, I should not be able to add much to interest you, for you don't know the people at all, and I only know their outside shell.

But I remember something upon which I am certain you are dying for information. You want to know how I like 'mangoes,' which from your earliest youth you have heard of as the 'most delicious fruit in the world.' After some trouble and much perseverance in eating them, I have got to think them very good fruit; but whereas I can understand raving about a pineapple, I can't understand raving over a mango. Outside the mango is like a large apple, ill-shaped, which is not to be wondered at, considering that inside it contains a big flat oval stone which it is difficult to cover symmetrically. When ripe, and exactly right, it is the colour of an apricot; when wrong, which is most often the case, it is green or pale yellow, and tastes strongly of turpentine; but unripe it can be made into a 'fool,' which you could not distinguish from gooseberry : that is a great merit. Eating it properly is quite an art. You have to turn it on one particular side and cut it the *flat* way of the stone, then you eat it out of its substantial skin with a spoon. If you wish (I am told) to enjoy it thoroughly, you should retire into a bath and bite it. I can't say I think it would be worth that trouble.

We have another fruit called a 'lechee'; it has a tough skin almost amounting to a shell, which comes off easily, and leaves a fruit the size and colour of a plover's egg, with a strong flavour of rosewater. Another fruit outside is like a potato, and inside looks and tastes like an over-ripe pear. A pommeloe, or very large coarse orange with a bitter taste, is rather nice and refreshing.

Now, after so much information, you will only want to know further that on Thursday I had a large garden party at home, and that on Friday I went to one at the Adjutant-General's (Sir Thomas Baker's) where all the space was taken up by a tennis ground, and where all but the four guests who were playing were confined to a gravel walk. The place is so far interesting that Miss Eden lived near there, and that out of compliment to her it is called 'Elysium.' On Saturday we went to a 'penny reading' for a charity. The place was crowded, and I never saw such a stream of rickshaws as that which came pouring down the steep hill to the theatre.

Thursday, 11th.—The Simla sky races began to-day, and a steeplechase was got through without an accident, though not without a difference of opinion, which is likely to lead to 'unpleasantness.' The Ilberts dined alone with us, and we all went on to a party given for us by the Rajah of Rutlam. I thought it a good party, well arranged, and very pretty and pleasant. He gave it in the rink which exists here for roller-skating. The room was decorated with carpets, embroideries, chandeliers, and baskets of ferns, and it was so large that there was plenty of room to have tables with photograph-books, chairs, and sofas all about it, while a raised place which surrounds the rink proper also made a good place to sit. Music went on all the evening, and people talked and moved about and seemed very happy. I was decorated with a wonderful gold braid ornament, and was given an embroidered bag full of spice. *I* must really send you one of these ' garlands' to see; they are beautifully made, and replace the flowers one gets elsewhere. I much prefer them, as they don't dirty one's gown at the time, and one can bring them home and keep them.

Friday, 12*th,* was also a busy day. It is the one morning I have for writing letters after the arrival of the mail, but at 11.30 Dr. Franklin came to give me his views upon the medical question, and directly after lunch *I* had Miss Stewart, Captain Turner, and Mrs. Franklin to rehearse their piece for my garden fête. This was no sooner over than we had to mount a very steep hill to the Military Secretary's house, Colonel Graham having a garden party there, and after that we had a little dinner at home.

Saturday, 13*th.*—We are all very busy preparing for the fish-pond, tying up parcels, painting jars, &c., &c.; but the weather ! Will it last till the 25th ? The monsoon has already broken at Bombay. How long will it take to travel up?

Monday, 15*th*.—We had such an interesting afternoon 'inspecting' Major Carré's mule battery from Jutogh. We had turned our backs on Simla, and were in a delightful spot in the heart of the mountains. The battery started from the top of one hill, crossed a ravine, and came up a very steep cliff on the other side. We rode up a narrow rough path, and stood at the top watching them as they threaded through the woods on the opposite hill, then came up, almost like flies on a wall, to where we were. The red turbans of the native drivers, and the white helmets of the soldiers, looked well among the trees. When they had reached a flat place on the very top, the guns were made ready for action. One mule carries the carriage, another the wheels, a third the barrel, a fourth ammunition, and some of the larger guns have another subdivision. The whole is put together instantly. Targets had been placed at different distances across the valley, and very good shooting was made with shell.

Thursday, 18*th*.—We went to the third lecture on nursing this afternoon; it was most practical and most amusing, for Mrs. Ilbert taught her class how to lift invalids in and out of bed, and how to change their sheets, and everybody had to try her 'prentice hand upon the only lady present who had on a habit, it being the least cumbrous garment. As that one was a stout young person in rude health, she was a considerable weight, and was dropped and flopped down upon the sofa in a way which would have killed any real patient; and then she submitted to being put in and out of ever so many nightgowns, and to having ever so many clean sheets pushed under her, and it was altogether very funny and very hard work. Everyone was busy; there were ladies learning to roll up sheets on the floor, ladies walking about two and two in apparently the most affectionate attitudes, or carrying one another upright like children in arms. These were various ways of moving patients who were not absolutely helpless. Everybody laughed very much, and everyone expressed an intention of finding some *light* amateur invalid at home to practise upon.

In the evening we had a large dinner, and a very nice dance lasting till twelve o'clock. People danced most vigorously, and did seem to enjoy themselves immensely.

Friday, 19*th*.—I had rehearsals of both the charity entertainments, and then went to visit the Mayo School. I was caught in a most fearful storm, beginning with dust and ending in waterspouts. I never saw such rain. The girls were riding, and, though they turned back at once, they got completely drenched. I do hope these are not *the* rains.

Sunday, 21*st*.—This was D.'s birthday, and so the A.D.C.s asked us to come down into the woods and have tea there. We had a fine morning for going to church, and then it began to pour, but was fine again at four, and we went down, down, down the khud until at last we arrived at one smooth flat little bit of grass surrounded by high wooded hills, and there we found—no tea ! It had gone wrong, but happily it was recovered before too late, and we sat on the ground—a real 'poggle-khana '—and had a very pleasant hour in this lovely spot. The Stewarts and the Durands came, and the A.D.C.s had provided a real birthday cake with good wishes in pink sugar on the top, so what could D. have wished for more ? He enjoyed his picnic very much, and we toiled up the hill again just in time for dinner.

Monday, 22nd, to Thursday, 25th.—The weather pre-occupies me fearfully. These must be the rains, and they come down in a desperate way sometimes, and then cease for a few fine hours ; but shall I hit upon those few fine hours for my fête or not ? It will be too hard if it rains, for here a shower is no joke, and cannot be overlooked or lightly passed through with a small umbrella ; if it is fine, everyone will come, and it will really be very amusing and money-making. I write this on the morning itself, and feel deeply the heavy clouds hovering overhead. Last night we had a re-hearsal of the two entertainments, which I will describe later. In the afternoon we had had another very good lecture, with practical illustrations upon all sorts of poultices and external applications ; and *that* afternoon was fine, not to say lovely, whereas this—but we shall see !

Thursday, 25th.—This afternoon too was not only

fine, it was lovely! The sky cleared its stormy brows, the clouds disappeared, and the sun beamed upon us! Greatly relieved in mind, we 'officials' set to work about three o'clock to arrange our various little establishments. The lawn was covered with Shamianas; there was a big one in the centre for the fish-pond; another at one end for the refreshment tables, while opposite at the further end I presided over a box full of parcels: 'Put in a rupee and take out what you like' was the plan of my box. Then there was a bank (for receiving our winnings and giving change) behind me, and a photographer beside me, and a weighing-machine near. There were raffles also, and a *very* few things to sell. People began to come at four o'clock, and remained till nearly 7.30. The band played outside; the fish-pond was besieged and entirely emptied; my box only held out for a short time; all the amusements were patronised; and the 'theatre' filled four times for the 'entertainments.' The only complaint made was that people could not spend enough money, and that they took home part of what they brought with them, but I was delighted to hear this, for our object was to extract money without pain. All sorts of people came, and all seemed to enjoy themselves, and we made 2,862 rupees (I suppose about 230*l*.), a large sum for Simla.

Friday, 26th.—I was almost pleased this morning to see that this is a bad day. It is delightful to know that my outdoor venture is safely over, and now I am prepared to try and admire the heavy clouds and their shadows on the hills, and the fluffy little bits they leave behind them in the valleys when they choose to lift for a short time.

This evening we gave a 'light music' concert, and not too much of that; and although we had far more guests at it than we could attempt to seat, they did not appear to mind, and the overflow stood about in door-ways and verandahs, and did not grumble. Captain Barrington Foote on these occasions is a host in himself, and he and a friend who are accustomed to sing and act together sang some very pretty and amusing duets. We finished up with the 'Torpedo and the Whale' out of 'Olivette.' This party was given for the Rajah of Rutlam, and in connection with him I must tell you that I have started My 'Female Medical Scheme.'

I have been working at it for some time, but did not intend to tell you about it until my plans were more thoroughly matured. But the Rajah, whose sympathy I enlisted in the matter, has given me a handsome subscription towards it, and Major Barrington Foote promises me the proceeds of a concert for my Fund, so now I shall make my scheme public. My idea is to form a National Association, with a Central Committee and a Central Fund, with branches in all parts of India, managed locally, to promote Female Medical Tuition, Medical Relief, and the establishment of Hospitals for Women all over the country, and to invite subscriptions for these objects.

As, however, I will send you all the papers connected with this work, I shall not tell you much about it in this journal. I do hope it will succeed, and that it will

be a real benefit to the women of this country. The
Fund is to be called 'The Countess of Dufferin's Fund
for supplying Female Medical Aid to the Women of India.'
When you come across people with loose cash, you may
mention it.

Sunday, 28th.—The monsoon indeed ! Fog not only
out of doors, but smoking in at the windows, pouring
rain, and no possibility of going to church until the
evening, when it cleared for a time, and then I never saw
anything more lovely than the lights and shadows on
the hills, the colours in the sky, two broad rainbows (we
are glad to have their assurance that this is not leading
up to a second deluge), and the clouds in the valleys
below. This respite did not last long—the rain came
on again and went hard at it for twenty-four hours.

Wednesday, July 1st.—It is actually fine, and so
people say to themselves, ' Perhaps the great rains have
not begun.' There are, however, a large supply of
clouds about, and nothing can be more beautiful than
the hills are between showers. Such a day as this is a
perfect study of light and shade. Sometimes the top of
a hill is covered with cloud, and then quite a bright
light seems to come from underneath and illumine all its
lower half; then on another hill there may be a streak
of sunshine sliding down its side ; then great waves of
bright green wood, succeeded by purple and blue ones, a
sort of opalescent tint everywhere, and clouds of every
variety, large and small, dark and light, hanging heavily
or floating lightly about.

All this I admired on my way home from Mrs. Ilbert's lecture ; but I ought not to attempt to describe such effects, for that is an impossible task. How tired you will be of the clouds and the rain before my monsoon is over !

Saturday, 4th.—An amusing afternoon, keeping Miss Nora Stewart's birthday. The party was in the afternoon at the Rink, and everyone seemed happy, and Sir Donald, who is always the gayest of the gay, enjoyed himself immensely and joined in everything. We had a small dinner with a little music. Did you ask after the weather ? Thank you, it's pouring nicely, and is quite as well as can be expected.

Sunday, 5th.—' It ' made morning church a difficulty, and evening church an impossibility, so I have not much to tell of this day.

Monday, 6th.—I managed to drive round Jakko, and to look in at a Monday Pop, coming home in time to read my mail before dinner. Afterwards we went to the play, and saw the ' Private Secretary ' really very well done, but the play here ends much too late. We did not get home till nearly one.

Wednesday, 8th.—Our last lecture at Mrs. Ilbert's ; presentation of 210 rupees for the hospital, with a few neat sentences on behalf of the company by Her Excelleney ; and then home to a dinner and a dance, where a lady rather amused me. I noticed her first after

dinner, when she lay back in an arm-chair deeply interested in His Excellency's conversation with other
people, and then during the evening she came and confided to some one near me that she had had such a nice
dinner, and such a nice man to take her in, and that
Simla was a heavenly place, and that she had lived seventeen years in India without coming here. Now she really
felt that all her previous life had been wasted!

The monsoon behaved in an admirable manner during
our party, and the evening was lovely.

Thursday, 9th, to Thursday, 16th.—My daily life
nowadays will really not bear journalising. A little *aperçu*
of it is all you could possibly stand. In fact, it would
read best in the form of a list of occupations, thus:—

Hindustani.—Lessons four times a week. Preparation
   every day.
Correspondence.—Days devoted to lady doctors. Inter-
   mittent attacks of private letter-writing, with five
   hours of it uninterruptedly on Fridays.
Entertainments.—'At home' every Tuesday morning.
   Dinners and dance or music every Wednesday fort-
   night.
Outdoor Dissipations.—A Monday Pop, and on Saturdays
   a 'variety entertainment' when wet, which becomes
   a gymkhana when fine. Occasional charity concerts.
Exercise.—A walk in a deluge, wetting one through in
   three minutes and penetrating the best umbrella.
   Riding mule or pony, and driving in a jinrickshaw,
   jhampan, or carriage.

Evening.—The young ones play ninepins, and D. and I read.

The morning amusements do not apply to him, for he is in his study all the day, and I never attempt to tell you about affairs of state.

I will mention Sunday this week, because we were preached at in two such very good sermons that the whole of Simla is talking about them, and most people plead guilty to the necessity of the attack made upon them. The first was upon the observance of Sunday, and the second upon our lives of dissipation.

It is quite true that the atmosphere of the place is one of pleasure-seeking. As the Archdeacon said, everything nowadays is 'urgent': our business is 'urgent,' our common occupations are 'urgent,' and our pleasures are '*most* urgent.' 'We must just show ourselves here,' and 'we must look in for a moment there,' and we talk as if 'poor society led a most precarious existence, and would come to an untimely end were we to desert it for a moment.'

He speaks so very well and earnestly, without any exaggeration or want of liberality, that his exhortations ought to do good; and I know of at least one person who hurried from a Sunday tea-party to second church, because after the morning sermon 'she really *must* go again.' That was a result of a homœopathic kind; . . . but alas! for my story, I find she did not go again, only *intended* to do so when she left her own house. What she did do was to exchange a lawn-tennis match, to which she had meant to go, for the milder dissipation of a little tea-party elsewhere—a result of a still more microscopic nature than I credited her with at first.

The other things I have done this week are these:—

I went to Major Marshall's to see a collection of butterflies. There are some very lovely ones, and we gained a certain amount of information there. I will only trouble you with one of the lightest facts. Some of the creatures, with the most gorgeous colours outside, shut themselves up so as to form the exact representation of a dead leaf, and so hide from their enemies ; there are quantities of them in the neighbourhood of a brewery here, and they actually have acquired such a taste for beer that they sit helpless on the casks, and can be caught with ease. These dissipated butterflies quite deserve to have a pin run through them, and to be shut up in glass cases, far from all temptation ; we shall be hearing next that they have taken to skittles !

Major Marshall's house is in the woods near here, where the ferns and the vegetation generally are quite lovely now. The rain covers everything with green; the walls disappear under a new growth of verdure ; the trunks and branches of trees are grown over with ferns ; and there are some most curious plants to be seen as well. One is a sort of tall green flower, out of which protrudes what appears to be the tail of a small snake. It is rather startling at first sight. Then another has a thick stem spotted exactly like the body of a serpent. I can imagine getting a ' turn ' from that. I may as well record here that I have not yet seen a live snake in India, nor a scorpion, nor any terrific spiders. I don't shake my shoes, or peep through my sleeves, or carefully examine my gloves before putting them on, and the only animal that I live in expectation of seeing and suffering from is a 'fish insect.' He habitually eats all your papers, all your clothes, has a particular taste for the noses in your best photographs, and soon runs through the thickest book; even he has treated me well so far, but I know the day may come when I shall find that some valuable garment or some precious picture has been devoured by him.

To go on with my doings. I had a committee meeting to arrange some matters respecting the nursing in the hospital here, and we also had a sort of examination at Mrs. Ilbert's upon her lectures, where Nelly's downright manner of explaining her way of looking after a patient, and the dulness of another pupil, were rather amusing. We are quite sorry these gatherings are over.

I must mention a further encouragement I have had for My Scheme by a donation of Rs. 4,000 from the Maharajah of Ulwar, and an 'order' from him for the training of two native students.

If I am industrious over my Hindustani, His Excellency is still more so over his Persian. He does work hard at it; but he has one advantage over me which I must tell you of. He is never allowed to stir without a policeman—a Persian-speaking policeman in a white turban and a calico overcoat, very imposing as to size, but very common-place as to dress. Wherever His Excellency goes that man has to be. He stands by at tennis; he appears at the church door when D. gets there. As sure as he pays a visit, or goes out to dinner, or to tea, or to the theatre, the policeman is bound to be there, and sometimes, when one has forgotten his very existence, one is startled by his sudden apparition ; and as nobody sees him go, or knows how he gets to a place, there is a sort of awe connected with his inevitable appearance there. When D. simply takes a walk, the policeman follows and walks like any other ordinary mortal; and then it is that D. profits by him, and, instead of resting his mind from his very heavy and anxious work while taking his exercise, struggles away to talk Persian and to learn words and pronunciations. I have no policeman, and so I get on more slowly with my conversation. I am not, however, learning ' under a bushel,' for last night I received a letter from the editor of a native paper, who, ' hearing that you are studying the vernacular,' suggests that his own paper, ' which is written in the best taste and the purest Urdu,' would be a good one for me to take in. If I follow his advice and read it, I shall have to add to my list of employments, ' To spelling out a column in a native paper—four hours.'

I send you a telegram which will certainly amuse you. It was addressed to a distinguished officer of the Royal Engineers, from Nari Gorge, by ' all the Babus, Sind and Peshin Railway,' and there is no question whatever as to its authenticity: ' All railway Babus assembled. To stay here is instantaneous death. What can Babu give in exchange for his soul? *In* anticipation of sanction we all leave to-night.' And they went too ! Cholera was raging at the place.

Sunday, 26th.—I have at last found a horse which I really like and am happy on; but it is, unfortunately,

Lord William's favourite polo pony, and I do not yet know if I can have it; meantime, Begum's nose has become slightly disjointed.

I have had some long interviews with 'authorities' about my Scheme—Sir Steuart Bayley and Dr. Simpson (the Surgeon-General), Mr. Mackenzie and Mr. Ilbert; and I am now trying to reduce it to writing, so that at least people may know what it is *not*. It was reported that I was going to abolish all civil surgeons and put women in their places, and that I intended to insist that no English nurses should be employed, but only natives. I am evidently credited with much more authority than I have found myself to possess.

Wednesday, 29th.—We had a dinner and a dance, which I overheard guests describing as ' exceedingly jolly.'

We have taken up whist as an evening amusement, and I am very glad of it, as a ' rubber ' is good for D., gives him a change, and prevents his studying Persian after dinner. One day we had a few people to tea in the tennis court to see some games. It is such a nice place now, and the Arabic and Persian inscriptions ornament it beautifully. Fifteen or twenty men come to play every day, and it is only closed to the public for a couple of hours in the afternoon.

Thursday, 30th.— After two very fine days the rain has begun again, so all we could do in the way of exercise was to go a sort of paddling walk to gather ferns —a new mania. We have set up little rockeries in front of our windows, and there is to be great rivalry as to whose is the best, whether from an artistic or a botanical point of view. It is quite delightful getting one's fingers well dirtied and feeling so countrified as one does when one grubs up roots without any implement and carries them home in a basket, and when, having said ' Na mangta ' (not wanted) to all offers of assistance from jemadars or followers of any sort, one escapes into the woods and does exactly as one likes—for a very short time. The ferns now are most lovely, and there seems to be an endless variety of them.

Saturday, August 1st.—To the great delight of the young men the weather ' permitted ' a gymkhana. True, there are few performers, and while one race was run by Captains Burn, Harbord, and Russell, the next was run by Captains Russell, Burn, and Harbord ; still everyone seems to like the afternoon and to enjoy the excuse afforded them for meeting, and this time there were no falls and some rather amusing ' events,' and everything went off well.

Tuesday, 4th.—My ' medical affairs ' are coming to a crisis, and I have had many interviews on the subject ; on Saturday I hope to settle the ' prospectus.' I shall be glad when all is in working order and when I have got over the plunge. I don't in the least mind the work, but I sometimes shudder over the publicity and wish it were a quieter little affair. The Maharajah of Kashmir sent me 500*l.* the other day, and *I* am ' opening an account,' starting cheque, receipt, and letter-books, and trying to be business-like from the beginning.

The weather is as usual rather wet, and it has changed its raining hours for the worse, coming down often in the afternoon, which it used generally to leave clear for us. Some days have been very lovely as studies—curious lights and shades on the hills, and peeps underneath heavy canopies of cloud on to the distant and sunny-looking plains.

A very pleasing and perfect English-speaking native lady who lives close to us has offered to come and help us with our Hindustani. She is called the Kunwari (or Princess) Harnam Singh. I have only just made her acquaintance, as she has been ill. Both she and her husband are Christians. She is remarkably nice and clever, so we ought to improve under her. I am reading quite a series of tracts and little moral stories, as the style of these is simple and more conversational than that of grander books.

Thursday, 6th.—This morning we went to the consecration of a very pretty little chapel of ease that has been built close to our grounds. It will be very convenient to us, as the church is rather far off.

Friday, 7th.—We went a second time to the ' Pirates of Penzance.' The performance was really very good, and there was a verse in a topical song which brought down the house. It said that when the Amir was made a G.C.S.I. and Sir P. Lumsden a G.C.B., and when there were difficulties here, and Komaroff was kicking up a row there, then ' *some one's* life was not a happy one.' We were all wondering how it would finish

up, as we knew they would not like to have said the
' Viceroy's.'

Saturday, 8th.—I had a great meeting about the
Scheme—a round table, and pens, and ink-bottles, and
paper, and Sir Steuart Bayley, Sir Charles Aitchison,
Mr. Mackenzie, Dr. Simpson, myself, and Major Cooper,
all sitting round with our various copies of the prospectus before us.   Mine was a very much corrected
one, as I had been collecting hints upon the subject,
so I read it out and suggested the alterations, and we
discussed until we agreed; and you shall soon see the
result!

I only had a short walk by way of exercise.

Sunday, 9th.—A more despairing look-out than ever;
absolutely nothing to be seen beyond the balcony, and a
drenching rain falling.   I don't think we should have
faced ordinary church, but we had promised to attend
the consecration of a native Christian church, so we set
off, and half-way had to desert the carriage for rickshaws, and in them we made the most terrible ascents
and descents through a bazaar.   Such turns and twists
and steep gradients you never saw.   Happily, after the
service it was fine, and we were able to climb up on our
own feet.   The service was in Hindustani.   My command of the language has scarcely arrived at the devotional stage, but I listened with extraordinary attention
to every word that fell from the clergymen's lips, to see
how much I could understand.   The Bishop was most
fluent, and I am in hopes that I carried away some

faint notion of his meaning. His Excellency had to content himself by picking out the Persian words in the discourse. In the afternoon we went to our new little chapel, and we had tea with Mrs. Cunningham, who lives close to it.

Monday, 10th, to Wednesday, 12th.—Monday and Tuesday were so wet that it was impossible to get out, and so on Wednesday morning we determined to seize a dry moment and have a ride. We had scarcely started when a deluge came on, but we got some exercise in spite of it, and came in very much draggled, or, to put it more poetically, like flowers bathed in dew.

I will not trouble you with any more Scheme, though it has kept me very busy this week. I am in hopes a lull will come now, as the prospectus will be out in a few days, and all the correcting of it and thinking it over is at an end. Major Cooper is my honorary secretary, and has had a very great deal to do. The Queen has consented to patronise the Scheme, which is a great help.

Thursday, 27th.—I do not think that I have ever told you how we manage here with regard to our household. D. and I, the two maids and the two girls, occupy the only beds there are in the house; but a few native servants sleep in the passages, ready to run any nocturnal messages we may have to send, while Goorkhas and policemen watch over us outside. Then all about the place there are cottages for the A.D.C.s and for the servants, barracks for the body-guard and the Goorkhas and for the mass of native servants. The

A.D.C.s have a sitting-room in the house, and have all their meals here. They live two and two in various cottages, and the Military Secretary has a really nice house on the top of a still higher hill than ours.

Every person keeps a lot of horses, and all the stables are under the direction of our coachman; but as each horse has a syce of his own, each A.D.C. has as many men as he has horses.

This morning mist and rain, and an incessant pattering on the roof. It is trying!

Friday, 28th.—We attended a performance at the theatre got up by the Babus, or clerks in the various offices, to obtain money to build a covered place for themselves at the Burning Ghaut. We had rather dreaded it, because we heard that on the first night it lasted from nine till two, because it was to be in Bengali, of which we know not a word, and because all the female parts were to be played by men; so we took the precaution of telling them that we should have to leave at eleven, but we did remain till half-past, and were quite sorry not to stay till the end. It really was most curious and interesting; and as the piece consisted of a series of scenes, and as we had a short abstract of the story in English which enabled us to understand the drift of each scene, the unknown tongue was rather an advantage than otherwise, for it added a sort of mystery to the performance, and made us feel as if we really were looking on at some ancient play.

When the curtain drew up, it revealed Ravana, the King of Ceylon, in grand array, sitting upon a very high throne, with all his courtiers squatting on the floor on either side of him, and one messenger all in white, and with his face buried in his hands, bowing before the king. A melancholy nasal song was going on which lasted for some time, and then the messenger with much wailing told the king that his son had been killed in battle. The king was deeply moved at this intelligence, but also a little annoyed to think that a son of his should have fallen by the hands of the son of the King of Oude. While he is expressing these sentiments, exit messenger a little suddenly, and enter Chittrangauda, the king's youngest wife. Her entry is peculiar; she is a good-sized man wrapped in women's garments, and she comes in falling, and flops down on her face full-length before the king. He consoles her, she goes out, the king prepares for war, and the curtain falls.

Act II. takes place in a pleasure-garden, and is devoid of incident. One man asks news of another, and is told of his brother's death, so he exits to prepare himself for the battlefield; then women come in and wander about, and either are consoled or refuse to be comforted. They are all tall and plain, and show their faces very little, and are the wives of personages in the drama.

Act *III*. The curtain draws up and reveals two goddesses, Doorga and Bejoya—melancholy women seated on the floor. Doorga wears a silver crown. Indra, the king of the celestial regions, and his wife come to consult these ladies and to tell them about the war, and Doorga says she will see what Siva says. Unfortunately that god is sleeping, so she employs a most alarmingly ugly Cupid to help her to awake him; and we then see

Siva's head and bare shoulders and his trident appearing above a rock in the background, and the overgrown Cupid (in a red uniform) takes deliberate aim with his bow and hits the god with his flower-tipped arrow. The Destroyer of Creation awakes, and a short conversation ensues.

The curtain is constantly going down, and a Volunteer band plays during the long intervals, the scenery changes every time, and all the acting is very quiet and methodical.

After this comes a scene in a tent, where Fakirs are sitting with whitened faces and long hair, and warriors and their wives come to consult them, and there is much bowing with foreheads to the ground ; and the women have now put on male attire for battle, and wear knickerbockers and short jackets and exhibit most pronounced figures, the work of the tailor, and then some one is advised to enter the temple, and prayers are made in front of the door, and finally the god Siva himself appears before it— rather a startling figure. A very fat man he is, with nothing on but a short petticoat, and a trident in his hand ; much local colour about him. Then there is some one whose mind has to be diverted, and so ' soorbalas ' try to charm him with songs and dancing. They are tall figures swathed in female garments; they move slowly about and get in his way when he attempts to leave them, but finally they give it up and run away and the man left alone enters the temple, and there we had to leave him.

I read the rest of the play, and I don't think we missed much. There was a battle, off the stage of course, and the news of it had to be brought to the king and to the women ; and the chief warrior fell, and the king, astounded, asked who killed him, and the messenger said that, having entered in disguise into the sacred shrine, Nicoomvilla killed him in an unjust battle —and the curtain falls for the last time.

I am sorry to say there was a very bad audience. The night was terribly wet, which was I suppose the reason, but the play, which was very well dressed (in spite of Siva) and well put upon the stage, was acted to empty benches.

D. and *I*, who both really like sight-seeing, enjoyed it much; it was all so strange and so ' behind the times.'

When *I* first came here, *I* said that Simla was suggestive of the Ark. The likeness increases, and I have the greatest sympathy now for Mr. and Mrs. Noah and their aides-de-camp, shut up in that erection for 150 days and over. How they must have hated the patter on the roof and the sh—sh down the sides of their habitation, and how tired they must have been of talking about their animals, and of wondering when they would all get out again ! What a thrilling incident the sending out of the dove must have been, and with what joy they must have wept over the bit of green leaf when it was brought them ! We invented an incident yesterday, and asked some people to tea in the tennis court ; and though cats and dogs were really coming down, all the guests arrived, and all seemed truly thankful for this excuse to get out, and for something to do. The doctor beat the Rajah, but he received rather heavy points from him.

Sunday, 30th.—Things (by which I mean the weather) improved a little, and in the afternoon we went to the church near us, and then on for a walk up to Observatory Hill, the site for the new house. As we climbed the hill the view was quite lovely, and we could distinctly see the plains, and very wet they looked; but by the time we reached our destination everything was enveloped in cloud. However, we sat down on a pile of wood and waited, and then, reflecting how much shut up we had been lately, we determined to be energetic and 'water-proof' this week, and to make expeditions and see something of the outer world; and, while these plans were forming, the fog did clear away and left rows of hills lying in layers of cotton-wool, with a little tiny attempt at a rainbow in one small cloud above, and the glistening plains in the distance below.

Monday, 31st.—Put a bit of our plan into execution. Determined to go and have tea at Mushobra, and there to spend a 'happy day.' Of course it was thought at first that it would require twenty men to convey our tea there, but I insisted upon 'roughing' it, and so two only were laden and set off; and directly after lunch the girls, Major Cooper, Doctor Findlay, and I started. (His Excellency declared wild horses should not take *him* there, and, besides, he is much too busy for long expeditions.) We drove up to a horrid tunnel which there is on the way, and then mounted our horses and had a nice but foggy ride out to the 'Gables,' an inn in the woods. There we found an excellent tea, with very many more things than we really wanted, so that *I* think one man might do next time, only that I suppose he will want company on the road. Then we took a walk, and afterwards rode home all the way. We enjoyed our little change.

Wednesday, Sept. 2nd.—People do say positively now, ' The rains are going,' so I do hope we shall come down from perpetual deluge and fogs to occasional storms. The shortest gleams of sunshine are most thankfully received, and we are beginning to talk of our tour ; the very idea of it is delightful. Think of emerging from the clouds and descending to Agra and Delhi and Lucknow and Cawnpore !

Thursday, 3rd, to Tuesday, 8th.—It is true the monsoon is really over. It no longer rains hopelessly, and when a heavy shower falls we say, ' It will soon clear,' with some assurance in our tone. Oh! it is a comfort ; you can't think how tired one gets of the gloom and the everlasting drip, and the impossibility of settling beforehand to do anything out of doors. This morning, therefore, when we found ourselves fog-bound and saw the ground soaking, we did not despair, nor did we put off our engagements for the afternoon, but allowed Colonel Collett to come and lunch, and ordered our horses at three to start on our fern expedition. The first thing I got the Professor to do was to come up to my rockery and to mark in a book for me all the varieties I had already collected, and against these I put private descriptions by which to know them again. Then we started off down the glen, riding some way, after which we took to our feet and to alpenstocks, and so descended the rougher path to the bottom. It is quite a new sensation to walk out with a naturalist, who seems to have several more pairs of eyes than you possess. Colonel Collett knows all the plants and trees and insects, and it was very interesting going about with him. We had a very long, hard walk, and finally reached Annandale, where we had tea to meet us, and very glad we were of it before riding up to Simla again. I got two or three new varieties of ferns, and am now tolerably perfect in about twenty long Latin names and varieties, which I look upon as a sort of little beginning for next year.

Friday, 18*th.*—Sir Alfred Lyall and Sir Lepel Griffin are staying with us ; that is to say, they sleep in one of our cottages and come here for their meals, for, as I have told you before, we have no spare room in our Viceregal cottage.

Saturday, 19*th.*—Ten thousand rupees to-night from the Maharajah of Jeypore, with a very nice letter upon the medical subject. As this is the largest subscription I have had yet, I chronicle it.

Thursday, 24*th.*—It had long been arranged that we were to camp out for a couple of nights for His Excellency to get some shooting, and we were to have started yesterday ; but it was so wet in the beginning of the week that we put it off one day so as to give the camp time to dry. I had forgotten, during this time of freedom from the trammels of state at Simla, that the moment we again stirred from our own door we should be put in charge of a deputy-commissioner and a police officer; but directly arrangements for a move came under discussion, then printed papers appeared on our tables, stating what officials were to go with us, what time we should start, what time we should arrive, what posts we should receive from Simla, &c., and it is only eight miles after all that we are going.

The day was lovely, and we left home after luncheon, riding; our commissioner met us on the road, and Sir Donald Stewart followed. The ride was through the hills, and very pretty and warm, with a nice bright sun shining on us. Our destination is called Dhamin, and we are to be the guests of the Rana of that place, whose privilege it is to spend a certain sum yearly in entertaining the Viceroy at a shoot! Honour and glory above his fellows is all he gets by it. He is a man of about 700*l.* or 800*l.* a year, and, as I saw when he met us on the road, a very nice-looking man, speaking a little English. We reached our camp at five. It is pitched on a hill, and is, of course, most comfortable : two tents, opening into each other, as dining and sitting-rooms, and a little street of small tents, prettily lined with blue and white. We each have one.

As soon as we arrived, the ' dolly,' or presentation from the Rajah, was brought forward. We stood at the door of the tent while trays of gold and silver, of rice, bananas, pomegranates, dishes of honey, bundles of sugar-cane, and ginger were laid before His Excellency, and a ram was dragged by its horns to be presented to him. He graciously accepted all except the money, which is always remitted, and then the Rana said there was another

dolly for the Lady Sahiba, and more trays and more
sheep were brought before me. We dined, and sat round
a bonfire, and looked at the moon, and then went to
bed. The only sounds to be heard an hour after were
the voices of the natives calling to each other from hill
to hill, a wild and rather melancholy sound.

Friday, 25*th*.—We have been out the whole day,
and have enjoyed the fresh air and the sunshine, and
the little change from the Simla platform on which we
have been stuck for six months. Breakfast was at
eight o'clock, and directly after it we started—I on my
mule, who is admirably suited for the sort of riding
here. She can go up and down staircases, and along
the dry rough beds of rivers, and through streams and
up narrow mountain paths, without ever slipping or
seeming to think the road at all extraordinary. The
girls were carried in jhampans, and only rode back.
Our way was through the hills, the weather perfectly
lovely, and the vegetation quite different from that of
Simla. Bananas, and rice, and ginger grow here, and
we saw one palm-tree, and the hills are covered with a
handsome sort of cactus, and there are new ferns, and,
in fact, the 2,000 feet we have descended make a great
difference in all one sees and feels. The shooting was
nothing to speak of—there were only twelve brace
killed, and ' much ado ' about killing them—but all the
guns were content, as rest from business and change
was what they really wanted, and these they got. What
appened was this : We all descended from our horses
in a valley, or rather in the bed of a river, surrounded

by hills, on whose tops we saw white figures, who, when
the guns were placed, began to shout and to descend on
all sides to drive the birds in. I suppose there were a
thousand beaters employed, and, as I told you, there
were about twenty-four birds killed. We went to three
different beats, and had lunch in the middle of the day.
One bird was a sort of partridge, and another a kind
of pheasant with most lovely plumage. A big umbrella
was held over D. while he shot, and he was surrounded by sympathising retainers, who were always
anxious that he should aim at anything that might be
sitting in the neighbourhood, or at any speck visible
upon the horizon, and who were perfectly indifferent to
the dangers there might be to any coolies in the line of
fire. The Rajah always kept at a distance under another
umbrella, and did not shoot.

We came across a very curious custom practised by
the hill people here. By the side of every stream we
saw a quantity of very small, very low, thatched sheds,
and, hearing these had something to do with babies, and
seeing many women approaching these places with
infants in their arms, we went to examine them, and
found that the stream is directed into a quantity of
little wooden troughs, and at the mouth of each trough
one of these little sheds is placed. The babies are made
to lie down with the crown of their heads just under
this miniature waterfall—what for, I can't make out.
They say it is to put them to sleep, but it seems an uncomfortable, laborious, and roundabout way of arriving
at repose! I crept into one or two to watch the process.
Sometimes the mother lay flat alongside, nursing the

child while the douche poured upon it. One woman told me she should stay there all day; others spoke of half-an-hour or an hour or two. Even in winter this treatment continues, and it must be painfully cold both for mothers and babies. I wonder whether during the next century my doctors will reach this barbaric custom and suppress it!

Amongst the followers were two men with falcons. I saw one kill a bird; but I think it is a most cruel sport to watch, and I prefer seeing the hawks at Barrackpore catch pieces of meat.

Saturday, 26th.—We again breakfasted early, and shot over three beats; there were no birds, but plenty of fresh air and sunshine. This place is ever so much warmer than Simla. We rode home in the afternoon, and passed on our way one Rajah, who has arrived here for the durbar the Viceroy holds on Thursday. The chief sat on a litter under a red dome, and was preceded by a number of men in scarlet, holding silver sticks. We shall see all the durbar very well from our balcony, as it will be held in a Shamiana on the lawn.

Sunday, 27th.—Mr. and Mrs. Grant Duff and their party arrived this evening from Madras, and, after some tea, were conveyed in rickshaws to the tops of the various hills where we lodge them. They descend for their meals, and scatter again at night.

Thursday, October 1st.—There was a durbar for the hill chiefs to-day, and it certainly was a very pretty sight. The Shamiana was placed on the lawn exactly opposite my windows, so that from the verandahs the whole ceremony could be seen perfectly. The tent was lined with pale blue and white ; there was a scarlet carpet on the floor ; the Viceroy's throne was at the far end of the tent, and the chiefs and their followers were ranged all down one side of it, while European officials sat on the other side. There had not been a durbar at Simla for nine years, so I believe the roads were crowded with spectators, and I shared my balcony view with a good many people. The chiefs began to arrive at eleven o'clock, and were conducted to their seats, and at twelve the Viceroy's procession marched straight from the house to the throne, the salute firing, and three military bands playing ' God save the Queen ' in unison. D., in red with all his collars on, was smart enough to satisfy even the Oriental idea. The whole thing looked like a picture : the open tent with the Viceroy on his throne, sitting in isolated splendour at one end, a line of the tall body-guard at his back and two attendants with yak-tails in their hands at either side of him ; then lines of natives in costume and officials in uniform filling the tent and sitting all in solemn silence. The first symptom of life in the tableau was when, having asked the Viceroy's per-mission to do so, the Foreign Secretary had each chief brought up in turn to be presented, and after him, one by one, the number of followers that his particular rank entitled him to bring with him, and each man offered gold nuzzars which the Viceroy touched. After this, a speech was made in English, and repeated in Hindustani, and then attar and pan were handed round, and the officials, bowing to the Viceroy, told him the ceremony was ended ; his procession was re-formed, and the chiefs gradually dispersed. These were all small men, and there were no splendid jewels, but for a country durbar it was a pretty one, and the sun shone upon the glittering dresses and showed off everything at its very best. D. has invited all these chiefs to meet him at Annandale for a gymkhana on Saturday; only two of them had the right to visit him, and he felt anxious to give the others an opportunity of speaking to him.

I have been able to send our guests to some dinners, garden parties, and to a fancy ball in Simla, so the week has passed away very satisfactorily, and they leave us on Monday morning. Mr. Grant Duff comes down from Inverarm to breakfast with us, and his conversation comes as a delightful break in the everyday small talk about dogs and horses, gymkhanas, and Simla gaieties.

Thursday, 8th.—I think I told you long ago that, before coming to Simla, I took a little country house here in which to spend Saturday and Sunday. But I soon came to the conclusion that it was quite useless to us, that we felt sufficiently countrified here, and that we certainly were warmer and more comfortable at home than we could possibly be in a miserable little wooden cottage on a distant peak—so I shall never again hire a house. But a ' standing camp ' is another luxury that is possible ; and as after the rains a little change is pleasant, I thought that I should like to see Naldera, the place where other Viceroys have had one, before I went down to the plains. This involved sleeping out one night, and I could not induce D. to come; but Nelly and Rachel and Major Cooper and I went on this expedition. It was made easy for us by Mrs. Ilbert, who gave us beds in her 'Retreat.' She and her husband and little children were alone there, with a most lovely view around them, and delightful woods for walking in. We rode out in the afternoon, getting there for tea, and we had a nice walk before it got dark.

Friday, 9th.—My instructor in photography insisted upon my taking the camera out with me, so I was obliged to get up early in the morning to take a few views. I felt extremely nervous over it, as I had never been left to my own devices before, and I did not wish to fail entirely. I may tell you now that my efforts were very successful.

After breakfast we started off on our horses and rode for about two hours, first through a sweet-smelling pine wood, with glimpses of lovely mountain scenery on either side, and then along a very curious open bit of country, where limestone rocks jut up through the soil like almonds in a pudding, and where there are stretches of grass like English downs. Naldera is in the midst of these downs—a hill covered with knots of trees, at the foot of which stand out some fine single firs and a very pretty picturesque little temple. While lunch was preparing we sat down to admire this place, so very unlike anything else to be seen at Simla, and I photographed the temple, of which I will send you a copy, as I am rather proud of my first unaided efforts in this line. We spent a very peaceful two hours there, and then

mounted the hill for luncheon, and after that meal sat
and looked at a fine view of the Sutlej winding like
a green ribbon through the plain below. The valley is
very unhealthy to live in, but very beautiful to look at.
We could not dawdle much, as we had a long ride before
us, and it soon gets dark and cold now, though the sunshine and the weather in the daytime are perfect at this
season.

Tea was provided for us at a half-way house, and
there we left our horses and returned home, first in
rickshaws, and the last bit of the way in carriages.

I think I must copy you out a paragraph in Lord
Randolph's letter to H.E.:—

' I am greatly interested in following the progress of
Lady Dufferin's Fund for providing Medical Aid to the
Women of India. *It* appears to be having a most remarkable and encouraging success, and will, I am sure,
be one of the conspicuous social reforms of the many
which will mark your reign.'

Tuesday, 13*th.*—I had a meeting of the Ripon
Hospital Committee this morning, and before retiring
from it myself made some suggestions for altering
its constitution. Now that I have my own Fund to
attend to, it is better for me not to be officially connected
with anything else except as patroness.

In the afternoon I went over the hospital itself.
The women's ward was full, but there are no nurses as
yet, and all the invalids are waited upon by their own
families.

In the evening His Excellency had a big farewell

dinner for the Commander-in-Chief, whose health he proposed. We are all so very sorry to lose Sir Donald.

Wednesday, 14*th.*—We went rather a long ride to the top of Tara Devi, a hill in the neighbourhood; from it there was a most splendid view of the snows, which are now looking quite beautiful. The weather this month is perfection, but we never can forget the rains.

I shall not write to you again from Simla. We leave it on Tuesday morning, and are now ' in our boxes.' Our rooms are dismantled, and to-day I say good-bye to people here. On the whole, I like the place very much; there is a monotony about it which makes the time pass quickly, and in fine weather it is very beautiful. The month of August, however, is most unpleasant, and I hope that it is not the time that I shall best remember when I prepare to return here.

Every year there are great changes in society, and next year we shall greatly miss both the Stewarts and the Archdeacon and his wife.

The new house is begun; it is on a beautiful site, and in two years time we hope to be more suitably lodged than we are at present.

CHAPTER V

AUTUMN TOUR, 1885: NAHUN, DELHI, RAJPUTANA, CENTRAL

INDIA, AGRA, AND LUCKNOW

OCTOBER 20 TO DECEMBER 16, 1885

Tuesday, October 20th.—We breakfasted at eight o'clock. At a quarter past the Viceroy signed the declaration of war with Burmah, and at half past we were saying good-bye to the Somités who had come to see us off; the band was playing, the Goorkha Guard was saluting, and *I* was trying to smile amiably, while I was really wondering how the horses would stand the thirty-one guns. They stood them admirably, and we were soon on our way down the tonga road.

Our drive lasted till 1.30, when we reached Dagshai, and were entertained at a very nice luncheon by the officers of the Highland Light *I*nfantry. I need scarcely tell you that our party is large, for we are always in charge of commissioners, district officers, and police officers, while the Foreign Secretary goes with us everywhere.

At Dagshai we leave behind us posts and telegrams, and start on our march; so we mount our horses after lunch and ride nine miles to our camp. The Rajah of

Nahun, whose guests we are, met us half-way and conducted us here. The roads have all been put in beautiful
order, so that the most nervous of us need not fear, and
the ride was extremely pleasant. We reached the camp
in time for five o'clock tea, which we found ready for us;
indeed, the whole camp is fitted with every luxury; bottles
of lavender-water, ink, paper, pins, scissors, every little
thing we can possibly want has been thought of, and in
D.'s tent and our dining-room are beautiful fireplaces
and fires in them! My tent is most spacious, and I am
writing now before dinner, while the natives outside are
chattering with all their might. I am expecting every
moment to hear a stentorian voice calling them to order.

The maids rode up, and are delighted so far. His
Excellency has been a little cold, but is warming, and
we all feel very well, though we are ordered to begin
each day with a dose of quinine, which I have undertaken
to make all my family swallow regularly.

The Rajah speaks English, and seems very nice. His
servants are all in bran-new red and gold liveries, and
he has some very fine police and soldiers guarding us.

We certainly are not very lucky in our weather. It
came on to blow in the evening, and all night our tents
were flapping about; energetic cold blasts made their
way through every crevice, and we had to roll up our
heads in flannel, while our pillows were knocked about
by the shaking canvas walls against which they leant.

Wednesday, 21st.—I was quite glad to find that all
were well this morning in spite of the cold. As soon as
I had got into a warm dress, jacket, and a fur cape, and

had climbed two or three high hills in the neighbourhood, I got warm and was ready for breakfast.

We all spent a very quiet morning, but got into our habits before lunch and rode off directly after. The march was thirteen miles, along a very good road, and we got to our new camp in time for tea. After dinner a fine leopard was brought in which had been shot in the neighbourhood.

Thursday, 22nd.—The morning, as before, spent in reading and writing, and then a long ride of about fifteen miles through lovely hills and fine woods to a new camp. This one is very picturesque, the tents being all on different levels, and the highest platform, on which our dining-room is pitched, being shaded by two enormous trees, and having a curious little temple upon it. The plains look quite near now, and have a very sandy and dusty appearance. The weather is beautiful, and we are gradually descending into warmth.

Friday, 23rd.—D. went out shooting before break-fast, and I took some photographs of our camp. Letters and telegrams unexpectedly follow us everywhere, and with Burmah on hand D. always has some business to do.

We again set off after lunch, but as I found the marches rather long, I began my journey in a jhampan, and only got on my horse six miles from Nahun.

The last four D. rode with our host the Rajah, and his sons and sirdars met us near the town. Nahun looked very white in the distance, and more like a camp than a town, on the top of a small hill covered with wood. When we reached the place we found a guard of honour of elephants with their howdahs on, and there were some baby ones standing under their mothers; people threw flowers at us, and soldiers lined the way up to the Rajah's palace, where we stay. It is a really good house, with a central room used as a durbar hall, and comfortable apartments all round. The views of hills and plains from the house are lovely. As we rode along yesterday the plains looked exactly like a sea when the tide is out, the coast line distinctly marked, green and rocky, and gradually rising higher and higher; the 'sea' part completely flat and sandy, with streaks of water showing here and there.

The Rajah speaks English well, and looks after all his affairs himself. He has his own foundry, makes all his bridges and roads himself, uses no forced labour, has only one wife, and is altogether enlightened. He will not, however, ask me to see that one wife, which is disappointing. I had his secretary sounded on the subject. but he said that some lady had asked before, and had been told that 'it was not the custom of the Rajpoots.'

The English mail came in.

Saturday, 24th.—I read in the orders for the day, ' At seven A.M. the Rajah will send four of his sirdars to enquire after the health of His Excellency. An aide-de-camp will receive them.' Of course they came and received a good report.

At eleven the Rajah himself came and 'was received in durbar;' offered his seventy-two mohurs, and went

through all the usual ceremonies. The Viceroy returned
his visit in the afternoon, and we met him later at the
palace door, where the Rajah had arranged all sorts of
sports for us to see. The 'barrack square,' where
they were held, is, for the hills, quite a large piece of
level ground; on all sides it was bounded by crowds
of human beings, while the Nahun army, cavalry and
infantry, occupied the centre. Military manœuvres
filled the first part of the programme, and we saw
some exercises which are now quite out of date elsewhere. Elephant fighting was the next sight. There
seemed to be nothing very vicious about it, and the
combatants received no greater hurt than a twinge of
tusk-ache. They walked up to each other, a man on
the neck of each, and, locking their tusks together, they
pushed and pushed till the losing one seemed about to
fall over. When they were hurt a little they cried out
and did not seem to like it at all. The tent-pegging and
lemon-cutting on horseback, which we saw next, were
not very good, and then came a troop of athletes, wearing a mere vestige of clothing, who tied themselves in
knots and twisted themselves about in all sorts of curious
ways. One rather novel way of performing the 'wheel'
we saw. Two men clasped each other so as to have
their heads in opposite directions, and when they went
'head over heels' they lighted first on one man's legs
and then on the other's. A curious band of wild-look-
ing hillmen came next, some playing musical instruments, the others, with bows and arrows and hatchets in
their hands, dancing about, and shooting at each other's
legs.

Amongst the musical instruments were some beautiful brass trumpets, quite five feet long. We are trying to get some of them for Clandeboye.

When these performances were over, we saw the Rajah's big elephant, which is said to be the largest in India. We had tea in the palace and waited there till it got a little dark, and until all the illuminations in the town were ready. As we looked out from the windows the view was lovely. An amphitheatre of hills on one side, the mysterious-looking plains in the hazy golden light of the sunset on the other, the white flat-roofed town below, with lines of light gradually appearing everywhere to mark its outline, all the inhabitants busily at work with their decorations, and then, passing through the narrow streets, an elephant with a silver howdah, in which sat—our maids!

We soon descended ourselves, and in procession rode through the bazaars, every house being lighted up with innumerable little oil lamps, till we came to a great tank, where we dismounted and sat on chairs to see fireworks.

They were all made at Nahun, and some of them were very good and curious. All sorts of spit-fire devices, wheels and rings, and lions and tigers, and fortifications which suddenly grew before our eyes in lines of light and sent off a regular cannonade from their walls. Their reflections in the water doubled their beauty. But the full moon rose, and our sight-seeing came to an end. We went home, entertained the five European inhabitants of the place at dinner, and then on a platform in the open air we saw a nautch. Plain women, with harsh voices, sang loudly, while they

gently moved backwards and forwards on the space
allotted to them; they chewed pan at intervals and
made faces, and no one could tell what they were singing about; and so when we had had enough we said so,
and the entertainment ended.

Sunday, 25th.—We had a quiet morning, but had to
start off again in the afternoon. This time we drove
most of the way, and so arrived at our new camp at
Majra with very little fatigue. The road lay through
the real jungle, with long grass and bushes between us
and the hills, where you might imagine any number of
tigers to be crouching. The camp is such a pretty one.
D. and I are in a cottage, and down a stretch of grass on
either side is a long street of tents. A very big tree
grows in the middle of this street, and looks very shady
and picturesque. Lord William arrived here for dinner,
which was an unexpected pleasure; he is so cheery, and
looks ten years younger than when he went to England.

Monday, 26th.—We have had a long day out in the
jungle, but I can only tell you about our preparations
for tiger shooting, for alas! we saw no tiger after all,
and so I have no great event to chronicle. Directly
after breakfast we dispersed ourselves over the backs of
thirteen elephants, and set off in a long procession
through the tall grass of the jungle, up and down
banks and through woods, not without occasional small
alarms, on my part, lest we should slip off behind or
before when the monster animal performed gymnastic
feats, or lest we should be swept off his back by some

great branch of a tree. We arrived safely at our destination and, descending from our elephants, proceeded
to place ourselves at our posts. When D.'s and mine
were pointed out to us, we looked up in the air and
saw two bedsteads tied very high up in a tree, on which
we were to sit in safety. With great difficulty I climbed
into mine, and then His Excellency got into his, and two
jemadars and two policemen perched on various branches
of the same tree, and the girls had a bed in another
tree, and some of the prudent people climbed more trees,
while others remained on the ground. Then a solemn
silence fell on all the human beings in the jungle, the
only noises to be heard being the occasional passage of a
vulture, or the jumping of a monkey in our neighbourhood. So we sat for nearly two hours, until at last in
the· distance came the faint sound of the beaters approaching, which sounds grew and grew until their shouts
and bugles and drums were quite close to us, and I
looked anxiously all round our tree to see if anything was
approaching. No—not one deer or bird, and much less a
tiger !

It was all over, and we descended from our tree ; and
finding that it was three o'clock, we naturally became
extremely hungry and thought only of lunch. This we
had on the ground in true picnic fashion, and then we
mounted our elephants again, still hoping to make something of a bag as we marched through the grass. A
few peacocks rose, but far from us, and no one got anything. It was all so new to us that we enjoyed it
much, and we are the only members of our party who
are not grumbling at the mismanagement of the beat,

or the folly of the tiger in keeping away from us. It was quite dark when we got home, having been out about eight hours.

Tuesday, 27th.—The Rajah said good-bye to us at ten o'clock, and we got into our tongas and left his dominions. He is a very nice man, and has entertained us right royally. We had a drive of thirty miles to do, and the road was somewhat rough and dusty; but the country, as we left the hills and came to grassy plains, big trees, and running rivers, delighted us—it looked so rich, and was such a complete change from Simla.

It really is much nicer to look up at moderate-sized hills, and to be able to move about on a level world, than to be perched on a high peak and to look *down* upon range after range of gigantic mountains. A river too is a refreshing sight, and the Jumna is a very rapid one. We crossed it on a pontoon bridge, which had been built expressly for the Viceroy. We lunched half-way, and then drove on to Dehra Dun, the country getting prettier at every step. It is a sort of tableland between the two last ranges of the Himalayas, and its climate is quite pleasant to live in all the year round. In sight of it is Mussoorie, another hill station, which appears to be at a much more reasonable distance from the world in general than Simla is.

Our horses and the body-guard spend the summer at Dehra Dun, so, in spite of the long drive we had just had, we started off directly we arrived to see the tables and the barracks. We are staying in the very pretty bungalow of the officer in charge of the body-guard, Captain Onslow.

Wednesday, 28th.—We left Dehra at nine in the morning, having a drive of forty-five miles before us. A little way from the village we stopped to see a tea-garden. It belongs to Sir H. Macpherson, and is on a small scale, the making all being done by hand, and not by machinery as it is in larger establishments. First we saw the crop growing—low, thick, compact, glossy-leaved bushes; then we saw the young shoots which had been picked, dried in the sun, and rubbed, and heated, and made up in their damp state into dirty-looking balls which are allowed to ferment, and then more drying and sifting is gone through, and the tea is ready for use. Green tea is not fermented at all, which is the only difference between it and black. The most delicate tea is made from the budding leaf, the second best from the leaf just unfolded, and so on till it is too coarse to be used.

We got through our long drive very well, and reached Saharanpore soon after tea. A change of dress was refreshing, and then lunch; afterwards D. went over the remount stables, and I went on to the Botanical Gardens, where he joined me. We had tea there, and examined various trees and creepers, &c. I mention the creepers particularly, for they are such overpowering plants. They wrap themselves round a big tree and smother and conceal it altogether, so that one has to look high up in the air to try and find what the original plant was.

I am writing this on my return from this expedition; and as I must begin a new letter at Delhi, I will tell you what we are going to do till we get there. We are spending this afternoon in the Commissioner's (Mr. Harrington's) house. We asked him not to have anyone to meet us, so we dine and lunch with him and his wife, and go off to our own train in the evening. We are to remain quiet till four in the morning, when the train will begin to move, and we shall find ourselves at Delhi pretty early, there to begin a new series of experiences.

I ought to say that the Harringtons have a very nice house in a charming district, broad level roads, fine trees, running water, all that we most admire, fresh from the hills as we are.

Thursday, 29th.—Even to think of writing about Delhi alarms me, and I fear I shall find it very difficult to give you much idea of the sights ; I must be content with attempting to record my own impressions, and I will not be historical, nor enter into too many particulars in guide-book fashion. We got here early in the morning, were met by all the celebrities of the place at the station, and were conveyed in carriages drawn by artillery horses to the Commissioner's house, 'Ludlow Castle.' If you read up the Mutiny, you will see that even our present home is historically interesting.

It is a good, comfortable Indian house, with large and rather dark rooms, and a park round it, where are small brickwork models of the places where batteries stood and did important work in that terrible year 1857. The weather is lovely, and we breakfasted under a Shamiana, and then the Viceroy saw native gentlemen, and we were left free till luncheon.

In the afternoon we began our real sight-seeing, going
first of all to the Fort. Its walls and gates are red sandstone ; they are very high, with a sort of ornamental
battlement along the top of the wall, and the gateways
are very massive, and almost like castles, with towers
and domes ; a deep moat runs round the walls ; the
gates themselves are brass, and are covered with large
spikes to prevent elephants from battering them in. The
Private Hall of Audience, with its adjacent baths, is
within the Fort, and is the most lovely thing in the way
of decoration that you can see. It is all white marble :
the heavy roof is supported by flat columns, which are completely covered with carving and gold enamel ; this gold
ornamentation gives a creamy look to the white marble,
which is beautiful. It is quite open on three sides, the
place where the celebrated Peacock Throne stood being
on the fourth. The baths, which are in separate buildings on either side, are in quite a different style and are
equally lovely. The walls, ceilings, and floors, are all
mosaic : a white marble ground, with coloured flowers, and
beautiful geometrical patterns laid in cornelian and other
stones—sadly destroyed in some places by the desecrat-
ing hands of people who like to carry away relics, but in
some rooms still perfect.

The Motee, or Pearl Mosque, is close by, and is a
little gem in pure white marble.

The Public Hall of Audience is a larger building on
the same principle—a back wall, and an arched roof
supported by pillars ; it is all red sandstone, and little
of the ancient decoration is left. There is only the Great
Mogul's Seat of Justice, which he entered from the back,

and which is white marble with a mosaic pattern on it, and on the wall behind it birds and fruits done in brilliant colours, also in mosaic. This lovely place is now used as a canteen, and next to these wonderful works of ancient days is pasted up a picture advertisement! D. went on to visit the Soldiers' Hospital, and afterwards joined me in the officers' mess-rooms, where we had tea. We knew the Colonel in Canada, when he was A.D.C. to his father, Sir O'Grady Haly.

We examined one of the great gates next, and then went on to the Jumma Masjid. It is a magnificent mosque; size and dignity, calm and repose being its characteristics. A broad flight of steps leads up to·it, the length of the lowest one being 149 feet. It is built in a great square, with four towers at the angles, and with open arched colonnades between the towers and the three gateways. Passing through the principal one, you find yourself in a paved court facing the inner mosque, which stands out grandly against the sky; at the prayer hour you hear the call to the people to come up, you see the picturesque crowd troop in, perform their ablutions in the central fountain, and kneel reverently in a long close line before the steps of the mosque, while the monotonous voice of the priest is heard reciting the prayer. Then you watch the various movements the worshippers make, and the attitudes of lowly supplication which they assume. I always do think that a number of Mahometans saying their prayers together is the most devotional sight one can imagine; I don't know any service that can compare with it as an expression of religious fervour.

Wrapping ourselves in cloaks, for it becomes cold directly the sun goes down, we went home and had a very little rest before dinner, after which we set off for the Municipal Hall to receive an address. We are nearly two miles from the town, and the whole distance and the whole place was illuminated in that peculiarly Indian way which is so effective. On either side of the road every wall, and pillar, and staircase, the fine old gates, the modern houses, and the newly put up arches were all outlined with fire, while coloured lamps hung from the trees, and wickerwork frames of different shapes were covered with tiny oil lamps. Can you imagine a whole city traced out in lines of light? *It* was beautiful. At the Municipal Hall an address in a lovely box was presented and replied to; we spoke to many people, and I put in a word for my Scheme to some gentlemen of the municipality; then we went out on a balcony and looked at fireworks, and then home to bed.

Friday, 30th.—We found that the French Governor of Pondicherry was staying here, so he and his wife and two 'suite' came to breakfast. He was very interesting and amusing, telling us of his political difficulties, and how Republican France has given universal suffrage to the natives in Pondicherry to elect one French Deputy, who consequently (being the voice of the whole people) is able to defy the mere majority in the Pondicherry Parliament of thirty members, who represent three classes of persons living in Pondicherry—namely, Frenchmen, native French citizens, and pure natives, who of course never all agree about anything. We sat and talked for a long time, and I then went to open a new Hospital for Women which is in missionary hands; it is doing good work here. On my way home I looked in at the Queen's Gardens, where there is a menagerie. It contains two very fierce tigers, and some monkeys, bears, and birds.

In the afternoon we drove off in our large brake to see some tombs. The old fort which we passed on the way is a magnificent ruin, and indeed for the whole five miles we went there was a succession of old walls and towers and tombs and little mosques, with remnants of their old ornamentation left, enough to make one think how splendid it must all have been in ancient days.

We first went into the tomb of Humayun, which was built for him by his wife. It is a large building full of rooms, in each of which some marble graves are to be found, and all the windows are perforated stone, each one a different pattern and carved so as to admit plenty of light. The next place we went to appealed to my feelings more than this rather massive monument; it was the tomb of Nizam-uddin, a saint of old. Here you come into solitary courts, with trunks and branches of trees protruding through the walls into their sacred precincts, and all the graves surrounded by carved white marble perforated walls and carved white marble doors, which are quite beautiful.

In one of these lies a Begum, who left orders that 'over this poor child of clay only God's grass should grow,' so surrounded by these poetic-looking walls is her tomb, with grass growing on it as she wished. These enclosures are mysterious and lovely—the workmanship so delicate, the material so precious and the general effect so dreamy and almost unreal, that you feel as if you must be peeping into another world.

Through these courts we passed to the edge of a large tank of very nasty-looking water, and here we saw a most curious sight. All round the tank were walls of various heights, and mosques, and cupolas, and numbers of men and boys climbing to the summit of each, and then jumping straight into the water below. Some of them dived fifty feet, and we could see their action perfectly. They start with their arms and legs stretched out like wings, and as they approach the water they stiffen themselves and go down feet foremost straight as an arrow. The sun was setting as we returned, and the great mosque I described to you yesterday, with its domes and minarets, and arched walls and massive gateway, looked so grand and calm against the golden sky. It is a building that grows upon one and impresses one more and more each time one sees it. In the evening His Excellency held a levée.

Saturday, 31st.—We have had a long day's sight-seeing, having driven out to the Kutub in the morning and only returned in the evening. I think it is one of the wonderful buildings of the world—a fragment only of what it was intended to be, but a fragment of gigantic size and great beauty! The prettiest story as to its original use is that it was built by the king to enable his daughter to see the river Jumna from its summit; it is one great minaret or tower of enormous height and beautiful proportions. It is built of a sort of red and yellow sandstone, with deeply cut carvings round the base and the top of each storey. The lower and most massive part is in alternate round and angular blocks; in the second storey the forms are all round, and the top storey is in angular pieces. There are 375 steps up to the top, and therefore, what we found more fatiguing, 375 down again. The building looks perfectly fresh; the colour of it is beautiful, and there is not a stain or a chip or a mark of age anywhere—yet it is more than 800 years old. A second minaret of equal size had been begun, and I suppose there would have been intermediate buildings, mosque fashion; but the Kutub itself now stands in its own solitary magnificence, the ruins around it belonging to a different epoch. They are very lovely too, some arches of beautiful shapes, carved pillars, &c.; one would like to spend several days pottering about amongst them. In the centre of one court is an iron pillar 'which rests on the back of the dragon which supports the world,' and by clasping your arms backwards round this pillar you can obtain a wish.

We had lunch in a tomb, and then went to see another of those mysterious shrines with small courts, and perforated marble walls, and big trees, and in one place a mass of lovely tiles; and on to another tank, where men jumped a hundred feet into the water below. A most curious sight it is! We timed them, and from the time they sprang they were about two seconds in the air before the splash came. One is quite relieved when each one reappears.

On our return journey we had tea at another tomb, and in the evening the principal officials here dined with us. Mr. McNabb, the Commissioner, in whose house we are, fell ill the day after our arrival. Delhi seems to be very unhealthy, and people are continually knocked up with attacks of fever. We are allowed to drink no water, and have to take quinine every day.

Sunday, November 1st.—We went to church in the morning, and in the afternoon we drove over the Mutiny ground, seeing the ridge, the gates, and various batteries. The battered walls and gates, and the scars left by the hurtling storm of iron shot, remain as they were when our troops marched in—a standing memorial of all our people did and suffered that dreadful year. Colonel Ewart, who went through the siege, was with us.

Monday, 2nd.—D. laid the foundation-stone of the new General Hospital here, which is to be called after him. A female wing is to be added to the original design.

We leave Delhi to-night, and mean to drive and ride about a little this afternoon; but, as we are not likely to see or do anything very interesting, I will send this off now.

The sun is extremely powerful in the day, but the weather is not too hot. It is generally about 75° in my sitting room.

Tuesday, 3rd.—I write to you from a native palace, where everything is very pretty and curious—that of the Maharajah of Ulwar.

We left Delhi at night, having spent the last hour

there in witnessing the performance of a native conjuror. The trick that amused us most was the following : He asked for some brandy, and when the bottle was brought he emptied it into a vessel of his own ; he also filled a small glass with it, and into that he put a few grains of different coloured powders and drank it off! A little while later he spat out the powders *dry*, and the large quantity of brandy was taken behind the scenes and carried off. It was a most transparent device for obtaining liquor. He had some horrible snakes, and it was rather curious to see a mongoose kill one; the activity of the little animal, and the way in which it seized the snake by the head, and turned and rolled itself over, and wriggled out of the coils in which the snake tried to envelope it with its tail, were extraordinary.

At eleven o'clock we went to the railway station, and as the narrow gauge is used in Rajpootana we did not have our own carriages, and are now travelling in very comfortable but much smaller ones. In the morning we stopped at eight o'clock to dress, and arrived here at nine. The Maharajah, with a carriage and four, cavalry, infantry, any number of bands, &c., met us and drove us to the palace. The grounds are beautifully kept, and the house is thoroughly Indian. The entrance-hall is a sitting-room, open on one side, with pillars supporting the roof, and the long narrow dining-room on the other is raised a few feet higher and is divided off by a low marble balustrade. There are gorgeous chandeliers, and various works of art in the way of pictures hung high up on the cornice. In front of the palace is a piece of water, and there are hills and woods round it.

My apartments are upstairs, or rather up a hill, for there are no stairs, only a sloping corridor, up which the Rajah can *ride* to his room. I have a long narrow drawing-room, with pillars and arches opening on to a passage and into an uncovered court, where one can sit most comfortably. The drawing-room combines all the colours of the rainbow in its decoration: orange curtains with blue fringes in the arches, red curtains in the windows, and yellow, blue, salmon, and green, &c., &c., in masses on the walls; blue glass chandeliers and coloured candle-shades and glass balls in the corners of the room: it all looks Eastern and unconventional; and I am glad it is not furnished in sage greens and faded blues like an English villa.

The Maharajah is a young man, is one of my chief 'medical' supporters, speaks English well, wears native dress, and is a very pleasant host. Colonel Peacock is the Resident; he has a nice wife and two daughters. Sir Edward Bradford, who holds a still higher post in Rajpootana, is also here.

The afternoon was spent in seeing the Maharajah's horses. He breeds them all himself, and has about 3,000 on his estate and about 500 here. The best ones were all marched past the door; some of them do tricks—jumping, walking on their hind legs, &c. Then we drove to a new fernery, saw some terribly fierce tigers in cages, and on to the stables and yards *full* of loose horses. A hurdle was put up in a gateway, and troops of horses jumped over it to their food on the other side. *It* was a very pretty sight.

The evening was more Arabian Nights like than ever.

We dined at the city palace, which has a fort-like entrance, high walls, gateways, and enclosed courts. The trees all the way along were hung with coloured lanterns, and when we reached the town the shops were similarly decorated.   Lime-lights were burnt on the arches, and as a background to the view there shone with myriads of lights a great peaked hill, with a fort on its summit booming forth the Viceroy's salute.   In the court, where we alighted, we found a guard of honour and the Maharajah's elephant carriage for us to see. *I*magine a beautiful gondola-like carriage, two storeys high, drawn by four elephants, all covered in gorgeous gold-embroidered cloths.   On certain occasions the Maharajah drives through the town in this, and sometimes he rides one of the trained horses, and goes down his streets performing a *pas-de-basque* step on horseback, to the great admiration of all his subjects.   This is a digression, however, and I must go on with our own experiences. Having passed through a passage, we found ourselves in another court and another scene of beauty.   The white walls of the palace enclosed this court, the further end of which was raised and had marble steps up to it and kiosks breaking the outline. *I*n the lower part of the court were the Maharajah's troops, their red coats against the white walls looking splendid.   They were ranged so as to leave a pathway, along which we walked.   All the lines of the building were illuminated, and the whole scene was something too bright and lovely.

As we mounted the steps we saw before us a suite of rooms open to the court, glittering with gold and light. One of these was the durbar hall, and His Excellency went and took his seat on the throne there, while we were admitted to a room at the back of the chairs of state, raised above them, but with open arches into the great hall. It was a most curious place, the whole decoration being painted and enamelled glass, very gorgeous and rather pretty.

The climax of our admiration was, however, only reached when we looked out of the windows of this room on to the most lovely bit of illumination I have ever seen. Immediately below us was a great tank with marble walls and with kiosks jutting out into the water on every side, and the whole way round this was a palisade of light! The effect was produced by a diamond-shaped lattice-work paling, in which at every diamond point a little oil lamp burned. This wall of soft-coloured light reflected in the water was too beautiful; and straight up behind it rose the illuminated hill.

From poetry to prose, and from the delight of the eye to an ordinary dinner! The Maharajah took me in and sat for a little while just behind me; he then went away for his own dinner, and only came back in time to propose the Queen's health.

The girls and I afterwards visited the zenana, and then proceeded to the top of the house to see the fireworks. The lights were out on the hill now, but the Fort was burning lime-lights, and the fireworks went off close to the tanks and were very successful.

Wednesday, 4th.—We have had such a long day—and the worst part of a journal is that, when there is much to say, there is no time to write, and I have to send you such hasty and imperfect accounts of everything. This was to be a tiger-shooting day, but again we drew an absolute blank. However, we were ready to start early, and we drove eight miles to the Silisehr lake—an artificial one—which supplies Ulwar with water. It is about four miles long, a most calm and peaceful sheet of water nearly surrounded by hills, and with a picturesque little castle on its banks, where we breakfasted. Then we started off on elephants—such a number of them, ' hacks ' and shikari (hunting) elephants—a great procession. We rode to cover on pads (a sort of flat bedstead, on which you sit as in an Irish car), and when we got to the beat, we mounted other animals, and got into howdahs. Thus we marched slowly through the jungle abreast, at first with some excitement, momentarily expecting to hear the tiger's roar ; but, as our hopes decreased, we simply looked about at the tall grass, which almost hid some of the elephants, and at the little woody places where perhaps the animal might be hiding, until finally we gave it up. And then we found that it was four o'clock, and that we had had no lunch, and that, moreover, the lunch was missing ! So we turned back, and in about half-an-hour we met the commissariat elephant. It was too late to sit down properly, unpack the boxes, &c., so a very funny scene was enacted. We all, sitting on our elephants, collected round the food, and about six men dived into the boxes and got out what they could ; bits of turkey were handed in the fingers from howdah to howdah, a pie slipped down between two elephants and was rescued with difficulty, soda-water bottles fell to the ground and were politely handed up by an elephant's trunk, loaves were sent as 'catches,' people drank out of bottles, and flung their manners to the winds, and everybody kept lurching and heaving about (for an elephant never stands still for an instant), and we all felt as if we were in a rolling sea. *It* was very amusing. We proceeded on our way home, and when it was quite dark we reached the lake and found a steam-launch waiting to take us up it. *I* was unwilling to leave the elephant, in whom I had acquired confidence, for a steam-launch, about which I felt doubtful, but the Viceroy commanded and *I* obeyed. I objected still more when I found a captain who is the head of some industrial school, who talked of his ship as 'it,' who asked the stoker to 'please to put on some more coal,' and whose language was entirely unnautical. While oppressed with these fears, *I* suddenly got a tremendous blow on the back, found myself and D. knocked forward, a great flap and a flounce, and a gigantic fish jumping about at our feet! We seized the first thing which came handy, and that happened to be a bran-new Newmarket coat which Lord William had just brought from England, and which he had lent to Helen, and in this aristocratic garment the fish was smothered. We went out for a tiger, but we only brought home a fish! The owner of the coat strongly objects to the smell left in it. We drove home, did not have dinner till nine o'clock, and were very tired, for the sun had been very powerful all day. After it we looked at some fine swords, and daggers, and arms, and jewels, and at some most valuable and beautiful illuminated books belonging to the Maharajah; one of them is worth

1,100*l*. The Maharajah is so cheery and nice, we like him immensely ; and he has a little Prime Minister, with a bright and pleasing expression, who trots about and appears at every turn like a beneficent fairy.

Thursday, 5*th.*—A jaunt in the train which I rather liked—a novel and a lazy attitude were refreshing after our long day out in the air yesterday.. We got to Ajmere at six in the evening, and the reception was very gay. There were crowds and crowds of people, and some smart dresses, and some lovely arches and new devices for illumination ; and the place itself is very pretty, with peaked hills, and a lake with old buildings on its banks. The address was read and answered as we left our carriage, and we drove up to Sir Edward Bradford's house, where we are staying. Lady Bradford has whooping-cough, and is far from well, so *I* have scarcely seen her yet. Their house almost hangs over the lake, and has a lovely view from it. The girls are in tents on the roof, and I fear our hosts are also turned out of doors to make room for us.

Friday, 6*th.*—I have just been watching D. receive the Rajah of Kishengur. Amongst his suite was a man in a most curious costume. He wore a simple muslin dress, with green ribbon braces across his body, and on his arms gold armour covering the hand and reaching above the elbow, a small close sort of cap richly decorated on his head, with a little plume in it, and in his hand he carried a shield. Two other Rajahs paid visits.

Some of them wore rather short tunics and gold belts, and many of their followers carried handsome shields.

In the afternoon we drove to see a very curious ruin which was originally a Jain temple, behind whose fine arched entrance a mosque has been built. It consists of rows and rows of beautifully carved pillars, which, it is said, were put up in two and a half days, and the mosque is therefore called 'Arhai ke din Jompri' (the two and a half days' shed). We then went on to look at the Mayo College, a fine handsome marble building, to be opened to-morrow. Perhaps you don't know what the Mayo College is. It is a Rajpootana Eton. The idea was suggested by Lord Mayo; the Rajpootana princes and nobles subscribed largely to endow it, and it has been very successful so far. Each prince has a house of his own in the grounds, which holds eight students; these he sends from his own State. They must all be of good family—men whom the Rajah rises to receive in durbar. It is such a pretty place, the new college being built of white marble, a fine statue of Lord Mayo standing before the door; and in the park, which is beautifully kept, are all the 'villas' belonging to the various States. Their different styles of architecture are Oriental, and, surrounded by rough hills as the place is, they look most picturesque; we stormed Major Loch's, the Provost's, house, and had tea there in his absence. After this came a review of the Meywar regiment. The men were once wild and lawless, but are now drilled into excellent and fine-looking soldiers.

There was a big dinner, a levée, and a reception in the

evening, and another wonderful sight in the way of illumination.

I told you that this house is situated on a lake which is over three miles round, and that there are the remains of palaces and colonnades at one end of it. When we looked out after dinner we saw a line of light round the whole lake, while the buildings were shaped out in fire. It was all so simple, with no coloured lamps or devices— merely the soft-coloured, brilliant line; and yet what a work of labour! Each tiny saucer is stuck on to a little mud-pie, which has to be made for it, the lamp has to be filled with oil and lighted and attended to, each one touches the other, and there is no break or gap in the line. There were, later in the evening, some fire-works in the town. It also was illuminated, but from the house we could only see the lake and the zigzag line which marked the road up a steep hill to the Fort.

Saturday, 7th.—A very interesting afternoon, spent in opening the Mayo College. When we entered the great hall we found it filled with people; the pupils sat in the front rows, and were all dressed in white, with coloured turbans and some jewels; their friends and other natives sat behind them, and then came the Europeans of the place. The hall is elaborately deco- rated in delicate colours, and is different from our idea of a 'schoolroom.' Major Loch read an address, to which D. replied in a very nice speech, giving good advice to the 'scions of ancient houses,' whom he saw before him, and, at the end, speaking of the Maharajah of

Ulwar as a good example of the first ruling prince who had been educated at the school, and who is employing so much personal industry, care, and intelligence in the administration of his State as to give complete satisfaction to the Supreme Government. The mention of his name was very enthusiastically received. When D. had pronounced the College to be open a salute was fired, and then I took his place and gave away the prizes. The great winner of the day, who carried off three medals and an armful of books, was called Zalim Sing and is a brother of the Maharajah of Jodhpore. The students gave me a book with views of the College and the dwelling-houses in the grounds. When we left the building D. spoke to the boys, and we went and looked at one of their rooms. Spartan simplicity prevails as to furniture—a bed, a chest, and a table being all that is allowed; but the walls were covered with little pictures and little glass balls arranged by the occupant. By this time all the houses were illuminated, and very lovely they looked, the different styles of their architecture marked out in light: magical domes and squares, horizontal and perpendicular lines, shining out through the darkness. We had tea with the Lochs, and then dined and started in the train for Chittore.

Sunday, 8th.—We reached this place (Chittore) in the morning; but though it is very interesting historically, it had not been arranged for us to stop here, so we simply sat down to one of the magnificent breakfasts in one of the magnificent camps which spring up at every turn in this wonderful country, and then got into carriages to drive seventy miles. Of course, exactly at the right time for luncheon, there was a halt in the jungle, and tents were to be seen; a banquet was found ready—the table was covered with flags bearing the Viceroy's name, the bills-of-fare were hand-painted with the flags of all nations; palms and shrubs, planted for the occasion, made a garden at the door, and we rested for an hour. Of course, also, there was tea at five, and at the place where this was laid the ceremonies connected with entering Udaipur began. The journey had been mostly through a flat and ugly country, but when at last we came to a fortified gateway and drove into the stronghold, and passed the wild men armed with bows and arrows who formed a guard of honour, it improved immensely. There were hills before us of curious shapes, some rising in one straight pyramid from the ground, others part of a chain of hills; there was a lake to be seen, palms and other trees growing. After driving for nearly an hour in this sort of scenery we reached the camp, three miles from the city, and D. got into one of the Rajah's carriages while *I.* followed in another, and a message was sent on to the Maharana (that is his correct title) to say that the Viceroy was coming. He met us a very short distance from this, and driving alongside of D. got out of his carriage and into the Viceroy's, and we all drove on. By this time we had every sort of escort and company on our way, and there were knots of people all along the road, the men shouting some welcome, and the women in groups, shyly holding out little brass pots with a bit of green in them, as is their custom on such occasions, and singing a little nasal song in the most

unmusical voices.   However, there is so much to delight
the eye, that the ear may well content itself with being
only amused.

As we neared the town, the sight became more and
more splendid and interesting. I always feel my pen
fail utterly when I have to describe an Indian crowd : the
masses of the people, the picturesque appearance of every
individual, the attitudes in which they place themselves,
the groups in windows and doors and amongst the arches
of quaint temples—the colouring and the interest of it
all defy description ; and when one passes on from the
ordinary inhabitants to the sirdars and the troops, one
finds it impossible to do more than enumerate some of the
various sights which one would wish to describe minutely.
There are the sirdars on horseback, the horse and the
man vying with each other as to which of them should
be the more gorgeously apparelled ; there are the followers standing by with long palm-branches or yak-tails
in hand; there are the men in chain armour, their horses
with heavy palls of the same; there are the wild troops,
who line the way and salute somewhat in *feu-de-joie*
fashion one after the other, irregularly ; there are the
camel batteries—a sort of old blunderbuss fixed on a revolving block on the hump of a camel ; there are the
sentries, who give themselves a word of command and
' present,' and there is one who, confounding the two
ideas, combines a wild hurrah and salaam with the
proper military manœuvre.   Then there are the Maharana's horses and elephants covered from head to foot
either with silver chains, or gold embroideries, or yak-
tails, or long fringes of silver and gold ; there are native

bands and great brass trumpets, and manifold uniforms, and a battlemented wall covered with people on one side of the way, while the great crowd I have been attempting to describe are on the other.

We are staying at the Residency, so we drove straight there, the guard of honour at the house being composed of 'Bhils.' They look rather like Goorkha soldiers, but are not quite so square in build, and have not got the Chinese type of face.

The Maharana has only been on his throne a year, and seems a most gentlemanlike, nice man. He never expected to be made the ruler, and was a poor man before coming to the throne, so all the state is new to him. He has only one wife, and will not take another, though his hand is eagerly sought for by great princes who have daughters or sisters to marry. The Maharanas of Udaipur are of the best Rajpoot blood, the 'Children of the Sun;' and as a Rajpoot princess can only marry a Rajpoot, it is difficult to find husbands for them all, and yet they are disgraced if they do not marry. This Ranee is now in an interesting condition, so I shall not be able to see her, and the question of son or daughter is a burning one in this State. I too shall be very anxious to know which it is, and so I am sure will you when I tell you the story. A long time ago there was a Maharana of Udaipur who had a lovely daughter, and the fame of her beauty spread so far that the great houses of Jeypore and Jodhpore were anxious to obtain her hand. They sent their splendid embassies, and the Maharana feared to decide between them, as civil war would have been the inevitable consequence; so he cut the Gordian knot by sacrificing the princess. 'What is a woman that there should be trouble on her account?' A Mahometan armed with a dagger was admitted to the zenana, the purdah was lifted, and there stood before him the beautiful princess. At the sight of her loveliness he threw the dagger down and fled. Then poison was resorted to, and the princess was told to drink it. In the grand manner of a Rajpoot woman she was ready for the sacrifice. Three times she swallowed a deadly draught, but never could retain it, and then they gave her opium, and she slept away. When the deed was known, a Rajpoot noble, full of indignation, exclaimed, 'May Meywar never have an heir,' and at the Maharana's death his Queen refused to be burnt for his sake, and a slave girl was chosen to accompany him to the grave. She rose in the flames and said, 'May Meywar never have an heir;' so the curse was twice repeated, and six Maharanas have reigned since, and no heir has been born to any one of them.

This man is a descendant of the prince who reigned before the curse was pronounced, so it will be interesting to see if the malediction passes on to him! There are certain families from whom the heir to the throne is chosen, and when the reigning prince dies the election is held at once. On hearing of his death, every man, except the possible heirs, shaves, and so little did this prince expect to be elected that he had already shaved when called to the throne, which is quite contrary to custom. The late Maharana's three widows have to sit for a whole year in the place where they hear of his death, so these poor things cannot move till December next.

They are given private notice of his demise in order that they may choose their corner and make their preparations, and then the official news comes, and they are shorn of their jewels, put into a dark dress, and retire from even the little world in which they usually live; so I cannot see them either.

The Residency is a charming house, and Colonel and Mrs. Biddulph are very nice hosts. A son of Lady Elizabeth Adeane is staying with them. D. had unfortunately a bad headache, and had to go to bed on arrival, while we went through the usual long dinner before we could rest; and we actually had to unpack and dress ourselves, for, though the ayahs started twelve hours before us, they dawdled on the way and did not get here till late. Perhaps it is good for us to rough it occasionally !

Monday, 9th.—The Maharana came to pay his visit this morning, and we peeped in at the solemn durbar. The dresses are always an' interesting part of it. Here they wear muslin gowns with very short waists, and with great scarves wound round their bodies much lower down, so that all the gathers of the skirts are above the scarf. Their turban is very neat, with a plain, smooth, slanting point in it; it looks as if it must be made up before, and not merely tied round the head.

When wearing their court dress they have voluminous petticoats, each one of which contains about 140 yards of muslin, is very heavy, and sways about as its wearer walks.

About an hour later D. went to pay his return visit

and saw more sirdars, and in the afternoon he rode about the town, joining us at teatime. Very few Europeans get here, as it is seventy miles from the railway. Lord Northbrook came privately, but no other Viceroy has visited it.

We have been out on the lake this afternoon, and have been quite carried away by the ideal beauty of this place. It is really enchanting. The natural scenery is beautiful : finely shaped hills surrounding a great lake ; and then white domes and battlemented walls and gateways, and a palace, and innumerable temples on either side rising straight from the water, and, in the centre of the lake, palace-islands with perforated marble screens and open arches, and kiosks and various-shaped pagodas, a tall palm or two rising above all, and green banana-leaves showing through the arches. All these buildings are pure white, but on the surrounding hills there are old forts and castles of a darker colour. I fear it is almost treason to say that this lake is a beautified Bosphorus ! But it does remind one of it. We landed on one of the island-palaces, and, getting up to the wall, saw just above the water a row of elephants' heads and trunks, these stone animals being supposed to support the building. Stepping through the first arch, we found ourselves in a labyrinth of little gardens, pieces of water, and covered pagodas, bits of carving, and rows of pillars, and staircases up to little turrets, and from every side lovely views of the hills and of the other palaces. There is one room in this island where the English ladies who were here at the time of the Mutiny took refuge, and were cared for by the father of one of this Maharana's sirdars.

It is a round room with inlaid marble walls, and I do hope it was not the English ladies who put down an English carpet and who hung some very common English pictures on its walls; but there they are, and of course the native who shows you over the place thinks they are the real treasures.

We rowed over to another island for tea. I am obliged to call it an island, but you must remember it is all palace, and that not an inch of earth is visible. Here there were some curious decorations on the walls, coloured glasses laid in—the old bits quite lovely, the modern restorations bad. This island-palace is built with the arched colonnade outside, and with square bits of water and flower-beds and fountains inside, and suites of rooms, one set very European and another rather curious, with paintings in the Japanese style on the walls. The great palace opposite this on the banks is a very massive building. Part of it is a huge square place, with no windows to be seen in it; that wing is the women's, who cannot enjoy the beauty of the lake on which they live, but must for ever look on small courts and enclosed gardens.

There is no escape from the inevitable long dinner which ends all our days, but when it was over we saw a strange sight. The Bhils, who are aboriginal inhabitants of this country, and who, at the present time, are either wild and troublesome neighbours or good soldiers, danced for us by torchlight. Their performance is very like the Kuttak dance which we saw at Rawal Pindi, only that, instead of swords, the men carry sticks. There were about two hundred of them, and they went round and round in a circle in a close mass, with a sort of swinging hop step, keeping perfect time with each other and with a tom-tom, which was the only music they had. They shouted and turned backwards and forwards as they moved, alternately striking the stick of the man before and that of the man behind them: this made a noise like castanets. The dancers were very wild-looking, and it was all most curious to look at, but the really interesting dancing was that of the women, for the Bhil women dance. I found I could not see them well, so I got inside their circle, and a more weird scene I never witnessed. The women are good looking, and are most picturesquely dressed, with large red veils covering their heads and skirts, the latter being generally dark blue, a *very* short jacket just over the bosom, and then a hiatus between it and the petticoat. Their arms are laden with bangles of all colours, and their legs are equally covered with brass ornaments. They held each other round the shoulders with one arm, and moved in lines of twenty, the lines overlapping each other and forming a circle. They sang a wild ditty as they danced, and the step and the song and their movements went together most beautifully. The step was like one 'chassé,' after which they beat time with their feet, and bowed down, the one at the end clapping her hands, and the others making a sweeping motion with the arm that was disengaged. Their dusky faces and their red garments, and their wild music and the perfect time and grace of their movements, made this a most striking sight.

Tuesday, 10*th*.—The beauties of this place have made me energetic, so I got up early and went out from seven till nine to try and take some photographs. Within half a mile on the lake there are fifty or sixty bits that one longs to do, they are all so lovely; and one might spend months in Udaipur without exhausting the carvings and the old temples and the endless variety of objects which excite one's admiration. However, I could only do a few, and I rather devoted myself to the palace—such a massive pile rising from the water, and so very unlike any other castle.

At twelve o'clock we went to see the inside of it, and a most quaint and odd interior it is. There are courts within its walls, where you see at a glance the life of the retainers, as they sit on the ground outside or squat in the open colonnades. Elephants and quantities of pigeons walk about there, and nothing seems to be considered out of place. Everything inside the palace is arranged to secure the utmost privacy, so all the rooms look either into a little court whose walls are glass mosaic in lovely patterns (one wall has panels, in each of which was a peacock, others have flowers or figures), or, as on the top of the palace, into a court where large trees and tall palms grow, with the most delicately carved marble pillars and baths, and a covered passage all round it. Some little rooms are lined with tiles, and many of them with the glass decoration peculiar to this country. The passages are so narrow we could only pass through them one at a time, and there is quite a long, narrow, steep, and slippery staircase up to each different room. The Maharana, who is a slight wiry man with a good expression and very pleasant manners, went about with us, and there was a young native who spoke English, and who, to my surprise, mooted the Female Medical question with me, and said with how much interest they all regarded it, and what a boon its success would confer upon the people. Two English doctors, sisters, have been here for years, and I had an interview with them yesterday, and to-day I lay the foundation-stone of a new hospital the Maharana is building for them. *It* will be a very pretty one, and he will spare no expense to make it nice. Mrs. Lonergan, the doctor, is married to the Commander-in-Chief here.

We have had a varied afternoon. First there was the Hospital function, which went off well. The Maharana presented me with a very nice address and a home-made trowel, which I shall value much as a gift from one of the ' Children of the Sun.'

We next proceeded to shoot boar, and an amusing sight it was. We were all either carried by men or elephants up a hill to a kind of tower, on the top of which we found chairs, and there we sat facing a high, steep hill, which rose straight before us. The beaters came along the side of the hill and drove the pigs towards us, while the gentlemen, who were with us in this safe place, shot at the animals. It was, however, very difficult shooting, for the pigs slipped in and out of bushes, and were much the same colour as the ground. We saw a great number, and three or four were got. Two hyenas also put in an appearance.   D. shot one, but he was unlucky in losing his spectacles on the way, and he could not see well.

And now leave the common-place world behind you, and fancy yourself launched on a smooth, mysterious lake, the stars shining above and a crescent moon looking down upon you—on either side of the way some old fort or temple marked out in fire, and before you a bridge of light.   This seems to be the gate to fairy-land ; for, passing through it, you come into a golden world, where the water is sown with stars, where brilliant and fragile structures rise in shining light on either side and from the centre of the lake, while their reflections look like solid palaces of gold.   I have tried to describe the beauty of this lake to you as seen in the daytime ; what it is at night, illuminated, you must really picture to yourself.   None of us have ever seen such a marvellous effect.   Passing through the bridge, there is on one side a battlemented wall, with a tower gateway, and then on every side domes, and cupolas, and minarets, and arcades, and flights of steps, and arched windows filled in with a latticework of stars—every idiosyncrasy of each particular style of architecture traced out in light, the solid building quite disappearing in the blaze, and, floating on the water in masses here and there, just as lilies might grow, little flower-lamps.   This was on our way to dinner. We dined in the palace, in a new and Europeanised part of it, with a great deal of Birmingham glasswork about it and English furniture in each drawing-room.   A Parsee contractor ' did us,' and as there is a decided family likeness between the banquets of all contractors, *I* won't say much as to the way in which we passed the next two hours. The Maharana came in at the end to propose the Queen's health.

After this we resumed the more poetical part of the entertainment, and sat on the roof, looking on to the lake, where by this time fiery dragons were starting out of the water, and showers of yellow and green and red and blue balls were falling from the sky, and long golden drops and gold dust were being scattered everywhere. I cannot use a common-place word to describe this scene, for even the fireworks—there, it would come—were refined ones and suited to the scene. Then chains of flowers were hung about our necks, and we were scented with rosewater and given parcels of ' pan,' and so rowed back again through the realms of light.

Wednesday, 11*th.*—Left Udaipur and drove seventy miles to Chittore, where we encamped for the night.

D. went off to see the ruins of that city, and as he says he would have gone a thousand miles to see them, I feel that of course I missed the one thing I ought to have seen. However, I have read the romantic history of the city, and I have looked at it in the distance.

Thursday, 12*th.*—We were in the train from nine till five, and, arriving at Indore, were met by Sir Lepel Griffin, the Maharajah Holkar, his two sons, the Rajah of Dhar, whose chains of emeralds were magnificent, and several other nobles. We drove through immense crowds of people and turbans, preceded by some of the 7th Dragoon Guards, to whom I had given their

Egyptian medals at Cairo. The Maharajah drove with the Viceroy, and I with Sir Lepel. Sir Lepel's house is charming and so prettily arranged, and he has taken great trouble with the grounds, and has made them very pretty too. There was some Bhil dancing in the garden after dinner.

Friday, 13*th.*—His Excellency had visits all the morning, and returned them all the afternoon. He had the pleasure of making one man supremely happy, and five more or less so. The happy man was, quite unexpectedly to himself, made a Rajah, which he had not been before, and he was delighted, and all his followers rose to express their joy ' on this great occasion.' He is now Rajah of Rajghar. The others received swords, medals, or ' robes of honour ' for various services.

I went to see the Maharanee of Holkar, a Mahratta lady. At the end of my visit I was wreathed in gold and silver and flower chains and bracelets, scented and given pan, and then I asked for her grandchildren to be brought to me ; they sang Sanscrit songs very nicely, and were dear little things.

The Maharajah Holkar gave an entertainment for us in the evening—fireworks, electric light, and supper, which came just an hour after dinner. The evening was very cold, and our host, in white muslin and a light burnous, which he pulled over his head, did not look nearly warm enough.

My friends, the children, were present at the fireworks, and sat by me, chattering away, and so happy.

I wonder if they will remember this night when, after a few years of liberty, they come to be shut up in a zenana.

It was this day year that we left England, and it was rather a strange coincidence that, in addition to ourselves, there were at dinner three of our fellow-passengers and the father and brother of two others.

Saturday, 14th.—D. got up early to have some black buck shooting—shooting conducted on the most deceitful principles. The sportsman goes in a bullock cart, and the innocent deer imagines he is ploughing, and, having no objection to agriculture, is not at all alarmed. When he has allowed the 'plough' to get near him, the sportsman slips out of the cart on to the ground, where he squats unobserved by the guileless deer, who, in the simplicity of his heart, continues his observation of the cart, and is shot dead by his deceiver. D. got one buck, and another fell as if quite dead, but on approaching it they found it was unwounded and was only stunned by a shot which had struck a bit off its horn.

D. received an address from the Municipality, who were most cordial in their remarks on the Female Medical scheme. We went next to open a college, which is in its infancy, but which is intended to be for Central India what the Mayo College is for Rajpootana; this one, however, does not start with an endowment of seven lacs, as the Mayo did. A native hospital was then visited; it is a very nice one, being on the cottage principle, each cottage quite detached from every other building.

We left Indore in the afternoon, accompanied to the station by the Maharajah Holkar, who clasped D. and Sir Lepel in his arms, saying to Sir Lepel, who, he knows, dislikes this exhibition of affection, 'Heart to heart, in spite of your English prejudices.'

We spent the night and all next day in the train, reaching Jodhpore at five o'clock on—

Sunday, 15*th*.—The railway to this place has only been open five years, and no Viceroy has yet visited it in state, so this is rather a grand occasion, and from the moment we left the railway station we passed into a thoroughly Oriental world. The Maharajah and his brothers met us there, all in their court dresses, those petticoats which *I* have mentioned before. The petticoats are in thick folds, and are all made of pink muslin ; halfway down the skirt they are tied in with a scarf, so that at the bottom they stand straight out and sway about as the wearer moves. They are so full that when a man rides in them they fall quite naturally over each leg as if they were ' divided,' but in a carriage they are most awkward, and no ball dress was ever so difficult to tuck in as was the Maharajah's skirt when he followed the Viceroy into the beautiful yellow carriage awaiting him. The headdress worn with this is also very peculiar. It is red and yellow, and rather pointed. The Maharajah wore the Star of India collar and ribbon. The drive to the camp was about a mile and a half long, and again we saw a wonderful crowd and a great quantity of men

in armour, camels, elephants, and soldiers, and such picturesque forts and city walls beyond. I had a delightful companion in my carriage—the heir-apparent, aged
six, dressed in red court petticoats, which he told me
he found hot, and which he had only put on to show me.
I never saw such a nice little creature. He never
stopped talking, and would issue orders to the escort,
telling them not to let their horses neigh, or to the
coachman to go slowly ; then he pointed out all the
sights to me, told me the names of his brother's horses,
examined my arm to see if I had any bangles on, asked
if my gloves were made of ' rubber,' exhibited his own
necklace, asked me if I had a little boy, and on hearing
I had he said he would send him a little carriage, but
that a good coachman must be got for it, and that then
he could drive along by me, and I must watch him when
he got in and out, and must have the horses well exercised.
He gesticulated all the time, and gave me a most vivid
description of a race, and was altogether a charming
little picture in his quaint dress, with his lively ways. I
should mention the harness on the carriage horses—silver
collars with bells, silver ornaments over their heads, and
all the traces covered with silver.

We had a quiet evening, General Hardinge and a
few others dining with us in our own tent. The Maharajah has about a hundred guests here, and the camp is
arranged just like ours at Rawal Pindi : grass has been
made to grow in the centre of it, fountains play, and
on either side the tents are pitched, our own special establishment being at one end. It is quite splendid : yellow
satin and gold chairs, screens, fans, clocks, albums, writing

cases, ornaments of all sorts and kinds adorn drawing-rooms and boudoirs and audience-chambers; and my bed-rooms and dressing-rooms are in a house built for the occasion, and highly decorated; so do we go on *crescendo* as our tour proceeds!

Monday, 16*th*.— The day began at seven o'clock with pig-sticking. We drove some way, and then *I* got on an elephant and the others on horseback, and the Maharajah showed me where to go, and I was in at the death. The chase and the sight of D. galloping wildly and prodding the poor animal were very exciting for about ten minutes, but we were four hours in the sun, and so I did not feel that I should care to renew the experience. D. enjoyed it immensely, and so did Nelly, who rode at a respectful distance. All the brothers 'Singh' (the Rajah's family), who are great sportsmen, were delighted at His Excellency's success.

At one o'clock I went to visit the ladies of the zenana. I drove there in one carriage with Pertab Singh and Mrs. Newman, while the girls followed in another. We had to get up to a sort of fort palace, a most picturesque and massive building on the top of a very high hill. When we had passed through the narrow streets of the town, which are only remarkable for most lovely bits of carving here and there, and come to the gate of the Fort, we had to get into chairs to be carried up. Mine was a massive silver sort of couch on poles, and looked a frightful weight; however, in it I was borne aloft through the great big Fort. It is a most curious and beautiful place—solid stone towers and walls, contrasted with lace-like carving. One bit that struck me most was a tower which, for sixty feet upwards, is a plain bit of solid masonry, but which then breaks into the most delicate and beautiful carving at the top, with balconies and windows, and every sort of ornament. Then there is one part of the palace, the front of which is a mass of carving. The zenana has no break in its carved face, even the windows being a lace-like pattern in stone.

Pertab Singh showed us the marble slab on which a new Maharajah sits when he mounts his throne, as well as some other rooms in the palace, but the outside of the building is much the most beautiful part of it.

The day was very hot, almost the hottest we have felt in India, so I thought that pig-sticking and a visit to the palace were enough for one day, and I did not go out again. The camp is furnished with thirty-three tricycles, and Nelly had a turn on one.

Tuesday, 17th.—The durbar was held to-day, and a wonderful sight it was. The tent is a most enormous one, so that, although there were 400 people in it, it was not filled, and, instead of the rows of seats being all straight, they were arranged in different directions, and one could see all the people much better than when they are placed in regular lines. In the tent there is a beautiful marble seat for two people, and behind it a white marble roof on pillars, with a raised floor. In this were two green velvet and gold chairs, one for me and one for the girls, so we had an excellent view of everything, and were much *en évidence;* though, in order to show that we had really nothing to do with it, we did not rise when the Viceroy came in, and the Maharajah took no notice of us. The whole court and all the sirdars were in those old court costumes. Most of the petticoats are pink, and the high headdress is red and yellow, but there are some who dress all in white. You may imagine how unlike anything we had ever seen before were these rows and rows of quaint figures. The Maharajah wore the ribbon and collar and star of the Star of India, and his petticoats were tied in with a red scarf. He had on some magnificent emeralds and pearls; beside him the dear little heir was seated in an arm-chair, which held legs, petticoats, and all. However, when the signal was given, he was helped down and waddled after his father to the door to meet the Viceroy, and then, when it was time for the sirdars to be presented, he came with his nuzzar, and, lively as he is, went through all the ceremonies in the most sedate manner. There were so many presentations that we had a longer time than usual for admiring everything. The newest feature in it was that a nautch-girl came to the door of the durbar tent, accompanied by three musicians, and there she sang. Her appearance added to the strangeness of the whole scene. The Viceroy and the Maharajah sat on the marble seat with carved lace-like sides, which was just in front of us. When all was over, the Maharajah and his family came over to our tent in order that I might do a photograph of them. I tried some groups, in which D. sat too, and then I took the child and the brothers, all in their dresses. The little boy was so good, but when it was over he said he was tired, and Pertab Singh, who seems to be a mother to him, undressed him before us, took off his jewels and his gown, and left him in a little shirt and trousers. When I lifted the frock I was astonished at its weight; it must really have been about a stone, there was so much material and so much gold on it. Everyone was, I am sure, delighted to get out of these clothes. In the afternoon we drove to Mandar, the ancient capital, where there is quite a crop of temples or buildings marking the places where the bodies of the Maharajahs have been burnt; some of them are very beautiful. Then we went on to see the work of which the reigning prince is most proud—a canal for supplying Jodhpore with water, and the supply stored up in a lake until wanted. As the country here is all sand and rock, very hot, and very dusty, and perfectly level, a little water occasionally must be invaluable.

The Maharajah gave a state banquet for us to-night. It was in a big Shamiana—one long table and a number of small ones; and, when we had finished eating, he came in to propose the Queen's health, and a little speech was made for him, welcoming all his guests and proposing the Viceroy's health, to which D. responded in terms which would have delighted the Rajah had he understood. After this came another Oriental scene. In the centre of the camp a couple of lawn-tennis grounds have been made, and when we came out of the Shamiana, we found a sort of long jewelled chain of clear glass lamps—red, green, and white—hanging from poles all round the courts, which had white cloths laid over them. Inside the magic circle were groups of men in armour sitting, and about 400 dancing girls, while men holding great torches lighted up the scene. The girls were in red and black and green, with quantities of tinsel and gold ornaments of all sorts about them, and their dancing and singing, though monotonous, like all similar Indian performances, was yet very pretty to look at when so many were doing it together. They waved their arms and turned about a little in the first figure ; in the second, they advanced towards each other, singing and clapping their hands ; and in the third, they twisted rather rapidly, their petticoats wrapping round them as they did so, and then, at a particular part of the tune, three put their hands together, palm to palm, and twirled again. Fireworks were going on in the distance, and the outlines of the city wall and of the great palace were illuminated.

The more we see of the camp and its arrangements, the more beautiful it looks ; and nothing is more wonderful than the great piece of really green grass they have got to grow down its centre. In the middle of it a good white marble bust of the Prince of Wales is set up.

Wednesday, 18*th.*—We had rather a pleasant afternoon, not being expected to do anything in particular, but only to wander about the camp, and ride tricycles and camels, and look at horses, and play with the heir-apparent. He looks upon me as his special friend, and accosts me every moment with ' Dekho Mem Sahib,' a sort of Hindustani ' I say.' The camel ride was very amusing ; the beasts were said to be remarkably easy ones, but we were kept jumping up and

down in our seats the whole time, and I was glad we
were not going a journey on them. After a quiet dinner
we were conducted to the train by all the family, and
we had quite a tender farewell from them. I don't
know how it is, but they inspire a *homey* feeling and one
of personal regard, and we were all very sorry to leave.
There is a kind of straightforward simplicity about all
the brothers which is pleasing, and the Maharajah,
though very solemn, is most kind. He presented D.
with a Marwar sword just before the train moved, and
when it did start we were pelted with masses of flowers
by him and by all the people present—a Marwar custom,
and their way of wishing one 'Godspeed.' The State of
Marwar is as big as Ireland, and the Maharajah has
about 400,000*l.* a year.

Thursday, 19*th.*—We go to sleep in one scene of magnificence to wake up in another. After travelling all
night we arrived at nine in the morning at Jeypore, the
capital of a still larger and richer State than the last. *I*
remember telling you of the Maharajah's visit to me in
Calcutta, and now we are his guests.

He and the Viceroy headed our procession in a
carriage with a gold-embroidered canopy over it, and
I followed in one much ornamented with gold and
silver fringe. We had a long drive to the Residency,
the road lined the whole way with troops, elephants,
camels, bullocks, men in armour, and bands, and music
of all sorts breaking out into 'God save the Queen' at
intervals, and crowds of spectators everywhere. Some of
the details of the procession were different from all we

have hitherto seen.   As we drove along, some wild-look-ing men holding swords and spears danced by the carriage, sometimes crossing their swords before the horses' noses, and jumping about very gracefully.   These are ascetic soldiers.   They belong to a sect which does not worship idols ; a priest is their leader, and they take the vow of celibacy.   I thought them very interesting.   Then the bullock-carts and bullock-batteries were curious.   The bullock is the animal known in the 'Zoo' as a 'Brahmin cow ; ' it is a handsome beast, pure white, with a hump on its back, and fine horns which in Rajpootana are generally painted red and polished so that they look like coral.   The carts in which these animals are har-nessed are very picturesque, with red or green painted canopies over them, and on this occasion the trappings and the horns of the bullocks matched the cart.   In the gun-carriages they looked very well.   They were standing in a very close row, and each bullock was completely covered with a red cloth edged with black, its white head alone being free.   In one place there were a number of lovely palanquins, red and gold and silver, carried by men.   The elephants were all magnificently clothed, and there were great numbers of them.

The Maharajah conducted the Viceroy to the Resi-dency, and then took his leave.   It is a large house in a pretty garden, and we have spacious apartments and are most comfortable.

Soon after breakfast I saw a regiment of men with trays on their heads passing my window, and found this was a ' dolly' for me ; so I went and looked at it, and took some sugarcandy, and said Thank you, and now

I suppose my servants are making themselves ill with so many sweets. I also 'touched and remitted' a great bag of money. At one o'clock the Maharajah paid his state visit to the Viceroy, who returned it in the afternoon.

You will begin to think that I am for ever describing to you the 'most beautiful thing I have ever seen,' but each place seems to have its own *spécialité*, and I am kept in a state of perpetual wonder and admiration, so I have to repeat that I have again seen a most splendid sight in the way of a durbar. It was held for the Viceroy's return visit to the Maharajah, and, being in a hall built for durbars, was better lighted than a tent can be, while the decorations of the building and the magnificent dresses of the gentlemen present seemed to harmonise, and to make the picture complete. The hall is open on three sides, the roof being supported on arches and pillars; the thrones are on the fourth side, and behind them is a balcony, where we sat. The Maharajah was seated facing the court, and on each side and behind him were rows and rows of his Thakurs (nobles), all gorgeous in gold, and velvets, and brocades, and jewels. We had time to admire the blaze of colour before a flutter in the court announced the approach of the Viceroy, and then we saw him being carried in a gorgeous palanquin—'served up in a gold dish,' he says. The Maharajah met him at the steps, and conducted him to the throne. When the presentations were over, a crowd of nautch-girls came in and, standing across the steps, filled in the fourth side of the square, so that the mass of colour was complete. They advanced in threes and fours with their

arms upraised, gently moving as they always do; and
when the time changed they all sang together a wild
chant, and while they sang the attar and pan and
wreaths were distributed. Then the Viceroy left, and
we drove through the town. It is quite unlike any other
Indian town, the streets being very wide and planned
like those of a modern city. It is, however, 150 years
old. The whole thing is painted pink, and to-day the
houses and balconies, roofs, windows, and pathways
were crowded with men, women, and children in gay
colours, and it all looked beautiful. The walls of the
houses seem to be very thin; they are generally ornamented at the top, and there is a good deal of open brickwork filling in windows, which looks pretty. I never saw
so many mottoes put up anywhere, nearly all of them in
English.

We drove afterwards to see a very damp and dark
garden, an Indian's idea of all that is delightful. It
only frightened me, and drove me to the quinine-bottle
on my return.

Friday, 20th.—We had rather a long and busy day.
At ten, I had an interview with Miss Swain, M.D., who
gave me many interesting details of her Indian experiences, and then D. and I went a round of institutions.
The School of Art interested us much, and there we saw
many of the special industries of the place being carried
on. Next we saw a museum, where they are beginning
to have a very good collection of things, and then we
visited the Maharajah's girls' school and his boys' college.
At the former I picked up a new medical pupil for Agra.

The little girls seated in rows looked very pretty, and I have been given rather a good photograph of them as they appear in school. D. heard the boys read English and Persian. These inspections went on till lunch-time, and directly afterwards we drove to see Amber, the ancient capital of this State. It is a most curious place, which quite carries one back to the middle ages. There is an enormous palace, with courtyards and great open squares and roof-tops, marble openwork screens and fine gateways, overlooking the ruins of the city. We drove home by moonlight, and as we passed through the town of Jeypore I thought it looked really lovely. The outlines of the buildings are so varied and so picturesque, and the streets so wide, that the town looks very handsome by a modified light, as you lose the pink colour and the rather thin appearance which the houses have in the daytime. The Rajah who laid out Jeypore so many years ago must have been a wonderful man— he was far in advance of his age in the matter of towns, and he was very fond of astronomy and had an observatory here. He also built a tower in order to see into the courtyard where lived a lady he loved.

Saturday, 21st.—I fear you will be rather startled when you hear the way in which I spent the early morning hours from seven till nine. I had better take you quickly over the shock by telling you at once that elephants, quails, partridges, rams, pigs, deer, buffalo, and cocks *fought* before us, and at the same time I will add that we only just saw their manner of attack, and that they were carried off, or dragged away, before any one animal could hurt another. The elephants began it. We were ushered through endless courts and passages, up staircases and ramps, and along walls in the palace till we reached a round tower overlooking a great yard, which was full of men in red, with spears in their hands, while the walls all round were covered with spectators. We first of all watched the fighting elephant being unloosed—a work which had to be performed with great precaution, and all round his neighbourhood were quantities of little holes into which the men disappeared if the elephant went at them. The second elephant, who is a fighter by profession and not by nature, had a mahout on his back, while the cross and quarrelsome one was simply turned loose in the arena. The two ran at each other and pushed and pushed till the one got the other up against a wall, where he nearly fell, and then the men sent off fireworks in front of them to separate them, as the elephant with the rider on had his adversary in such a corner that he could have killed him. As it was, no one was the least the worse of the encounter. After this we wandered again ' for miles ' up and down and through the palace, and from the very top looked at the view of the town and of the surrounding hills and forts, and then on to another court where a quantity of richly caparisoned horses were shown off. Some of them did circus tricks, and two men with long spears did rather a pretty exercise on horseback. Two quails were next put down before us, and they began to jump at each other as canaries do in a cage, but they did not even get badly pecked, as we examined them afterwards. Rams and buffaloes follow the same method; they run at each other, and, their heads having met with a thud, they go on pushing till the men in attendance pull them apart. There were some little pigs, carried in men's arms, who upset each other with their snouts, but, having no tusks, they merely showed that it ' was their nature to,' and did no harm. The older pigs were rather fierce, so I got their performance stopped at once. Two hog-deer were brought forward, very curious-shaped animals that I had never seen before, but they were very friendly, and would not even pretend to fight. Though there was a total absence of cruelty in the performances, and though it was worth seeing as a peep into a bygone world, I feel almost sorry we had been present, for it does seem rather barbarous. Nor did the afternoon improve upon the morning. True, I first visited the Albert Hall, and saw there the things that are going to the Exhibition in London, arranged as they will be there —so when you visit it you can imagine how I walked about it too—and then I went on to a hospital and inspected it ; a very nice one it is, and I really hope that I may very soon see a good English lady doctor there. His Excellency meantime was out shooting, and when we joined him we found he had slain a black buck. Of course that is too European a sport to be cruel, but what we saw was a cheetah, or hunting leopard, kill a deer. The animal was in a cart, hooded, and we drove after it to a place where deer were grazing. The bullock-carts did not frighten them at all, and when we were pretty close the cheetah was unhooded, and immediately made for and chased the deer. It sprang upon one and pulled it down quickly, and the men despatched it. They had, however, to coax off the cheetah by giving it some of the blood to drink in a pan, and while it was so engaged they put the hood over its eyes again.

The evening was another scene of beautiful illumination, nautch-dancing, and fireworks. We dined at the Maharajah's palace. All the way to the town the trees were hung with coloured lamps, and when we got there we found straight lines of light running along the buildings. In one place in particular the effect was lovely. There is a square with a fountain in the centre, and all the wide streets go at right angles from it. Looking down them we saw these long lines of light, while in the square itself a temple was shaped out in fire, and behind it all rose a high hill with a golden palace on its summit and a golden 'Welcome' on its side. The word is marked out in letters fifty feet high by eight wide, and was originally done for the Prince of Wales. In the daytime the letters are white and suggestive of some advertisement, but illuminated they are lovely.

The dinner in the palace was very pretty too. It was in one of those great open places in a court—a roof supported on rows of arches and pillars. When we entered first we only saw a drawing-room, but a curtain fell to the ground and revealed the banquet spread. The colouring of the inside of the building is very brilliant, and red purdahs were let down in the outer arches, so it was quite warm and beautifully lighted. The Maharajah came in, as usual, at the end for the toasts, and the Viceroy was able to say that he had had the pleasure of investing him with his full powers during this visit. Rajahs are kept to a certain extent in leading-strings until they have proved their capacity for ruling.

The nautch which followed was pretty, because so many girls danced in it, and they had a few new figures. One was a snake dance, where they held the end of a veil in their mouths, making it look like a pipe, and then they pretended to be charming the snake, and swayed about as if following its movements.

After this we looked at some old books and arms, and moved on to a very pretty open gallery looking into a garden. Fountains were playing, illuminations were to be seen everywhere, and fireworks began. I never heard such noisy ones. If we had been besieging Jeypore we could not have made more fuss over it, and there was rather too much smoke for the light that accompanied it. I think they used too much powder. However, the whole entertainment was very magnificent and a great success. The Maharajah is very quiet and nice, and kind as a host.

Sunday, 22nd.—We walked quietly away from Jeypore this morning, getting into the train at a small station outside the Residency garden, and travelled till five o'clock, when we reached Bhurtpore.

It is quite a different place from the great city we have just left, and as we drove through the town it seemed a mere village, the crowds of inhabitants swarming on the low roofs and in the little shops being the most interesting part of it. I have already described to you the Maharajah of Bhurtpore, who visited us at Calcutta. He has made splendid preparations for us, and the Residency looks as if it had been furnished throughout with new and lovely things. I have been quite relieved to hear that they are standing decorations, for I never like to see the Rajahs put to great expense for our sakes—white satin blinds to the windows where muslin would do, and so on, through numberless extravagances.

Colonel and Mrs. Euan Smith—he is the Resident—are very pleasant hosts. She plays beautifully, and they have shown great taste in the decoration of the rooms.

Monday, 23rd.—This was a duck-shooting day. The gentlemen went out early and we joined them for luncheon, and sat about on the edge of a marsh watching the sport.

In the evening the dinner at the palace took place. It is quite curious how, with illuminations and fireworks everywhere, each place contrives to invent some entirely new variety. The illuminations here were in their way as pretty as anything we have seen, and we were able to calculate that, had the lamps been arranged in one long row, there would have been sixteen miles of them, one foot between each. The way it was done was this: from the Residency to the town there was a strong paling on each side of the road, with three rows of lights on each, and in the town the whole way down the narrow streets, and with no break in them, there were high palings with five rows of lamps, so that we seemed literally to drive through two walls of fire. There was an arch made of wooden latticework, 100 feet high and proportionately thick, which was one great mass of light;

this and the palace decorations are not included in my sixteen miles. The gateway to the palace, too, was exceedingly pretty, and the garden in the courtyard was all lighted up. The dinner was very well managed and was good and short, and the usual speeches went off well. The fireworks were very good, some of the best we have seen. There were two gigantic serpents who spat stars at each other, and some other novelties, besides some lovely sheafs of rockets. Three fires in the town burst out during the performance, but no one minded them in the least—'Oh, it's only a thatched roof, it is all right.' We drove home again through the walls of flame, and were pleased to find it only ten o'clock. To my great comfort and satisfaction I find that the horses belonging to Rajahs stand any amount of noise, fire, and confusion. I don't know how I should have survived these drives if they had had any nerves at all.

Tuesday, 24th.—We made an expedition, which took up the whole day, to visit the Fort and Palace of Deeg. We only saw from the outside the very massive walls and towers, and the great moat round the fort, but we spent many hours in the palace and its gardens. The latter are pleasanter and better kept than most I have seen, and there are very pretty low, trim hedges, and hundreds of fountains. They were turned on for us, and we got shut up in one corner by the splash and spray, and were kept close prisoners until they could be turned off again. There are several palaces in this garden, all of them looking out on to series of fountains, and all of them with the central hall open to the front

and supported on carved arches and pillars.   The open-
work carving in some of the windows was beautiful, and
in one little marble palace there is a dado inlaid with
colour which is lovely.   We were kept wandering about
for some time, and then discovered that the camels and
the elephants who carried our lunch had not arrived,
which was sad news to hungry people ; however, they
appeared at last, and after fortifying ourselves we were
conveyed to a high place to look on at an elephant fight.
Had I been told it was play or affection I could quite
have believed it.   They walked so quietly up to each
other, touched their trunks, as if to say, ' How do you
do ? ' gave each other a little push, stopped and examined
a pot which lay near to see what was in it, casually
had another push, considered whether or not they
would climb on to a little mound that was near them,
and then pushed again.   They are, however, such
great heavy beasts that one is always afraid of seeing
them hurt themselves.   The drive to Deeg was twenty
miles, and we did not get home till eight o'clock.

Wednesday, 25*th*.—We left Bhurtpore in the morning,
and on our way to Agra we visited a most interesting
and curious place called Futtehpore Sikri.   The Emperor
Akbar built it, intending it to be the capital of India ;
but it proved to be very unhealthy, and there was no
supply of water, so that it was very soon deserted, and
one sees there the spectacle of a desolate place in perfect
preservation.   The first thing to see is a most wonderful
mosque, such a great size and so beautiful.   The story
is that Akbar and his Queen arrived at this place

having just lost twin children, and it was prophesied
that they should never have another son.   However, a
holy man who lived here said that if some one gave up
his life as a sacrifice, then an heir would be born, upon
which the holy man's own child (of six months old)
spoke and said, 'I will give mine,' and died upon the
spot.   In memorial of this circumstance Akbar built
this mosque.   It is of red sandstone, the chief ornamentation round the doorways and cornices being white
marble let into the stone in mosaic patterns.   There is
one immense and splendid gateway, and a great court is
enclosed by the various buildings and covered passages,
and in the centre is a perfect gem in white marble,
which contains the sheik's tomb.   The outer walls are
carved in lace-like patterns, and in the inner chamber
is a sort of four-post bed, which is the grave; it is all
inlaid with mother-of-pearl, while the floor and walls are
marble.

The other buildings of interest are the houses of
Akbar's wives—little separate establishments; they are
of red sandstone, and the walls are carved from ceiling
to floor.   There is one curious place which is a five-
storeyed open court, each platform getting smaller till
the top one is a mere little summer-house; each one
is supported on rows and rows of pillars; from these
one looks down into a court where the Great Mogul
used to sit and play chess with live pieces, and close
to this place is a hall where he transacted business.
In the centre of it is a pillar on the top of which he
sat, and from that central spot four narrow passages
run to the four corners of the room.   In each corner

(it is said) sat one of his ministers, and from this seat of vantage he sent his orders north, south, east, and west, while the crowds of applicants or lookers-on remained below. We had only just time to see all this, to have luncheon, and to drive on to Agra so as to arrive there before dark. The Maharajah of Bhurtpore came with us, and also stays at Agra during our visit.

We are staying in our own camp, and are going to have a very quiet evening so as to be fresh for a new series of sight-seeing here. D. has been up early both yesterday and to-day for duck and buck shooting, and we have had very long drives, so we have earned a rest.

Thursday, 26th.—Perhaps I shall remember a few more details presently, but just now I can only think of the 'Taj.' The whole day furnishes but this one idea—I have seen the Taj ! You know that it was built by the Emperor Shah Jehan as a tomb for his wife, Mumtaz Mahall (the Pride of the Palace), and that he and she lie side by side within its walls. It is of white marble, and its ornamentation consists of the plain material carved, of flowers inlaid with agate, jasper, and other precious stones, and of inscriptions in the beautiful Persian character, the letters being in black marble ; it is raised on a high terrace, which has a great minaret at each corner, and according to our ideas it is more of a mosque than a tomb; it is enclosed in a walled garden, which is arranged in stiff alleys with cypress and other dark trees, and with water and fountains down the centre. You enter through a red sandstone gateway, and across this silent garden see before you the Taj. I won't attempt to describe it further. It is as if the building had a soul, as if it had been created, and not made, so mysterious is its fascination. You can't imagine a time when it was not there, or a time when busy workmen, or noise, or untidiness, or bustle, surrounded it; you feel that you could not bear to see a hammer or a tool of any kind approach it, and that it is only as a dream, as something unreal and almost sacred, that you can think of it. And there is nothing anywhere to mar the effect. When you enter and look upon the graves of Shah Jehan and his 'Chosen of the Palace,' surrounded by a marvellously beautiful screen of white marble, some one sings a chord which bursts forth in a volume of sound from the roof like an organ or a choir of angels. The echo lasts for fifteen seconds, and so quickly do the sounds succeed each other that the chord given out note by note below comes in one harmonious whole from above, and when one note alone is sung it is impossible to say where the human voice ends and the echo begins. So the Taj exerts its charm upon you, and having seen it by day you return to see it by moonlight, and wish to see it again by sunrise, and feel that, did you live at Agra, whenever you wished for peace or rest, whenever you felt sad or sorry, you would come and commune with the Taj. That is why I say that it is like a building with a soul; it exerts a fascination over everyone who sees it that its pure white colour and perfect proportions are scarcely sufficient to account for.

We also visited the Fort and palace, but having seen the same thing in a more beautiful form at Delhi I will

not tell you much about these.   There is a mosque—
court, and surrounding walls, all in white marble—which
is fine, and which has a certain grand simplicity about
it, but D. thought the details rather coarse as compared
with some others we have visited.

We were accompanied here by one of that terrible
species of bores—a guide.   'Forty-five ladies sat on this
side please, and forty-five on that, and they could see
everything please, but no one could see them—yes;'
'That is a sundial please, but the dial is gone—yes;'
'The Government restored this in 187- please'—i.e.
covered the red sandstone Hall of Audience with white
plaster!

Friday, 27th.—D. and I. visited the College and
Medical School officially; but as I am going through
it more thoroughly on Monday I will not say anything
about it now.   In the afternoon D. went to receive a
municipal address, which amused him rather, because
when he hinted at the possible necessity of imposing
additional taxation, the people cheered loudly.   I called
on Lady Lyall, and then we all met at Itmad-ud-
Doulah's Tomb.   In the distance it looks like an ivory
inlaid box, and close at hand it is very beautiful, more
completely covered with ornament than almost anything
we have seen : every bit of the whole building is inlaid
with coloured marbles, the dado in a larger and coarser
pattern, and all the rest in more delicate designs ; there
is also some very fine pierced carving and some of the
most lovely raised bas-relief marble work I ever saw.
The guide-book account of the tomb says : 'The lower

hall containing the tomb is a parallelogram of marble inlaid with coloured stones, chiefly in arabesque, with a few large flowers. It stands on a sandstone terrace 149 feet square. Four bold kiosks stand at the four corners, and in the centre is a small pavilion of rich pierced work covered with an oblong dome topped with two light pinnacles.' This tomb was erected by Itmad-ud-Doulah's daughter, Nur Jahan, wife of the Emperor Jehangir.

Rachel is reported to have said one day, 'I do so like old tombs because one always finds tea there.' This one was no exception to the rule.

I think I have forgotten to tell you that we are in our own camp now. It is quite flat and uninteresting being at home and in British territory. The men in armour, the illuminations and fireworks, and all the Oriental splendour of our progress through Rajpootana, have faded away as in a dream!

Saturday, 28th.—The Viceroy had a very hard day indeed—interviews, durbars, and institutions without end. I did not do so much, but I started with him in the morning, and after two of his visits we went to the Roman Catholic College and Convent, and to the gaol, where they make most lovely carpets, and then D. went to the Agra College, where he answered three addresses, and I returned home to have a conversation with Dr. Moir, the Officiating Principal of the Female Medical School. The Viceroy got back in time to receive, one after the other, the Maharajahs of Bhurtpore and Dholpore, and Prince Napoleon, who came to luncheon.

At three o'clock D. plunged into more interviews, and I
went to see the wife and mother of the Maharajah of
Dholpore.   The Maharajah himself was dressed for visiting and for receiving the Viceroy, and had on the most
magnificent pearls, about four rows round his neck,
and two long chains, and a sort of breastplate and
epaulettes, all of larger pearls.   When D. had paid his
visit we went for a short ride, and in the evening we
had a dinner.   Prince Napoleon dined.

Sunday, 29th.—You will have begun to think that
Sunday had dropped out of our weeks, for we were
travelling on the last two.   We were very glad to find
ourselves quiet for this one.   The changes of temperature try everyone, so hot in the day and so cold at
night, and we have all borne them better than some
other people in our camp.   We went to church in
the morning, and had meant to go once more to the
Taj, but I did not go out again, and at six in the
evening I received Sir Frederick Roberts, who had just
arrived from England, and who stays with us for a few
days.

Monday, 30th.—I visited a zenana school and a
dispensary, and went thoroughly through the Female
Medical College, where the girls were at work, listening
to lectures, attending to patients, taking pulses and tem-
peratures, &c.   However, *I* think I had better not drag
this subject into my journal, else you will have far too
much of it, as it occupies a great deal of my time and
attention.

In the afternoon we went with D. to visit the Maharajah of Bhurtpore, as he wanted to show us a new house he has just built, and then on to Sikandra, where is the tomb of Akbar. We were all in the proper frame of mind, and were prepared to be much impressed, but we were disappointed with it, and did not greatly admire it. The ornamentation is coarse, and I suppose we have seen too many lovely things lately not to have become a little critical; it is, however, considered very beautiful.

We had a dinner for the new Commander-in-Chief, and gave a 'drum' to the Agra people, and just as we were going to bed we got the very best news from Burmah. D. has been so anxious that there should be little bloodshed, and he was greatly relieved and pleased to find how well the whole thing has been managed. Everything had been done so quickly that I imagine the Burmese found their breath taken away; only one officer and three men have been killed, and I fancy very few on the other side have lost their lives. It is exactly six weeks since war was declared.

Tuesday, December 1st.—Three telegrams arrived this morning. One contained the Queen's congratulations on the success of the Burmese campaign : ' I am commanded by the Queen to express to Your Excellency the pleasure with which Her Majesty has received the news of the result of the military operations in the *Irrawaddy* Valley so effectively organised by Your Excellency's Government, and so brilliantly carried out by Her

Majesty's forces under the command of General Prendergast.'   The next telegram said : ' Her Majesty's Government offer to Your Excellency cordial congratulations
on the conspicuous success which has attended the expedition against the King of Burmah, and are glad to
express their profound satisfaction that the immediate
objects of the military operations have been attained
with so little loss of life.'   The third telegram told us of
the Duke of Somerset's death.   D. was very fond of
him, and he had always been most kind and friendly
to me.   Every fresh blank made amongst those we left
just a year ago is sad to us, and D. feels too the gradual
dying out of those amongst whom his mother spent her
youth.

The journey from Agra is quite short, and we arrived
at Gwalior in time for luncheon.   Our visit is more than
usually interesting, because the Viceroy is going to give
the Fort back to Scindia.   He has been wanting it for
years ; and when one sees how close it is to his palace,
and how completely it commands his town and his home,
one can quite understand what a thorn in his side it must
have been.   Now it is to be put into his own hands, and
he gives in return another fort and cantonment farther
away from his capital.   I believe he has only once been
into the fortress here, which shows how much he has felt
the position, for he is a Mahratta chief, a great soldier,
has a large army of his own, and cares only for it.   We
are staying in his palace—a very fine new building, with
one magnificent room, in which we lost ourselves last
night.   We were about twenty people, and were illuminated by 900 candles, and were indefinitely reproduced in

mirrors, which are opposite to each other all the way down the room.

In the afternoon D. had to be visited by and to visit the Maharajah, so his time was filled, and I thought we ladies had better go and see the Fort in the cool of the day, instead of waiting till the morning. It looks like a ' Gibraltar ' guarding this place, and is a very large and massive pile. When we reached the gate, we got on an elephant to go up the very steep ascent, and passed through more gates and along a narrow road with carvings in the rock, and then under the palace, which is very curious, and which has the remains of most brilliant decorations in coloured tiles. The rooms inside are small, but are covered with stone carvings in quite a different style from the marble work of Agra ; and at the farther end of the Fort are two temples, specimens of the oldest Hindoo architecture. They are entirely covered with deeply cut patterns in the stone, and with figures, all of which have been more or less defaced by the Mahometans, who object to representations of living creatures. These temples are put together without mortar or plaster of any kind, and are most interesting. Another very remarkable feature of this Fort is the rock sculpture, gigantic figures in stone carved in the solid rock. Most of them represent Brobdingnagian human beings, standing stiffly and undraped against the side of the hill. One cannot conceive anything more different in the way of design, execution, form, and character than the tombs and palaces we have been seeing hitherto and these old Hindoo temples and carvings at Gwalior. The rock sculptures are supposed to have been cut in 1467, but the infallible guide-book gives A.D. 274 as the date of the founding of Gwalior. It also says that the largest figure is fifty-seven feet high, and it is well to mention this, as you may have no idea. of what I mean by ' large.'

Wednesday, 2nd.—I had intended to revisit the Fort with D. in the morning, but we have been rather tried by the changing climates we have gone through, and so I thought it more prudent to avoid the hot sun and to have a quiet morning, especially as Nelly seemed a little feverish, and is better at home.

The durbar was held at three o'clock, in the great drawing-room I have mentioned before. The thrones were at one end, and the natives and soldiers in long lines on either side filled it, leaving only a pathway down the middle. It was a very fine sight. Scindia met the Viceroy in the centre of the room, and they walked hand in hand to the thrones, and soon after they had seated themselves the Viceroy read out the Foreign Office dispatch handing over the Fort to the Maharajah; and Mr. Durand repeated the same in Hindustani. Scindia made a short reply in a very low voice, and the whole thing was over. Though the Maharajah showed very little pleasure or emotion of any kind, we all knew that the great wish of his life had been fulfilled. He said to the Resident as he left, ' Now *I* must go and tell my boy,' the heir, a child of nine, to whom he is devoted, but whom we have not seen, as he is ill.

There was a great banquet in the evening, seventy-our people at table, and at the end of it Scindia came

in to propose the Queen's health, and the Viceroy's.
In his reply D. said that in the morning, speaking
as the Queen's representative, and in the name of the
Government, he had used the official and somewhat cold
and formal language necessary upon such an occasion,
but that now in his own person, as the friend and guest
of the Maharajah, he wished to congratulate him warmly
upon the signal mark of favour he had that day received
at the hands of his Sovereign.   Scindia really did look
pleased and happy, and a number of his sirdars had
come with him, whose gay dresses brightened up the
room considerably, so that the party was quite cheerful.
Fancy, however, the face of official *India*, when at
the end of H.E.'s speech a gentleman suddenly got up
and passed a eulogium on the Maharajah.   One would
have thought the end of the world had come, such looks
of blank amazement passed around !   Poor man, he was
brought to a state of ' abject apology ' soon after, and I
don't think he has heard the end of it yet : happily his
speech was short.   There were illuminations and fireworks, and so ended a great day for Scindia.

Thursday, 3rd.—We did not leave Gwalior till after
luncheon, so I drove about in the morning to see the
town, which is called Lashkar.   There are some pretty
carved arches and windows, but it is not a really interesting place.   We left with all the usual ceremonies, and
passed again through Scindia's army.   *It* is a pity that
he has put his men into helmets instead of turbans ;
a very white helmet, of a very ugly shape, which never
by any chance fits its owner, looks very bad on the top

of a dark face and a head of long black hair. All our native troops look so remarkably well in their puggarees that I wonder he does not see how much more soldierly and becoming their headdress is.

After two hours in the train we reached Dholpore, and spent a very pleasant afternoon there. The Maharajah lives in the Residency House, as he has no palace; it is a red stone house, very new looking, and not pretty outside, and seems to be set down in some fields, for there is no attempt at garden about it. Inside it is nicely furnished, and is very English-looking. The Maharajah is a perfect gentleman in every way, and I am told he is an excellent rider and sportsman. There was nothing to be seen here except some caged tigers and a herd of black bucks. The latter were in a great yard, which was intersected by low mud walls, and when a man on horseback rode after them, they positively flew over these walls, and nothing could be prettier than their graceful movements. We could see the way they doubled up for the flight, and when they were on the level ground they gave great jumps every few steps in the most light and airy manner.

After this display D. was carried off to another house, to interview the Maharajah's mother with a purdah between them. It seems that every Viceroy visits her. They had a most successful meeting. D. said to her that as she and I were members of the same Order (Crown of India) we must be sisters, and then that as we were sisters he must be her brother, and must come behind the purdah—all of which delighted her and she laughed heartily. Another great joke was that he told her he heard a man's voice behind the purdah (her little grandson's), which sent her into fresh fits of laughter, and she said to her son that 'This was something like conversation, and so very much better than the usual "How are you? I am glad to see you."' Then she sent him round a rose, and he told her that the rose would fade and the scent pass away, but that the remembrance of her gracious act would for ever remain in his heart— but that Her Highness had put him in a great difficulty, as on his return home his wife would certainly make a point of finding out who gave him the flower. D. also told her that she was the first *I*ndian princess he had conversed with, and that her grandson was the youngest prince who had ever presented him with a nuzzar. All this was quite a new way of talking, as I imagine all previous interviews had been very formal, and I believe she was delighted.

The dinner was not large, and, as the programme for the day said, the ' usual speeches ' followed. D. manages on these occasions to say something appropriate, and puts in some commendations with a *soupçon* of good advice to the Maharajah. After dinner we sat out on the steps, and saw a very amusing procession which is peculiar to Dholpore. Led horses came first, and then camels, and elephants most splendidly dressed and with beautiful howdahs on. One of these, as he passed, waved a pocket-handkerchief in his trunk, and said 'Hurrah,' and another carried a pole with a burning torch at each end of it. After the elephants came palanquins, in which sat people dressed as kings and queens and wearing masks, and little boys with masks on jumped about the road, and one car passed with two white and silver clad women standing up in it, and then a crowd of nautch-girls danced before us. We asked for the procession to come round again, and the elephants had just re-appeared upon the scene, when the fireworks began and frightened them so much that they turned tail and fled, nearly upsetting us as they ran. The fireworks were good, and some most impetuous fire-fountains were pretty, while the fire-balloons were also so successful that they appeared to form new and magnificent constellations in the sky.

Having enjoyed the evening very much, we were conducted to the train, where we spent the night, on our way to Lucknow.

Friday, 4th.—Sir Alfred Lyall, the members of the Municipal Committee, and about eleven of the ex-King of Onde's family, met the Viceroy at the Lucknow station. The Oude people had splendid jewels on their heads. One man wore a tiara on a turban with a brim to it, and drops of big emeralds hung from the edge of it all round his head. The municipal address was a particularly good one, and *I* don't say so only because it was so *very* nice to me and so cordial about my Scheme, but because it also spoke so very sensibly and with such good feeling about its own municipal duties. The Viceroy's reply was much to the point, and was an interesting one, as he entered a little into the political part of the Burmese question.

We then drove to the Government House, where we are staying with Sir Alfred and Lady Lyall, and D. held a levée at noon.

In the afternoon I gave new colours to the 2nd Battalion, Leicestershire Regiment, and made a very short speech. The ceremony is always a pretty one. The regiment gave a ball in the evening, but I had refused it for myself, and D. was to have taken the girls. At the last moment, however, Rachel could not go on account of her grandfather's death, and Nelly had not been very well the last two days, so I kept her at home, and it ended in D.'s looking in for about ten minutes and then coming home.

Saturday, 5th.—We all went to see an Exhibition ; it contains specimens of various industries in this part of India, of things going to London, and of a small loan collection. We found it very interesting. After inspecting it we saw a 'Musical Ride,' the 17th Lancers being the performers, and in the afternoon Lady Lyall had a garden party. D. had not felt well all day, and by this time he had some fever and a terrible headache, so he had to go to bed with the intention of getting up after dinner and going out to hold a durbar, or large reception. He insisted that he must go whatever happened. However, Sir Alfred Lyall assured him that it could be postponed, and so he consented to remain at home, which was fortunate, as he could scarcely speak by nine o'clock ; and, though I am sure he would have managed to go through it, he would have been much the worse for the exertion.

Sunday, 6th.—We have had to alter our plans somewhat, but I shall scarcely know till the evening how far they must be changed. D. is no worse this morning, but at any rate we must stay another day here, and must cut Cawnpore out of our programme.

It is a great disappointment to him losing this afternoon's visit to the Residency, for he has been looking forward to that for months, and General Wilson is here on purpose to show it to him, and the survivors of the Baillie Guard have come up to Lucknow for the occasion ; nor can this be merely put off till another time, for General Wilson leaves Lucknow to-night, and India in March, and the Baillie Guard are old and cannot again be summoned from their various homes. General Wilson, too, was greatly disappointed at not showing it to the Viceroy himself, for this was his own last view of a spot associated in his mind with so many miseries, so much gallantry, and such painful interest ; and it quite affected him to see again these old Baillie Guard men, whose behaviour at the siege of Lucknow he considers unsurpassed in the world's history. They were drawn up at the gate when we arrived, for I went with him, but we did not speak to them till our return, as General Wilson felt that if once he began to talk to them he would never get away. Old and feeble many of them looked, but they all had medals on their breasts and bore a soldierly appearance. They were pleased to see him, but remarked that his beard had grown white since they knew him, and then, after we had explained to them how sorry the Viceroy was to be unable to see them, they were photographed in a group. One can only appreciate their share in the defence when one sees how close the enemy were to them, how they could actually talk together, and how these men were coaxed and threatened by their own countrymen and co-religionists without the wall, and how, though uncertain whether the few Englishmen shut up in the Residency were not the only ones remaining in the country, they yet remained faithful. General Wilson was Assistant-Adjutant-General at the time, and was consequently the very best possible person to describe the whole scene, for it was his duty to be going about all day within the defences, while the other officers and men were confined each to his own particular post; and for the 145 days they were shut up, a man at one end of the place had no idea what was going on at the other. Of course it would be useless to attempt to give you a real account of what you can read in books, but *I* will just go through our walk with General Wilson and tell you a little about it.

The first thing one has to do is to imagine what the place was in 1857. Now, for miles round the Residency are green fields and trees; *then* it was a dense bazaar up to the very gates, and it is quite astonishing to see *how* close the besiegers were. There was no walled fort or city, but a sort of large garden, in which were a few gentlemen's houses and a church, completely overlooked by surrounding houses, and there was only a hastily raised mud wall to divide the enemy from the defenders. The foe outside could see every movement inside, and could take exact aim at individuals walking about. There was one path in particular which it was most dangerous to cross, as ' Johannes' House ' commanded it, and all the protection that was possible was the stretching across the road a

piece of canvas which made the besieger's shot a chance
one and not a certainty.   The men had to fight all day
and work all night, as, being so overlooked, nothing could
be done in the light; funerals, getting out stores, re-
pairing defences, every internal arrangement was necessarily carried on in the dark.   At the present moment
the Residency is a very pretty place—gay flowers, picturesque ruins—but it must have been dried up, barren,
and terrible then.   Seeing ruins made is a very different matter from contemplating them calmly years
after the destruction is accomplished.

The first place we looked at, to the right of the gateway, was the house defended by the Baillie Guard, within
speaking distance of the enemy.   It is marked all over
with shot, and bullets seem even to have taken headers
into inner courts, where people might have expected to
be safe, and left their marks there.   We next saw the
banqueting hall, the lower rooms of which were used as
a hospital, while officers lived above ; the top storey of
every building was considered unsafe for women, so they
were in a cellar below, out of which they dared not move.
In this building we saw the place where the dead were
carried each day and left till night.   Then we walked
on to the Residency House itself, saw the room where
Sir Henry Lawrence received his death-wound, General
Wilson being with him at the time.   A shell burst in it,
took off the leg of a punkah-boy sitting there, wounded
Sir Henry mortally, and rent off a portion of General
Wilson's clothes.   The smoke made it pitch dark, and
he said to Sir Henry, ' Are you hurt ? '   ' I am killed,'
he replied.   On this building the English flag floated

every day; it might be shot down or torn, but as sure as the morning dawned it was in its place again. Next came a spot where an officer and fifty men lived in a hole in the ground, all the time watching the low mud wall and having constant conflicts with the enemy. Then the church, with the doorway cut behind the altar, out of which the stores were got at night, and all round which one sees the tombstones of those who died: memorials of them, but not marking their actual resting-places, as no distinctions were made, and all were buried together. The most interesting is that of 'Sir Henry Lawrence, who tried to do his duty. May the Lord have mercy on his soul.' After this we visited some buildings which were outside the Residency, but within the defences, and in which women lived below and men above, surrounded always by hot fighting. We saw the spot where 'Johannes' House' was, and listened to a vivid description of the manner in which it was blown up; and so on we went from post to post, General Wilson giving us a little account of all that happened in the most interesting way, straight from his heart as it seemed to come, and without any unnecessary details. The last house we saw was the one in which Sir Henry Lawrence breathed his last. The rebels, seeing that some important person was carried there, immediately turned their guns on it, and his nephew, George Lawrence, was wounded at the door of the room where his uncle lay dying.

When the Mutiny was over the native city was destroyed, and they say that great sums of money must be buried on the spot, for the panic-stricken inhabitants fled and left all, and when they returned again they found a grass plain, and could not possibly tell where their houses had been, or where their treasure was. Now, I really must not say any more about this, but you see it was very disappointing that D. missed it. He still has some fever, and so we have given up all the functions here, as well as going to Cawnpore and Benares, and now hope to leave this on Thursday, and to go straight to Calcutta.

Monday, 7th.—I went to the Exhibition for an hour in the morning, as it was a zenana day, and *I* had promised to go. Most of the ' zenana ' ladies were English, but there were I suppose about thirty really purdah who may have liked to see me. The rest of the day I nursed D., who keeps nearly to the same point, neither better nor worse.

Tuesday, 8th.—I did not go out till six o'clock, when I went with the rest of the party to see the *I*mambarah illuminated. It is a hall, a courtyard, and a mosque, which fell into our hands at the time of the Mutiny, and was only given back to the Mahometans last year. The outside was brilliantly illuminated, and the great room, which is 163 feet long and 49 feet high, and which is, they say, the biggest room in the world, was also lighted up. It contains the tomb of its founder, and is a semi-sacred place. I felt quite sorry that, so much trouble having been taken, I was the only person to profit by it, and *I* was nearly covered up in the gold garland prepared for the Viceroy.

Wednesday, 9th.—D. is decidedly better to-day ; but as

he is not allowed to travel till next Monday, I will send this off now. I had intended our tour to have been so beautifully rounded off at Calcutta on the 12th, the very day we arrived there last year, but this fever altered all our plans.

Saturday, 12th.—I have already given you an account of my doings last Sunday ; but, as this whole week has been one of beef-tea, quinine, arrowroot, thermometer, doctors, nurses, hot bottles, and pulse, I begin again from Saturday, 5th, just to tell you that I have passed almost my whole time in the sick-room, and that fireworks, illuminations, and grand processions no longer occur daily.

I did the nursing myself for two or three days, and discovered a wonderful capacity for waking up at odd moments, but then the doctor interfered, and I got a nice respectable Eurasian woman to help me.

D.'s temperature never went quite up to 102°, but it hovered about 100° for many days, and it is only to-day (12th) that it was normal.

It is a great mercy for us that we were here, for Lady Lyall is so kind, and an invalid has everything of the best in this most hospitable house.

Talking of Indian houses reminds me that perhaps I have never told you their great peculiarity, which is the public character of all the rooms. I have not yet been in one room, whether in my own house at Calcutta or in anybody else's abode, in which you could say, 'Well, no one can come in here.' You may lock one door, or two doors, or three, or four, or five, but then there are the one, two, three, four, or five windows opening on

to the verandah, along which everyone may pass, and
if your servants think you particularly want to be alone
their natural curiosity leads them to creep in silently and
constantly by one of the unguarded entrances—to show
you some extraordinary attention.

Wednesday, 16*th.*—Monday was a bad day with D.,
and it was a relief on Tuesday morning to hear that we
might start for home.   He was weak and had to be carried
to the carriage, but he seemed no worse for the journey,
and was able to walk and to put on an air of convalescence
when we got to Calcutta.   We remained in the train, but
did not travel by night, and we arrived this afternoon.
We thought it best to spare D. a public entry, so we
meekly and modestly drove up with a pair of horses, no
troops out and no fuss, but a great crowd of natives in
the street.

At Government House we had the joy of finding
Archie, also Fred and Blanche and their baby boy awaiting us !   They have just arrived from England.

Thus ends our first year in India.   In the way of
business it has been a most eventful one, crisis after crisis
coming on.   The Bengal Rent Bill, the Afghan compli-
cation, the strengthening of our frontier, the Burmese
War, and many minor difficulties have all had to be dealt
with.   We sincerely hope that the coming year may be
a less eventful one.

CHAPTER VI

December 17th to 24th.—Our second season at Calcutta starts with much unpacking. There are the things
which were left behind last March, there are those which
have come from Simla, those which have been on tour,
and the new clothes arrived from England; they are all
soldered up in tin and wrapped in paper and screwed
down in wooden cases, so that even when they have
been dug out they have to be sorted and put here and
there, and we have to try to remember where this picture hung, where that bit of china lay, and to wonder
what we can do with all the old papers and letters and
photographs and bills and other accumulations of the
year. I assure you it is no joke, especially when we
recollect that we are only re-settling for two or three
months, and that in a very few weeks the packing-cases
will have to be filled again. It makes me understand
how people come to be lazy about beautifying and
arranging this lovely house, and how a spirit of ' anything will do for such a short time ' creeps in. When
one first arrives in the country, one imagines this palace

is to be one's home, but six months in the Simla cottage soon undeceive one.

The new clothes are of course deeply interesting— they are our great stand-by for the year; and as we certainly have to pay for them, though we have been unable to choose them, it is equally certain that we must wear them, whether we like them or no.

The only difference in our house-arrangements down-stairs is that, having created a little room at the back of my drawing-room which I meant to give Terence, I have taken it as a business-room for myself. I thought the ' Fund ' would make me untidy, and that it was necessary to have a barren-looking chamber in which baskets of papers for the Honorary Secretary of the Central Com-mittee, &c., &c., could be set forth and remain undis-turbed. My own pink drawing-room, into which this room opens, has been re-covered with silk, and over that with chintz, so that on ordinary occasions I look less smart than before, when I was always in silk, but then at dinner parties my chairs and sofas will burst forth into most lovely blushes! Mixed up with these house-hold and wardrobe preoccupations has been some care to be taken of the Viceroy, whose levées and drawing-rooms have been a subject of anxiety to us. He recovers his strength slowly, and at last we persuaded him to put off the levée for ten days, and to be content with the drawing-room now. We had it on the 22nd, and it was D.'s first appearance since his illness.

The Calcutta races began on Wednesday, and for the first time in my life I saw a really exciting race. Lord William brought out two horses from England, and one broke down yesterday, which was a great disappointment and loss, and so we were anxious that the other should win to-day. The horses all kept together till near the end, and then *Metal* came on and won amidst great applause and tremendous excitement.

Christmas Day, 1885.—Again this year we had the good fortune to receive our English letters on Christmas morning. It is so nice because it makes one feel less far away when the good wishes and the remembrances from home come exactly on the right day. The enlarged family party also made itself felt, as when we came down to breakfast there were more people to exchange greetings with, and there were more mysterious parcels lying about. The breakfast-table was laden with gifts from Hermie and Victoria, and from you, and from all of us here to each other, and there were toys for the baby, who, however, did not much appreciate any of them.

In the afternoon we went down to the Botanical Gardens in the launch, and walked about there, and saw some of our countrymen and women dancing quadrilles and waltzes on the grass, some of the men looking rather unsteady after their lunch, others performing most wonderful steps. We drove back on Lord William's coach.

After dinner my ' children' insisted upon having snapdragon and Christmas games of that kind, so we all joined. Lady Sykes was the only stranger, and she was quite ready to play.

D. is quite well now, but he has to take care not to get a chill, and it is really very wintry weather.

Barrackpore: Sunday, December 27th.—The weather is decidedly colder than it was last year, and the Bougainvilleas and the convolvulus are doubtful about coming out. Still Barrackpore looks lovely, and we enjoy it as much as ever.

In the afternoon we went to see the elephants, and were amused by the performance of one in the water. A man stood on its back, and made it go right under and then roll round while he balanced himself upon its slippery side as men in a circus do on a revolving globe; and when it came out of the water it was made to jump, an elephantine hop; and the mahout told us that this obedient animal had twice sent him into hospital by taking him up in his trunk and injuring him. I do not wonder that this beast is sometimes savage, for man has behaved badly to him, having blinded him on purpose to make him milder and more useful.

Monday, 28th.—The household were greatly excited this morning, as they went out hunting for the first time with Lord Herbrand's hounds. The girls and all were off at 6.30, and seem to have enjoyed themselves immensely; they had a short run after a fox, and eventually killed a cat. Lord Herbrand has just bought a pack with a view to hunting jackal at Barrackpore, and this adds greatly in the eyes of many people to the attractions of the place.

Friday, January 1st, 1886.—The last week of the old year was spent quietly enough—riding, driving, a race or two, a little polo, a committee-meeting, an infinite amount of letter-writing and bill-paying, a few visits from various people, civilities to guests, and such like ' common tasks ' filled the seven days, and on the last night of it we had rather a pleasant dinner. It was extremely well chosen (by me), and there were several tourists to give variety to it, and we had a Hungarian violinist who played beautifully for us in the evening, and then our guests dispersed, some to see the new year in at a dance, and some at church, while we meant to sleep it in, but were kept awake by the jingling of bells and the shrieks of steam-whistles. In the evening we had the usual big dinner—seventy-eight men and five ladies. It was rather pleasant this year, as I knew most of our guests. We could just fit into the Marble Hall without overflowing beyond the pillars, and the banquet looked bright, and was well and quickly served.

When we five ladies went up to the drawing-room we found some of the native officials who don't dine waiting there, and *I* had some very interesting conversation with one of them on the subject of my Scheme. In the evening, too, the Maharajah of Durbungha told me he was going to build and establish a female dispensary, and *I* am to go and lay the stone (his place is only twenty hours off—a mere nothing). He had been to speak to D. about this before, and *I* am greatly pleased at the idea, as of course my great wish is to see native gentlemen do the thing for themselves—and these new establishments started by them are far more valuable than money subscribed to my Fund.

Tuesday, 5th.—Sir George Bowen, with a son and a daughter, arrived from Hong Kong on Sunday. Monday was a hard day for D., and we had to leave Barrackpore early, as we had so much business on hand. We breakfasted on board the launch as we came down, which was rather pleasant. The girls had been out hunting still earlier, but on this occasion had neither 'found' nor 'killed.'

At eleven o'clock the Council met on most important business. Sir Auckland Colvin made a financial statement bringing in an Income-Tax Bill, and D. spoke afterwards, justifying the measure and explaining the policy of the Government. The Viceroy's speech seems to have given great satisfaction to all those who were present, and I now begin to doubt whether the execrations which I expected to see heaped upon his devoted head will be uttered in a very violent manner by the press. In the evening he had a very large levée. I believe there were about 1,500 gentlemen at it—the house was overflowing with them; they passed, I am told, on an average of about sixty every three minutes, and when we wanted to go to bed—I mean we ladies, who for the evening were behind the purdah—my guests could not get to their chambers at all. First they tried to get through the drawing-room—the entrance to it was barricaded, and it was full of men; the second floor was the scene of the levée itself; and the bottom of the house was the fullest of all, for everyone assembled there to await their carriages and to get their coats, which lay in gigantic bundles on the floor ; so the ladies made their way up again, and, finding themselves condemned to remain alone in the ball-room till the levée should be over, and being tempted by the waltzes and the polkas which the band was discoursing, set to and danced together in the dim light reflected from the drawing-room. Our own rooms lay on the side of the house to which access was possible, and we had said good-night to them, thinking they would get round to theirs through the lower regions.

Wednesday, 6th.—My Committee and *I* made all our arrangements for the public meeting we are to have here on the 27th. *I* do not trouble you with much, ' Fund ' information, but I have one meeting every week, and often see individuals on particular points, write and receive letters, and keep a record of all that I do, with regard to this matter, in a very dry and business-like way.

As soon as *I* was free in the afternoon I went off with some of my family to a little garden party at Mrs. Hope's, and in the evening we had the state ball. I thought it went off very well—not at all too crowded, very good dancing, satisfactory supper—so I am in hopes people enjoyed it.

Thursday, 7th.—Terence and Mr. Rosen arrived early this morning. They had two very rough days on their way out, during which two passengers put on their best bonnets, packed their trunks, and prepared to take to the boats.

Archie was in waiting on His Excellency for the first time, and came in for a full day. First of all he sat in an office from 10 to 1.30, receiving Government secretaries at intervals and showing them in to the Viceroy ; then came a durbar for the new Maharajah of Kashmir, a not very satisfactory chief, said to be very superstitious, and to go to bed encircled by chalk lines to keep the spirits off. I meant to have looked on at this ceremony, but a doctoress who came to see me kept me until it was all over, and so I missed it; but as all the people are in mourning for the late Maharajah they wore white, and the dresses were not worth seeing. Directly after lunch H.E. returned the visit, and then, coming back for me, we all went off to present colours to the 18th Regiment of Bengal Infantry. The manœuvres, and my speech, and the whole ceremony went off well, and 'one of the oldest native regiments in Her Majesty's Indian army' looked very fine and soldierlike. Mr. Wingfield and Mr. Vincent dined with us. We were rather sleepy after last night's ball and our long day's work, and were glad to go to bed early.

Friday, 8th.—We all went off in the afternoon to see the ex-King of Onde's gardens. He is an old gentleman, who is described to me as being utterly devoid of every moral sense. He never does any good to anybody, and he spends his monthly lac of rupees in keeping 25,000 pigeons, whose food costs him 400*l.* a year; in buying sick creatures which the animal merchants sell him just before they reach their last gasp; in building houses for those of them that survive; and in the partial maintenance of several hundred ladies. These latter have often complained to the Government about his treatment of them, but, in answer to an official remonstrance against their inordinate numbers, he added ninety more to his zenana the day he received it. The place is curious to see, viewed as this ex-king's hobby, but in itself is merely a small zoological garden. The pigeons, who fly in flocks and obey signals, are pretty, and there are whole fleets of pelicans sailing about on tanks, and long-legged birds with decidedly light fantastic toes who hop about ridiculously, and peacocks perching in the trees, and fox-houses which smell atrociously, and dwarfish-looking woolly camels who provide material for soft shawls, and rams who must get terrific headaches as they clash their foreheads together with a portentous thud, and real live poisonous snakes who, being tumbled out of the earthen pots in which they live, sit up glaring viciously and licking their lips as they gaze around; they are picked up with an iron hook, and caught by the tail and put back again by men who seem to have little fear, though it made me shudder to see them handle such dangerous reptiles. The less poisonous snakes live in a palace built for them of concrete, and wriggle in and out of this erection, and fascinate toads which are found in their neighbourhood, placed there by some kindly hand. Close to this serpent-palace is a cottage for a few queens.

I need not tell you that the King of Oude has *not* subscribed to my Fund, and you would be horrified if you could see the holes in which his retainers live outside his walls.

Well, we walked about and looked at all the creatures, and were spit at by llamas and screeched at by the parrots, and then drove home again and prepared for a big party—a 'drum' to which native gentlemen come as well as all the European society here. We had it in the Marble Hall, which looked very fine, and it was quite full, and the dresses and the varieties of people looked very gay, and I liked it, and I think it was a success. The Maharajah of Kashmir came, and politely said we had introduced him into Paradise.

Tuesday, 19*th*.—D. has gone to Delhi for the manœuvres, and during his absence we have taken an extra day or two at Barrackpore, and I really believe that the more I see of it the more delightful I think it. We do so enjoy the flowers—lovely roses of gigantic size in the greatest profusion, and violets, and such convolvulus and Bougainvilleas and Bignonias climbing all about! It is a most perfect little place.

Thursday, 21*st*.—D. returned from Delhi, and I must now try and tell you all he has told me of his adventures there. He arrived at the little house he had taken for himself near the camp on Sunday night. On Monday he received visits from the foreign representatives, the Commander-in-Chief, &c., and there were some sports in the afternoon. Sir Frederick Roberts opened them by a successful tent-pegging feat, and that was very effective, as everybody said no other commander-in-chief in the world could have attempted such a thing; and the day seems to have been fine and pleasant. As he could do nothing for them himself, D. proposed to breakfast with the foreign officers in their camp on Tuesday morning, which pleased them much, and over the coffee he was inspired to propose the healths of all their emperors, kings, or chiefs, with a nice allusion to each one; finally, his inspiration led him to wind up by saying that he regretted that his visit to Burmah

would prevent his entertaining them himself, but that
he would commission his daughter to give them a ball at
Calcutta, so that they might see how effective was the
artillery of our ladies' eyes, and so on.   He pretended to
be much alarmed as to what I should say to all this,
and was astonished at the comparative calmness with
which I heard it ; but the reaction came later, for it did
not dawn upon me for twenty-four hours that anyone
took the ball part of it *au sérieux*, and when I saw
in the telegram that these gentlemen were coming to
Calcutta for Lady Helen Blackwood's ball, I only remarked sententiously that 'Viceroys must not joke.'
At last it was borne in upon me that it was no joke,
and so, after a little consideration, I asked D. to put off
starting for Burmah for one day, and to have this ball
the night before our departure.   So we telegraphed to
the foreign officers to say that, if they could so arrange
it, we hoped they would dine with us on Saturday and
come to a ball on Monday, and that we would remain
here to receive them—and they have accepted ; but, as
you may perceive, *I* have got far away from D.'s breakfast on Tuesday morning.   Whatever the fate of the
ball may be, the speech was a great success, and, when
it was over, devoutly hoping that the weather would
keep up, everyone set off for the great review.   The
Viceroy in a frock-coat and tall hat was the one un-
uniformed person present.   Everybody else was gorgeous.
But what is the use of gorgeousness when the rain comes
down in torrents ?   What is the use of having a lovely
tricolour puggaree round your helmet, as the Frenchman
had, if it melts into streams of red and blue over your

face ?—or of deep red cuffs, like the Prussians, if they only serve to dye your hands ? The second Russian officer, a Chevalier Garde, got hit by his horse's head as he was mounting, and had to retire for the day. Lord Reay was ill, and D. insisted on his going home too, but everybody else sat for four hours in the drenching rain. The Viceroy gained great renown for the cheerful manner in which he bore his fate. He put on no great-coat, and at the end people said he looked as smart as when he arrived. The A.D.C.s were very cold, and had difficulty in preventing their horses from sitting down, while some of the steeds had to be supported by draughts of whisky. Fred says he felt the water running down his back into his boots, and then heard the sound of it inside the leather. The poor troops did splendidly, and the only regiment which marched badly might be excused, for the men's loose slippers stuck in the mud. Was it not unfortunate and provoking?

In the evening there was a damp reception in the Commander-in-Chief's camp; and the next morning the troops, looking as clean and smart as ever, lined the streets for the Viceroy's departure, and the foreign officers and military grandees appeared in full dress at the station.

Tuesday, 26th.—Doctor Findlay and Lord Herbrand have been away for a week looking for tiger in the Sunderbunds; the former returned to-day, but Lord Herbrand remains in pursuit of a terrible man-eater who has killed twenty-three men in the last nine months. This beast was absent from his accustomed haunts for some days, but he had just returned before Dr. Findlay left, and so Lord Herbrand was encouraged to wait for him, as the whole neighbourhood is desperately anxious that he should be killed.

Dr. Findlay had only shot some alligators and some deer, the latter being brought to his feet by a man who imitated a monkey and so attracted the deer to the tree in which he was jumping about and chattering. The clever deer said to themselves, 'That monkey will knock down the leaves and the fruit; come, let us stand under the place where he is;' and this reasoning brought them to their death. The pursuit after tiger in the Sunderbunds is very exciting; the jungle is so thick that, even though the sportsman can see nothing, he may feel pretty sure that one is quite close to him, and in this case they found afterwards, by the foot-marks, that a tiger had actually been following them all day. Lord Herbrand spent twenty-four hours in a cage, and Dr. Findlay joined him for twelve of them, but they both went to sleep at last, and then woke to find that the tiger had certainly been to see them, as his marks were all round the bars through which they meant to shoot him. It sounds creepy, I think.

I have not told you about the racing here this year, which seems to be nearly as dangerous a sport as can be indulged in. At one steeplechase Captain Leonard Gordon had a severe fall, and is still wearing a sling; and last week, out of eight horses, five fell, one was killed and one broke its tail, so I am in hopes that steeplechases will go out of fashion. At the flat races yesterday two horses had a collision, and the jockeys were both badly hurt. The ground is so frightfully hard here that a fall becomes very serious—and I suppose all the riders are not fine performers.

Wednesday, 27th.—Lord Herbrand returned home without his tiger ; seven roamed about him and ate four bullocks which he had set as bait for them, but he never got a chance of shooting at them.

This was a great day for me, and rather a nervous one. The big meeting inaugurating my Fund took place, the Viceroy in the chair. I never felt so much anxiety at a public meeting before, but now this Scheme is really started, and I trust it may go on as well as it has begun. The meeting lasted till 7.30, and we had to hurry home, dress for dinner, and go off afterwards to a ball at Belvedere. D., Nelly, and *I* remained there only one hour ; Rachel, Blanche, and some others came away later, and Archie and the rest of the party stayed till the end. We had the best of it, however, for at eleven o'clock the weather was lovely ; after twelve there were showers, and still later a downpour which made supper in a tent very disagreeable and most injurious to gowns ; indeed, at the very end the tent came down, burying a drummer-boy, crushing the viands, and getting a hole burnt in itself.

Saturday, 30th.—I was to have had a meeting of my Committee on Friday to wind up some of my affairs before starting for Burmah, but the Legislative Council sat so long that neither Mr. Ilbert nor Sir Steuart Bayley could come, and we were not able to get through much business. I was therefore obliged to have another to-day. We are beginning to meet with some of the little troubles that one must expect in working such a large concern.

I rode out early this morning to see the *Clive*, the ship in which we go to Burmah. We take some horses with us. It would astonish the English mind to see what globe-trotters our horses are. They did a great part of our tour this autumn. They went to the Delhi Manœuvres, and now they are coming to Mandalay.

The foreign officers have arrived, and we had a state dinner and a concert for them ; the Hungarian violinist Remenyi played, and we had a very pleasant evening— eighty people at dinner, and about sixty more afterwards. The music was in the drawing-room and a buffet in the ball-room, which opens into it with pillars, so that those who preferred talking to listening were able to stroll away and be happy in their own way.

Tuesday, February 2nd.—I do not know whether you have read about the revolution in Nepaul and the murder of the Maharajah Sir Runodip Singh, the Prime Minister and ruler, which took place last November. He was lying on a bed in a small room in his palace, when four of his nephews came in, and, pretending to show him a new rifle, shot him dead. His wife, the Bari Maharani, and the Jethi Maharani, the mother of the real heir, took refuge in the Residency, went on into British terri-tory, and are now in Calcutta. The Bari Maharani wrote and asked me to see them, and I was allowed to do so as an expression of sympathy with them in their grief. Unfortunately the widow was ill, and could not come,

but the Jethi Maharani, who saw the man shot, and who
is also a widow, came, and a more extraordinary figure I
never saw.   Her appearance deserves minute description.
My first view of her was that of a mass of light gauze
above, and a pair of legs clothed in loose white trousers
below.   Having conducted this avalanche of gauze to a
sofa, I had time to study details.   The thin pink and
yellow striped material was not a petticoat, and I am
quite at a loss to imagine how it was put on, or how
many hundred yards were in it.   It looked just as if a
great piece had been unrolled, and unrolled, in a heap
on the floor, and then picked up and half wound round
and half carried by the wearer.   When she sat down
it was in a great fluff, and when she got up she took it
in her arms, and it overflowed everything, except the
trousers.   The body was made tight, and she wore
pink mittens on her hands.   Another wonderful part
of her was her head.   Her hair is jet black, and it was
combed up from the back, and two very thick plaits
were arranged across the front, one on the top of the
other.   She had a straight fringe, and one long thin
corkscrew curl on each side of her face.   On her cheek
there was a large round red mark painted, and during
the interview she kept putting her finger, wrapped in her
handkerchief very carefully, first into the corner of one
eye and then into the other.   I really did not see that
she was stopping her tears until later when she broke
down a little more.   Her brother, who wore uniform and
a small round cap with a chin-strap, was very deaf.
He and an English doctor who was interpreting for me
stood in front.   She and I sat side by side on the

sofa, and the maid, who was dressed like her mistress and who had a terrible squint, stood behind. I spoke to the doctor, and the doctor whispered into the ear of the brother, who, folding his hands before him, whispered into the ear of his sister; and we none of us said much to the purpose.

Then I took her hand and walked with her to the top of the staircase, and then ran to a window to see how she would get her skirts into the carriage.

Last night we had such a pretty ball to the foreign officers. New lights were put up over all the archways, the men were in uniform and the ladies very smart, and everything looked as nice as possible; but I have no time to write more to-day, as I am off to Burmah to-morrow, and I leave this behind me to be posted next mail.

CHAPTER VII

BURMAH AND MADRAS

FEBRUARY 3 TO MARCH 8, 1886

Wednesday, February 3rd.—We bade farewell to the stay-at-home portion of our family this morning, and set off on our way to Burmah, with Archie, Lord W. Beresford, Major Cooper, the Doctor, Mr. Mackenzie Wallace, and Mr. McFerran in attendance.   A short journey by train and half an hour in the launch brought us to the *Clive*, a fine ship belonging to the Indian Marine.   We were joined by the Commander-in-Chief and his suite of four officers, and by Miss Moore, whom we are taking to Rangoon.   Captain Hext, a sort of Indian First Lord and an Honorary A.D.C. to the Viceroy, is in command of us.   We have our own servants, our own cooks, our own horses, cows, calves, chickens, sheep, and quails on board.   The sea is calm, and we make a prosperous start, go on smoothly all day, and drop our pilot in the evening; all dine together, and then sleep comfortably in our spacious cabins.

Saturday, 6th.—I do not mean to give you a detailed account of an uneventful, and therefore pleasant, voyage.

We enjoyed it very much; and although we did not get quite away from posts and telegrams, we did have a certain amount of rest. All Wednesday we had hanging over us the possibility of sending letters by the pilot, and all Friday the necessity of trying to catch the mail on Saturday morning, and then to-day came telegrams about the new Ministry, vague utterances upon the *Irish* Question, and in fact all sorts and kinds of information more or less interesting. Without going into too much detail, however, you may like to know a little about our voyage.

We entertain all the officers on board, so we have a long dinner-table, and for breakfast and lunch place it on deck; then we read, and talk, and play quoits, and have a little singing, and I am rather industrious and finish off an article upon my Scheme which has been hanging like a log round my neck. Sir Frederick Roberts disappears a good deal either to sleep or to write; Colonel Chapman is not very well, and Major Chamberlain is always miserable at sea, so that the army is in a much less flourishing condition than the civil department. The Viceroy himself is, of course, quite the sailor.

This morning, after catching the mail, we had some hours to spare before entering the Rangoon river, so we anchored and read all those telegrams before alluded to; and later on, Mr. Bernard, the Commissioner, came on board, and D. and he discussed the Burmese Question together; and we changed from yachting into Viceregal clothes, and the steamer moved on, and every moment the scene became more lively and more interesting.

The river itself is simply liquid mud, flowing at an extremely rapid rate; the banks are low and green, and no high land is visible anywhere. All sorts of picturesque boats are moving about. There are big rice-boats laden with their merchandise, and crowds of tiny row-boats with two men in each, the boat having a very sharp point at the bow, which widens out into two points at the stern in triangular fashion; the men are extinguished in large hats with pointed crowns. These little boats come out to bargain with the larger ones, and when the bargain is made a flag is stuck on the rice-boat to show which firm has purchased its cargo. As we advance we gradually catch sight of the great Pagoda at Rangoon— it is just like a big bell, and is the only building to be seen from a distance—and then the men-of-war come in sight, and the reception begins. The ships are dressed, the yards are manned, and great clouds of smoke and booming cannon announce the Viceroy's approach. We could only get up to the landing-place very slowly, as the current was strong, so we had plenty of time to examine the scene. The banks were a perfect mass of people, and there were gardens and palm-trees, and very pretty Swiss-cottage sort of houses beyond them, and more crowds visible in the distance; then on the wharf, which was laid with red cloth, were Infantry, Regulars and Volunteers, and bishops, and ladies, and town councillors, all waiting, and behind them what do you think? Why, the gateway of Killyleagh and the tower on the Town Rock, all in canvas, but exact representations of the solid stone.

The prolonged agony of arrival being over, we landed

and the Viceroy inspected the Guards and made a speech to the Volunteers, and all the people round were presented to him, and I gazed at the Town Councillors, whose hair is arranged in a tight knot at the top of their heads with a fillet of muslin tied round it, and then we walked on through the gateway and found ourselves in a great covered place full of European and Burmese ladies and gentlemen, and an address was read and replied to. I was given a bouquet, and then on we walked to the carriage.

We were escorted by quite a regiment of mounted Volunteers, the chargers being the smallest ponies you ever saw a man ride, and we drove at a foot pace for three miles to the Resident's house. Such a drive!—the streets packed with a picturesque crowd of Indians, Burmese, Chinamen, Karens, &c., &c., for the number of nationalities is too great to be learnt in a day, and all the people so good-humoured and merry-looking, and dressed in such gay colours. Almost each nationality had put up an arch, and each arch was double, and was filled with the people who had put it up— the Chinese arch with Chinese people, the Burman arch with Burmese people, and so on; and generally, as we went through, a bouquet, or a wreath of flowers, or a shower of rose-leaves, was thrown into the carriage. One arch was full of the ladies of the place; and very pretty and smart they' looked—perhaps a little like big dolls out of a Japanese shop. They all had flowers in their hair, and a very tight petticoat, and their bodies tied round under the arms with a sort of bandage, the arms and neck being bare, or merely covered by a transparent jacket. They either carry or throw over their shoulders a bright-coloured soft silk scarf. They look very decent and modest in their dress, for they have no more figure than the above-named dolls, and the 'bandage' therefore is quite sufficient and quite proper.

As we got out of the town we passed the houses of the richer inhabitants, such very pretty wooden villas surrounded by nice gardens, with porches covered with creepers; and at last we arrived here, feeling quite tired after the excitement of the day. Not that the day was over by any means. Oh no, the dinner and reception were to come. But I have not yet told you about the weather, and you must be quite longing to know whether it rained or not. It did not rain, and it was delightfully sunny and pleasant; but had we kept to our original programme, and had we not waited at Calcutta to enter- tain the foreign officers, we should have come in for the Viceroy's usual downpour. *It* did rain here for four days, and the arches were put up with difficulty. The Burmese ones are most delicate structures, and with seven roofs taper away into nothing at the top. This is the Royal shape, and this is the first time a seven-roofed pagoda has been put up for such a purpose. Now that poor Theebaw has been extinguished, I suppose the people look forward to seeing no more Royal visitor than a Viceroy, so they have given him the seven roofs.

It is fine weather, but it is not warm, and we suffer from all the preparations that have been made to keep the house cool. Take my bed-room, for instance. A wide open-work lattice runs round the top of it, a large open archway lets in the air over each door, a strip of wood in the centre of the wall separates it from other rooms in which the same airy system is carried out; the windows are made without glass, and punkahs hang both outside and inside the mosquito-curtains.

There was a big dinner of sixty people, which lasted two hours, and I don't think there can be sixty doors in the room, but there appeared to be one at each person's back, and still the punkahs were kept going. D. had a little cold, and I was quite frightened about him, and asked to have this cold-giving machine stopped for a few minutes, but he shook his head at me, and it went on again. The party was cold too; the room was quite open, and it was chilly in the extreme—in fact, hot sal volatile and a mustard-poultice were the results; but we did our duty. We were introduced to everybody, and found out exactly what they thought of the weather, and they feared we must find it very hot after Calcutta; and when we explained with pride that we enjoyed much greater warmth there, they were sorry for us, and glad that they did not live in such a hot climate. I also found out that the whole society have been in Rangoon about one year, which seems curious; but whether they have been here one year or fifty, as about three people have, they all feel hot.

I will now throw in some little scraps of information for your benefit.

The Burmese women are great personages, and play a great part in their households. They choose their own husbands and divorce them when they like, retaining their own property and all that they have earned; they are at liberty to marry again, whether as widows or as *divorcées.* Mr. Bernard told me that when the last census came in, he thought the number of women who said they could read and write was small, so he made enquiries, and from all parts of the country young ladies replied that they did not like to say they could read, lest young gentlemen, learning the fact, should write to them.

The Karens, whom I mentioned casually, are said to be the pre-Burman inhabitants of the country. Great numbers of them are Christians, and they are a more plodding and steady race than the Burmese.

You may also like to know that my room is swarming with lizards, that Major Cooper has killed a scorpion in his, and that a humming-bird has built its nest in the silk tassel of a Chinese lantern in the verandah, and did not even mind its being lighted last night. I have forgotten to tell you sooner that we are staying with Mr. and Mrs. Bernard. He is the Chief Commissioner of Lower Burmah, and he will go up to Mandalay with us. Both he and his wife are very nice, and have been most kind and hospitable to us.

I must end abruptly here, for the mails go off unexpectedly, and I am called upon at all sorts of odd times to be ready with my letters. I am quite sorry to send off such a meagre account of my first Burmese experiences.

Sunday, 7th.—After a very quiet morning spent in the house, we went for a drive before evening church. Through a real willow-pattern garden we made our way to the entrance of the great Pagoda. This is guarded by two gigantic and grotesque white stone dogs, their faces painted red and blue. Passing them, we walked up a great flight of steps through a colonnade covered in by a series of seven-roofed pinnacles. I cannot find out the correct name for this style of building, but the roofs gradually diminish to a point, and one sees them in all Chinese pictures. When, as in this case, they rise one after the other up the side of a hill, they look very pretty indeed. Within this covered way were all sorts of people with stalls, selling little coloured candles which people buy and offer to Buddha; dolls and curious toys, and paper flowers were also for sale, and there were groups of the blind, the halt, and the maimed, and lepers asking charity.

The nuns, who all seem to be old women, and who are clad in white, with bare, bald heads, sit by the way too, telling their beads, and monks are to be seen everywhere.

Every Burman has for some time during his life to be a Pohngee, or monk. He may remain in the monastery a day, a year, or his whole life, but his entrance is always a great function, and it seems to be something like the Sikh baptism or like our own Confirmation. The proper thing to do is to remain at least one season of Lent in a retreat, but the moment a man feels that he cannot keep the vows he returns to the world. These monks all wear the most picturesque yellow drapery, and of course there were numbers of them all about the Pagoda.

The Pagoda is in the centre of a plateau which is quite covered with temples to Buddha. It is one of the most extraordinary and unquiet-looking places I ever saw. I could not help thinking of the calm simplicity of the Taj, and contrasting it with the glitter and the odds and ends of buildings here. I don't suppose greater contrasts could be imagined ; yet it is very grand in its way. The Pagoda itself is like a gigantic hand-bell. It is gilt, and is 370 feet high and 11,000 feet in circumference. It is solid, and was built to hold three hairs from the Lord Buddha's head. All round it is a row of smaller ' hand-bells,' each one a 'work of merit ; ' that is to say, each is put up by a Buddhist to purchase for himself some advantage in a future state. Outside these comes a row of gilt trees, bearing glass fruits, and lastly elephants, and men in white stucco kneel holding trays for offerings.

The rest of the plateau is covered with innumerable buildings ; some are seven-roofed temples full of images of Buddha, some contain large bells which the worshippers strike when they have done praying. The carving of the seven roofs is always most elaborate. There are also posts surmounted by the sacred goose, from which sausage-shaped flags float out into the air, and cells built round the sacred peepul-tree, with an image of Buddha in each cell. Buddha is everywhere, and there are often thirty or forty images of him in one temple ; he is always sitting there with the same calm smile upon his face, and is seldom in a recumbent attitude.

The strange living figures—monks, nuns, men, and brightly dressed women—moving about add greatly to the beauty of the scene, not to mention the babies, who are most attractive—babies in pink silk shirts toddling about, or babies unadorned except by a little top-knot on their heads ; they are brown and fat and fascinating.

Both men and women have beautiful glossy black hair, and are very proud of it ; the men wear it at the top of their heads, and the women have their chignons lower down, and generally ornament them with flowers.

We saw a game of football going on, which was remarkably pretty and lively. The ball is made of wickerwork, and must not be touched by the arm or hand during the game. One man begins and plays ball with it, catching it on his knee, foot, or shoulder, and then suddenly throws it on to another, who keeps it up as long as he can, or until it pleases him to send it further. They played this game close to the Pagoda.

We had just time to drive a short way by a lake before going on to church. It was six o'clock in the evening and really cold, so I begged that the punkahs might be stopped, but even so it was draughty, and D. made his cold worse.

Monday, 8th.— We left Rangoon early, Mrs. Bernard and Miss Moore remaining there, but Mr. Bernard coming with us. We had seven hours in the train, reaching Prome at 5.30. At all the stations on the way the villagers came to see us, the place was decorated, and a bouquet or basket of flowers was brought me. Once we saw a Burmese band. The bandmaster sat in a carved wooden circle, round the inside of which drums of all sizes were hung, and he played upon these, with his hands flying about from one to the other, and looked just like some one performing a very grand piece on a piano. Another man in another circle played cymbals, and outside there were men who struck split bamboos together with great precision and in excellent time. The music was very pleasant.

At Prome we descended from the railway to the wharf through a beautifully made covered way with pinnacled roofs like those at the Pagoda, and Burmese officials squatted on one side, while Burmese ladies squatted on the other. The road was lined by troops who had just come from Calcutta, and we had also a number of Blue-jackets with us.

The river steamer is splendid—its only fault lies in the preparations for keeping up a perpetual draught; and as the mornings, evenings, and nights are extremely cold, as we go at the rate of fourteen knots an hour through the water, and as the Viceroy has a cold, this is unfortunate. Our accommodation is all in the bow. The bow itself makes a delightful sitting-room for us, and there we have six cabins or small rooms which D. and I, Archie and Mr. McFerran divide between us. One is my boudoir, and it has such smart furniture—such plush tables, stuffed arm-chairs, gold-headed scent-bottles! The dining-room and all the other cabins are towards the centre of the vessel.

Everything had been so well arranged for us, but imagine the captain's feelings when we arrived with 100 servants whom he had never heard of! They have all been stowed in somehow.

We were thirty-six at dinner the first night, as we asked the officials at Prome to dine. One of our guests was a Countess Calliarveris; she has married an Italian, but she is a real native who was educated in England. She is very lively and well mannered.

Tuesday, 9th.—D. had to stay in bed for his cold, which was a great pity, as the middle of the day was lovely—such a balmy air, and the river so pretty to look at. The Irrawaddy is a fine river, and, without being very striking, the scenery is interesting—white sandy shores, rocky banks, fair-sized hills, and always plenty of trees.

We cannot travel at night, so we anchored in the evening opposite to the Fort of Minhla, which is one of the few places where there was a little fighting before the taking of Mandalay. I went ashore to see it. The fort is simply a square with a second inner wall, on the top· of which our officers now have their tents. One charge was made to take it, and when our men reached the top the Burmese fled, some down narrow stairs, some dropping over the wall. They cannot stand fixed bayonets for a second. Close to the fort are some pagodas. In the twilight the place is like a great graveyard, and I almost wonder Colonel Baker likes to sleep there; his tent looks as though it were pitched among tombs.

These pagodas are not gilt, and they are all much the same size—about as tall as a cottage. Very few Buddhas remain here, and those that do have lost their heads, for the very first night the Mahometan soldiers got in, they defaced every image.

The officers who have been shut up in this small place for more than two months were very glad of a little change, so I asked eight of them to dinner.

Wednesday, 10th.—Another delightful day on the

river. D. enjoyed it much. The scenery was more varied to-day, and in the evening, when we sighted Pagan, it was really lovely. This city was the ancient capital, but it is now deserted, and is simply a great town of pagodas. They reach for many miles, and you may imagine how picturesque they look. They are not all the bell shape, and are many of them square or octagonal, each storey decreasing in size, the whole ending in a point. This mysterious-looking town, reflected in the river, and with a red sunset light over it, was very striking.

The navigation of the river is most exciting, for it very low at this season, and we are perpetually avoiding sand-banks. We have a pilot-ship in front, and when we watch the turns and twists she has to make, we can scarcely believe that our great long vessel can follow safely in her wake. We heard this morning that the *Irrawaddy*, a vessel of the Indian Marine, has gone ashore and sunk somewhere on our route.

We did not stop till after dark, and so I could not land. Four officers came off to dine.

Thursday, 11th.—At about twelve o'clock a little steamer appeared in sight, and brought General Prendergast and Colonel Sladen on board. The former is a very straightforward-looking soldier. Colonel Sladen was the last English Resident in British Burmah, and he had just returned in time to see King Theebaw's exit, and remained at the Palace with the Royal family during the last night. He lays the blame of all Theebaw's evil doings upon his wife, Soopaya-Lât, whom the English call ' Selina Sophia.   She managed everything, and all the money from taxes and other sources was brought to her.   Her mother, also a very masterful woman, is exiled too.   Theebaw writes that he is very happy and comfortable, and that he has even been provided with a doctor, so much care do we take of him.

I landed at Mingyan, the last place where any resistance was made to our troops.   In the distance it looked very pretty, a town of spires; but on shore I only saw the military arrangements, as we had not time to go sight-seeing.

The *Peel,* a vessel which was following us with a guard of 100 soldiers for the Viceroy, went ashore last night, and we do not know if she has got off.

Blackwell and D.'s Persian policeman both have a touch of fever; it really is a work of difficulty to get safely through the varieties of temperature and the draughts we are exposed to.

I sat between General Prendergast and Mr. Gordon at dinner.   The latter is an unsuccessful candidate at the last election.   He has come here to see about railways, and has a passage in our pilot-boat.   General Prendergast is very nice.   He seems to have been quite the right man in the right place—very kind, but determined.   It is, of course, very interesting to hear all the details of the taking of Mandalay, but I must not weary you with a too voluminous report of our proceedings and of all we hear.

Friday, 12th.—The outlook this morning was very curious.   There were the noses of all the junks sunk by the Burmese peeping out of the water all round us, and there was our own ship *Irrawaddy* settling on the sand-bank ; and in the narrow channel we had to twist in and out of these dangers with the greatest care. The banks, covered with pagodas, are lovely. We were off Ava at nine o'clock, and every little hill was crowned by a snow-white monument, while there were groups of them in some places, and below a beautifully-carved wooden monastery. Out of every bit of jungle rises a spire, and it is impossible to convey the effect of it all. You can't bear to take your eyes off the scenery for a minute, lest you should lose some specially characteristic building. Burmah looks rather like a country of cemeteries, if you imagine each tombstone to be about the size of the Albert Memorial.

We reached Mandalay about twelve o'clock. The town is three miles from the river, so that all we saw from the ship was a reception-hall which had been put up for the occasion, some British tents, and next to us on the river a most wonderful old barge. It is two boats joined together, with a seven-roofed pinnacle over the centre, two large gilt ornaments at the stern, and two great gold and silver gods at the prow.

We were to go ashore at three ; and before then we watched the Burmans coming and going, men and women. They wore very gay colours, and some of them had men carrying big hats umbrella-fashion over their heads. When all was ready, we marched up the steps from the steamer to the entrance of the hall, the way being lined by British sailors, and through it, just as the Viceroy does at a durbar, to two thrones placed side by side upon a daïs. They had embroidered peacocks on the back, and were set with imitation stones; a white canopy, the emblem of royalty, was hung over us. It was a very odd sensation to come and 'King and Queen' it in this way, and I felt rather like an actor in a play. We all sat in solemn silence, while the Viceroy's salute was fired—a great assembly of soldiers, politicals, and Burmans!

The thirty-one guns over, Colonel Sladen bowed before His Excellency, and said there was an address to be presented. This one was from the European inhabitants of Mandalay. It was in a long box and was written on narrow slips of bamboo, which the reader handed one by one to some one near as he finished each bit. D. replied to this address. Then came some Burmese merchants to present another, and we heard the language for the first time. It is read in a very sing-song manner, and with a very long drawl on an occasional word, which has a funny effect. The Burmese all sat on chairs at this durbar, as D. said he only expected the same marks of respect from them that he did from Europeans and Indians, so they squat no longer.

When all was over we walked out again, treading on the roses which some Burmese women threw upon our path, and getting into our carriage started for the Palace. The whole three miles was lined with troops; there was a very strong escort, besides our own body-guard, who look real giants in this country of small men and ponies.

Outside the city all the houses are mere matting sheds, and the people look very poor and naked. But the city walls are beautiful and of a rich colour, being built of brownish-red bricks. They are in perfect repair, and form a great square, each side a mile and a half long. The whole wall has a plain indented border, and at stated intervals along it are those lovely many-roofed pagodas—large ones at the corners and in the centre, and smaller ones between. There is something very grand and simple about the whole, and a moat right round it, wide as a river and full of water, adds to the effect. We drove through the finest gateway, and soon came to a high palisade which encloses the Palace ; there gilded minarets and shining pinnacles and golden carved roofs began to appear, and when we descended from the carriage we found ourselves at the entrance of King Theebaw's Hall of Audience.

I must, however, go back to tell you that two wonderful arches were put up for us on the way. They were filled with people, and we stopped in each to receive addresses. On one side of the first were the gentlemen who read the address, and on the other were dancing-girls singing and posturing, and wonderful to behold. In the second arch—tables were spread on either side with fruit and flowers, and wooden figures dressed up as women stood by.

The great Audience Hall is all gold—great teak pillars gilt. At one end is Theebaw's throne, and doors open directly behind it, through which he used suddenly to appear and look upon the crowd bowed before him with their faces to the ground. When we entered there were four men playing drums, and I think it was one of the most comic things I ever saw. The

drums were hanging up and had white muslin petticoats round them, and the men who played them
danced about and made grimaces, and threatened them
with their fists as if they were living things and as
if they were having a good joke together. There was
one old gentleman in particular who seemed to be a
first-rate actor, and who certainly had great fun with
his drum. I could have looked at them for hours,
were life less full of seeing and doing than it is at
present.

Then we walked on through the Palace. A marvellous
place it is. What is not gold is a sort of glass mosaic
which is very bright and effective. There are glass
latticework sides to some of the rooms, and golden
pillars, and glasswork pillars, and great mirrors; and
outside, golden roofs beautifully carved, and more gold
and glass palings, acres of gilt roofing, and shining
pinnacles, and forests of teak pillars all gold !

One very fine room has been arranged by our officers
as a drawing-room for me, and it has in it some of the
pretty things collected from various parts of the Palace :
fine china bowls in which the Burmese had been cooking; glass-work pagoda boxes, containing vessels for
water ; poor Soopaya-Lât's triple pier-glass, which shuts
up and has a peacock on the back of it, and other things
which I shall have time to inspect later. We mounted a
high tower, from which we could see the whole Palace and
its surroundings. It was nearly sunset, and the light
on the seven-roofed pinnacle over the royal abode, and
the glittering of the many smaller ones, and the great
expanse of fantastic-shaped roofs with their carved and

gilt eaves, gave one a fine idea of the size and beauty of
the Palace. The view itself was lovely, for the whole
enclosure within those splendid city walls is full of trees ;
the Shan Mountains rise beyond, and there are strange
pagodas or temples everywhere. There is the ' Incomparable Pagoda,' which is quite white, and which rises
from the ground in diminishing squares, and near it
another very celebrated golden bell-shaped pagoda surrounded by eleven hundred small shrines.

Just before leaving the Palace—for we have decided
to remain most of our time on the steamer and only to
spend two nights there—we saw some Burmese dancers
for a few minutes. When we entered the circular building
where they perform, they were all seated, a mass of gold
and silver and bright colour, and then they came forward in two lines and danced before us. The row of
men were dressed as princes. They wore very high
pointed gold hats poised on their heads, and held on by
straps which had large gold wings covering their ears.
They had very big silver Charles I. collars, and gold
and silver stiff leaf-like aprons. They were completely
clothed and very brilliant.

The women were just the figures you know so well in
pictures. Their dancing is much more interesting than
that of Indian nautch-girls ; still it consists almost
entirely in bending about the body into extraordinary
positions, many of them suggestive of a bad pain somewhere. The movement which is the most admired is
made with the arm, and consists in bending the elbow
the wrong way ; it looks as if it had a double joint.
The dancers all have thin little arms, and they twist

them and their fingers about all the time.   Their petticoats are very long and very tight, but they manage
them well.   The dance is a sort of play which goes on
for hours, so we only saw the prelude, and the male
and female dancers were just beginning a figure together
when we had to go.

The Head-quarters Staff is settled in the Palace, and
we were to have stayed there, but the ship is considered
more healthy ;   we are, however, going there on Monday
for a little.

Saturday, 13*th*.—We went out this morning to see
the Queen's Monastery.   The central building, which is
most elaborately carved, is all gilded ; and the surrounding houses are equally beautifully carved in plain wood.
Every house in Burmah is raised on piles, and in this
case, where the pillars are solid teak covered with gold,
the ground-floor has the appearance of a magnificent
hall of columns.   At the corners it is supported by
carved dragons ; flights of stairs outside lead up to the
first-floor, round which, forming a verandah, there is an
elaborately carved paling in solid wood.

We were told the Bishop would see us, so we were
taken into the room where he sat surrounded by his
monks.   Don't imagine him with lawn sleeves or an
apron.   No ; he had a quite bald head, and a beautiful
yellow toga wrapped round him, which was over one
shoulder and under the other arm.   This room almost
defies description—the columns, walls, doors, ceilings,
all gold.   About the height of a man's shoulder from
the floor the pillars have round them a broad band of

raised carving set with diamonds, or what appear to be
diamonds. At one end, on a shining daïs, sits the
calm, smiling Buddha. All the doors are carved with
figures in relief, and every little morsel of wood you
look at is a perfectly carved figure or design, and all
gold. The only touch of any other colour you get is
from below, when you see the red lining of the roofs; a
very beautiful red it is, and it is used in every place
where there is not gold. The many diminishing roofs
along the city wall are of this deep red just tipped
with gold.

In the afternoon His Excellency received all the
Burmese Ministers. He first saw them together, and
then had two of them here separately. They were both
presented to me. The Prime Minister did not desert the
King, but saw him safely off, and has since worked with
us. He seems a bright old man, and he told the other
when he went back that he need not fear to go and
see the Viceroy, as he had passed safely through the
fire. They were pleased to hear that I intended to
give a party for the ladies, and the second one said he
had just lost his only daughter, and that his wife was
very unhappy and could not come, but she would be
sorry not to see me. Their dress is a long piece of silk
tied round the body, the wide ends hanging like a petticoat in front, a wisp of muslin tied round their heads,
a knot of hair in the centre, and a white jacket.

When the business interviews were over, we went to
see the ' Incomparable Pagoda.' The great hall in the
centre is like what I have described before—a golden
room with great pillars, jewelled bands round them, a

big Buddha sitting there.   The outside of this is ugly; a staring white place built in diminishing squares, the top of each battlemented.   There are gold and plain carved houses attached to this; and in one we saw a beautiful white marble Buddha with gold cap, shirt, and finger-tips.

We next went to look at a pagoda which I certainly like better than the one at Rangoon, and it is most curious.   The pagoda itself is again a gigantic hand-bell, but without any tawdry accompaniments.   It is all gilt.   Forming a great square round it are eleven hundred white pagodas, or small buildings, each one with a slab of marble upright in it, most beautifully inscribed on both sides with pieces of ' scripture.'   I went half-way up the outside of the great pagoda, and was delighted with the view; all these strange white cupolas in the foreground, the trees and rising pinnacles, and gold roofs and the distant mountains—it made one really feel as if one must be dreaming.

I confess, however, that this evening I feel almost tired of gold.   I never conceived such masses of it before, and can't understand it all at once.

I must tell you a little more about the glass mosaic which is often used on the side walls of buildings, and of which there is so much in the Palace.   Some of it is composed of pieces of glass imbedded in a gold ground. Sometimes it is laid on an open latticework and edged with gold.   In other places it is cut and set with coloured bits like jewels, or round panels, the centre of them being artificial flowers with glass over them.   This is the least successful form, but even this is very effective when a whole wall is done with it ; and I think that when it is mixed with gold on the outside of buildings it looks like silver and is very splendid.

There were some very funny groups of people about while the Ministers were here. Five men, for instance, sitting under one big hat which a servant carries over his master's head when he walks ; an occasional elephant passing with his passenger sitting in a basket on his back, and a particular elephant stepping over a rope lying on the ground, which was the most comic sight of all—he felt it and shook it, and finally lifted each great foot as high as ever he could, as though he had the trunk of a giant tree to pass over instead of a mere thread !

Sunday, 14*th.*—I went to church this morning in King Theebaw's Audience Hall. The Army Chaplain stood in front of his throne, and all the soldiers in lines between the columns.

In the afternoon we made a charming expedition to see the great bell at Mengdoon, which is only second in size to the Moscow bell. A smaller steamer came alongside ours to take us there, and we lunched on our way across the river. All the Special Reporters, both those who draw and those who write, went with us. We also had a strong guard of sailors, who formed a cordon round the place while we roamed about and saw the sights.

The biggest pagoda in the world was to have been built here, but an earthquake put an end to the whole design ; and all that is to be seen now is a solid mass of brick masonry rent by this convulsion of nature, and the hind-quarters of two gigantic lion-dogs which were to have guarded the entrance. The square block is, even in its unfinished state, a very great performance, and with wood and river and small pagodas near, the place is very pretty. The big bell is close by, and is half resting on the ground and half hung between pillars grown over with ivy. Lying in the jungle we found some carved wooden ladies, who were shouldered by the sailors and carried off with a view to their taking up a position some day in the hall at Clande- boye. We had one or two people at dinner, amongst them Monsieur Andreino, the Italian Consul, who so narrowly escaped from Theebaw's clutches !

Monday, 15*th.*—We came up to the Palace to-day to stay, and very nice and pleasant it is. There is my drawing-room with its twenty-eight beautiful golden pillars, and its gold and glass latticework sides. There is my bed-room with its golden pillars and little matting partitions, and in both rooms a lofty roof, the rafters all gilt. In the drawing-room a number of white canopies hang about and form occasional ceilings, and show that it is a royal abode.

We looked at the 'Prize.' Very poor prize it is ! Theebaw's ladies were much too sharp for our soldiers, and managed to walk off with everything. There is positively only one jewel, and that is French—it is a necklace of small diamonds and rubies, and an ornament for the hair in the shape of a peacock, to match ; one very big, but bad emerald, and three large good ones ; that is absolutely all. There are a number of Geneva watches, and some small French ornaments, but nothing even worth buying as souvenirs, for these odds and ends are European things.

At three o'clock D. had a levée. He stood in front of Theebaw's throne (which, as I told you, is only a daïs), with a row of body-guard behind him and another row in front, and much 'brilliant Staff' around and about him; and the 'Illustrated' on one side, and the 'Graphic' on the other, busy scribbling away; themselves a good subject for a caricature in their evening coats and big sun hats. I was behind the throne, looking through some carved brass doors, where I could criticise the casual nods which some officers give as they pass by. I saw the Burmese Ministers trying not to squat, and the Chinese residents bending double, and the native officers presenting their swords, and then unfortunately there was some mistake and the levée was supposed to be over, and the Viceroy put on his helmet, and I fled back to my room, saying to myself, ' Only two Burmese; is it a demonstration ? ' Then it turned out that all the Burmese who had a right to come were there, but had got into some out-of-the-way corner. The Viceroy resumed his place, and they all passed by, but I missed seeing them.

After this ceremony plain clothes were put on, and we rode out. We visited all the sick and wounded in the hospitals : such hospitals !—more gold pillars and carved roofs. They are really admirable buildings for the purpose. They are all raised from the ground, and are open to the air on every side. Not a single man in hospital has died from a wound, and all the sick do well.

Then we started to go up Mandalay Hill. The city takes its name from this hill, which rises direct from the plain and commands a great extent of country. There is a rough sort of staircase up to the top, and some people rode, but I walked both up and down, and it was a steep pull! Half-way up there is a gigantic gold figure of Buddha. It is about forty feet high, and it is pointing to the spot where the palace was to be built, and where it now is. At the top there are more Buddhas. Our soldiers have a signalling station there, and I believe this is the place to hear news, for they learn at once all that is going on. On coming down we looked at a sitting figure of Buddha which is twenty-four feet high, and which has a house all to itself. The whole way round this building are hundreds of small temples, each with a Buddha in it, and when you look down a row you can see these kneeling figures the whole way along.

In the evening we had a Burmese play. It was held in the ' Umbrella Room,' a name which exactly describes its construction. A small pasteboard mountain close to the stick is all the scenery, and the spectators sit all the way round the edge of the open umbrella, except at one part where the actors are collected. One of these Burmese plays lasts about three days, and the actors like to go through everything in a long-drawn manner, so I felt rather ashamed of the way in which we hurried them from scene to scene that we might see as much as possible.

The story was that of a princess who was to be given to the one out of seven suitors who could bend a certain bow and shoot an arrow from it. Mixed up with this

simple theme were evil spirits and clowns who lengthened
it out.   Each prince had a little scene to himself to introduce him : he marshalled his followers ; he had a certain
amount of chaff with the maids of honour ; and he was to
be presented to the king, which all took time.   Then the
ladies appeared, and the princess (an elderly *prima donna*)
waved herself about and began to sing what turned out
to be an ode to the Viceroy and me.   *It* spoke of my
dress as being worth millions, and of the diamonds in
my hair, and I felt that the expectations of the composer
must have been sadly disappointed at sight of the real
thing !   All the actors' dresses were very fine, really handsome, for this ' Opera ' is supported by the State, and a
Minister has, or had, charge of the department.   It was
a very pretty scene.   At first one thinks that moving
about in a dress which is as tight as it can well be—like
one trouser leg—cannot be pretty, but the women are
so supple that their movements become graceful.   The
prima donna carried a small fan and a silk scarf in her
hand, and she ended off her song very prettily, making
first of all an English ' salaam ' before us, and then a
Burmese salutation with her face to the ground.   The
ease with which men and women squat is most remarkable.   There was a good deal of fun in the acting
too.   A clown, who wore a silver collar and a petticoat,
was very funny, and the women were charming and very
lively when they scoffed the unsuccessful suitors.   This
sort of play would make an admirable successor to the
' Mikado,' if it could be produced in London.

I forgot to tell you that we saw Theebaw's state
coat, which is⋅ very like what the dancing ' princes '

wear. D. is going to send it to the South Kensington Museum.

Tuesday, 16*th*.—We got up early and rode four miles to a place where marble Buddhas were being made. The ride was the most interesting part, as we passed through the Mandalay ' Covent Garden,' and saw all the people buying and selling vegetables, and the pohngees (monks) going about, as they do every morning, to collect food from the faithful. To put something into a pohn- .
gee's pot is a work of merit which every Burman should perform daily. Afterwards *I* was taken to see the palace storehouse. Although there is nothing valuable, there are any amount of odds and ends purchased from Europe : scores of photograph-books, sewing-machines, photograph-frames, fans, toys, and lacquer boxes of all kinds, and scent enough to furnish a shop. A little auction was held here to-day, by the Prize Committee, and I believe the rubbish went at enormous prices.

In the afternoon I had the most successful party you can imagine. I was just a little afraid that the Burmese ladies might not come, but at four o'clock about sixty of them appeared, all swathed in lovely colours and soft silks, diamond and pearl necklaces, and flowers in their black hair ; earrings too, which *I* must mention particularly, for they are straight tubes of amber, glass, jade, or gold, pushed through the lobe of the ear—they are as thick as a lady's thumb, and about an inch long. Some of these are set at one end with big stones, but some are hollow. D. and I stood at the door and welcomed our guests one by one. They had to come up three steps into the room, and as their garments are open all the way down the front, it requires some management to walk up with propriety. They do manage them so well that you never would know that the petti-coat is not joined unless you were told it. As we shook hands with them, they bolted past us, and immediately squatted on the floor, which I now find is a most admir-able arrangement, doing away entirely with the stiff circle into which the best regulated chairs will form on such occasions. The first time, however, that I saw all my guests thus seated I was rather startled, and wondered how I was to pass the time for them. I began by sitting on a very low chair near the Ministers' wives, and giving them a cup of tea and a biscuit, asking them a few questions meantime and admiring their jewellery. When they had gained sufficient courage, they asked me my age, which, according to Burmese etiquette, is an essential mark of politeness, and then we got on beautifully. I enquired if they would like to look at the things in the room, so we all got up, and I showed them the Queen's triple looking-glass, which was a great success, and they were highly amused at seeing themselves on three sides all at once. I next produced a musical box, and the ice being now entirely broken they asked me to let them see some of the other rooms ; so, with a brilliant following, I marched about exhibiting Theebaw's Palace to his late subjects. They were most cheerful, and said they had been in the Palace before, ' but not like this.'

The next part of the programme was some dancing, and, still with my train behind me, I repaired to the

Umbrella Room. There they sat on the floor, leaning forward with their elbows on the ground and enjoying it thoroughly. The principal lady advised me as to the best dances, and I got her to ask for them. Several times they said to me (according to the translator) that it was very 'jolly,' and that they were so pleased to have come; and towards the end they told me that I had only got to send for them when there was any more dancing, and they would come at once. Their husbands had told them not to smoke before me, so the very enormous cigar, which is generally in the mouth of man, woman, and child, did not appear on this occasion. They were quite unwilling to go away, so I think I am justified in saying that the party was a success. There were also some Mahometan ladies at it, but the only peculiarity I could see about them was that they would only take the tea from Mussulman hands: and I don't know why they should have this prejudice. They were dressed like the others, and are in fact Burmese.

I must mention one other function, which took place to-day. The Viceroy received the ' Archbishop ' and a great suite of ' chaplains,' all of them with shaven heads, yellow robes, and each one with a large fan in his hand to shade him from the sun.

Wednesday, 17*th.*—D. went into the bazaar before breakfast, and all the morning did a great deal of business, while I amused myself with photography and with looking about the Palace. We took a little ride in the evening, and ended up with a dinner to the Head-quarters Staff. D. proposed General Prendergast's and Mr. Bernard's healths in a speech which you will read in the 'Times,' to which they both replied. It was all very nice; but as the guests were heads of departments they could not applaud their own praises, and so it seemed to me rather solemn.

Thursday, 18th.—I got either cold or sun in my eye, and had to go about with a green patch over it, unable to read or write, so I was rather glad that I was to see the French nuns who are settled here. They came in the morning and gossiped for some time. They saw a great deal of Soopaya-Lât, the late Queen, and I will tell you all they told me about her, and what I have heard from others. She seems really to have been like a queen of ancient history.

A Burmese king is expected to marry his half-sister, so that the royal blood may be kept pure, though her child does not necessarily become king—and Soopaya-Lât bore this relation to the King; but she had an elder sister whom Theebaw should have married, and it was only because they were already betrothed that his engagement to her was allowed to stand, and to the great misfortune of the country she became Queen. If the people here are to be believed, all poor Theebaw's crimes of commission and of omission were due to her; he never was allowed out of her sight, never did anything or gave an order except at her suggestion. He did not drink as he was said to do, for no wine-bottles full or empty were found in the Palace.

They both lived in small back rooms, sitting all day side by side on the ground, and if he moved away she used to tell him to come back quickly. They seldom went about the Palace, and only appeared on state occasions in the large apartments. She was a very violent and passionate woman, governed entirely by impulse and caprice, thinking herself the very greatest person in all the world, and unable to conceive the possibility of misfortune or retribution falling upon her. She had maids of honour and eunuchs about her, and she had a wonderful talent for keeping them employed. Her followers were like ants, always busy, always fetching or carrying, or in some way fulfilling her behests. The King had a guard of women, who were relieved at stated hours like soldiers; but Soopaya-Lât took good care of him, and if he looked at another woman, woe betide that unfortunate creature. That she employed 'refined cruelty' and that she tortured her victims seems certain; and the nuns told me that they have sat with her in one room while women were being beaten in the next, and that the Queen and her Court were highly amused at their cries, and treated it all as the most enjoyable fête. A bed, with all the necessary machinery for letting its occupier down into a cellar below, was found, but of course no one knows whether it was used or not.

A former queen and a princess had been in prison and in chains for six years, and they could not imagine what had happened when our soldiers opened the doors and released them. They are now in absolute poverty. As the Bishop said of Soopaya-Lât, '*If* she liked you, she loved you; if she hated you, she killed you.' The wives of officials lived in constant terror lest their own or their husbands' lives should be taken.

The nuns had curious relations with the Queen, and I think these good ladies have got themselves into rather a mess, for they had some large business transactions with her. The Queen used to send constantly for them. Some days she made them translate to her all the French novels that could be found; other days she displayed her jewels—such diamonds and rubies! The nuns described dazzling heaps of them covering the floor. Other times she gave them commissions: they were to send to Paris, to Calcutta, to Rangoon, to get jewels and every other sort of thing that came into her head—watches without end, photograph-albums, frames, and stuffs. The nuns did it, and at first they got paid, but the last two years Soopaya-Lât has paid nothing, and there is, I believe, a considerable sum due for jewels and other unpaid goods.

These ladies did a good deal of needlework for the Queen too. One time she thought trousers made a good dress for women, so they set to work and trousered the whole Court. As a rule, she wore the ordinary Burmese dress herself, but she had a magnificent 'uniform' for state occasions. It was a long and very heavy coat, with stiff points like fins at the sides, and it was covered with gold and precious stones. When she and Theebaw sat in their grand dresses on the throne, the floor of the room was covered by a multitude of people, all with their faces to the ground, and if the Queen saw anywhere in the most distant corner a person who was less prostrate than he, or she, ought to be, she sent him from the room and he 'heard of it' afterwards.

She gave quantities of presents to the persons she

liked, and one of her amusements was on one of these state occasions, or fête days, to sit on the daïs, with a great pile of money before her, and to call people up to take as much as they could carry in their two hands. Their efforts to get big handfuls caused her much amusement, and then she would throw pieces about the room and enjoy seeing the scramble that ensued. She would go on for a whole night doing this, laughing to see her subjects grovelling before her; thus she spent large sums of money.

I. can't make out that she had much amusement in the daytime. She was fond of music, and if there were any European ladies at Mandalay, she used to get them to come and play the piano to her, but they had to do so kneeling. A photographer used to be sent for sometimes, and he was kept photographing all the ladies of her Court the whole day long. Another day she would look through all her albums, and study the very ugly photographs therein. I saw numbers of them, and bought one.

The Queen wished to travel, but she said that, although other sovereigns did so, it would not do for her. She meant, however, to make her children go about. The King was very devoted to her, but was dreadfully afraid of her. He has also married her youngest sister at Soopaya's desire. She told the nuns that she was fond of her sister and wished her to be as happy as she herself was, and so she had got the King to marry her.

When Theebaw left the Palace, his hands were crossed before him, and he had a wife on each side; he thus led them out, and seems to have behaved with considerable dignity.   What a terribly dramatic ending to Soopaya's greatness !   Not even a gold coach to go away in ; only a square box of a vehicle, in which she and the King and her mother all crowded together.   They were followed by women carrying trays full of goods, but many of these ran away and escaped with the things.

General Prendergast brought me a lovely little image of Buddha, which he said he and the officers of the army wished to give me as a souvenir of my visit to Mandalay ; and they gave D. the original and the translation of Lord Dalhousie's Despatch when he addressed his ultimatum to the Burmese.

We left the Palace in state at five o'clock, and drove down to the reception-hall which had been put up for our arrival; there English officers and the Burmese Ministers were collected.   The latter stood in a row before the Viceroy, and he told them then that their country had been taken over by the English people, and that we expect them now to show loyalty and devotion to their new Sovereign.   Then we shook hands with them and went on board.   The ' Prime Minister ' wanted to give me some silk, and Archie a sword, but we could not take them.

The Burmese appear to be a most pleasing, nice people to do with, but some of their very virtues make them difficult to govern and to depend upon.   Their police are no good, and they neither stand and fight nor quite give way.   However, for better, for worse, Burmah is annexed.   It seems a rich country, and Mandalay is a lovely place, and we, at any rate, have had a delightful visit there. The soldiers hitherto have had an exciting time too, but now that the glamour is worn off, they have a dull and rather dreary prospect before them.

D. has done an immensity of business : things could not have been settled without his coming here. The last act he performed before leaving was rather curious and picturesque to look at. He had promised to return to the Bishop and his monks some Buddhas which they considered specially sacred, so these were all laid out together, and the yellow-robed brethren stood by, and D. handed their images over to them, and then a crowd of coolies rushed in and carried them all off.

We are once more on board our ship, and hope sincerely to get down the river without sticking.

Friday, 19th.—My last entry expressed a wish which has not been fulfilled. We did go on a sand-bank, and did stick there for a whole day. Our pilot-steamer and all our men were busy from morn till eve hauling, and tugging, and laying out anchors and taking them in again, and we just managed to get off before dark.

The stoppage was long enough to put out all our arrangements, and we have had to alter our plans, so that we shall not reach Calcutta as soon as we intended.

Life on board need not be recorded. Happily our mail came in, and brought us news of all our belongings in various parts of the world, and our letters were highly appreciated.

As *I* have nothing to say of ourselves, it may amuse you to know what Theebaw is doing, as described in official papers by the officer in charge of him. He is greatly occupied about the coming baby. He wonders what clothes it had better wear, and he has ordered a gold dish set with rubies to be made for its reception. He is also much troubled about the nurses, who are for ever on the eve of leaving him and returning to Burmah; one, having made up her mind to go, begged to be allowed to get out of the house as quickly as possible, as it would, under the circumstances, be too hot to hold her. Another woman, who superintends these nurses, climbed a tree and could not be got down till she was threatened by Theebaw himself, when she descended 'like a squirrel.'

The Queen expected her European monthly nurse to crawl in her presence, but that she refused to do; and even the ayahs, who have done it so far, say their knees are sore and they cannot go on.

There! I have sent you a great supply of Mandalay gossip.

Tuesday, 23rd.—The remainder of our voyage was uneventful, and after a day in the train we reached Rangoon yesterday.

In the afternoon we attended 'sports.' It was such a very pretty fête. We assembled at the edge of a charming little lake, with bridges and islands, and green banks and fine trees about it, and a fringe of gay-coloured people adorning it all. First there were races; sixteen or seventeen men rowing in a very long and narrow boat, shrieking, and splashing the water with a very rapid stroke. At the winning-post a long stick was stuck into a hollow bamboo, and whichever boat carried off this stick was declared the winner. When we had seen enough of this we went through the pavilion where we sat, and on the other side of it we found thirty very young girls, arranged in a square, squatting on a carpet there, and ready to perform. The spectators were in crowds all round them. These children wore heavy wreaths of flowers on their heads, quantities of jewels, pink silk jackets, and red and yellow short petticoats, made in the tight Burmese fashion. The curious part of it is that they are all the daughters of the Burmese aristocracy, who come out thus to perform for any great official, to do him honour, and they are all drilled like ballet-dancers. They were sitting on the floor, and during half the dance they remained in this posture, swaying about, and moving their arms and hands, and singing, all very exactly in time. Then they got up and danced very gracefully and nicely. After this we saw some older girls go through the same sort of performance, and then there were children, one of whom pretended to be a tiger and to eat up a princess, while a supernatural creature of some sort came to save her.

We also saw the game of football, about which I told you before. The men, who are not athletes or specialists of any sort, play with wonderful dexterity. The ball must not touch the arm below the elbow, or the hand, and they throw it from foot to knee and from knee to shoulder, then let it run down the back and throw it up again with the heel, back to the shoulder, from one side of the neck to the other, and so on as if it was possessed. I believe they can play even better than they did to-day, but they had put on some extra clothes in my honour, which rather encumbered their movements. The ball is very light, and is made of wickerwork.

A dinner and a levée ended the day.

Wednesday, 24th.—At eight o'clock in the morning we laid the foundation-stone of the Cathedral of Rangoon. Directly after breakfast the Viceroy saw the Commander-in-Chief on business. At twelve I had a Medical Association meeting, and at one I saw a lady by appointment. At three I went to give prizes at a school, and the Viceroy had a durbar, received memorials, and made fifteen speeches in reply ; this function lasted two hours. At five we received Burmese Christian ladies, and a large assembly of Karen Christians. At six His Excellency went to call on the Admiral; at eight there was a dinner, and at 9.30 a ball.

Having thus carried you breathlessly through a day of Viceregal duty, I will try to tell you a little about the most interesting features of it. At the foundation-stone ceremony this morning there were representatives of eleven different nationalities, with their Christian clergy and teachers. D. laid the stone, and made a nice little speech on the subject.

My deputation was interesting and satisfactory to me. Something in the nature of a Maternity Charity will be begun at once here, and I think some pupils will also be sent to the Calcutta Medical School. The doctors in Rangoon are most energetic, and are doing all they can to promote the work. Burmese ladies and gentlemen were present, and three pupils for a midwifery class came too. They are nice, strong-looking girls, and as Burmese women are business-like and energetic, this seems a most promising place to make a good beginning in. The medical treatment in Burmah too is especially barbarous, and I may mention to you one example of it. After the birth of a child the mother is subjected for about seven days to a roasting fire. Wood is piled up for the purpose, and she is nearly baked and dried up. I know that the ex-Queen was treated in this fashion, and I suppose she had the best advice that could be got.

The durbar was much more of a business assembly than it is in India. The Burman recipe is, ' When you catch your Viceroy hold him tight, and make him listen to your grievances.' Accordingly D. was caught, and did listen and reply from three till five. It must have been rather interesting, but I had to go to the school and heard nothing of it.

The school, which is a missionary one, seems very successful, and certainly the Burmese are a nice and satisfactory people to work for. The girls all look bright and intelligent, and they are active and good-tempered. I noticed one peculiarity in their costume. They all had a loose coloured handkerchief, which was generally hung over the shoulder, and to 'one end of which was attached a little bunch of gold keys. It is rather a pretty ornament. Many of these school children had beautiful diamonds, and there was one tiny Chinese-Burman who was a picture!—a little thing of about four, in brilliant Chinese dress, trousers and slippers, with a tight band of black velvet two inches broad fitted round her head. A bead fringe hung over the forehead, and the band was covered with a design in elaborately worked red gold ;

inside this there was a knot of black hair stuck through in every direction with artificial flowers ; and her cheeks were rouged.

I gave prizes, and saw the children at tea, and then I came back to meet the Christian Karens.

They dress differently, look stronger, and are a more persevering people than the Burmans ; and I think I told you before in what great numbers they have become Christians—how they pay their own clergy and even send out missions to other people. It appears that, according to some old tradition of theirs, they believed that a white-faced creature would some time appear on their horizon and would bring them a book, and so when the missionaries came they saw the fulfilment of the prophecy, opened their arms to them, and are now a large Christian community. Their friendliness struck one as very pleasant. They did not treat me as a stranger, but all rushed to try and shake hands with me, and to make their babies do so too ; and the whole crowd of them looked so happy together. They are very fond of music, and one of the schools of big girls sang to us so well. They can sing by sight, and each had a book of songs copied by herself. The clergyman said that the only punishment he had to resort to in the school was to forbid the delinquent singing. They brought us specimens of their garments, and gave us a curious sort of gong elongated into a tube, which they cast themselves.

Some Burmese Christian ladies also came to see me, and were very pleasant and nice.

D. went down to the *Bacchante* to visit the Admiral, Sir Frederick Richards, and was delighted with his visit.

The yards were manned, and the ship was illuminated by the electric light, and looked beautiful.

The Rangoon ball was a great success. It was held in a magnificent large room, in which 700 people manœuvred with ease. I could not help thinking of the one, two, or three exits to a ball-room with which we are content at home, and counted forty large doors all round this one. But where it shone was in its really scientific arrangements for flirtation. There it was unsurpassed ; and a General, whom I took round the ' dark places,' kept saying, ' Well, I have been forty years in *India*, and I never saw anything like this ! ' ' This ' was a long covered way made of latticework, and arranged with small compartments on either side, shut in with plants and red and white curtains, and each little niche just big enough for two. Need *I.* say that the light was of that quality usually known as ' dim religious ' ?

I made a sort of state promenade down these alleys, giving a shock to each couple as I passed, and discovering the Military Secretary in the last one. *I.* hear I also greatly discomposed a lofty official, who confided to a friend that he never would have gone there had he known Her Excellency would pass through. Outside these arbours were open and well-lighted places for four, with whist-tables.

The variety of the costume at the ball was very great. There were the Burmese people, Jews, who wear a p cu-liar and rather pretty dress, Parsees, and others. The dancing was kept up with great spirit. The supper was beautifully arranged. A gigantic structure big enough to seat 700 was put up and lined with red and white, and all the men were given cards beforehand, showing exactly where they were to sit; so there was no confusion, and the whole assembly sat down quietly, and were admirably served. Our healths were drunk, and His Excellency's little speech was a great success, everyone being delighted at his expression of a hope that when he returned to Burmah he should find the ladies ' more beautiful and younger than ever.'

We got home at two o'clock, very much pleased with everything; but D. was rather tired—seventeen speeches, many of them requiring considerable thought, in addition to all social duties, is hard work.

Thursday, 25th.—We spent our last morning at Rangoon in sight-seeing. We went first to look at the elephants at work in the timber-yards. I am never quite sure whether to consider an elephant a remarkably clever animal or an extraordinarily stupid one. He does his work admirably, but then he need not do it at all; and it seems stupid of him not to know his own powers, and to allow himself to be ordered about and controlled by a creature who looks like a fly on his back. In the timber-yard all his strength and his ignorance of it are displayed to perfection. In a sea of mud on the banks of the river lie great trunks of trees which no other beast could move. There the elephants work obedient to the voice and to the little stick of the men on their backs, hauling, pushing, piling up, and neatly arranging these fallen trees, as if they really understood all about it—picking their steps, seeming to understand the very best way of attacking each load, and never upsetting anything or making a mistake. We also saw an elephant diving for a lost log in the river, and admired the dexterity of the mahout, who sat tight while the great body on which he was riding rolled and pitched in the water. The elephant, having found the timber, raised it with his trunk and then balanced it on his tusks. In the yard they use tusks and trunk and forehead to pull and push, and arrange the timber in heaps.

From the elephants to the School of Art, where silver bowls were being made and wood was being carved. These two industries are specialties of Burmah. The silver work is really beautiful, but the duty on sending it home is so great as almost to prevent any sale for it there. There will be some specimens in the Exhibition.

After this the Viceroy insisted upon walking through the bazaars. He declares he is kept in purdah like a Hindoo lady, and that he will not submit, and will see the outside world. The expedition was very amusing, and when we had convinced the accompanying police that we did not wish to have the people beaten out of our way we saw plenty of them, for they were only too anxious to see us, and were also I think much amused at our eccentricities. The Viceroy made a sort of tasting progress through the food bazaar. He tasted pickled tea, and palm-sugar, and betel-nut, and every queer sort of seed or mess he came near, while the Burmese ladies sat aloft amidst their goods and smiled upon him.

Then we passed on to the 'dry goods' department, which we found unmistakably Manchesterian; but

Manchester goods presided over by foreign ladies and naked babies are interesting, and Manchester manufacturers study the tastes of their customers, and I have some lovely cotton pocket-handkerchiefs, with a Burmese peacock spreading its tail over the whole centre, which are nevertheless produced by Lancashire looms.

Home to lunch, and then a state departure. The streets were lined with soldiers and were full of people, and our last impression of Burmah was as gay and friendly as our first. Killyleagh still stood upon the shore; the men-of-war manned yards and saluted; all our new acquaintances came to see us off, and so we steamed away.

Mr. and Mrs. Bernard have been most kind to us, and have made our visit very pleasant.

Monday, March 1st.—Madras was sighted about ten o'clock, and by twelve we were enjoying all the excitement of arrival in a foreign port : new boats, new people, new harbour arrangements, ships dressed, town buried in bunting, telegrams coming off, unaccustomed ropes being hauled about the decks, extra sweepings going on—a general break-up of our quiet sea-going life.

Spoilt children of fortune that we are, we felt seriously aggrieved because our letters did not reach us at once, and an A.D.C. was bustled off to see what the postal authorities could be thinking of. However, the bag arrived before his return, and we were at lunch when the cry that 'Major Cooper is coming off in a catamaran' roused us, and caused us all to rush to the side to see the sight.

A catamaran is two logs of wood lashed together, forming a very small and narrow raft, and as the Major sat on his tiny craft the waves washed over his feet and wetted him to the waist every second. Archie's 'Ha-ha' must have reached him a long way off.

I may as well tell you at once that these catamarans are the only boats that can go about here in bad weather. The rower wears a ' fool's cap,' in which he carries letters, and when he encounters a big wave he leaves his boat, slips through the wave himself, and picks up his catamaran on the other side of it.

We had our letters to read, and D. had to study all the Madras addresses, but still there was plenty of time to ' look around '; and we were well amused till the time arrived for us to land. We were anchored inside the breakwater, a wall of massive concrete blocks, which was toppled over like a pack of cards three or four years ago in a storm ; it is now being rebuilt on a new principle. Then some very large deep barges, the planks of which are sewn together to give elasticity and the interstices stuffed with straw, came out for us, with a guard of honour of the 'Mosquito fleet,' as the catamarans are called, on either side of them ; two of the ' fool's cap' men, and a flag as big as the boat itself, on each one. The big barges and the tiny boats bobbed and rolled about though the day was calm, and we had to get on board with precaution, waiting for the right moment to jump.

Mr. and Mrs. Grant Duff met us on the pier, and we went down it in a glorified tramway, and were deposited under an awning where the rank and beauty and fashion of Madras awaited us. I was given a magnificent

bouquet-holder with flowers in it, and the Viceroy received about eight addresses in beautiful boxes. Only one was read, and he answered them all in one speech.

Two carriages and four drove us through crowds of people and many arches to Government House. *It* seemed to me about the warmest reception D. has met with anywhere. The people were more demonstrative and less silent than most Indian crowds. Ten thousand children were collected in one place, and I believe they were all fed that day by one man. Another native fed great numbers of poor; these were nice ways of doing honour to the occasion.

The Government House is a very handsome one; the weather is warm enough to make punkahs agreeable, and we dined in a verandah, and were fanned by them without grumbling.

Separated from the house there is a very fine banqueting hall, and there the Viceroy had a levée first, and we both held a drawing-room afterwards.

The Madras papers were amusing upon the subject of my curtsey, and described how *I* 'stood erect' and then 'sunk the fourth of my height,' while the young ladies who passed me ' slantingdicularly ' were unable to imitate me successfully.

Tuesday, 2nd.—I visited the Caste Hospital which has just been opened in Madras. Many people doubted at first whether purdah women would go into it, but Mrs. Grant Duff has taken great pains to establish it, and there are already twenty in-patients and five hundred out-patients attending it.

D. was receiving native gentlemen all the morning, and in the afternoon we went to an Art Exhibition and then drove along by the sea. I was not prepared for anything so pretty, and Madras seems to me to be really a nice town and a pleasant one to live in. There is scarcely any town proper, as every house is surrounded by quite a park of its own, so there are no *streets*, and the distances are great; but all these 'country seats' look very comfortable, and there is the beautiful sea, and this splendid drive along the shore. I also think that the outside view of Madras society gives one a favourable impression of it; everyone looks smart, and those I have talked to are pleasant people.

The ball was really very pretty. It was in the banqueting hall, a room which in any country would be considered a fine one. It has a gallery round it, and there are two storeys of white pillars supporting the roof. It is of course very lofty. Coloured banners hung above the gallery, and between the lower row of columns were large red pots with pretty light ferns in them. Everything else was white with the exception of the crimson dais at one end, and a bank of ice and ferns at the other. Along the walls, underneath the gallery, are some large portraits.

Supper was in tents lighted by electricity, and a very pretty novelty was a light inside each bouquet of flowers on the table. The roses and leaves arranged in dishes, with this artificial sunshine lighting them up, looked lovely.

The Southern Cross saw us home.

Wednesday, 3rd.—In the morning I visited Lady

Hobart's school for Mahometan girls, and afterwards had
a very interesting conversation with a Mrs. Firth, who
thoroughly understands the native life here, and who has
started a great number of very useful charities worked
on most practical principles.

The whole afternoon was spent in receiving native
ladies. They came one by one, and the function lasted
three hours. First, there was a dear old lady who came
here years ago as a bride in great state from her own
home, escorted by troops, and the object of an enormous
outlay, and who has never got over the grandeur of that
day, or recovered from the shock of finding herself a
widow at sixteen shorn of all that made life pleasant to
her. Then there was another lady with a sad story.
The money all spent, no son to inherit the family
estates, and a husband at death's door, with the prospect
of leaving his wife and family houseless and with 150
rupees a month as their income. She is a really nice,
handsome and lady-like woman, but very unhappy.

I have not time to tell you about all the others.
One grey-haired and kindly person said to me, 'I
am so glad you asked us to come and see you, for our
husbands will not let us go anywhere else, and perhaps
now they will see that we may be trusted out.' Another
told me about the pleasure her brother had felt in seeing
the Viceroy, and how he had wept over the kindness with
which he had been received. He is a great invalid, and
she said that when he came back from his visit, he had
forgotten all about his pain. She wore a sort of gold
dressing-gown, gold and green shawl, and a round gold
hat. Some of the ladies brought their grandchildren,

nice little girls. All the Indian women I meet are gentle and attractive and very sympathetic, and I long to know more of them.

We dined here, a large party, and afterwards started off to drive six miles to Guindy, which is the Governor of Madras' 'Barrackpore.' It was illuminated, and the house is very pretty, so are the gardens in which we sauntered for a little, and then came in for dancing; six miles home again !

Thursday, 4th.—I paid my return visits to the two Indian ladies.

The nearest male relative, the husband of an adopted daughter, met me at the first house, and supported me upstairs, and the old lady met me at the threshold of an outer room, and handed me to a seat of honour under a great canopy in an inner drawing-room. After a little small talk I was put into a heavy garland of flowers, a bouquet was handed to me, and a bottle of scent given, and *I* was led out again. Scent in a bottle was a very great improvement upon the ordinary custom of covering one with attar of roses, a perfume which oppresses me for the whole day after. At the next house I was received in the hall by the poor old dying husband. It was a very touching sight. He is quite paralysed and had to be held up by men, but he looked such a gentleman, and he had a white turban on with a diamond ornament on it to give a dressed appearance to his other white garments. He showed me a crippled hand, and he is quite helpless and almost unable to speak, so I do hope he will be no worse for the exertion he made to appear.

The lady and her daughters and grandchildren were all very nice, but she was very sad and tearful over her future prospects, and I felt very sorry for them all. Her wreaths and bouquets were adorned by the most wonderful tinsel peacocks, so you may imagine how very grand I looked as I descended the stairs robed in flowers, with a peacock on each shoulder, one perched upon my bouquet, flower bracelets on my arms, and bottles of scent and packets of ' pan ' in my hand.

These visits occupied the morning. After lunch I received the Nizam of Hyderabad, who paid me a private visit.

When he had gone I went with Mrs. Grant Duff to visit a very fine native hospital. The whole thing has been built by one man (the same who fed the poor people), and all the wards are most clean and bright and cheerful and well arranged. In connection with it is a leper hospital. I went through the female part of it, as these poor creatures enjoy any little change, such as the sight of a new face. It is dreadfully sad to see young girls and children there, and to know that they must get worse, suffering more and more, and becoming more and more repulsive in appearance every year they live. Twelve years is the longest time they do live after they have been attacked by the disease.

These native gentlemen have made a very nice park in the neighbourhood of this hospital for the poor of the district, with a fernery on an island, and nice plants and walks and fountains. They are always adding something to it, and I was very glad to have seen this whole institution, which is entirely native.

I am unable to give you D.'s diary with mine. We are obliged each 'to go our own way,' but he is busy nearly all day seeing people, and this afternoon he drove out to Guindy with Mr. Grant Duff.

In the evening there was a state dinner, and we left to go on board directly after it.

Our departure was so pretty and curious. We drove to the pier escorted by gentlemen Volunteers, and when we got there the whole place was lighted up with lime-lights and torches; the flags were flying and everything looked most brilliant, and when we had said good-bye and got into the barges, the 'Mosquito fleet' surrounded us in full force, looking more quaint than ever. Figures in 'fool's caps' and night-gowns, two sitting on each plank, with a blazing lime-light between them, making them sometimes of a rosy red and sometimes of an unearthly blue, were on every side of us, paddling with all their might and shouting Hip, hip, hurrah! and all the other barges in the harbour had torches on board, and the shore was glorified with coloured lights, and so we made a most novel and amusing passage to our ship, and here we are now on our way to Calcutta.

The Governor and Mrs. Grant Duff were most charming hosts, and we liked Madras and our visit very much indeed.

Monday, 8th.—We have had a fine passage, the weather quite cool, and now we are approaching Calcutta and have just passed a P. and O. steamer which left this morning. As we passed the ship was dressed, the passengers cheered, and we all waved handkerchiefs at each other.

We had such a grand landing at Calcutta to-day.

For many years Viceroys have arrived at a railway station, but in old times when they came by sea they used to disembark at Prinsep's Ghat, and on this occasion we did so too.

The *mise en scène* is very superior to that of the station; here a magnificent river, filled with splendid ships, all dressed with flags, and every variety of boat and launch flying about, Calcutta itself on either bank, and the Ghat covered with red cloth, flags, and smart spectators. We went ashore at 5.30, and were met by the great officials in their best uniforms, and by Blanche in her best gown, and we walked up the crimson pathway, speaking to people as we went along, and treading upon flowers that were thrown at our feet.

END OF THE FIRST VOLUME

PRINTED BY
SPOTTISWOODE AND CO., NEW-STREET SQUARE
LONDON

Lightning Source UK Ltd.
Milton Keynes UK
UKHW032017280119
336360UK00013B/1451/P